A TWIST OF LUCK

SHIFTER CITY FATED MATES

BOOK 2

JAYMIN EVE

CONTENT WARNING

Your mental health is important to me! If you need any specific information about what might be included, please contact me at jaymineve@gmail.com

Triggers include:

- Death of a parent
- Abuse by a parent
- Past trauma/flashbacks
- Panic attacks
- Scenes of sexual nature with dominant alpha males
- Violence
- Stalking
- Kidnapping
- Forced bonding (not from the main pack)

STAY UP TO DATE

You can keep up to date with my releases by following me on Instagram, joining my Facebook group The Nerd Herd, or subscribing to my newsletter.

This is where you'll get all updates and information about my worlds and publishing schedule.

CATCH UP ON THE WORLD

Emmeline is a wolf shifter in a world where all packs live in cities, with multiple alphas, betas, deltas, and rarer: omegas. These designations form quintets, packs of five, and are governed by alpha councils. Emme is an omega, just like her mom, who was killed by a pack of alphas when Emme was fourteen. This was the catalyst for her to run from the cities and the alphas who controlled them. She swore she would never end up like her mom.

Fast forward over a decade and Emme has been moving between human cities, avoiding the five major pack cities at all costs, and keeping her head down. An unfortunate series of events finds her in the path of an alpha with tracking capabilities. She runs again, but he tracks her and drags her to Golden Claw, the largest of the five pack cities.

Here, she faces the Alpha Council, charged as being a rogue—a shifter without a pack city affiliation. But when they discover she's an omega, they are less inclined to give her the usual sentence of death.

When one of the most powerful alphas scents Emme as his true mate, it's Emme's worst nightmare, as she believes that if she bonds with an alpha she'll be killed the same way her mom was. Her mom's pack was a scent match too, and they still murdered her.

When she finds out that this alpha is one of four alphas in her scent match, she believes her life is over. Quintets are usually made up of one alpha and a mix of delta and betas. Her pack, though, consists of four alpha males, making it strong, and *dangerous*, especially for an omega.

Just like her mom's.

Emme has no choice but to reject the alphas, which receives mixed reactions from the four.

Hunter, the entitled alpha, doesn't give up when he sets his mind to something, and he's determined to win her into the pack by whatever means necessary. He convinces her to move into their pack house for a while, save up some money, and not worry. He also promises not to bond her without her explicitly begging for it. Hunter is an obsessive and possessive alpha stalker, with an end goal of keeping his pack safe, and as strong as they can be. Also... hand tattoo. That is all.

Kellan, the golden retriever alpha, comes in with his sweet and kind soul (though don't underestimate his ability to rip another shifter's head from his shoulders if he looks the wrong way at Emme). Kellan would follow her through this life and into the next no hesitation. Emme, who has been alone her whole life, is won over by Kellan's sweet and unconditional obsession with her.

Slade is a scary dragon shifter. Cold and clinical, he has an observational interest in Emme. She certainly intrigues him. He keeps an eye on her through security cameras, and is as strong a stalker as Hunter, just in a less forceful way. For now.

Finley, a bear shifter, doesn't take her rejection well. It triggered his childhood trauma where he was rejected and hurt by his family. He decides she is toxic to them all, and he's determined not to have her in their lives.

Once she's in the pack house, bonds start to form between Emme, Kellan, and Hunter, despite her best efforts to reject them. As an omega, who can stand outside of normal pack dominance, she is desired amongst alphas, and her pack is determined to keep her safe. During one attempted kidnapping by the guard on the Reeves pack security team, she fights back long enough for Hunter and Kellan to arrive and destroy the shifter, which seals another portion of their relationship. Emme grows even closer to those two.

While investigating the attempted kidnapping to find the source (the guard was a hired hand), the end of *A Curse of Fate* finds Emme and Slade on motorbikes, heading to an interrogation. On the way, they're blown up by a rocket, and an injured Emme is thrown into the back of a van before she blacks out. When she wakes again, she's in a basement cell, bars blocking her exit. Slade is across from her, in another cell, restrained by magical bands.

When her kidnapper steps into the room, she freaks out because it's the entitled alpha of her mom's old pack. They've been searching for her, and when she showed up on the pack register for Golden City, they took their opportunity to track her down.

This is where *A Twist of Luck* begins.

This is dedicated to those who enjoy a buffet of alpha personalities.

The Hunter
The Lumbersnack
The Cinnamon Roll
The Stalker

Eat up.

CHAPTER 1

Kicking through the bodies sprawled at my feet, I ignored the stench of blood, shit, and death permeating the air. I stopped in front of the only one still breathing, blood spattered from his mouth as he coughed, and knowing he wouldn't be alive much longer, I pressed my boot against his chest. "Who took her? Who took my omega?" My rage was a living entity, seeping into those harshly bitten out words, but he was too injured to even register my lethal intentions.

Behind me, Kellan growled from where he paced, alternating between his own fury, and an overwhelming sorrow that almost brought him to his knees. Finley kept him propped up, focusing on Kellan rather than his own feelings. The bear shifter hadn't said one word since we'd tracked down everyone involved in the attack on our pack mates, but he'd been by our side the entire time.

The alpha on the ground gurgled once more, and I pressed harder with my boot. "If you answer me, I'll end your suffering fast," I promised him. "Or you can feel more agony than you thought was possible in your final minutes."

Another cough, the blood darker and congealed this time, which meant he was almost done. His pulse was sluggish too. This motherfucker had better not check out on me before I could make good on my promises.

I was an alpha of my word, after all.

"Sil—Silver City."

I almost missed what he said as he choked on his words, but he got there in the end. I felt a coil of satisfaction—my first emotion other than rage and fear since the attack. I'd been in the final Summit meetings when I'd felt the explosion. I might not have been bonded to Emmeline Anders, the final of our quintet, and our omega, but my wolf had a strong bond to Slade. I'd felt his pain and fury as he'd taken the blast. Not even one minute later, Kellan had rung me in a frantic mess, and we were at the site of the attack twenty minutes later.

But it had been too late.

Slade had dropped a ton of bodies, but not enough to prevent them from being taken.

The attackers must have had a veritable army on their side. I had no idea how they'd even made it into the city. We might have tracked down the rest of these hired mercenaries, but someone from Golden Claw let them into the city. We had a fucking traitor, and while my focus was on finding Emme and Slade, whoever betrayed us would pray to the goddess for death.

"We need to bring in our enforcer squads and go after them," Warrick said, as he kicked one of the fallen shifters in the side. He was an entitled alpha who had befriended my omega, and while he pissed me off to no end, he was also too powerful to turn away as an ally. Especially while Emme was in trouble.

"We don't have fucking time," Finley snarled, and I almost detected a hint of panic in his first words.

Warrick wiped a hand over his face, smearing a few of the spatters of blood he'd picked up in our fights with the mercs. "They've got a decent head start on us, but we know where to go now. In Silver City, you'll be able to track them easier."

"Fin is right," I snapped. "If we bring in the squads, we need to go through the Alpha Council or it turns into an act of war. The legal route will take time, and I'm not willing to wait another second. We're heading to Silver City unofficially, which means weapons and a plan."

"Weapons aren't an issue," Kellan all but howled, his wolf strong in his words. He ran his hand through his hair over and over until it stood on end. "You know I have a decent stash of Reeves Industries tech, along with guns and blades."

Kellan was a weapons expert. His dad—a former enforcer—had taught him to shoot, wield a blade, crossbow, and multiple other weapons, along with fight training. Kellan went even further by collecting his favorite range of weapons, which would come in handy today.

"Make sure you pack Taser S," I told him.

Kellan was the inspiration for my patented technology, which could zap a shifter and keep them stuck in a form between beast and man, shifting back and forth constantly. It wasn't completely debilitating against an alpha—I'd never invent a weapon that could be used to hurt my pack. But it would still stun them long enough to give us an advantage.

We were definitely up against other alphas. I could scent their power all over the scene of the attack.

"I'll pack everything useful," Kellan said with a nod, his eyes focusing as he got on board with the plan.

"Go and help him, Fin," I said. "We'll head for the airport within the hour."

Our Gulfstream G700 had been fueled and waiting since the attack. I'd had a feeling the alphas would take Emme and

Slade as far from Golden Claw as they could. Get out from under us, and where we were our most powerful.

Silver City was a five-hour flight, and it was already nearing morning—none of us had slept since Emme was taken, and I doubted I would again until she was safe. Slade too, but my dragon brother was a tough bastard who could take care of himself.

"I'm coming too," Warrick said shortly. "I'll be at your place in twenty-five minutes. Don't leave without me."

I preferred to keep this within my own pack, but I wouldn't turn down the help when I had no idea what we were up against. "We won't wait. Don't be fucking late."

With a snarl, Warrick turned and raced toward his Range Rover, disappearing in a cloud of dust. Finley and Kellan slapped a hand on my shoulder and left in Finley's TRX, and I stood in a field of dust and dead shifters.

The one I'd questioned remained alive and coughing up a lung, and I crouched down until I was eye to eye with him, his body propped against a tree. My wolf claws appeared in a partial shift, and I tore out his throat in the quick death I'd promised.

Wiping my hand on my suit pants, I retrieved my phone from my pocket and dialed my assistant. "Casey, I need a cleanup team out by the racetrack. At least a dozen bodies."

There was no hesitation in her reply. "On it, boss."

Casey had been with me for over ten years because she took whatever I threw at her and made it better. Without question. In this situation, I needed the bodies to go away so I didn't have to deal with the rest of the Alpha Council before we headed for Silver City.

When I reached my bike, I cleaned my hands more thoroughly on a towel from my bag while I mentally ran over the plan. We'd land in Silver City just after lunch, then we'd track our pack mates using tech and our beasts to follow the bond.

When I figured out where they were, the approach would be crucial. We'd have to take our time or risk spooking their attackers, which could put our pack in danger. I wouldn't make any firm decisions until I saw who and what guarded Emme and Slade.

Slade especially.

They held the strongest alpha in the world, and if he hadn't escaped and torn them to pieces, they knew what it took to keep him contained. The most likely scenario was that they had a witch on their side and used magical restraints. My brother, Slade Riverson, was the last dragon shifter in the world, and while most magic would simply bounce off his skin, if they found a strong enough witch...

Whipping out my phone, I sent Kellan a text to also bring the ShiftLar, an iron-laced armored vest I'd invented to shield against low level magic and spells. His reply came through instantly, and satisfied with our plan, I kicked my leg over my bike and started the engine.

As the powerful motor thrummed under me, I dialed the one number I'd never wanted to use again. "Hunter." The purr of her voice was familiar, even though I hadn't heard it in almost five years. Jewels was born and raised in Mexico but barely had an accent. The witch was well over fifty years old, *while looking twenty-five*, and had lived in America for at least half those years. "It's been a long time, love. To what do I owe the pleasure?"

"I need your help."

Four simple words shouldn't burn, but here the fuck we were. For Emme, I'd burn in a much hotter hell than Jewels Amaro.

My bike was loud as I took off along the main road back to

town, my phone pressed between my ear and shoulder. Jewels' silence was weighty, and I let her have the moment. As the entitled alpha of our quintet, I was used to commanding and getting what I needed immediately, but that wouldn't work with Jewels. She played a whole different game, and I frankly wasn't in the mindset for it today. But I had no choice.

I was almost back at the house by the time she responded. "I've waited a long time to hear those words, *mi corazón*."

Gritting my teeth against the urge to insult her, I instead responded calmly. "You know I wouldn't call unless it was urgent. They took Slade."

She'd always had a soft spot for the dragon. Her need to *fix* broken alphas would have been her downfall if she wasn't so damn powerful.

"My dragon is hurt?" There was a stronger purr in her voice now, the accent bleeding through as her magic almost reached me, sending my wolf into an uneasy stir. Shifters might have been created from a witch's curse, merging human and beast, but that didn't mean I enjoyed the trickling of icy magic down my spine.

"I don't know if he's hurt or not. We tracked down some of the mercenaries, but Slade had already been taken to Silver City, according to the intel we received. You know the only way they can hold him is with magical restraints, and I don't want to go in underprepared. Will you help us?"

"Give me five minutes." She hung up abruptly, and I was happy to be off the phone.

In the garage, I left my bike in its usual spot and forced my gaze to move past the empty spots where Slade and Emme's bikes should have sat. Both were totaled in the attack, lying in broken heaps out in the open desert lands.

Kellan had blamed himself for a solid fifteen minutes when he'd found the crumpled remains of the pink bike he'd gifted

Emme, tearing into the wreckage until it was scattered across the sand. They'd need a metal detector to find all the parts now.

That destruction was nothing on what we'd bring if our pack mates weren't returned to us. In perfect condition. Our tenuous holds on our beasts would snap and we'd ravage this fucking world to the ground without a single care for the fallout. The only reason I hadn't lost it yet was my ability to focus on retrieving my pack. But eternal darkness hovered at the back of my mind.

A darkness that if let loose would make even my father look like a saint.

"Weapons and ShiftLar are packed," Kellan shouted as I marched into the main foyer, my dirty boots slapping against the marble. "I grabbed some clothes for you, so just shower and change into Tactical gear before we head out."

"Warrick here yet?" I asked.

He shook his head, blue eyes wide and focused as he peered through the front door to doublecheck. "Not yet." Kellan was dressed in black cargo pants, boots, and a fitted shirt. He had the armored vest strapped over his chest, and multiple weapons already secured around his body.

"I meant what I said. I'm not waiting for him."

Kellan nodded, as Finley bit out harshly, "Nope, no waiting."

Finley wore black too, but his vest wasn't strapped properly yet, and he had no weapons. Our bear shifter could fight, but he preferred to use his hands. His expression remained neutral as he watched me and then Kellan, and I had no idea what he felt deep inside. He'd fallen into hating Emme for her rejection, which had triggered him back to his shitty upbringing. His parents were on par with my dad, and that was fucking saying something. He was here though, and clearly prepared to fight for our pack.

Which was more than enough for now.

"I'll get cleaned up," I said, kicking off my boots. Florence, our housekeeper, wouldn't freak if I tracked blood and dirt through the house—she was far too used to it—but I didn't want to leave a ton of work for her.

Taking the stairs four at a time to reach my bedroom, I threw off my clothes and dove under the icy spray of the shower. It took me a full five minutes to get all the blood out of my hair, and when I was clean, I pulled out one of my rarely used enforcer outfits. I hadn't dressed in black tactical gear since the day I quit to take over as entitled alpha and the CEO of Reeves Industries.

As the thick material of the pants and shirt settled over my skin, I enjoyed the sensation of being out of suits for once. Shame it had to be under these circumstances. Slade had been trying to get me to run with his squad all year, but I'd been too busy. Another one of my regrets.

"Hunter!" Kellan's shout echoed up through the house as I ran down two sets of stairs, jumping the last flight to land in the foyer. "What the fuck is that crazy bitch doing here?"

The front door was open, and I saw Warrick first, followed by a tiny blond witch. "Kellan, baby," Jewels crooned. "You know I love you. I never meant to curse you to pee a little every time you laughed."

Kellan growled, his hands shifting to claws as he launched for her, only to bounce back off her magical protection field. "Enough!" I snapped. "Kellan, we need Jewels. They clearly have magic on their side. And considering you slept with her sister and bailed, you're lucky she lifted the curse after a week. Let's call it a fair exchange and move the hell on."

Jewels threw her head back and laughed loudly. "Goddess, have I missed you boys. Just like old times, right?"

She went to throw her arms around me and I sidestepped the embrace. "Not like old times at all," I warned her. "This is a normal exchange, where we pay you for your services."

She opened her mouth, but I wasn't about to let her dictate any of the terms. "With cash only. We pay you an exorbitant amount of money and you back us up with magic. Deal?"

Jewels was pretty, with full pink lips, olive skin, dark eyes, and wavy blond hair, but as she pouted all I felt was annoyance. The witch couldn't hold a candle to my omega, and it pissed me right off that we even had to call in an outsider to help with pack business.

For Emme and Slade. I would need that reminder a lot over the next twenty-four hours.

"Fine, Hunter, you big meanie." The pout disappeared and she was all business. "This is a freebie anyway. I owe Slade. For him, I'll level those fuckers to the ground."

This was the Jewels we needed, and even Kellan looked appeased as his dominance simmered down. We all knew that with her assistance we had a much stronger chance of successfully retrieving our mates.

"Let's do it, then," Finley said shortly, heading out the door. "We're wasting time."

We followed him to where the Range Rover sat out front, the ass end slammed with the weight of the weapons. As I started the engine, I cursed how long it would take us to get to Silver City. Even with our powerful plane, it was too long. If it was only me, I would have convinced Jewels to use witch portals, but she couldn't take us all without wiping herself out for days. Which meant traveling the old-fashioned way.

Hold on, little omega. We're coming for you.

CHAPTER 2

EMME

"You have been a burden to me from the day you were born, Emmeline Anders. I wish I'd done exactly what your daddy wanted and tore you from the womb before you took your first breath."

Tears burned my eyes as Momma spewed venom all over me. I knew better than to openly cry and sob, but today it hurt more than usual. Today I felt it all the way to my exhausted, lonely eight-year-old bones as I cowered in the corner. Momma had never treated me well, but she was extra mean this year with the sneering faces of her pack to back her up.

Alpha Blaine Rogers stepped forward, the entitled alpha of the pack. I feared him the most, with his dark, angry eyes. "Maybe your little princess needs to be taught a proper lesson in obedience, Omega."

They always called her "omega." I was fairly sure they didn't even know her actual name. Or care what it was. The only part they cared about was her being an omega, and I prayed with every part of my being that when my wolf finally appeared, I wasn't the same designation.

Momma lifted her head and simpered at the big shifter. "What did you have in mind, Alpha?"

Blaine examined me. I was already pressed as hard as my slight frame could go into the corner, but I found myself trying to scoot back further. If his smug smirk was any indication, he enjoyed my fear.

"A reminder she won't forget, perhaps," he said, rubbing his chin like one of the villains from the cartoons I snuck into the living room to watch whenever the pack left the house. Crappy old television or not, it was one of my few glimpses of the outside world.

"Whatever my alpha thinks is suitable, I'm happy to agree to."

Momma popped up on her toes and started to kiss him, and I heard the rumbles and grunts from the rest of the pack as they leaned toward Momma. But no one touched her except Blaine.

"Hewie, grab my hunting blade," Blaine said when he pulled back from licking Momma's face. The very sight turned my stomach, and if I'd eaten at all today, I'd have vomited all over the floor. Alphas not only scared me, they were gross.

Hewie, Josiah, and Donnie left the room, and Hewie returned with a giant blade in his hand. It was sheathed in a leather holder that I'd seen clipped to Blaine's belt more than once. When the entitled alpha took the sheathed blade, he caressed it softly, and then unclipped the loop and pulled the long hunting knife free. The handle was white and carved, and while it looked old, the blade was wickedly sharp.

Warmth trickled between my legs, and I realized I'd peed myself. Again, a lack of food and water had saved me from more than a trickle, but it was enough to send shame cutting through my fear.

My body lurched forward as I held my hands up. "I promise. I promise, Momma," I screamed. "I won't ever leave my room without permission again. I won't sneak food from the pack's stores. I'm sorry. I was just so hungry."

She stared down in disgust, before her booted foot shot out and *she shoved me back. "You disgusting little shit. You say you're sorry, and then you do it again."*

Because I'm starving, I wanted to shout again, but I swallowed my anger. I always swallowed my anger.

Hewie left again, apparently uninterested, and Blaine and Momma stepped forward. "Hold her," Blaine snarled, and all I saw was the glint of a blade as it sliced toward me. "The silver will ensure the little princess remembers this for the rest of her life. Her wolf will be too late to save her."

"Emmeline! Focus on me, Omega. Focus!"

The roar shook me from the memory, and I sucked in deep breaths, over and over, my mind stuck in the past as I fought to focus on the present. My panic attack tore at me with the force of a tsunami, and I hadn't even noticed that Blaine Rogers, who'd been standing in front of me minutes ago, was gone from my cell.

After the attack in Golden Claw, I'd woken up here, in what looked like a basement turned prison. Two cells stood on either side of the room, with a large path between them that led up to a set of stairs. From where I was chained, I could not see much more than that.

What I could see though, was the cell across from me.

Furious, unearthly green eyes were locked on my face, as low rumbles filled the room. Slade's godlike beauty was enough to briefly break through my panic, and I stopped clawing at my face in an attempt to rip those memories free.

But I couldn't slow my breathing.

I couldn't halt the fear response.

"Listen to me, Emmeline," the dragon shifter commanded, his huge body locked down with multiple chains and witch cuffs. "We are going to get out of here. I will not let him hurt you."

Slade was one of the four alphas who were my scent match

and goddess chosen mates. Mates, who thanks to Blaine and those assholes who destroyed my mother, I'd been rejecting from the moment I met them.

I'd rejected them to never end up like mom, who had given away all her power to her alphas. Not that any of my scent matches were remotely like the Rogers pack.

At least not yet.

An omega could share their power when bonded into an alpha pack, and my understanding was that this process would change and corrupt the alphas who received it. For this reason alone, I'd spent most of my life running from the shifter cities so I'd never end up in a pack.

Only to encounter one alpha, who'd changed everything.

He'd dragged me to Golden Claw, where I'd been scented by one of my true mates, and despite my immediate rejection, I'd somehow ended up living with them. Living with and liking most of them. I'd even contemplated, briefly, the possibility of letting myself belong to *and with* my pack, right around the time Blaine blasted me and Slade off our bikes and dragged us here to his secret lair. It was a timely and painful reminder of what I'd been fighting against all along.

When I'd woken in this basement cell, Blaine had appeared, and I'd found myself screaming into a waking nightmare. Back to the day he'd carved his blade through my back, leaving a thick ropey scar as a forever reminder.

Scars. Pain. Fear.

Small, mewling sobs escaped me as I used my arms to drag myself closer to the wall. My back had been damaged in the initial attack, and my legs still weren't responding. Slade's rumbles picked up in intensity, but they sounded muffled as the panic dragged me back under.

The blade sliced into my spine, the scent of metal surrounding me as I screamed and choked on spit. I'd never felt pain so intense, even with all the beatings Momma had given me.

The roar grew louder as I prayed for oblivion. I'd have taken another knife to my body before I chose to experience suppressed trauma exploding from my psyche again.

It consumed me in a black hole of despair.

Heat and roars shattered through the room as the floors and walls rattled; small pebbles of mortar and debris rained down over me.

I gasped when strong arms wrapped around my shoulders, and I fought against the hold until the scent of toasted marshmallow filled me, blending with my chocolate and honey tones. My wolf howled and scraped against the magical bands holding us, wanting to shift closer to her mate, fighting against our restrictions.

Chains clanked as Slade pulled me closer, and as if he'd somehow used magic too, his touch had my hysteria dying down into choked sobs. "Calm," he murmured, in his low, slightly accented rumble. "Calm yourself, Emmeline. You are not alone. I will not let them harm you."

Not alone.

That sentiment echoed through my mind, louder than those ghosts of the past.

Slade's energy was like liquid lava, burning into my skin, but it didn't bother me. The heat helped to slow the tremors racking my frame, and as he held me I found myself doing exactly as he'd commanded: calming.

I had very little experience with hugs, but I was starting to learn that when they came from my alphas, they were one of the nicest moments of my life. Surrounded by warmth and energy, comforted and content. Especially with Slade, who was coldly aloof most of the time.

Even as the last of my tremors subsided, he never let go, his massive frame protectively shielding me from whatever could enter through the now-broken bars of my cell.

When my tense muscles finally released, I fully collapsed against him, spent and broken. A few soft sobs escaped as I clung to my anchor in the storm. It wasn't until he reached behind me and tore my chains from the wall—using one hand like they weren't embedded in four feet of concrete—that I remembered a super important detail about the dragon shifter.

He hated to be touched. *Oh shit.*

Slade had a strong touch aversion, and while I had no idea what had specifically caused it, I knew it was trauma from his past. The dragon, with his genius computer brain, was cold and formal most of the time, but not today. Today, he'd saved me, and at great personal cost.

Pulling away, I blinked to clear the haze over my vision and see him clearly. His thick black hair was disheveled, blood streaking his throat where the magically enhanced neck band had cut into his skin. I could only assume that happened when he'd torn his own chains from the wall in his cell.

Bands still encased his wrists, waist, and both ankles. These magical bands stopped him from shifting into his beast, but he'd clearly retained enough strength to wrench the chains from the wall.

As Slade adjusted his position, keeping me close, I noticed he still wore his black leather jacket from when we'd taken out the motorbikes. The shirt beneath was torn up, exposing a lot of his bronze skin, and allowing hints of his tattoos to peek through. I swore I saw a realistic jewel-like green eye near his right pec, but I couldn't make out the rest. At least there were no visible injuries, even though I'd seen him take the brunt of the blast and get blown off his bike.

I'd lost my jacket during the attack, which hurt almost as

much as the memories of the past assaulting me. The jacket had been a gift from Kellan.

My beautiful Kellan. He'd be freaking out not knowing if we were okay or not, and I hoped that the rest of our pack didn't put themselves in danger while they tracked us down.

I had no doubt they would come after us. For the first time in my life, I had a pack, and they would rain down hell on Blaine and co when they got here.

"Slade, are you okay?" I rasped, my voice busted up from all the screaming I'd done. "You're touching me. You don't have to make yourself uncomfortable. I'm fine now."

Despite wanting to remain in his comforting embrace, I tried to scramble away, but my useless legs hindered my progress. I was slower to heal than a regular shifter due to years of suppressing my beast.

"Stop," he commanded, more bite in his tone. Had I been anyone other than an omega, I wouldn't have had any choice but to obey this bark of dominance from the strongest alpha in the world. But omegas stood outside the normal dominance hierarchy—one of our lovely superpowers—which made it quite the statement when I *chose* to obey my alphas.

"I don't want to make you uncomfortable," I said, voice barely audible.

Slade ignored my feeble attempts to remove myself from his arms. "Rest," he murmured, still with the single word commands. "I need you at full strength to get out of here. I can't shift until these chains are removed, and I would be risking your safety if I took on the number of shifters I sense above us. We must plan and heal, Emmeline. I will hold you until you can hold yourself."

My stomach whirled and flipped at those words, along with the overwhelming sensation of being held by Slade. Until this moment, I'd never so much as grazed his skin, and now his near seven-foot frame was wrapped around me, binding all my shattered pieces together.

Just five more minutes, I told myself, soaking in the comfort of not being alone in a house of alphas who starred center stage in my worst nightmares.

"All along," I mumbled, half delirious, "I thought I was hiding from my pack. From what would happen if I ever bonded."

A deep, reverberating sound echoed from Slade's chest. "Who were you really hiding from? Who are these alphas who took us?"

"My mom's old pack," I said as the edge of my vision darkened, pure exhaustion tugging at my consciousness. Every part of me was in danger, but here in Slade's arms I could forget about it for five minutes. For five minutes, I was safe.

CHAPTER 3

EMME

I must have fallen asleep at some point, the stress and exhaustion too much for my body to take any longer, and when I came to, all I could see were Slade's broad shoulders. He stood in front of the destroyed cell bars, snapping at someone on the other side. "What's your point?"

"You smashed both fucking cells."

I couldn't see who spoke, but it wasn't the deep timbre of Blaine's voice. It sounded like Donnie, who had a very slight lisp on s words. It was weird recalling even these small details when I'd spent years purging this pack from my memories.

"Correct. And if you don't want me to add you to the carnage, you will bring us food and water."

Slade's voice never rose above a rumble, but still a shiver traced down my spine. Apparently, a dragon needed *no* inflection to get his point across.

Donnie spluttered. "We... We n-need to s-secure you against the wall again first."

Slade's huge shoulders lifted in what looked like a casual shrug. "You can absolutely try. Keeping in mind that I haven't attacked yet or attempted to escape, so there's no real need. If my beast feels remotely threatened, and that includes any movements toward my omega, I won't remain so calm."

There was a crack against the floor, which sounded like Donnie stomping his foot as he muttered, "Fine, I'll be back with food and water."

His footsteps echoed as he walked away, and I tested out my ability to move my legs, relieved that not only did they move but there was minimal pain. I'd really screwed up in keeping my wolf so suppressed, and it wasn't only my restricted healing. My senses were dulled, and I was less powerful overall.

"You need more sleep, Snow," Slade growled, interrupting my thoughts, and I wondered how he'd even known I was awake. He hadn't turned from where he protectively blocked me with his huge frame.

"Snow?" I questioned, forcing myself to stand so I could arch my back and stretch out aching muscles.

"Your wolf's fur is the whitest I've ever seen," he explained, as he finally glanced my way, his expression neutral. His eyes burned though. "It reminds me of the purity of snow, and your arctic blue eyes only add to the vibe."

Scooting closer, I took extra care not to touch the dragon. I was under no illusion that his break from character to comfort me during my panic attack meant I had a free-for-all to touch him now. "When did you see me shift?"

From my new position, I could finally see the full carnage from where he'd torn the bars from the concrete floor and ceiling. There was nothing stopping us from walking out of here and up the stairs, outside of the veritable army that awaited up there. Slade had already calculated the odds, and with us vastly outnumbered, his dominance tempered by the magical bands, and unable to shift, he'd decided it was best to stay put.

Maybe he was waiting for our pack to show up too. Who knew how long that'd take though.

"Your very first run with Warrick and Cora," he told me, turning back to the stairs, "and then again when you shifted in your room. I've been watching you in one way or another since you arrived in Golden Claw."

Okay, then. "Are you saying that Hunter isn't the only stalker I have to deal with in the pack?"

It occurred to me halfway through that sentence that accusing *Scary Shifter* of being a stalker might not be my smartest move, but hey, if he wanted to kill me, he could have done so long ago. I figured I was fairly safe for the moment.

"Every alpha in your pack has their way of keeping track of you, Emmeline," he said nonchalantly. "Mine is just more thorough."

I found it very hard to believe that Finley, the bear shifter who hated my guts, bothered to think about me at all. But the rest... yeah, it made sense that they'd be keeping tabs on me in their own ways.

Deciding we had more pressing issues to worry about, I directed the conversation back to the current situation. "What do you think my mom's pack want with us? Why didn't they leave you behind if I was the target?"

"You were the target," he confirmed without hesitation. "They brought me because they knew I'd track them the moment they left with you. They've done their research, they know of my skills, and were prepared to keep me locked down. There was a reason they waited until you were alone with me."

"The others won't be able to track us?"

Maybe he wasn't waiting for them to show up at all. It was stupid of me to just sit here and wait for a rescue anyway. I'd spent most of my life fighting my own battles, but my self-preservation had taken a back seat lately as I fell into pack mentality. It was a heady, dangerous, and addictive feeling to not be alone and have others at your back.

A feeling I really couldn't afford to indulge in.

"Not like I could," Slade said. "It will take them longer."

Slade was a computer genius, and according to Hunter, if he had even a sliver of your digital identity, he could track you anywhere in the world. At this stage, it appeared he had a lot of mine.

"So, they took you as well to ensure they had enough time with me to do… what, exactly? What do they have planned?" For the first time since I woke up, my brain was back online, and I needed answers. "Do you think this pack has been tracking me for almost twelve years since Mom died? There's no possible way, right? They'd have to be the worst trackers in existence."

I'd never seen the slightest hint of their presence anywhere until I'd been captured and sent to Golden Claw. That was when I'd been registered with the pack cities, which was most likely the catalyst to catapult me back onto Blaine's radar.

Slade turned from his vigilant position keeping an eye on the stairs, and I was once again ensnared in the vibrant green of his eyes. The color and reflection were so unnatural, like jewels had been shined, polished, and slotted into his perfect, godly face.

Every part of Slade was too much, and yet I could never get enough at the same time.

"I don't think they were tracking you at all." He confirmed my previous thoughts. "From what I've gathered, and I only had them under surveillance right before the attack, they became aware of you again when you were brought before our Alpha Council. I would hazard a guess that the attack by our guard was instigated through them, and when that failed, they waited for the chaos of the Summit to enter our city without raising any suspicions."

His gaze returned to the stairs once more, and I sucked in a low, ragged breath, willing my heartrate to level out. "If you had them under surveillance, how did you not know they were part of the Summit?"

The lowest rumble sounded in his chest, and once again I was struck by the fact that loud did not equal menacing when it came to this alpha. "They sent lackies first. None of them arrived until the day of the attack, and I was occupied keeping an eye on you. They must have traveled via witch magic to our borders so as not to leave a digital trace, and then lay in wait for the opportunity to cross into Golden Claw."

The rasp on *claw* told me how angry he was that they'd slipped past his surveillance. I almost reached out and touched his arm, catching myself at the last minute. "You did nothing wrong, Slade, and you're here now keeping me safe. I have little doubt that I'd have already been dragged upstairs by these assholes if you weren't standing as guard dragon between us."

Footsteps echoed from above, and as his expression hardened, he jerked his head to tell me to get behind him. Which I immediately did, because I was vastly outmatched against other alphas. "General magic doesn't work on me the same as it does other shifters," Slade murmured. "But if they have strong enough spells at their disposal, they will be able to hold me until they get to you. It won't hold me forever though, so don't give up. No matter what happens, I will come for you."

His promise burned into my chest, and with it came a sense of calm. My anchor remained, and I would cling to the comfort of Slade for as long as possible.

Peering around his side, I waited as the steps grew louder, until Donnie hurried down the stairs. The stocky blond shifter held a large tray in his hands, and there were no witches or other alphas in sight. I should find it odd that he was appeasing Slade's request without any fanfare, but the dragon had a way about him—even while suppressed—that commanded even other alphas.

And omegas.

"Here," Donnie snapped, dropping the tray on the ground a few feet from Slade. His focus was on the largest threat in the room, and he hadn't noticed me. "We have provided food. We will be back soon to discuss our proposal regarding the omega. Please ensure she's awake and ready to chat."

Slade moved so fast that I swore he flashed in and out of existence, crossing six feet of concrete floor to punch Donnie right in the face. The other alpha's face exploded, blood and bone splattering everywhere. Slade leaned down and hoisted him into the air before *throwing him up the stairs* like he was a fucking tennis ball.

There was a thud when he connected with the door at the top of the stairs, and then he tumbled back down to land near the basement floor. Slade stared at the knocked-out—*maybe dead*—alpha at his feet, gave him a bit of a kick, and then leaned over to scoop up the tray.

"Food is safe," he said when he reached me, and I just blinked, tension holding me in stasis.

"G-great."

He placed the tray on the floor before me, and then leaned back against the remaining bars, his stare unblinking as he watched me. There was an immediate vibe that if I didn't start to eat soon, he would take great pleasure in feeding me. Blindly, I reached out and grabbed the first bowl, which happened to be a salad.

My nose wrinkled as I stared into the leaves and horse chow. *Dammit.* I mean, I was hungry, but I wasn't sure I was hungry *enough* to swallow this shit down. No doubt the alphas remembered my dislike of herbivore food and made sure to include it out of spite.

Now I wanted to kick Donnie.

As I glared at the bowl, Slade reached out and plucked it from my grasp, replacing it with a larger bowl filled with what looked like stew. Beef stew, to be more accurate, the broth dark and thick, with *thank the goddess* only a few carrots and potatoes as vegetable filler.

My stomach woke with a vengeance, and foregoing utensils I tipped the bowl up and drank it from the side. It was too salty and not meaty enough, but it wasn't a salad, so I wouldn't complain.

I paused when Slade turned and threw the salad at the wall, the bowl smashing and scattering the offending greenery everywhere. I was reminded that Slade preferred a mostly meat-based diet too.

"You want some?" I said, holding the second half of the stew out to him. "It's a lot better than that salad."

The alpha tilted his head, observing me in that calculating way of his. It was a stare that always appeared to take in more than he should from a simple glance. "You're still hungry. You will finish it."

I shouldn't have been surprised—the alphas in my pack were quite diligent in waiting for me to eat before they did—but somehow I was. "I'd rather share," I admitted, staring into the thick broth once more. "You're bigger and need strength. I can't fight these guys off."

My gaze flicked to where Donnie remained sprawled in a bloody mess. "I need you."

I turned back in time to see Slade's eyes darken, but he didn't take the bowl. "I can last without food for weeks before any weakness touches me."

While that was a cool trick, it didn't satisfy me or my wolf. "You were injured in the explosion. You've expended a lot of energy healing and keeping me safe. I bet you haven't even slept. Don't push me on this, dragon. Eat the fucking food."

A flicker of a smile ghosted over his lips, so fast that I probably imagined it, but he did reach out and grasp the bowl. There was the briefest graze of our fingers, which set off an entire kaleidoscope of butterflies in my gut. "Whatever you need, Snow."

Oh. *Fuck*. The way that sentence rumbled from his lips had my body reacting in a way that was highly inappropriate for our current situation.

My body curved forward right as the door at the top of the stairs exploded inward, and I almost didn't care that we now had a much more pressing issue to deal with.

I was too busy falling into a dragon's thrall.

CHAPTER 4

SLADE

The more time I spent around the omega, the more intrigued I became. I'd reached a point where my brain was ninety percent occupied with unravelling the mystery of her and her life. I wanted to know it all: how she grew up, how it had shaped her, how she had so much fire when normally an omega was unassuming and accepting—especially of her alpha.

Omegas stood outside of the normal hierarchy in pack dominance, and while we were never plainly told why, it was reasoned that they kept our beasts from taking us over. They kept an alpha from losing control. It was *never* reasoned that their ability to withstand commands could be used as a factor in ruling against or *controlling* alphas.

Though, I'd theorized that maybe that was the exact reason.

Our omega was calm and levelheaded, even as she fought against the odds. She did calm my beast, as much as the dragon could ever be calmed, but it felt as if there was more to her as well.

Her compassion especially was a surprise, *and* an irritation at how easily it could get her into trouble. I was a dangerous shifter, and she'd already let her guard down multiple times in moments of vulnerability around me.

She could never show that same *softness* with another pack. It wasn't safe. And I had a newly vested interest in keeping her safe.

"Don't push me on this, dragon. Eat the fucking food."

My dragon rumbled but he wasn't upset. Her fire enticed us, and I almost smiled. Emme was an adorable kitten compared to my beast, but I'd let her have her dominance for the moment, especially if it kept her from spiraling into another panic attack.

I never wanted to see that look on her face again as she clawed at her skin, fighting an enemy that I couldn't destroy—an enemy in her mind.

"Whatever you need, Snow," I said, reaching for the bowl. Her pretty lips parted; her pupils dilated as I leaned into her and grasped the bowl. She followed my movements, arching forward toward me right as the door was kicked in at the top of the stairs.

The alpha who had upset her before started down the stairs. *Blaine.* She'd been yelping his name in her panic, and I wanted to tear his head from his shoulders just for breathing the same air as her.

Not bothering to pay him any attention—he was no match for me—I kept my gaze locked on Emmeline. I had a small obsession with observing the constant and quickly changing expressions on her face. She didn't have any skill in shielding her emotions, flashing everything she felt to the world, which was a part of her I craved.

Somehow, though, she still remained a mystery.

I loved a good mystery.

Blaine reached the bottom of the stairs and let out what he

must have thought was an impressive growl as he hovered close to his unconscious pack mate. I had no idea what his issue was; the pathetic excuse for an alpha was still alive. He'd probably even make a full recovery, if his healing was up to par.

I'd been downright generous. They should thank me by leaving us alone until I figured out the safest way to take them all down without Emme getting hurt.

"I'm going to fucking kill you, dragon scum."

For fuck's sake. Gnats were annoying until you swatted them dead.

Apparently, I hadn't delivered enough of a warning with the last one, and with a sigh I set down the stew. As I turned to deal with him, Emme shifted closer to me, her arms trembling as her sweet scent turned acrid with fear.

She hadn't reacted this way with the other troglodyte, but the entitled alpha bothered her.

This time, when my dragon reared up, he was most definitely irritated. "What did he do to you?" I hissed, barely restraining my beast. "Tell me exactly what he did. *In detail.* Leave nothing out."

It was yet to be tested if the magically enhanced cuffs would stop my shift—there wasn't enough space in this room to try. Hence why I'd been calculating the risks of all the other escape options. But if they threatened Emme in any way, my restraint would end.

"He—" she gasped, and with it, another surge of rage built in the fires in my gut. The fires were always churning and burning with the power of my ancestors, but her fear was a fuel I'd never experienced. I hadn't lost control in years, but today... I was on the verge.

Eyes unfocused, Emme reached over her shoulder and rubbed her thick, ropey scar. Shifting my stance, my arm shot out to grasp the entitled alpha by the throat. With very little effort, I lifted him until only the tips of his boots dragged on the ground, and slowly hauled him closer. "What did he do to you, Snow? Tell me everything, and I'll make his death nice and slow."

My grip tightened, and he scraped at my hand, even going so far as to partially shift his claws, but it didn't break my hold. "He helped Mom carve me up," Emmeline whimpered. "To teach me a lesson. He destroyed her in the end as well. He's a monster."

As I tightened my grip, sulfur filtered through the open door at the top of the stairs, and the magically enhanced chains encasing me lit up with energy. I was zapped with enough force to knock out a normal shifter, which loosened my grip, allowing the other alpha to scoot away. He grabbed his pack mate from the floor and hightailed it up the stairs. *Pathetic.*

Turning away from the sight of him retreating with his tail between his legs, my heart almost stopped as Emme swayed and then tilted forward. I caught her before she hit the floor, my skin itching at the sensation of our touch, but oddly it was far less consuming than usual. *Easily ignored.* Especially as I focused on checking her vitals, hoping the witch's zap of power hadn't done any permanent damage.

A quick assessment indicated that outside of being unconscious, her pulse and heartrate were normal, and her scent, while shrouded in the sulfuric stench of magic, was also normal.

That was why my attack, and our escape, had to wait until my plan was solid. Not that we could wait too long and give them time to add to their forces.

It was a fine timeline, and I would make sure it was *just right* for my omega.

Emme took ten minutes to rouse. I used that time to plan

my attack while monitoring her pulse and heart rate… and freely touching her as if it wasn't completely out of character. I'd spent years expecting every brush across my skin to hurt, and it would take lifetimes to break that instinct. Not that I'd ever bothered to try rerouting my brain when it came to touch, but for a moment I wished to be less broken.

"Slade," she mumbled.

It amused me that she'd never used our titles correctly. We were all strong enough for an entitled *Alpha* before our names. Not that Emmeline gave a shit, and for that, she made me proud.

"I'm here," I said, as I gave her eighty percent of my attention, while the other twenty remained upstairs, where I tracked the dozen or so members of their army. I'd hurt their numbers back in Golden Claw, but not enough. "How are you feeling? They have a witch, or at least access to spells that can debilitate us through these chains. I need to figure out how to remove them before we attempt an escape."

She pushed herself up and glanced around, her face pale as her striking eyes darkened. "Is it possible to remove magically enhanced cuffs without using magic itself?"

I'd been working on the one around my right ankle since we arrived here, and had dented and damaged the mechanism, but I couldn't sever the final connection. "I'm not sure. Shifting would break them, but I don't have the space. I'll keep working on it while you keep healing. Finish the food for fuel… even the salad." I'd smashed the first pile of grass, but there was a second bowl on the tray.

She grimaced, but didn't argue, shuffling forward to pick up the scattered tray. She opened one of the water bottles and took a huge gulp before handing the second bottle over to me. Our fingers brushed as I took it, and she startled, while I forced myself not to react.

The urge to lash out or scrape off my skin was present, but much less than I'd ever felt before. It was almost a non-issue. I'd never have believed that anyone could desensitize me to their touch within hours—it took Hunter years to even be able to brush by me without copping a fist to the face. The rest of our pack was the same. If I initiated the contact, it was different, but they could never touch me first.

Emmeline collapsed against the wall, a bowl of salad in her hands as she grumpily shoveled the greenery into her face. She looked so put out eating lettuce, and the pout on her lips distracted me from my task.

Yep, my fascination continued to grow, and I was starting to wonder if my usual *limited* tolerance for shifters would not have the same limit with Emmeline.

"You want some?" she asked, holding the bowl out toward me. A glimmer of hope that I'd take it away shone on her face.

I almost laughed. An actual, amused laugh.

When I removed the bowl from her hands, she released the most relieved sigh I'd ever heard, and my restrained chuckle from before escaped. Her relief altered into shock, and she stared at me like she'd never seen another shifter before. Ignoring her, I dropped the repulsive greenery on the tray and returned to my task of releasing this cuff.

It took her a few seconds to recover from her shock, as she watched me closely from her peripherals. Eventually, she got to her feet and started to pace—another oddity for an omega, with her incessant need to move. "Are your injuries fully healed?" I asked, sensing no more pain but needing her confirmation.

There was a pause as she tested out her limbs and did a few jumps on the spot. "I still have a couple of mild aches, but otherwise, everything appears to be in working order. I think my healing has improved since letting my wolf out more."

It would continue to improve through the years, but she'd never grow to what she could have been. The most fundamental growth periods were during our first shifts, and she'd been locked down by her mother and pack. It'd be a celebration when their entire pack was dead.

"We need to make a run for it soon," I said, digging in the side of the cuff. "Our only issue is the witch magic. These cuffs give them a direct link to our shifter side, and my normal resistance is weakened. We need to take their witch out first. If she's unconscious or dead, her magic won't be as effective."

"What if it's not an actual witch?" Emme mused as she tilted her head. "You said they could just have access to spells she left behind."

In my experience, most witches wouldn't leave their magic in shifters hands, but I'd also never met any pack receiving as much magical help as the Rogers pack. There was a bigger connection here between this pack and the witches. One that I hadn't managed to uncover in my research.

"They could have access to spells," I finally admitted. "Which is why I'm going to attack first, while you remain down here. I'm strong enough that even if the witch is up there, she'll have to use a lot of her power to knock me down. If she's not up there, they'll have to exhaust their stores of energy to stop me. Either way, it's going to assist in us eventually getting out of here."

Emme's expression turned uneasy, her eyes a piercing, icy blue. Her face was easy-to-read, but her true worry and fear lingered deepest in her eyes. "I don't like the thought of you going up there without me," she said, rubbing the bridge of her nose and bringing my attention to the spatter of freckles across her cheeks. Who knew freckles could also be fascinating. "What if you get hurt? What if they kill you? I'd never even know."

No one ever worried about me, and for very good reason. "If they can kill me, then there's no hope for your survival, Snow. You should worry about yourself if that scenario comes to pass."

Her expression fell and she immediately shut down as she crossed her arms over her chest and nodded. "Yeah, okay. Makes sense."

I examined her briefly, trying to understand what I'd said to upset her. The varying depth of emotions most shifters experienced were not familiar to me. I lived in a world of black and white, facts and figures, data and code. Emmeline Anders was all color and grayscale, spontaneity and beauty. It was a foreign language.

Ironic, considering I could speak almost every language known to shifters.

Just not Emmeline Anders, apparently.

CHAPTER 5

EMME

Slade returned to working the cuff on his ankle, which he'd transformed into a mangled mess of metal, even as it remained around his black pants. I took another sip of water and continued my new favorite pastime: watching the dragon shifter and debating if I'd ever break through his contained exterior.

Whenever I made even a small dent, he'd retreat and ice me out again, which only had me trying harder. "I really don't like the idea of you heading up there without me."

He'd already explained his reasons why, and they made perfect sense. Both of us agreed that in a physical sense, I would be less than zero help. There was no debating that after what I'd seen him do to Donnie and Blaine. He *was* underestimating how great my moral support was, though.

"You must be protected," was all he said, and while a part of me swooned another part was annoyed.

I'd survived a lot on my own. Slade believed me to be a frail, pathetic omega with zero dominance. Next thing you know he'd call me *cute* as he bopped me on the nose, and I could store the full trifecta of shifter loserdom under my belt.

I started to pace, enjoying the use of my legs, even as the chains still attached to my cuffs clanked. "What are they waiting for?" I growled, my voice healed up enough for a decent growl again.

Slade didn't look up as he tore away another strip of the outer layers of metal. "If I had to guess, which I don't particularly like to do, they're reassessing and figuring out how to keep me contained now that I've busted through their cage. They're probably also regretting bringing me along for the ride, though it was their only logical choice at the time."

"What if they'd killed you?"

The sound that emerged from him was a dark, twisted version of a laugh. "I'm not easy to kill, which is the only reason I'm here with you."

Thank the goddess that Slade was on my side.

There was another clank and creak as he tore metal away, and when his head jerked up and he stilled, I froze as well. "There's only a few of them left in the house," he finally said, and my pulse raced at the predatory tilt to his head.

I wasn't the prey he tracked today, but my instinctive fight or flight response remained the same.

His eyes darkened, black threading through the green, and he jumped to his feet so fast that he was gone before I choked out a gasp. He moved like liquid, flowing from one spot to the next, and I wondered if my reflexes were even slower than I'd originally thought. Or was he just that much faster than a regular alpha? Either way, it threw me completely off balance.

"Now's the time," he said. "There aren't enough left to stop me. I want you to wait here while I clear the path. I will call for you, Emmeline. Do not move until then."

I opened my mouth to protest being left behind, but he was already up the freakin' stairs.

In like, two seconds.

I really needed to add cardio into my daily life, but now was not the time to compare our abilities. Slade couldn't... uh, there had to be shit he couldn't do as well as me. Like... menstruate.

Yes! I was an expert at that, and speaking of, I was due any day, so it'd be excellent if that didn't happen while I was in captivity. My periods usually knocked me down for at least a day with terrible bleeding and cramps, and there was no way to hide the scent of blood in a house of alphas.

Yeah, okay, so clearly I wasn't even an expert at menstruation, but I was still better at it than Slade.

Shuffling closer to the base of the stairs, I peered up at the broken door and frame, the edge of the handle just in sight as it swung on one hinge. Straining to hear any sound or a scuffle, I was disconcerted by the eerie quiet keeping me company.

I'd just placed my foot on the bottom step when Slade appeared above.

"You might as well come up here," he said shortly, and I wasted no time scurrying up the stairs, emerging into a small, old-fashioned kitchen with pink, white, and yellow flowered wallpaper and wood cabinets painted in a brighter yellow. "What happened?" I hissed, looking around for Blaine and the others, but the room was empty. The entire house felt empty.

Slade's expression remained ten shades of pissed off, which unfairly only made him look hotter. His gaze moved toward the back door. "As soon as I emerged from the basement, the few remaining rats bailed, leaving the entire house locked down with magic. I checked every room, and we're alone. This is just a larger prison, and I have no doubt they'll be back soon with a big enough army to take me out."

Fucking excellent.

"Okay, so is there any way for us to break through this magical lock before they return? How strong is it?"

When he exhaled, I was surrounded by the ashy sweetness of his scent and my knees weakened. I reached out, and as casually as possible, pressed my hand to a flowered panel of wall, needing the support. Hopefully, he wouldn't notice me using the house to prop myself up.

"Strong enough that this house had to be built with magic in its very foundation. Maybe in the soil beneath the foundation. I might be able to break through; it's just going to depend on how much time we have before they return."

I could work with that. "How can I help?"

He glanced around the small kitchen. "Search out food, anything with high protein and fats. I need to fuel my energy as I battle the magic. It will be draining."

Having an actual way to help bolstered my mood, and I immediately headed for the fridge. "On it. You get to work figuring out how you'll break us out of here, and I'll figure out food."

When I reached the ancient fridge, which would have been white at some point in its life but was now yellowed with age, I opened the door and got blasted with excessive cold air. The thermostat was out, but at least everything inside looked fresh.

"How did they even get access to all of this magic?" I asked as I yanked out the pound of beef strips and mince from the middle shelf, along with a bunch of *useless* vegetables, which I'd only use to bulk up the dish. Thankfully, there were at least a few potatoes, which made the green, purple, and orange produce look positively pathetic in comparison. When did purple carrots even become a thing? Their very existence was wrong. Along with orange ones.

When I mentioned as such to Slade, he almost cracked a smile. "Purple carrots are actually the heritage varieties, around a long time before the more modern orange."

That made me dislike them even more. "So... what you're

saying is they're the ones that started this nonsense with vegetables?"

With a shake of his head, Slade ignored my vendetta against vegetables and answered my question from before. "I'm not sure what connection they have to the magical community. My research didn't indicate that these alphas were particularly exceptional in either the financial or dominance worlds." He huffed, and I glanced over my shoulder to find him slamming his shoulder against the door. I paused my gathering of ingredients to observe him closer. "I'm searching for a weak point," he explained, and I almost heard him over the sound of my ovaries weeping. In my fertile time, with my period approaching, and this god of a shifter smashing down walls, I was in a world of trouble. "There'll be one somewhere, which is our best chance for a quick escape."

Right, *right*. "Hope you find it soon," I lied.

With a shake of my head, I left Slade to his *work* and started to open all the cupboards to find a large enough pot for the food. I also lucked out with a bag of rice and spices, and hoped I could pull it all together.

The cooktop was as ancient as everything else in the kitchen. The electric element took fifteen minutes to even start heating, by which point Slade had left the room.

I heard him banging on walls, and tried not to think about his muscled arms as he hoisted the house about. I focused on making this the best meal that I could. Frying up the vegetables in oil, I added salt and seasonings, before browning the meat. I finished with water and extra seasonings, letting it all simmer for a while. In another pot, I cooked rice to add to the dish.

I'd learned how to cook through my years in diners and restaurants, but this meal was all *winging it and hoping for the best*. The aim here was to create as much of a meal as possible, to keep Slade fueled up. As nice as it was to see him go all alpha and beat up the walls, I really did want us out of here before the Rogers pack returned.

After twenty minutes the kitchen smelled delicious, and I lifted the lid to inhale the fragrant aroma. There were only a couple of dusty spoons in a drawer, which I rinsed to have my first taste.

A burst of beef hit my tongue, rich and hearty, with only a slight undercurrent of vegetables. The potatoes hadn't broken down yet, but they would eventually, thickening the liquid. It wasn't the best concoction I'd ever tasted but it would do. We couldn't exactly be picky under the circumstances, and I was never going to come close to the quality of Gerald's cooking.

Placing the lid back on to give it a little more time to simmer away, I wandered out of the kitchen and into the living room. Slade was in the corner, using an iron fire poker to jab at the edge of an old bay window. Like the fridge, the paint on the sill and walls would have been white a long time ago, but was now yellowing with flakes of paint fluttering to the dusty wood floors with each jab from the poker.

"Found the weak spot," Slade said as I shuffled closer. "The spell doesn't wrap around quite as neatly here, and I should have this wide enough for us to leave in approximately twelve to eighteen hours. With four hours of sleep factored in."

I reached out toward the wall, but when he growled, I halted, my hand hovering a few inches from it. "Don't touch the perimeter. It's live with magic and will zap your cuffs again. I don't have time to care for you while unconscious."

"Shit, sorry. I should have expected that." My brain had been offline since I'd woken up to find Blaine Rogers standing over me. As heat filled my cheeks, I quickly changed the subject. "The food should be ready in about ten minutes. Do you want me to feed you while you continue to work?"

Slade's head jerked up, and I found myself locked in the laser focus of his piercing gaze. "Feed me?" He rumbled it with so much confusion, as if I'd spoken in a foreign language and he was attempting to translate the meaning.

"Yep," I nodded, barely hiding my grin. "It usually happens with babies, but you don't have to worry, I won't make any airplane noises as I spoon the food in. Unless you want me to, of course."

He blinked a few times before he shook his head. "I'm capable of fighting the energy and eating at the same time. Just leave the bowl close by."

Goddess, this guy needed to relax before he gave himself a stress induced heart attack. "Right on it, sir."

I snapped to attention with an exaggerated salute, and Slade narrowed his eyes, but I hurried away before he could tear me a new asshole. Thankfully his strict timeline for pummeling a hole in the magical wall had him mostly occupied.

Back in the kitchen, I turned off the element but left the lid on the dishes to steam through for a few more minutes. I found a mixing bowl large enough for Slade's portion and spooned in the rice first, then added a huge portion of the stew, focusing mostly on the meat.

When I returned to the living room, I was pleased to see long beams of light peeking through the gap he'd made beside the window, and while we were a long way from fitting through, it was progress.

"Here's your food," I said as I moved closer.

For the first time ever, I noticed a light sheen of sweat on Slade's forehead, face and neck, mingling with the remnants of the blood from the neck cuff. His scent was stronger as well, and I wasn't impressed when the lower half of my body started waking up and fluttering about.

Not the time, vagina. It was really not the time.

"Thank you," he huffed, jerking me out of my horny daze. He indicated with a nod that I should place the bowl near the window. "That shelf will work for me."

Gently setting the steaming meal down, I rested the spoon against the side. "Where's yours?" he asked as his frown deepened. "If that's all the food you made, you will eat your portion first."

"I ate not long ago," I reminded him, "and you're the one tunneling us out of here with a fucking teaspoon. You need the sustenance. I'll be fine."

I was heading back to the kitchen to fetch him a glass of water when his rumble had me tripping over my own feet. *How in the fuck did he do that?* It wasn't even dominance... it was something else. "You will eat with me, Emmeline. Now."

Drawing in the deepest breath I could manage while my body was all but locked down by this controlling lizard, I said with faked calm, "I'm not hungry, Slade. I don't need to eat."

"Lies," he replied with a bite. "Don't ever lie to me, Snow. I can hear your stomach and sense your need. You will eat before I touch the dish."

These freakin' alphas and their controlling tendencies.

"Fine," I sighed, deciding we didn't have the time or energy for this fight. At my compliance, he released me from whatever hold he'd had over me with his growl, and I grumbled all the way into the kitchen.

Grumbled and glowed, my body invigorated in a way that I only felt around my pack. The care of these alphas brought parts of me long suppressed to life.

Fire and need, anger and hope, desire and despair. A plethora of contradictory emotions swirled within me, and I'd never felt so alive.

CHAPTER 6

EMME

The next eight hours were spent in a stringent routine. Slade removed the chains connected to our cuffs to make life easier, but other than that, he worked in silence while I dished up food and water, replacing the bowl of rice and stew until there was nothing left. The magical cuffs, while annoying, didn't hinder either of us in our tasks.

Weirdly though, it wasn't an uncomfortable silence. We kept each other company and it was almost... pleasant.

Around midnight, a sharp cramp in my lower stomach rocked through me, and I excused myself to use the bathroom, groaning at the spots of red on the toilet paper. As an omega and shifter, we were fertile for the week before we bled and during the first few days of our periods.

I'd always been very consistent with my fertile time—every six weeks—with the pain and blood finishing in four or five days. Despite the faint cramps and overall general neediness I'd had recently, I'd been hoping this portion of my cycle would give me another day.

Periods wouldn't be an issue if I wasn't in a house with no

pads, tampons, or painkillers. "*Fuck*," I muttered, as I opened every drawer again, triple-searching in desperation. Slade had said he'd be done in a few hours, so I'd just have to tough it out and use toilet paper until then.

Wouldn't be the first time.

Bundling up layers of paper in my underwear, I pulled my jeans back up and rubbed my hand over my stomach. The discomfort would continue to worsen over the next two to twenty hours, and without painkillers I'd struggle to sleep. Again, though, a few hours without sleep wouldn't kill me. I was tougher than this, and if we got out of here before the Rogers pack returned, then any amount of pain and blood would be worth it.

When I returned to the living room, the hole was now big enough to get my head and shoulders through but was still a way off for Slade's massive form. Holding my stomach, I sank gingerly onto the old, dusty couch, its floral patterns all the rage in the eighties.

Slade lifted his arm to smash into the corner again, only to pause, his nostrils flaring as he turned from the window. "Are you hurt? I smell blood."

Ah, fucking excellent. Alphas and their sense of smell.

"I have my period," I said shortly, nipping this shit in the bud immediately. I also refused to feel embarrassed about a perfectly normal biological occurrence. "There's nothing but toilet paper in the house, which isn't the best for absorbing the scent. But I'm not injured."

I had no idea how the generally reserved shifter would take this information, but to my surprise he didn't blink an eye. "Are you in pain?"

He'd warned me not to lie to him, and I took the warning seriously. "Moderate discomfort, which will most likely grow worse over the next few hours. How long until we're out of here?"

Slade rolled his thick shoulders, rotating them as if to work out muscle fatigue. "I'll continue for another two hours, take the four hours of required rest, and then have us out of here by morning. Just hold on for a few more hours, Snow. I promise I'll get you out of here."

"I trust you." Another truth.

Despite every shifter in the world, even my own pack, warning me that Slade was a loose cannon and couldn't be trusted, my gut *and wolf* said differently. My wolf couldn't always be trusted when it came to her pack, but when my gut backed her up, it felt like a safe bet.

"You don't want to bond with me, do you?"

The words slipped out, and it took me a second to realize I'd said the quiet part out loud—the part that was my realization of why I trusted this alpha. Slade showed no inclination that he wanted me or my power, and it was… nice.

Slade met my gaze, his biceps bunching as he slammed the iron shovel into the spot he was working on—the poker had snapped two hours ago. "No. I don't." There was no tone to tell me why, just the matter-of-fact statement.

I remained quiet in the hopes he'd expand on his reasons, but he didn't, and I wasn't about to push. I'd never expanded on my reasons for not wanting to bond either, and despite the ache in my chest at his rejection, I wasn't a hypocrite. I had absolutely no grounds to demand anything more from him.

Half an hour later, exhaustion eve got the better of me, and despite the pain shooting through my uterus, I slid down on my side and curled up in a ball. "Wake me when it's time for you to rest," I said around a yawn. "I can keep an eye out for the *assholes to return*." My last words were mumbled, but I heard his grunt, which I took as alpha speak for *Okay*.

My sleep was fitful, the pain keeping me from falling too deeply. Add in the chilly winds streaming in through the ever-widening opening in the wall, and it was an uncomfortable rest. At some point, while dreaming about bleeding to death in the snow, a band of heat pressed against my stomach, and it brought such blessed relief that every tense muscle in my body relaxed.

Half asleep, I remained too drowsy to explore where the heat originated from, and when I eventually woke, it was to find a dragon shifter on the floor in front of me, his head very close to mine—I could smell his sweet scent—as he pressed his hand against my shirt.

No other part of him touched me except that one huge hand spanned across my stomach, the natural heat he exuded easing my pain. Despite the uncomfortable way he was sprawled across the hardwood floors, he appeared to be asleep, his chest rising and falling rhythmically.

Scared to move and disturb him, I let my gaze drift around the living room to find that the hole was now large enough for me to escape through, and—

A face appeared in the gap, and I almost screamed, only managing to stifle the sound at the last second. The early morning light reflected off familiar blond hair, and warmth flooded more than just my stomach.

Kellan!

I met his wide-eyed and shocked stare, which would have been comical if I wasn't so fucking relieved to see him. Hunter's snarling, gorgeous face appeared next, and I caught a glimpse of Finley standing a few feet back.

"You okay?" Slade rumbled, and I jumped, wondering if he was ever asleep enough not to be aware of his surroundings.

"Yep," I squeaked. "Our pack found us."

Another rumble, his chest shaking the couch. "I sensed

them as soon as the witch appeared. Her magic is strong enough to leave an echo."

Witch? "The bad witch?" I shot back, lifting panicked eyes toward Kellan.

"No," Slade said, straightening. "This one is on our side."

Oh, right. Hunter must have figured out that magic was involved, and in his control-freak, anal retentive ways, he had already planned ahead and brought his own magical weapon.

Slade shifted away from me, and when his heated palm left my gut, an intense cramp almost took me down. Along with a gush of blood from between my thighs.

Shit. I should have changed the paper hours ago, but apparently I'd been too busy enjoying my dragon hot-water bottle.

"You tell them what happened while I clean myself up," I said to Slade as I stumbled to my feet. He grunted in return, and I was pleased to see we were on the same page.

"Pretty girl," Kellan called, his voice hoarse, dragging my attention back to him. His features were strained as he met my gaze. "Where are you going?"

Deciding a little blood on my clothes wasn't that big of a deal, I segued toward the opening, my heart bursting to life in my chest as I basked in a dose of golden sunshine. "Don't touch the walls," I warned him as he leaned closer, even though I wasn't sure he'd get zapped without the cuffs and bands.

He nodded. "Yeah, the witch already told us that the house was warded."

The way he said *witch* indicated he wasn't a fan. Odd for my normally happy and accepting alpha.

Through the gap, I noticed he was dressed as if they were heading into war. His all-black outfit included a heavy armored vest that made his already broad chest look massive.

He also had weapons strapped across his body, and no lie, I never even knew he owned a gun.

It was a gloriously sexy look on Golden Boy, minus the matching dark circles under his eyes. "I can't believe you guys tracked us down so quickly," I breathed, reaching through to touch his face. "I missed you so damn much."

He closed his eyes briefly as my icy fingers landed on his warm cheeks, letting out a long blissful sigh. "How could you ever doubt we wouldn't find you fast, Shortcake. We haven't stopped searching for you from the second we felt the attack." He opened his eyes again, expression sobering. "Where are the alphas who took you? I feel a great desire to end them in the most painful way possible."

Leaning forward, careful not to bump the walls, I kissed him on the lips. Just one gentle taste that I needed more than my next breath. "Slade will explain everything. Give me a second in the bathroom and I'll be right back."

His nostrils flared slightly, and the blue of his eyes darkened as he met mine. "Period," I murmured, not wanting him to worry.

Kellan's expression softened. "Okay, pretty girl. I'll be waiting right here. I'm not leaving your side for the rest of my life."

I snorted. *Elegantly.* Like a lady. "What if I die first?"

"Not a chance. Absolutely unacceptable. We will die together, and I'll accept nothing less."

A month ago, his declaration would have had me freaked out and running for the hills, but today, all I felt was a comforting warmth in my chest. "I'll hold you to that, Golden. Now, don't go anywhere."

I pulled away from him and almost crashed into Slade, who stood closer than I'd expected. "Be right back," I called, noticing Hunter in the background arguing in low tones with a blond chick—the witch I would guess.

I did my best not to run through the many reasons she was connected to my pack or why my wolf wanted to scratch her face off. We needed a magical ally, and I wouldn't let my jealous beast ruin that. Provided she kept her hands to herself, we'd be just fine.

In the bathroom, I spent a good fifteen minutes cleaning up the blood on my underwear and pants, thankful the material was dark enough to hide the stain. Changing out the paper for more, folded even thicker this time, I got dressed again and washed my face in the icy trickle of water from the rusty faucet.

What I really needed was a long, hot shower, and access to all my toiletries. There was hope, with the rest of the pack arriving, that we'd be out of here shortly and on our way back home. Rogers Pack clearly hadn't returned with their army in time, and for that, I was eternally grateful.

Ignoring the pessimistic voice in the back of my mind that felt it was all too convenient, I focused on the positives. The most important was that Slade and I weren't alone.

We'd be back home and safe very soon.

Home.

At some point over the past weeks, I'd started to think of the alpha's gorgeous house with its white cladding and gray stone as *my* home, while continuously reminding myself that this happy bubble couldn't last. One day, the alphas would grow tired of my inability to bond with them, and they'd either force me or reject me.

Both options ended with me having to run, which I already knew would feel like cutting out a vital organ and expecting to keep living without it. Just a bleeding, gaping hole in my person that would never be repaired. As much as I was glad to have met these alphas and learned that there were decent and amazing shifters out there, I wasn't sure I'd survive now I knew what I had to lose.

When I ventured back into the living room, I found the rest of the wall and window were gone, and my entire pack—including Warrick, who I hadn't even known was here—standing in the threshold.

"Warrick," I cried. "I can't believe you're here." The entitled alpha who'd given me my first glimpse of a true pack and home, pressed his hand to his chest.

"We've been worried about you, Emme. I'm so happy to see you're okay."

Kellan distracted me when he side-stepped Hunter and hauled me into his arms. He gave the most perfect hugs, and my chest was doing that stupid heaving sensation again.

I'd never get used to being held like this, with so much strength and need. It was my eternal undoing. With a groan, I sank into his energy, ignoring the pain in my lower half, exacerbated by his tight embrace.

"Remember how I told you I lost ten years off my life when you were attacked by our security," Kellan rasped brokenly, pulling back far enough to see my nod. "Yeah, well, it was a hundred years when you were blasted off your bike and kidnapped out from under us. I'm running out of years, Shortcake. Can you pretty please with sunshine on top not get taken again."

This alpha was the perfect dose of good endorphins. "I'll do my very best," I chuckled, relieved to feel happiness once more.

Slade left Hunter's side and I wasn't the only one who gasped when he pressed his hand against the center of my back, over the material of my shirt. His warmth was so much stronger than Kellan's, and it was a relief to my aching uterus once more.

"She's in pain, Kel," he said in his softly menacing way. "Loosen your grip."

Kellan immediately released me from his firm grasp, his expression falling into concerned lines as he examined me. "Baby, I'm sorry. You should have said something."

With a shake of my head, I buried my face in his chest. "You could never hurt me, Golden Boy. Never. This is exactly where I want to be, held as tightly against you as shifterly possible."

For a second, everything was right in my world, but I knew it wouldn't last for long.

I had an evil alpha pack and their magical witch to deal with.

Well, two witches apparently. Time to find out who blondie was.

CHAPTER 7

EMME

Hunter's expression reminded me of an icy winter morning, frosty and biting, as he observed me. We hadn't had a chance to talk yet, as he'd been occupied with the witch, but now I had his full focus.

Like with Kellan, seeing the massive alpha kitted out in full black including armored vests and weapons was a new, sexy experience. He usually wore suits, and I'd thought that was his hottest look, but this... oh fuck, this was so much hotter. His six-foot-six frame looked massive, topped off by heavy shitkicker boots. Not to mention the stormy darkness in his gold-threaded irises, letting us all know his wolf was present.

"Jewels can release the cuffs," he said, indicating toward my wrists.

"Of course," she purred, hurrying for Slade, only to pause when he leveled a furious stare in her direction.

"Remove Emme's first," the dragon shifter ordered, and if that expression had been directed at me, I'd have sprinted the other way.

Jewels released an exaggerated huff as she turned to me,

moving much slower. "Hello, Omega," she said, just the slightest hint of an accent in her husky tones.

My wolf was annoyed at how tiny and blond she was, all pale curls and richly tanned skin. Her dark eyes examined me as closely as I was examining her, and while she didn't look older than me, her energy felt ancient. Instinct told me she was a powerful witch, and I hated her connection to my pack. Magic felt wrong against our beasts, and I wouldn't want that sulfuric scent of her magic to taint any of us.

It was hard to dislike her as much when she released me from the itchy, irritating cuffs though. "Ahhh, that feels so good," I said, rubbing my reddened skin. "Thank you for your help."

"No worries. Your mates pay *very* well for my services."

And what in the hell did that mean? She better be talking about cash... Or we were going to have a larger problem.

When she released Slade's cuffs, I noticed her tuck the discarded magical bands into the pocket of her jeans, and despite their bulkiness, they somehow fit perfectly.

Finley stood a few feet away, arms crossed, wearing his usual grouchy expression. His glorious hair was out, angled down just below his ears and sliding toward his jawline. He didn't have a weapon, but wore the same tactical uniform as the others. It did add to his appeal, and even scowling, there was no taking away from his beauty.

If I had to guess, the moody bear was pissed off that I'd survived and would live to annoy him another day. Warrick, though, who stood by his side, was all smiles. "Cora is going to be so relieved when I tell her you're okay," he told me.

"Thank you for coming with them," I said again, touched that he'd come into a dangerous situation that involved alphas and magic for me.

The entitled alpha shook his head as his forehead

wrinkled. "Sweetheart, you're part of our extended family. Cora and the others are going out of their minds with worry."

Cora was my newly claimed best friend, and I equally liked the other members of Warrick's pack too. They did feel a little like extended family. I would have to call them when we finished dealing with our current situation.

Hunter stepped into the conversation finally: "We need every detail from when you were taken to the moment we appeared." The fury he'd barely contained since they'd arrived finally boiled over. I tried not to feel bothered that unlike the last time I was attacked, he hadn't touched me once since they'd tracked me down.

Subconsciously, a part of me had been waiting for a dose of the entitled alpha's claiming touch. A part of me needed it to right my omega and beast.

"I'll tell you everything I know, but I was unconscious for a lot of it."

As uneasy as it was to remain here, lingering on the edge of our enemy's house, this information was important. I didn't want to have to run from my mom's pack for the rest of my life, and now that they knew of my existence and city affiliation, they'd come after me again. No doubt they wanted to use my power the same way they'd used mom's. Which I could never let happen.

I needed the alphas' help.

Kellan stroked my back in a soothing rhythm as I started to explain: "It was my mom's old pack: the Rogers pack. Blaine is the entitled alpha, and then there's Josiah, Donnie, and Hewie, all alphas as well. I don't know anything else about them these days—I haven't seen them since I was fourteen when they destroyed my mom and I took off. That was the last time I was around shifters until I was dragged to Golden Claw. Slade believes they found me through my registration with the cities, which makes sense."

"What do they want with you?" Hunter asked, his expression unchanging, but I felt the surge in his energy.

"Most likely the same thing they wanted from my mom. To bond an omega and use me for their own gain."

It was as much of the truth as I could reveal, without telling them everything they did to Mom—what they took from her, and the tragic ending that was the result.

Finley released a disparaging sound, and I found myself leaning to the side to see around Hunter and meet his glare. I'd spent most of our brief time together ignoring his moody, surly ass, but today I couldn't hold back. "Do you have something to say, Finley Thornton? Let it all out, you big grouchy asshole."

The handsome shifter's face wasn't drawn like Kellan's or racked in worry like Hunter's. He appeared to be the pinnacle of virility, and even dressed as he was, he gave off woodsman vibes with his light brown skin, shiny chestnut hair, and whiskey eyes.

I'd felt a connection to him from the first moment I stared into his fractured gaze, but his attitude was frankly starting to piss me off.

"Nothing of any importance to say," he said calmy, showing no sign he was offended by being called an asshole. "It's just hard to believe that you didn't do anything to get yourself into this situation. You've been so determined to escape us, Ice Queen." I started at the nickname, which was the first he'd ever given me. Typically, it was not a nice one.

He grinned, showing me all his perfect, white teeth. "Ah, that struck a nerve, did it? Well, Slade called you Snow, and it reminded me that you're as cold and unforgiving as that element, and just as deadly."

Even though I knew that wasn't the reason for Slade's

nickname—his was actual perfection—I could see why Finley took it that way. As I'd said before, he was an asshole.

"Have I tried to escape though?" I shot back. "Think about it, meathead. In all the time I've been in Golden Claw, have I attempted even *once* to escape?"

The answer to that was no, and he couldn't remotely argue it. I'd justified my lack of escape attempts in multiple ways: the alphas hadn't been pushing me to bond; I needed to get a stash of cash together; it'd be easier once they trusted me and left me alone. But still, even with all of that, the number one reason was how good it felt to be with them. I'd been desperately consuming this pack and family life, all the while fearing the day it would come to an end.

"You might not have had an opportunity yet, but you've made it very clear that you want to leave. You haven't even bonded with Kellan, who you hang off constantly, or created any sort of permanent place in our pack. You're still just using us until you have your chance to escape. We're not a fucking stopgap on your way to something better."

Hunter moved forward, as if to stand as a barrier between us, but I placed my hand on his chest to hold him back. His chest rumbled, but he didn't fight me. This was my battle with Finley, and I didn't need help. *Yet*. "There's nothing better than this pack," I told Finley softly. "Nothing. And I have a very good reason for not wanting to bond, and that reason has little to do with how much I want Kellan, Hunter, or Slade."

I deliberately didn't say his name, but once again he showed no sign of reaction.

Fucker. I wished I could be this indifferent, but it was impossible.

"And what pray tell is this very serious reason you've never shared with us?"

Staying with them meant my death. If I revealed that

though, I would have to elaborate on the why, and once they knew they could gain power from our bonding...

Every shifter wanted more power—it was the core component of our beasts. Especially alphas.

"I didn't ask to be dragged to Golden Claw," I bit out through gritted teeth in an attempt to keep my voice steady. "And I didn't ask to live in your house. Hunter all but forced me into it. In the end, I think I've been more than gracious with the way you've all dominated and controlled my life. Maybe you need to look harder at your own actions and worry less about hating me. As far as I can tell, you're the one with a problem, when I've done nothing to you. *Nothing!*"

With his expression darkening, Finley took a step toward me, and it was intimidating to be in the shadow of a massive alpha. It was also the first time we'd been this close, and the strong scent of vanilla cherry melded into my chocolate honey like we'd been made for each other. "You're my only fucking problem, Ice Queen—"

"You're out of line, Fin," Kellan growled, stepping between us before I could say another word. "You have to stop blaming Emme for both your own trauma and for other shifters' actions. This..." He waved his hand around "...was not her fault. She didn't ask to be taken."

Finley shrugged, his expression smoothing as he got himself under control. "She didn't *not* ask to be taken. If we were all bonded, we could have tracked her. Thankfully, once we found the city, with the help of the witch and our connection to Slade, we managed to track them down. But even the most uneducated shifter knows a completed quintet is the strongest. It's almost as if *Emmeline* doesn't really care if she's stolen from us."

"Enough!" Slade silenced the room, and I noticed witchy pouting even harder. She'd been enjoying the drama of the bear tearing into me. "Firstly, don't presume to know why I call her Snow. That's between Emme and me. Secondly, you're being an asshole and it's not the time. I can confirm that Emme had nothing to do with orchestrating our kidnapping, and she was quite hurt in the process. Her spine was broken, amongst other injuries."

Finley's head jerked back, and this time when he looked me over, I could not mistake the concern in his expression. It was briefly there, oh so briefly, but my body thrummed from that one intense visual scan.

Goddess knew I wouldn't survive if I had his full, undivided attention in a positive way.

"And thirdly..." Slade continued. "We need to get back to the issue at hand: do we wait for the pack to return, or should we head out and track them down ourselves?"

"They won't be back, my darling dragon," the witch said with a shrug, and my wolf briefly debated clawing her eyes out. "There are magical boobytraps all over the yard that we triggered upon arrival. My guess is that they'll disappear for a few weeks to regroup and replan. They won't take you on with your full pack."

"Boobytraps," Hunter snapped, giving the area a sharp once-over, his dominance stronger than ever. His wolf flashed until the gold almost drowned out the storminess of his eyes. "What the fuck does that mean? I felt nothing when we approached."

She shook her head, pursing her lips. "Sorry, that wasn't the correct adjective. More like alerts. *Security*. They'd be alerted if anyone escaped, but it works the opposite way as well. They felt our arrival before we reached the house."

The entitled alpha looked frustrated with this information.

"What city are we even in?" I asked, trying not to dwell on my fight with Finley, even though his words swirled like missiles in my head. Targeted and painful every time they hit.

"Silver City," Hunter said, stepping closer to me, the hard expression he'd worn since they arrived finally easing. "The pack who took you make their home here, and two of the alphas are on the council. The entire pack is unusually dominant and connected within the community. It'd be foolish to hunt them here, in their own territory. We need to plan first."

I nodded, already agreeing. "They have a lot of magic on their side too, though we never saw signs of a witch."

Jewels looked around, sniffing the air. "There's no recognizable essence here. I don't know the witch they're using, which is... odd."

Kellan cursed. "How the hell are these alphas so powerful and magically connected? It makes no sense. We've never even heard of them before—I thought we held the most powerful pack spot."

There was a huff from the dragon shifter. "Only the two with council seats came up on my radar." He sounded annoyed. "They're keeping their exploits offline as much as possible, which makes sense now that I know what they've been planning." He turned his piercing green gaze on Kellan. "And we are the most powerful, because I am the most powerful. But that pack is not to be underestimated. They're dabbling heavily in magic, *and* have full use of Reeves Industries tech, which means they're rich enough to buy the best."

Hunter growled, inching closer to me again, until I could feel his energy racing over my skin. The urge to lean forward and bury my face against his chest was strong. I wanted to soak up his comforting and supportive presence for a few seconds. "Sounds like we need to be more careful with who we allow to buy from us," he said, the rumble unmistakable in his tone. "These bastards must have loved using *our* technology to attack and contain our pack mates. Makes me want to ensure they're buried ten feet under in a permanent dirt nap."

Finally, *fucking finally,* Hunter wrapped his arms around me and hauled me up into his chest. He must have heard Slade's advice to be gentle, as his hold wasn't as tight as normal, and I sank against him, realizing how out of sorts I'd been with his distance. He'd been in full entitled alpha mode, but I finally sensed a small snippet of *my* Hunter returning—the one who had claimed me with a tattoo and who cared for and protected me with every part of himself; who'd saved me from the guard by destroying him where he stood.

My Hunter.

"Were the Rogers pack this powerful when your mom was their mate?" he asked in a low uncertain voice, his mouth close to my cheek as he breathed me in. "Do you have any theories of where their strength originates?"

I had theories alright, and maybe it was the emotional upheaval from my kidnapping, or the way he hugged me so perfectly, but for the first time I was on the verge of revealing the truth.

I wanted to stop hiding what happened to Mom and what I feared would also happen to me.

To trust that we could all work this out *together.*

Taking a deep breath, I lifted my head and said, "Mom's pack knows exactly what an omega's power can do—"

Slade's roar cut me off, and I smelled sulfur a second before the most eerie, surreal energy washed through the living room.

A force hit me in the side, and still wrapped around Hunter, I was thrown into the yard as the house blasted to pieces around us, raining down debris in its wake.

"*Conquesta marina tulula mergan,*" Jewels shouted as we

flew, her magic cushioning our landing on the icy dirt. Even with her magical help, we still should have felt more impact from an explosion, and I couldn't figure out why we weren't injured until I was hauled to my feet by Hunter. We both turned to see a giant, scaled form blocking the side of the house.

Or where the house used to be.

It was Slade. In his dragon form.

Holy goddess. He'd shifted and taken the brunt of the magical attack, leaving the rest of us safe and uninjured. I stepped forward, concerned he'd been hurt, only to pause as I took in the sheer size of his beast.

He was massive, maybe fifty times the size of me, towering high into the sky as the sunlight reflected off his scales, which were mostly green with black-tipped edges. "Slade," I whispered, gazing up and up and up to find his colossal head.

The dragon's long neck swung around, his gaze snapping toward me, and I drowned in the depths of sharp, biting green eyes that never blinked as they held me in place. The green that appeared so unnatural in his bipedal form felt just right in this mystical, incredible beast.

My mind whirled, and I swear my soul left my body when his long neck bent to bring massive rows of razor-sharp teeth closer to my face. The heat he exuded left my face feeling raw and slightly singed.

"Slade," Hunter murmured in a low, soothing tone as he shuffled closer to my back, apparently hesitant to move any faster. "What are you doing? Control your beast."

The dragon's huge chest rumbled, and we were blasted with wafts of fire-touched air. Tension filled the yard, and even Hunter stopped moving. In fact, the only one of us who appeared to even be breathing was the dragon.

He was graceful as he moved forward, his thick, heavy legs

stomping down the browned bushes that made up the bulk of the yard. He was so massive that when he stopped in front of me, I stood under his front legs and chest, and my head didn't touch him.

My body refused to obey my command to move as paralyzing fear held me in place. Was this the moment Slade decided I was an annoyance and a risk to his pack and gulped me up?

He sniffed me, heat blasting my face again until I was sweating, and when his nose brushed across my stomach, I sucked it in harshly. "Uh, g-good d-dragon," I stuttered, my voice barely working too. "You don't want to eat me, right? I'm way too scrawny to satisfy your big appetite."

He huffed again, blasting hot air right at my stomach, and the ache of my period eased.

I had no idea if that had been his intention all along, but as I stared into his unblinking eyes, the fear thrumming through me eased. Without thought, I reached out toward him. It was more than a want, it was a desperate, driving need to connect us.

Just before my hand made contact, Hunter noticed my intentions and roared as he dove for me, but he was too late.

CHAPTER 8

EMME

Slade swung his head in a graceful arc and smashed into Hunter's side, sending him flying. I choked on a scream as the entitled alpha flipped a few times, landing smoothly on his feet, his expression resigned rather than furious.

"What do we do?" Kellan shouted, his gaze whipping back and forth between Hunter and the dragon. "Is he going to hurt her?"

Hunter growled, deep and menacing, but he didn't move toward us again. "Do not approach them. Slade's dragon isn't attacking yet, and it appears at least for now that he recognizes his mate. Still, never forget that the man is not in control of the beast."

The dragon's giant head and scary teeth appeared back in my line of sight. The two of us examined each other for many long seconds. The urge to touch him hadn't gone anywhere, but this time I moved slower. It wasn't that I thought I could startle a dragon, but I wanted to give him time to move away from my touch.

The dragon's gaze remained firmly on my face, as if he were

committing my features to memory. My palm connected to the smooth scaled surface between his eyes, before slowly sliding down to the end of his nose. The scales felt near indestructible, hard and hot beneath my touch. They reminded me of diamonds, especially as they reflected brightly in the early morning light.

The beast released a smokier huff, and I coughed for a second. All the while I continued to stroke his scales, feeling almost relaxed at the sensation. "Look at you," I murmured, leaning closer until my face was pressed against the side of his head, just below his eye. Which was almost the size of my entire head on its own. "You're just a big snuggly beast, aren't you?"

Another huff, one that almost sounded amused.

"Emme, for the love of my sanity, can you please step away from the most dangerous shifter beast in the world." Hunter's words were strained, which entertained me to no end.

"Don't worry yourself, Daddy Alpha. I'm perfectly safe with Slade. He's had more than enough opportunities to murder me over the past however many weeks, and I'm still standing here."

Kellan's laughter was a mix of amusement and strain. "That's a great theory, pretty girl, but the dragon and the man are two separate entities. Maybe it's best to not keep testing the beast's limits on your first meeting."

Ignoring the worried alphas in my life, I scratched my nails gently down the long, thick jaw. "Are you dangerous?" I asked him in a low, soothing tone. "I mean, I know you're dangerous, but not to me, right? These silly alphas are all worried over nothing."

Another of his amused snorts, and I was hit with a strong blast of that same, mystical energy from before, and in a flash the beast was gone. In his place stood a nearly seven-foot-tall shifter.

Jerking myself backwards, I landed on my ass, the fear returning with Slade's bipedal form. There was a scary facet to this shifter no matter what form he chose.

He stomped forward in two steps to stand over the top of me again, and *holy goddess of the shift*. He was completely and utterly naked.

My breaths huffed in and out as I took in his massive cock and heavy balls, hanging over the top of my head. *What in the weapon of mass destruction was happening here?*

It wasn't that I was surprised to find Slade's jewels matched the rest of him. He was the biggest shifter I'd ever seen in my life, and that was the biggest dick I'd ever seen in my life.

It made sense.

But there was more than just the size... *Slade was pierced.*

From the tip of his thick head all the way down to his even thicker base. I counted eight piercings, but there could have been more. Gah, and that view wasn't even fully erect, because as I stared, his second beast continued to lengthen. *Come on*, there was no way that would ever fit a normal shifter...

I scrambled to my feet to distract myself from *all of that*, breathing harshly as I met his gaze. His *furious* gaze. "Don't ever fucking do that again," he snapped, his chest heaving.

I wasn't sure I'd ever seen Slade this angry; he'd mostly been ambivalent and cold around me and his pack, but as he stood before me, he was all fire.

"Do what?" I choked out, unsure if he was referring to the way I'd eyeballed his pierced shaft like we were about to become better acquainted.

"The dragon is not a fucking pet," he snarled, his hands trembling at his side.

Oh, right. The dragon. Beast number one.

"If he seeks you out," Slade continued, "remain still and quiet, and if you value your life, never, under any circumstances, touch him. I won't be able to stop him if you annoy him. He's killed for far less."

"He… he didn't seem to mind me."

Slade scoffed, the green of his eyes chilly. "He might not have my touch aversion, but then again, who would have ever gotten close enough to know that before you. Stupid, Omega. Stupid will get you killed."

With a shake of his head, he turned and walked away, and I got a glimpse of broad shoulders and his strong back, leading down to two, bronze and perfect ass cheeks. *Goddess be damned.* The shifter was a piece of perfection, and I'd been so caught up in *all of that* I'd missed what his tattoos on his chest were of.

The annoying witch distracted me as she made a weird weepy sound. "I'll go after our dragon and make sure he's okay."

The urge to reach out and grab handfuls of her perfect blond hair and yank her back was strong, even knowing I had no right to get possessive over that dragon, or any of these alphas.

"It's your neck," Finley told her with a harsh laugh.

Forcing myself to stop staring at the spot Slade disappeared to, I hoped that all the progress I'd made with the dragon during our time together was not completely undone. The thought of going back to what we'd been when we first met was a jab far sharper than period pain.

As if sensing my distress, Kellan and Hunter pressed in on either side of me, holding me between their alpha heat and soothing energy. Neither of them said a word, but they felt more relaxed now that the drama of the dragon had passed. "I wasn't in any danger, guys," I whispered, somewhat pleased by their protectiveness. "I don't know what you're all on about, but that dragon is a sweetheart. I'm keeping him, and there's nothing you can say to change my mind."

Hunter's rumble was menacing, and Kellan's was strained, as they wrapped me up a little tighter.

"You're going to be the death of me," the entitled alpha sighed, craning his neck to breathe me in, his nose running along my skin. When he pulled away, I stared into the clouds of his stormy eyes. "Promise me you won't seek Slade out in any form. He doesn't think like other shifters. There's an animalistic quality to how he assesses every situation, and oftentimes that part of him wins over the more human-based empathy and logic."

I took his warning seriously, because if Hunter, who was the second toughest, scariest alpha I knew, was worried, then I would be as well. Still, I really did want to keep the dragon. I'd figure out the way to make it safe for all of us.

Warrick, who I'd all but forgotten was even here, said, "What's the plan with these alphas? They just tried to destroy us through a magical explosion. It's not safe to keep lingering here in Silver City."

"What do you suggest?" Finley asked, shooting the entitled alpha a droll stare. "If you're going to bring up the obvious, you need to offer a solution."

Warrick didn't bite back. "We need to inform the Alpha Council?" he said, offering his solution. "Now that Emme and Slade are safe, we can go through the official channels, and enlist our own army."

Warrick and Slade led two enforcer groups, which were filled with the most elite of shifters, trained and prepared to protect our city. They would be a great asset to have on our side against the Rogers pack.

"The council is already looking into it," Slade said as he reappeared fully dressed in his usual black fatigues and boots. The witch strolled along beside him, and I was relieved to see her keeping a decent distance from the dragon. Even if he was no doubt wearing clothes she'd conjured... *okay, yeah, I wanted to smash her face in again.*

Hunter's hand traced up and down my spine for a second before he moved away to speak directly with Slade. "How do you know the council is looking into it?"

Kellan took advantage of the space Hunter left and pulled me back against his chest, his heart beating faster than usual. It hadn't escaped my notice that he hadn't said a word since I'd scared them half to death by petting a dragon.

I slid my hand over and threaded my fingers through his, binding us together as I rested against him. He exhaled his tension, his much larger frame engulfing mine. "It's okay, Golden Boy," I murmured, my gaze on Hunter and Slade, who remained in an intense discussion about the council. "I'm okay, and I'm not going anywhere." Not today anyway.

"I've waited a lifetime for you, Emmeline," he whispered close to my ear. "And if I've learned anything since you came into my life, it's that if you're not alive then I'm not alive. I refuse to do this shit without you. *I can't do this without you.* That's just how it is now and forever."

My chest clenched like it was in a vise; the wheezed sob that spilled from my lips was loud enough to draw the attention of everyone in the yard. I attempted to spin in Kellan's hold, wanting to see if his expression matched the broken shards of his voice, but he held me too tightly to move.

He slowly rocked us back and forth. "It's okay, baby," he murmured, so low I doubted the other alphas would hear. "It just means I will stand between you and death always. I'm not worried about living without you, because it won't happen.

The only reason I didn't jump in with the dragon was the risk of provoking him. Along with the fact that I've seen Slade lose it before, and his beast was calm with you. Maybe calmer than I'd ever seen him."

The thought of Kellan dying had my knees giving out; it was lucky he held me, or I'd have hit the ground. "No!" I finally managed to get a word out. "I refuse to let you stand between me and danger. I refuse to let you die first. That doesn't fucking work for me."

With each statement, I got louder, which had Hunter prowling toward us. "What's happening between you two?" he asked as his gaze settled on Kellan. "Emme's wolf is going mental."

Kellan's chest rumbled, the movement reverberating through me. "I was just reminding Emme that her heart beats for more than one now."

Hunter's expression shuttered, becoming difficult to read as he reached out and clasped a hand on Kellan's shoulder. It was a nice moment between the pair, and I didn't expect Hunter to jerk us into his hold, leaving me sandwiched between their hugs.

They did that a lot, holding me between them. These alphas, who had shown me affection and interest from almost our first meeting. And I wasn't mad about it.

If anything, it had me craving a time I could be between them in a *different* way.

A reality I wasn't sure would ever truly be mine, but a girl could dream.

CHAPTER 9

EMME

Further discussion ended with the sound of sirens in the distance. Not a huge surprise considering the house had been blown half to pieces, and despite the size of the house blocks here, we were clearly still in suburbia.

"Silver City enforcers are on the way," Slade said, tilting his head back as he listened closely. "A dozen or more. We need to leave."

Kellan and Hunter wasted no time ushering me into one of the blacked-out SUVs they'd parked a few blocks from the house. "As out of character as it feels to leave without a fight," Hunter said getting in the driver's side, "if we want to go through official channels, we can't be caught here."

"I'm already erasing all trace of our presence in this city," Slade added as he slid into the passenger seat, Hunter's phone in his hand. It reminded me that we'd lost our phones in the initial attack. I was sad to lose the group chats—they were secretly one of my favorite parts of pack life.

"Excellent," our entitled alpha said as Kellan and Finley jumped in the car. Jewels and Warrick were in the second car, and I was relieved to have my pack with me. Even if two of them remained distant, it was better than them not being here at all.

Especially when all of our scents mingled together.

Hunter's mocha goodness had me desperate for a hit of caffeine; Slade's toasted marshmallow had me dreaming of nights under the stars; Kellan's cinnamon and caramel were scents I associated with home and love; and Finley's vanilla cherry was the least familiar but no less potent.

All of them merged flawlessly and smelled even better when combined with my chocolate and honey. If we bonded, our scents would mingle even stronger to inform shifters that we were a completed quintet. That, along with the bites I'd wear, would also be a deterrent to other alphas.

As unfair as it was, males—especially alpha males—rarely had to defend themselves against advances. If they said no, very few shifters could force them. Females weren't quite as lucky, hence why our mates marked our throats and shoulders. A clear sign of a claim.

The silence was heavy during the drive to the airport, with Hunter keeping us well above the speed limit, seemingly unconcerned that we might be pulled over. Kellan, who sat beside me in the middle row, reached out during the drive to play with the ends of my long, strawberry blond hair. His face was calm and contented as he stared out his window, and I was relieved that the pain and worry he'd worn upon his arrival, had faded from his features.

It had been a stressful and fucked-up few days, and I was already excited by the prospect of time spent in recovery with the alphas. Eventually, we'd have to deal with the council and the Rogers pack, but only after we'd recuperated from this. *Hopefully*.

Staring out the window too, I took in Silver City, which appeared far less developed than Golden Claw, with only a few buildings on the horizon standing above a story or two. There were no giant skyscrapers like the Reeves Industries and Thenguard Shipping buildings. Mostly, the infrastructure consisted of large housing blocks interspersed with forests. Like Golden Claw, it was chilly outside, but without our sunshine. Silver City, for its shiny name, was actually gray and dull. I couldn't wait to return back home.

I'd come a long way from the day that alpha scented me in Florida and changed my entire life. Weirdly, it almost felt like a lucky break now to have been dragged kicking and screaming into a world I never expected to experience. I finally understood what it felt like to truly belong to more than myself.

"Did you guys miss a hockey game?" I asked suddenly, realizing that life would have been going on as per normal, even as we were in the middle of a shitshow.

Finley was the one who answered, shocking the crap out of me. "We did. I left Coach a very cryptic message, which I'm sure will get our asses kicked when we return, but he was aware that there'd been an attack on our pack."

His statement was delivered without his usual ire, and I let myself appreciate his deep husky voice. A voice I very much enjoyed when he wasn't using it as a weapon to eviscerate me.

"I'm sor—"

"Don't apologize," Hunter snapped. "You didn't do anything wrong, and none of us consider hockey to be more important than our pack."

Finley sighed, and I was hit with a gust of cherry-vanilla, but he didn't correct Hunter. We were all more than aware of how his priorities lay. I wasn't even a close second to hockey. I wasn't even on the list.

Kellan's wolf energy surged stronger as he reached over and unclicked my seatbelt, hauling me out of my chair and into his lap. My heart leapt briefly into my throat but settled as I sank into his firm chest and thighs. I was so instantly relaxed I could have taken a quick nap... It felt *good* to be close to him.

Hunter eyed Kellan closely, and I'd have been worried about his lack of focus on the semi-busy street, but I'd seen him do this before. Our entitled leader apparently had eyes on the side of his head because he never hit anything, even while distracted. "What did I say about slobbering all over Emme...?"

Kellan, as usual, took no offense. "Firstly, you're one to talk, bro. Who went all alpha wolf on her when she was attacked by Jones? I couldn't even see her pretty freckles through all the bruises and marks you left on her skin. And secondly, I'm not slobbering on her. I'm adoring her. I'm fucking obsessed with her, and I'll never stop showing her. She'd have to kill me first, and if that's her choice, I still stand by my obsession."

Did I just melt into a pile of goo? I'd never been adored. Or obsessed over. Or... loved. Not even for one minute in my life before I met these alphas. I had no idea what to do with the overabundance of emotions scorching through me and burning my eyeballs.

Crying was not advisable when in close confinement with alphas, so I channeled the surge of feelings into the only available release: twisting in my seat and pressing my lips to Kellan's.

He released a low groan from deep in his chest, before a puff of air escaped his lungs, as if he'd been too overwhelmed to even breathe. His mouth parted in a slow, perfect motion, and I was dragged into the kiss. There was no hurried desperation as I'd felt in other kisses with the alphas. This was a slow devouring. A consummation, as I was surrounded by not only the sweetness of his taste, but the buzz of his energy.

This was our wolves connecting on a spiritual level.

His fingers bit into my thighs as Kellan yanked me around

to straddle him on the chair. He slouched to give us more room, and I barely stifled my moan as I rocked against him.

I'd had sex half a dozen times in my life. With humans. It was always completely forgettable, and eventually I decided my cheap ass vibrator was far superior, and stopped even bothering.

The feeling of Kellan between my thighs, though, told me in no uncertain terms that what I'd experienced in the human world had nothing on being with a shifter. With an alpha. *My alpha.*

Unfortunately, today I was not only bleeding quite profusely, we were also in *a car with the rest of our pack.* Two facts that doused my arousal fast as I gasped and tried to lurch away.

Kellan slid one hand up my spine and into my hair, tightening his grip at the base of my skull. The tugging sensation against my scalp was mimicked by another one much, *much* lower. "It's natural, pretty girl," he murmured against my lips, and for a brief, *insane* second, I thought he was referring to fucking in front of the pack. "None of us are turned off by blood."

Goddess of a shifter, *and* I was right back to almost combusting.

When the whimper spilled from between my lips, I pulled away to catch my breath, and for no reason at all, my gaze met Finley's, who sat right behind Kellan's chair.

The bear shifter looked stiff and uncomfortable, but for a change the whiskey of his eyes was light and bright, those thick lashes framing their beauty as he stared me down.

At first glance I'd have said disgust lined his expression, but as I caught the slight flare of his nostrils and noted the deepening cherry-vanilla of his scent, I had to reassess.

He almost looked like he was in pain.

Our gazes remained locked, until he growled all bearlike: "Get us to the fucking airport. I don't need to see this shit right in front of me."

Kellan buried his face against my chest and laughed lightly. "Leave the shade of green for Slade, Fin. It's not a good look on you."

Slade grunted from the front, and while he didn't turn around for me to see any other reaction, it felt like the interior grew hotter with each passing second.

Was it suddenly hard to breathe in here? Did Hunter switch the air off?

I hit the button to lower the window, desperate for waft of cool fall air, and a slight escape from the intensity pulsing like it had its own heartbeat.

Silence descended once more, and Kellan didn't appear to be worried, as he absentmindedly stroked my side, the calming rhythm lowering my pulse. This shifter had been telling me from the start that he was *all in* with me, and somewhere along the lines... I'd started to feel the exact same way about him. Like I couldn't exist without him in my life.

It was terrifying to know my happiness and future were tied up in these four alphas, especially with bonding the inevitable ending for us. I needed to tell them the truth, so we could all fight it together. It was exhausting fighting fate on my own.

I'd almost spilled it back at the clearing, and maybe this was the topic we needed right now, to fill the awkward silence. With their help, I might even be able to go through the omega books from Chelsea. She was the only other omega in Golden Claw, and her reference texts remained stacked in the corner of my room, untouched.

"I want to tell you all what happened to my mom." I blurted out before I could second-guess myself. Even as fear thrummed through my veins like injected poison. "Explain what her pack did to her and why I've been running from the cities."

Hunter's eyes left the road again, and Slade turned as much as he could in the seat, his shoulders too wide to maneuver more than thirty degrees.

"You don't have to if you're not ready," Kellan assured me, sitting straighter and bringing me closer to his face. "We can be patient for as long as you need. There's no pressure. For anything."

Gah, perfect Golden. I was fairly sure I was in love with this alpha, and for that alone I'd take the risk. "I want you all to understand why I ran from you. Why I've had to fight against this pull between us. Because I promise, I feel it too. I've just had no choice but to take a different path. It's been a really fucking lonely, sad, pathetic existence. Fate dealt me a bit of a run of shitty luck."

Hunter's tone was soft and gruff at the same time, which perfectly summed up this alpha: "There's nothing you could tell us that would change the way we feel, little omega. Nothing. We want to be part of the solution to your problems. Let us be the solution."

Of course, our resident genius inventor believed there was no problem he couldn't fix. I hoped this time he was right.

"It's not as simple as letting you all fix it, because this might be beyond..." I choked up, my cheeks heating even as the cool air from the now open window slapped against my skin. Kellan ran his hands up and down my back, soothing me once more. "This is a secret that omegas do not want others to know. Hence why it's not common knowledge, or at least I don't believe it is."

"Can you fucking spit it out already, Icy," Finley growled, and I was simply *thrilled* that he had a shortened version of my name that was somehow even meaner. "It clearly affects us as much as you, and the fact that you've been keeping it from us and rejecting us—"

He didn't get to finish tearing strips off me as Hunter cursed and slammed on the brakes, jerking us to the right. A wash of pungent sulfur flowed in through the window as magic wrapped around the vehicle.

I screamed as we were flipped into a deadly tumble across Silver City streets. It was only Kellan's hold on me that kept me from being flung into the ceiling, even though I still managed to hit the edge of the door and the hard lines of his body armor multiple times.

When the momentum finally came to a halt, we were the right way up at least, but before we even caught our breaths, Kellan's door was ripped off, and we copped the full force of the witch's magical blast. I was slower to react, as instinct had me lifting my hands to call on my wolf, who was slightly more resistant to magic. Kellan, though, was already two steps ahead of me.

As I threw my arms up, he did exactly as he'd promised me earlier: moved my half-shifted beast out of the way and placed himself between me and danger. When the magic hit his face, his entire body shuddered and collapsed.

With a howl, I lost control of my wolf and lunged straight for the witch outside the door.

CHAPTER 10

EMME

There'd been no thoughts when I lunged, just an overwhelming need to destroy the threat to my pack. My wolf had complete control, and even as I screamed and cried in the back of my mind for Kellan, her focus remained on the target. Fangs sank into skin, and blood filled my mouth. I must have taken the witch by surprise to land a direct hit to her shoulder, and I took advantage of that by tearing into her flesh, with its hint of death and decay.

Witch tasted disgusting, but I didn't stop as a frenzy took over.

I growled and shook my prey, tearing through muscle and cracking bone. There was a rumbling roar from nearby, and I smelled Slade a heartbeat before his huge form appeared behind the witch. He hadn't shifted to his dragon, but he didn't need to as he gripped the witch's head with both hands, their span completely covering her skull.

"Release," he commanded me in a guttural rasp, his blazing gaze locked on mine.

Obeying, because Slade had my beast in a metaphorical hold, I relaxed my jaw and fell to the ground, my paws catching on the shattered glass from the blown-out car windows. Sensing Slade wanted more space, I backed up until my tail hit the side of the car, the sulfuric release of magic choking all fresh air around us. But it didn't appear to bother Slade.

When a magical avalanche of energy exploded from the witch, he simply tensed his forearms and crushed her skull in his bare hands.

In. His. Bare. Hands.

It took a single breath of time for him to kill her.

My beast stilled, staring up at her alpha, and she had no sense at all to fear him. Nope, she wanted to rub against his leg and mark him with her scent. *Down, girl.* Not the freaking time.

"Omega!"

The snap of Finley's voice had my gaze jerking from Slade and past Hunter, who stood behind the dragon, ready to back him in whatever way needed. Finley was beside me, near the back of the vehicle, and there was no sign of Kellan except one leg flung from the open door.

A mournful howl rocked through my chest and poured from my jaws. *No! Nooooooo! Please, goddess, no.* He couldn't be dead.

I refused to believe it.

The witch had just knocked him out because that blast was meant for me, and the Rogers pack didn't want me dead. There was no way she'd use a killing blast.

Right? *Right!?*

Pushing forward, I got the top half of my wolf into the car, sniffing along Kellan's unconscious form. When I picked up the steady thrum of his heartbeat, my entire body shuddered. He was still alive, thank mercy, but his scent... it was tainted with the sulfuric magic. *What did that bitch do to him?*

"Jewels," Hunter bellowed, and I peered from the car to

find the blond witch and Warrick racing toward us, their SUV awkwardly parked with both doors open.

Jewels ground to a halt beside the dead witch on the ground. "Matilda," she gulped, her expression morphing from shock to horror to fury in a span of five seconds. "Oh, I'm glad you killed her, even if her coven is going to shit a brick."

Slade didn't even lift an eyebrow; I'd never seen a less worried shifter in my life. "Check on Kellan," he ordered her, voice harder than the witch's expression. "He was hit with magic when she attacked, and he hasn't regained consciousness. His scent is tainted with sulfur."

She obeyed Slade like he had a hold over her too, moving toward the open door. My beast reacted defensively, rumbles and growls ripping from my chest as I bared my teeth at her. I'd already chowed down on one witchy bitch today and had no issue making it two.

Even if they did taste dried up and gross.

Jewels eyed me closely, and I was aware that half my white fur was speckled in the blood of the other witch, but she didn't flinch. "Stand down, Omega," she said as a tingle of her magic reached me, "I'm the only one who has a chance of helping him through a magical attack."

That wasn't completely true. I'd seen Mom help her pack recover from a magical attack, but as I wasn't bonded to Kellan and couldn't use my strength to bolster his, I had to step aside.

I backed up, keeping my piercing gaze firmly locked on her. Hunter clearly trusted her enough to bring her along, which was the only reason I wasn't attacking now. But if she made one move to do *anything* other than assess or help Kellan, I'd fucking end her.

She kept her dark eyes locked on me for at least thirty seconds, and I swore there was a white glow behind her irises. Freaky bitch.

When she finally turned her attention to Kellan, she ran her hands over the top of his chest, slowing over his sternum, before moving forward again. The scent of her magic was subtle, and I had no idea if it was due to her being stronger or older than the other witch.

"She hit him with a simple knockout and containment spell," Jewels finally said, which should have been good news, but her expression wasn't giving happy feelings.

Her brow furrowed as she turned to where Hunter waited impatiently by the open door.

"What aren't you telling us?" he said in a low, forceful tone.

Her worried expression didn't ease, and I was forced to pace round and round in my small section of the car. "The spell wasn't designed for Kellan," she finally said with a heavy sigh. "Which means it's reacting erratically inside him, especially as he's a powerful alpha. Two powerful *foreign* magics do not like to mix."

She returned her gaze to Kellan, and my wolf shuddered on the spot as panic almost took me down. "What else?" Finley asked from outside the car. I couldn't see him from my spot trapped in here, but I heard him just fine. "Tell us how we can fix it."

His usual angry, bear-like rasp was tinged with the same panic I felt. The very thought that Kellan was hurt or.... worse. *Nope.* Finley and I weren't capable of dealing with this, but for our Golden Boy we'd figure out how to keep it together.

"This spell was keyed to the witch you just killed," Jewels added somberly. "It's a simple spell to remove, if you were the one who cast it. Its sole purpose was to keep a shifter unconscious during transport."

Translation: it was designed to keep me unconscious until I was delivered to the Rogers pack. A pack of alphas too chickenshit to even be here and fight their own battles.

Hunter gripped the frame of the door, crushing the dinged metal in his hands. "Are you telling me that with this witch dead, there's nothing we can do to help Kellan? That he'll remain in this unconscious state forever?"

Jewels eyes were shiny as she swallowed roughly, and while I wanted to cover my ears for whatever she said next, in this form, I was forced to hear the bad news.

"No," she whispered, shaking her head roughly. "He won't remain like this forever."

Hunter released the car and his left hand shot out to wrap around her throat. It wasn't my claiming hand, and it wasn't in the sexy, dominant way he usually acted with me. This hold was brutal and cruel, his expression unyielding as his eyes flashed gold. "What. Do. You. Mean. Jewels?" Each word was dragged out through his gritted teeth, his jaw already elongating into his wolf.

"Eve—eventu—" she coughed, unable to speak around his crushing grip. Hunter flexed his fingers, relieving just enough pressure for her to spit it out. "Eventually the spell will kill him. The... they're not des—" Another cough "...designed for long-term use."

Hunter dragged her from the car until she dangled before him, looking even more tiny and doll-like in his massive grip. "Unacceptable. You will figure out how to fix him or I will destroy you, your bloodline, and anyone your family has interacted with in the last century. Do you understand? I will wipe you from existence, as if you were never here at all."

Even though Jewels was clearly a powerful witch, pure panic lined her face as she struggled against his hold. To no avail. "O-okay. I'll figure it out."

Slade and Finley stepped in on either side of Hunter, and the three of them were visibly intimidating as they faced off against Jewels. I *almost* felt sorry for the witch, while still feeling relief that she had an *extra incentive* to give the task of saving Kellan her entire focus.

I refused to believe that this attack, which had been meant for me, was the end for Kellan. Naïve or not, I would not accept that fate.

Why did he put himself between me and the attack? I fucking hated that. I hated anyone standing between me and danger.

This was my fault... well, my stupid mother's fault. Which I'd inherited.

These alphas didn't deserve to be hurt because they were unlucky enough to be scent matched to me. I'd tried to warn them, and if they'd have just let me go when I first came into their lives, none of this would have happened to them.

As if he'd heard that thought, Hunter's dark and gold-flecked gaze snapped toward me. That alpha-laden stare held my wolf in thrall, both sides of me terrified *and excited* by the ferality he exuded. "Kellan needs you now, Omega. Don't even fucking think of running because the shit has hit the fan."

My wolf shook again, fury and pain driving my body to the brink. To the brink of what, I had no idea. Sanity, exhaustion, pain, panic.

In my wolf form, there was no way for me to tell Hunter that if I had to run to save them, there was nothing that would stop me. For the first time, my need to escape wasn't about saving myself, and I found that *saving my pack* was an even stronger driving force.

These alphas deserved to be protected.

Slade, in one of his weirdly intuitive moments, figured out exactly where my head was at. "She thinks it's her fault," he said, as he watched me closely. "She wants to run to protect us from other magic and the dangers this Rogers Pack might bring into our lives."

I couldn't for the life of me understand why he made that

sound like the stupidest choice ever. Two of four alphas had been attacked in only the few weeks I'd known them.

Because of me.

"She will not run. She will not leave Kellan when he's hurt and needs her." Hunter said it so matter-of-factly, and there they went again, knowing me better than anyone else ever had.

Jewels let out a gasping cough as Hunter finally released her; he enjoyed making his point in a manner that left no room for interpretation. His dominance didn't allow for space to negotiate or misunderstand.

I'd never really had his fury directed my way, and I wondered how he'd act if I got on his bad side. Would I be the exception to his usual brutal means of achieving his end desires?

Or would it be even worse for me?

"This isn't your fault, little omega." The familiar drawl of my nickname from Hunter eased my panic. "The witch will figure out how to heal him, and we will be a completed quintet once more."

Warrick, who had wisely remained on the periphery, was hesitant as he said, "The council is ready for our updates when we return. The Rogers pack and any witch working with them will pay for this."

Hunter acknowledged that with a single nod, before he glanced around the street. We weren't on a main road, but there were a few curious faces visible in the nearby houses. Word would spread quickly—the Reeves pack was worldwide famous, and no amount of Slade's digital erasing would completely kill this story.

"We need clothes for Emmeline," Finley said to Jewels as she scrambled from the car.

While his aim was no doubt to avoid seeing me naked, it

was considerate of him to think of me at all. Jewels' face remained pale, and a twitch in the corner of her eye indicated that she wasn't happy.

With a wave of her hand, the scattered remains of my torn clothes were repaired, looking clean and new as they folded themselves neatly on the seat. I'd wait until we were on the plane to get dressed, mostly because I had no more paper for my period. The blood was less potent when I was in my beast form.

Moving closer to Kellan, I gently licked across his cheeks as I whimpered. I wished he was the one who had shifted and destroyed his clothes, and I was the one unconscious.

My life wasn't worth shit compared to that alpha—the world needed more Kellans.

I needed *my* Kellan.

This might not directly be her fault, but at their core, all witches were cut from the same cloth, so I had no sympathy for Jewels. She better figure out how to heal Kellan, or Hunter would be the least of her problems.

CHAPTER 11

EMME

The flight to Golden Claw took five hours. I'd never been on a private plane before, and I'd have been thrilled to explore the Reeves pack's incredible jet, if it wasn't for the fact that one of my favorite shifters in the entire universe was hurt.

Hunter had placed Kellan in the private bedroom at the back of the plane, and I refused to leave his side, lying next to him and whispering to him for the entire journey.

I had no idea if he could hear me, but I needed him to know that he wasn't alone.

Exhaustion eventually got the better of me, and I drifted off holding his hand, only stirring when someone lifted me off the bed. "No," I mumbled as my hand slipped from Kellan's. "Kellan."

A rich coffee scent surrounded me as Hunter drew me into his firm chest, his nose sliding along my cheek. "Kellan is right here with us," he murmured. "You can sleep, and we'll make sure he stays by your side."

My exhaustion and Hunter's comforting scent tugged me

back into the darkness, content in the knowledge that this alpha kept his promises.

When I woke up again it was in a panic, worried that I'd missed an update. The rapid beat of my heart slowed when I felt the familiar heat of the alpha beside me. Kellan looked like he was just sleeping, his gorgeous face serene. They'd removed all his body armor and weapons, leaving him in just a plain white shirt. As I snuggled in beside him on the bed, it was hard to believe he suffered from any magical attack.

They had to figure out how to save him. There was no other option here.

A cramp in my gut reminded me that I was only day two-ish into my period, and as I glanced down hoping I hadn't bled all over the bed, I noticed that someone had placed a towel under me.

Hunter no doubt; he was a surprisingly thoughtful entitled alpha.

Leaning over, I pressed my lips to Kellan's cheek. "I'm here with you, Golden Boy."

It was the hundredth time I'd whispered that to him, and I would continue to remind him until the witch figured out how to heal him. All magic had a price and a counterspell, but she was working on a limited timeframe. Which terrified me.

"I shouldn't have killed her."

I jerked my head to find Slade sprawled in a huge armchair in the corner, his long legs extended in front of him. *Fuck.* How in the hell had I missed a giant shifter just sitting there?

His face was impassive as he watched us, but his eyes

blazed. "You probably saved the rest of our lives," I reminded him, my voice broken up. "You didn't do anything wrong."

His expression remained unchanged. "My first instinct is always violence. The dragon solves our problems with death and destruction, and now Kellan suffers due to my inability to find another path."

Pulling myself up to sit, I kept one hand on Kellan's chest, while patting the bed beside me with the other. Slade's eyebrows drew together, as if he had no idea what I wanted from him, and I didn't push. I let him take his time.

When he stood, the room shrank around him, and I marveled at this massive, scary-ass shifter finally showing me a sliver of his vulnerability. I was starting to comprehend the true disconnect between Slade and his dragon, and I wondered if this was partly the reason for his coldly calculating need to control the world around him. Was it all a means to help with the internal chaos he could not repair?

Or maybe I was pretending to be a pseudo-therapist and should stick with serving drinks at Luxuria.

When Slade sat, he kept a small distance between us, but we were close enough for me to feel his heat. It reminded me of his comforting presence in the prison house, and how he'd saved our lives when said house exploded. And then again with the witch.

"This is not your fault," I repeated, firmer this time. "As I told Hunter when he killed Jones, if your instinct is to protect your pack, and there was every chance that witch could have used killing magic on the rest of us, then you did the right thing by destroying her. You protected us and made the hard choices so the rest of us didn't have to."

Slade's gaze was intense, trapping me in what felt like a beam of green light. I couldn't look away, even as I struggled to convey all my feelings. "You are not a monster, Slade Riverson.

You are a protector. Your dragon saved us from the blast. Don't tell me that wasn't pure instinct. Not even you could have premeditated and moved that quickly."

He tilted his head to the side and lifted his hand. There was a breath of sensation against my cheek, and my eyes closed involuntarily. I heard a whispered, "Thank you," and by the time I opened my eyes again, Slade was gone and all that remained was his scent. His scent and the sense—*hope*—that maybe I'd finally gotten through to him.

Even in my dazed state, my bladder reminded me that I needed the bathroom, and after brushing my hand gently down Kellan's chest, I swung my legs off the bed and picked up the stained towel to take with me. I hadn't paid attention to which room we were in, but as I glanced around at the light blue walls, one of which was completely covered in mounted weapons, combined with the caramel scent, I knew it was Kellan's.

I'd had no idea he was *this* into weapons, and it hurt me that we'd had such a short amount of time together. There was so much more to learn... I *needed* more. I needed forever.

As I moved toward his bathroom, I heard footsteps which were followed by Finley's scent. I paused, bundling the towel up tighter as I debated hurrying away or remaining where I was. In the end, I let Finley decide what he wanted.

When he froze in the doorway, his broken stare took me in as I hovered and bled all over myself. Eventually my patience ran out. "I'm going to shower. Can you stay with Kel? I don't want him to be alone."

He responded with a deep, bear-like rumble, and then a grunt. Ah, lovely. "Great, thank you."

I forced myself to calmly stride around the bed and toward the exit, my legs aching as the last few days took its toll on my body. It went back even longer than that, really, if you considered the first attempted kidnapping. Or getting dragged to Golden Claw and meeting my scent matches—

You know what, it had been a fucked-up month, while also one of the best in my life.

As I passed Finley, I held my breath, not emotionally ready for a full hit of his scent. In my room I closed the door and breathed in the clean, cool air. Florence had been in to tidy, and she'd opened my blinds and shutters, letting in the crisp afternoon breeze.

After dropping the towel into my laundry hamper, I was heading for the bathroom when I noticed a large basket sitting on the end of the bed. Upon closer inspection I found it was filled with an array of period related products, including underwear, cups, discs, tampons, pads, painkillers, a hot water bottle, chocolate, and snacks.

I blinked and stared, wondering how they'd managed to get all of this in the short time since we'd returned from Silver City. My throat grew unbearably tight and my eyes watered, my emotionally fragile state unable to hold the tears at bay.

With plans to sob my guts out in the shower, I took a second to sniff the basket, surprised to find Slade's scent was the most prominent. With just a hint of Hunter's too. Our entitled alpha took the care of his pack very seriously, and I'd anticipated this would have come from him, but the dragon was unexpected.

Piece by piece, day by day, these alphas chipped away at the protective barriers I'd been erecting around my heart— rewiring the parts of my brain that had been determined to never rely on or feel attached to this pack.

At this stage, if I had to leave them for any reason, it would be akin to an addict weaning off their drug of choice. Mine was apparently dominant, possessive alpha males.

Leaving the basket for after my shower, I entered the

bathroom and cranked the water as hot as I could. My skin itched, and I couldn't wait to scrub myself clean. When I stepped under the stream of water, heat engulfed me, and trails of red ran down the drain. Not all of that was from my period; that witch's blood had remained in my hair, and it was somewhat cathartic to watch the last of her disappear.

Fuck her. How dare she hurt my Kellan.

The first sob was loud, ripping from my chest as I curled in on myself. Fuck her. *FUCK HER!* She needed to be here so I could kill her again, tear her to pieces to assuage this pain crippling me. My knees buckled, and I would have crumpled to the tiled floor, but strong arms caught me as I went down.

More sobs burst from me, gut-wrenching in their intensity, and my tears fell so fast that I was blinded. Not that I needed to see to know who was with me. Both logic and scent told me it was Hunter, the one who held me in the shower when my world destructed.

"I've got you, baby girl," he whispered. "Fall apart. Fall all the fucking way apart and trust me to hold the pieces. Until I put you back together."

My scream was guttural, and I didn't restrain myself as I raged and cried and hated on the world. My stomach heaved, and I would have vomited if there'd been anything in my gut. I hadn't been able to eat a single thing on the plane, too focused on Kellan.

Hunter's hold never wavered as he wrapped me tighter, both of us pressed against the shower wall, as I screamed against his chest. He did exactly as he said and held my pieces, until eventually I quietly sobbed through my pain.

Without letting me go, Hunter reached out for my washcloth, added some of the peach-scented bodywash, and gently dragged it over my skin. He washed away blood I'd missed, and down my thighs where new blood slid, and not even once did he show any reaction to my period or my brokenness.

If anything, he was gentler than ever as he caressed my stomach, the slow soothing swirls of the cloth feeling like heaven, and as my eyes fluttered closed, I realized that Hunter was putting me back together. Another promise he'd kept.

"Kellan is going to be okay," he murmured as he continued to soothe and clean me. I was too wrecked to do more than trace my fingernails gently up and down his biceps, moving over the geometric pattern of his tattoo, while listening to his calming and reassuring words. "I refuse to ever lose a member of my pack. I've kept you all alive up to this point, and that's not going to change with our Golden Boy. Do you understand, Emmeline? Kellan has no choice but to recover, because I never admit defeat."

My chest tightened. "He took that blast for me. He sacrif —" I couldn't finish.

"He did, and he'd be so fucking happy with himself if he was awake," Hunter replied, his huge chest rumbling under my face. "You'd tell him he was a good boy and give him a hug, and he'd be swinging his dick around, about to come in his pants. I promise, that's still our future. This is not the last we've seen of his annoying ass."

I chuckled hoarsely, surprised I could still find anything humorous. "He's perfect, you know."

Hunter stilled, the cloth pausing on the small of my back. "I know, baby girl. I fucking know."

We stayed together under the beating water for a long time, and when he dried me off, there was a sense of peace in my soul that almost equaled the pain.

CHAPTER 12

EMME

Hunter left me to get dressed, and when I was outfitted in comfy sweats and Kellan's hoodie, I headed back down the hall to the blue room. I didn't want to disturb Finley's time with his brother, so I slowly poked my head around the corner.

What I saw had my chest tightening once more, and tears rimming my already swollen eyes.

Finley had dragged the chair Slade had been in earlier closer to the bed, and with his head bowed, his huge fist gripped the front of Kellan's shirt. He didn't speak or even look up, he just held on to him. Even from the doorway, I felt the pain and desperation bleeding off the bear shifter, and was thankful I'd had my breakdown in the shower already, or I'd be an actual mess on the floor.

Knowing Finley wouldn't appreciate me interrupting his moment with Kellan, or witnessing his pain, I started to back away. Despite my socked feet not making a sound on the wood floors, Finley's head still shot up, and once again I drowned in the whiskey depths of his eyes.

His thick, dark lashes fluttered as he sucked in a ragged

breath, and then exhaled just as heavily. "I need to get to practice," he murmured, and it was weird to hear his husky voice without any bite. Apparently, he was too wrecked to even hate me today. "You'll stay with him?"

"Yes, of course. I don't plan on leaving his side except when absolutely necessary."

Finley released his brother suddenly, his fingers flexing as if they were stiff from how tightly he'd been holding on. "He'd like that."

As he stood, he gave Kellan's supine form one last look, before he strode from the room. When he passed me, I barely felt his usual Grouchy Bear anger. It bothered me to see him grieving but at least he had hockey to help. I might not know him well, but I knew that the ice was his therapy and salvation, and he needed both more than ever today.

When he was gone, I hurried over to Kellan, placing my hand on his chest and sighing at the steady thrumming of his heart. "Hey, Golden Boy. I missed you." Leaning over, I nuzzled against his cheek. "Daddy Alpha is out of sorts with you like this. Not that he hasn't always taken care of me when I needed it, *and even when I didn't*, but today he was extra gentle. Slade is beating himself up that this is his fault, and Finley is falling apart, so I need you to stay strong until we can figure out how to heal you." I swallowed roughly, choked up once more. So much for expelling my pain in the shower; it was an endless pit at the moment. "You promised you'd follow me through this world and into the next, and I'm holding you to that promise. I need you, Kel. I'm not sure I can live my crappy existence without you in it."

I was absolutely sure I couldn't.

I'd been shocked when he'd said that if I didn't exist then he didn't exist—I'd never had anyone care that much about my existence. But now I perfectly understood the sentiment; I couldn't imagine living in a world without Kellan. I refused to imagine it.

I needed to ask Hunter if they'd found my phone on the back road of Golden Claw. I wanted to scroll through the group chats and escape from reality for a while.

For the next few hours, I sat with Kellan. I spoke to him until my voice was hoarse and I'd run out of shit to say. I told him every detail of my woeful childhood, and the dreams I'd held for years. The only truths I kept from him was what my mom's pack did to her, and how she died. The words got stuck in my throat every time I attempted to spill those final secrets.

Twice now, I'd tried to tell the alphas this truth, and twice the universe had intervened in the most explosive way. It almost felt like a sign to keep my mouth shut. With Kellan stuck in a magical spell of containment, it really didn't feel that important anyway. The truth, and my past, weren't going anywhere, and I had many more pressing issues to worry about.

Through all my conversations, Kellan never moved, flinched, or shifted. It was as if he lay in the deepest of deep sleeps, and as grateful as I was to hear the steady beat of his heart, it wasn't enough. I missed his dark blue eyes, and how they turned violet when he was aroused or angry. I missed the animation in his face when he teased me or his pack brothers. I missed the lightness he brought to this house filled with more serious alphas.

I missed him.

Florence brought food for me in the early evening, and I managed to eat a few bites and drink some water before my stomach rebelled. The only reason I ate at all was that Kellan would be upset with me for not looking after myself.

When my legs cramped from sitting for so long, I got up and walked around his room, taking in the small personal touches. Along with his impressive wall of weapons, I loved the greenery he had scattered around. Every corner, shelf, and window ledge had a leafy green plant, giving his space a homey and cozy feel.

Stopping by the main wall, where he'd mounted dozens of swords, guns, knives, crossbows, and axes, I wondered what had inspired his love for weapons. There were even a pair of scythes that looked like they'd been stolen straight out of a reaper's hands. It felt odd to correlate the easygoing, sweet alpha with his murder wall. But… then again, I couldn't forget how he'd held Sorenson off the ground like he was a child that day. There was a streak of darkness in my golden alpha, and I liked that part of him just as much.

"You like weapons, Kel?" I asked with a chuckle, looking over my shoulder. "I hope I get to see you in action one day."

It was my own fault that I knew so little about the alphas. I'd been afraid to learn too much and find out they weren't monsters; it was easier to keep my distance that way. But now I wanted to know it all. Did Kellan just collect weapons or was he trained to use them as well? Were those rough patches across his palms, the ones I'd traced for hours over the last few hours, from more than just hockey and working out? If so, when did he start? What were his parents and siblings like? He'd told me he had brothers who lived in the family compound, but I hadn't had a chance to meet them yet.

For the first time, I really wanted the whole picture.

When I moved on from the murder wall, I stopped at the overflowing bookshelf tucked into a corner. Along with two crowded shelves of hockey trophies and medals, there were many paperbacks squished into every other available space. Despite my poor reading skills, I picked up a few of the novels, curious to know what genres Kellan enjoyed. I'd never seen him with a book in his hands, but no one had this many if they didn't enjoy reading.

On both covers I grabbed there was a half-naked couple embracing. A weird gurgling laugh escaped me.

Romance.

I lifted another to see the title *Bonekissed*, with a similar suggestive couple pose. Book after book held the same vibe, mostly fantasy, with vampires, fae, shifters, and witches. *What the heck was a fae?* Even more importantly, Kellan enjoyed reading romance, which was overall less surprising than his wall of weapons. It also explained why he always had the most perfect and romantic lines up his sleeve. He'd been trained by the best of the best.

According to Kerry Anne, who'd been my manager at Wahl's Diner in San Diego, romance books were the ultimate guides for males. I'd never seen her without a book in her hand during her breaks, and she'd tell me the plots while we worked. She also introduced me to audiobooks, which I'd been able to afford approximately once a year.

I was hit with the urge to read the same stories as Kellan, but it would take me months to finish this book. My best hope was that he'd wake up soon and tell me the plots of his favorites, sharing that way with me.

"I can help you."

I spun around, clutching a book about a stalking vampire to my chest. "With what?" I asked, looking around quickly before returning my focus to Slade, who was perched in the doorway.

"I can help you with your reading."

Annoyed embarrassment filled me, coating my cheeks red. I'd mentioned my lack of schooling and weak reading skills before, but Slade was the one shifter who saw deeper into my true weaknesses and vulnerabilities.

He always saw deeper.

"It's not just a lack of schooling," I said, forcing myself to breathe evenly in the hope of willing my embarrassment away. "My brain is kind of fucked up. Letters and words mix all around, and I can't seem to make lines of text stay straight. They jump up and down the page."

Slade's expression never shifted. "Yes. I've noticed the way you squint at the page. Based on the symptoms I've compiled, I believe you're dyslexic."

He said it so matter-of-factly, and I tried not to let my shock and distress spill across my face. "You think I'm dyslexic?"

I'd heard the term before of course, but only in passing as customers chatted about their children and school. I wasn't sure what it actually meant, or how it was related to my reading inability.

Slade nodded. "Yes. It's a reading disorder that affects many. There's nothing wrong with you, and you're not stupid."

Through my continued shame, because a *disorder* didn't sound like an affliction to brag about, there was also a sliver of suspicion at his reference to being stupid. I'd been telling Kellan about it only a few minutes before I got off the bed, as part of my task to share with him all my life's secrets.

I discreetly glanced up, but couldn't see any cameras, so maybe it was a simple coincidence.

"Dyslexia is a reading disorder," Slade repeated. "It has no correlation to your intellect. You just need to understand how your brain works and find the tools to help overcome the obstacles. I believe I can help you."

Despite the years of hating my own flaws, a part of me was hopeful that maybe there was a way to improve. "I'm almost twenty-six," I whispered.

A rumble rocked Slade's chest. "Yes, on the twelfth of December."

Another spike of suspicion, since I was fairly sure my birth had never been recorded, and I sure as shit hadn't told them.

"Yes. Don't you think I might be too old to learn how to read now." Just talking about this had my heart beating faster. I'd spent years not drawing attention to my weaknesses. But when Slade acted so matter-of-fact, it did help me look at it clinically too. "I've made it work for most of my life. No point trying to force a round peg into a square hole when I'm already grown and dealing."

Slade straightened, and when he stepped into the room, the atmosphere danced with new tension. "You could learn to be a nuclear physicist *now*. Or a cardiovascular surgeon *now*. Or how to build rocket ships *now*. There's nothing you can't learn, Snow. If you're brave enough to take the chance." His shrug was elegant, despite his massive, muscled shoulders. "If you're afraid or can't be bothered though, I won't waste my time."

The jab wasn't as sharp as others he'd directed my way before, and for the most part I was glad that the dragon never tempered his words. He gave you his exact, unfiltered thoughts.

He gave you his truth.

He walked away before I could respond, leaving me to wonder if I should add *dyslexia research* to the list of shit I had to do over the next few weeks. The irony of needing to *read* information to find out about my *reading disorder* wasn't lost on me. Along with omega research, my brain was going to start screaming at me.

Neither of which was as important as making sure Kellan woke up.

CHAPTER 13

EMME

The next time I fell asleep, it was in the chair, my head resting on the bed beside Kellan, my hand wrapped tightly around his. When voices jerked me awake, I had no idea how long I'd slept for, but there were heavy shadows lining the walls, with just two oyster lamps on his bedsides casting light around the room.

I wiped a hand over my face and shook myself awake as voices and steps grew louder. I was relieved to see Hunter's head pop through the doorway first. "Are you okay if Jewels, Tyson, and Julien check in on Kel?"

It took me a beat to even remember who Tyson and Julien were, since Kellan had only mentioned them a few times in passing. *His brothers.* Along with the witch, who would hopefully have some answers.

"Of course," I said, jumping to my feet and backing up a few steps. "Has Jewels figured out a counterspell yet?"

I hated the lines of stress on Hunter's face as he shook his head. "Not yet. She needs to do a few more tests and take a sliver of his essence to confer with others in her coven."

When he stepped into the room, I was moving toward him

before I thought about it. Hunter represented comfort and protection, and my body needed a dose of his particular brand of care.

There was strain in my legs and back from hours of sitting in a chair, and I hoped my healing would kick in soon. Hunter didn't show any sign that he noticed my stiff gait, his focus on the tray of food on the dresser. "While they're here," he said, "you're going to eat a proper dinner."

He leaned down, and I shivered at the sensation of his breath brushing over my lips. "My wolf is losing his shit, little omega. You will let me take care of you, or I will force the issue."

Damn him. Hunter probably read romance novels as well, but his were definitely of the dark, obsessive variety.

"Let's hear what Jewels has to say first," I replied, desperate for even a flake of hope that Kellan would wake up. "Not to mention that this is my first time meeting his brothers. Do you think they're going to hate me for what happened to Kel?"

Hunter's eyes flashed gold and he rumbled, a deep, spine-chilling sound that sent goosebumps over my skin. "Not if they value their lives." He wrapped his hands around my biceps and dragged me closer. "Don't ever say that again. This is not your fault."

I could promise not to say it, but that didn't mean I believed it. When I remained silent, he huffed out his annoyance, but for a change, didn't push like a bull at a gate. "Come on, let's hear what the witch has to say so I can get you fed."

He pulled me back into his body as he called out, "Enter." Ah, the arrogance of an entitled alpha who had to fear nothing and no one.

My gaze fell to the bed, and the rise and fall of Kellan's

broad chest. Well, even alphas weren't immune from death. It was just harder to kill them.

Jewels wandered through first, bringing with her that tinge of rotten eggs. Magic left its mark, even when it wasn't dark. I'd heard that dark magic smelled like decaying corpses and was easy to recognize. Hopefully I never experienced the difference.

The witch was followed by two large shifters, and I immediately knew which was Julien with his alpha energy, and which was Tyson, who was clearly a strong beta. Both looked like Kellan, just with a different variation of blond hair and blue eyes.

Jewels made her way to the bed, while the Jackson brothers approached Hunter and me. Julien, who looked a few years older than Kellan, had dirty-blond hair and eyes in hues of midnight blue. "Emmeline," he said softly, his gaze running over me, and I wished I didn't look such a wreck for this meeting. "I'm honored to finally meet you." I stiffened as he reached out to hug me.

Hunter rumbled his annoyance. "Family or not, if you touch her, I will rip your fucking arms off."

Julien shot Hunter a grin, unperturbed, though he did back away. His smile reminded me of our easygoing Kellan, which hurt my heart like a shot straight through it.

"I'm happily mated, Alpha Hunter," Julien reminded him. "You know that. I'd just like to meet the shifter who changed my brother's existence. I owe her everything for the happiness she's brought Kellan."

Hunter grunted. "No problem with that. Just show your gratitude from a distance."

Julien held both hands up in surrender. "Fair enough." He winked at me, and I shot him a warm smile, relieved he didn't appear to hate me on sight.

"I'm so happy to meet you," I said, including Tyson, who had dark blond hair and a greener tinge to his blue eyes. "Both of you. Kellan is an extraordinary shifter, and I know that must have come from having a wonderful family."

"Wait until Mom and Dad meet you," Tyson said with a chuckle, rubbing a hand over his handsome face. "They're going to drive you crazy with all the hugs and love. Their baby finally finding his romantic match is their dream."

He sobered and slowly turned toward the bed, where Jewels was running her hands above Kellan's chest, her eyes closed and lips moving.

"Are they going to fly out here to Golden Claw?" I asked, knowing they remained in Thorny Gardens with the rest of their quintet.

Julien's expression sobered. "We haven't told them yet. I didn't want them to worry before we knew for sure what we were facing here. But best believe, the second they hear, they'll be on the next plane."

"I'll send the jet," Hunter offered, more easygoing now that no one was trying to touch me. "Just tell me when you need it there."

Julien clapped him on the shoulder. "Thank you. We'll go sit with Rocket now."

Rocket. There was a story there, and I wanted Kellan awake so he could tell me it.

The brothers wandered over to their brother and stood on the opposite side of the bed to the witch. While it wasn't hard to tell the three Jackson boys apart, their familial connection was also obvious. My heart ached, and I silently prayed for Kellan to open his eyes.

Hunter remained at my side, supporting me with his hold, while we waited for Jewels to finish up her magical assessment. "It has progressed a little," she said as she straightened. "Nothing to be concerned about. But we must decide on a plan and solution within a few weeks, or it'll be too late to reverse the effects."

"And do you have a solution?" Julien asked, his voice breaking on the last word. "Or at least a plan to work toward one?"

Her eyes flashed with white light as she glared at him. "Of course. I'm working on a plan and gathering magic from others to help. It's tricky to reverse spells like this one, as it's keyed to the energy of another witch—one who is dead and can't be forced to revoke her magic." The scent of Jewels' magic exploded through the room, and my nose wrinkled. "I have what I need for now."

When she met Hunter's gaze, she swallowed roughly, and her magic faded away. "You're lucky I like your pack, Alpha Hunter," she breathed. "I wouldn't do this for just anyone."

When I stole a quick glance toward Hunter, I found his expression neutral bordering on bored. He responded with a grunt, so I elbowed him, and his eyes widened in astonishment as if no one had ever thought to strike him.

He wasn't the only one either, as the others stared like we were a new phenomenon popped up from the depths of the underworld. "What Hunter meant with his alpha grunt is thank you," I told Jewels, forcing a smile. "We really appreciate everything you're doing to save Kellan."

Her expression turned shrewd as she ran her gaze over me, searching deeper in a way that had my skin prickling. "You're welcome. I'll be in touch soon."

When she left, the scent of magic completely faded, and all of us breathed a sigh of relief.

"Do you mind if we sit with Kel for a couple of hours," Tyson asked as he settled into the chair. "We need to catch up with our little rocket."

Hunter swept me up into his arms as he headed for the door. "Take all the time you need. My *vicious* little omega needs to eat and rest. She won't leave him alone, but if you're watching over him..."

Julien and Tyson were smiling broadly as they watched Hunter alpha-handle me like I was a bag of potatoes, but whatever they thought of his actions, they kept it to themselves. "We've got a lot to catch him up on," Tyson said, shrugging off his jacket and pulling over another chair from Kellan's desk. "You take your time with dinner and *whatever else*."

Before I could protest, or give Kellan one more hug, Hunter exited the room with me firmly contained in his arms. "I'm fine," I protested. "You're being a big, overprotective alpha. Which is unnecessary."

Hunter ground to a halt, and I gulped at the surge of heat and dominance that poured off him. "You were kidnapped right out from under me," he bit out, slowly, deliberately. "Taken and held hostage. Attacked by a fucking witch. And now you're not eating or sleeping properly. Don't make me fail as your alpha more than I already have, Emmeline. Don't ask it of me. Not even for you will I let you keep spiraling into an abyss of darkness."

Whoa... *Whoa!* "You're not a failure," I said, swallowing hard to keep my voice clear. "Not in all the time I've known you. You keep us together and safe, Hunter. Don't think I haven't seen all you do. I've seen it, and I admire you for it."

I wanted to be the one who cared for him as well, but it was hard when eventually *we* would come to an end. One day they'd get sick of this half-bonded-quintet situation we had going on. They'd get sick of my trauma, drama, and issues.

They'd get sick of me.

"Will you eat for me, Emme?"

Deciding this wasn't a battle worth fighting I nodded. "Yes, I'll eat and rest. Kellan will be okay with his brothers for a few hours." It was a reassurance for myself as much as anyone else.

A purr of satisfaction lit up Hunter's chest. "That's my good girl. Come on, Florence has been helping Gerald prepare their best dishes in the hopes that you'll eat."

That alone had me wanting to eat whatever was offered. These shifters showed me in their own ways that they cared, and I wouldn't throw it in their faces.

Not even when grief was my driving force, leaving my stomach in a shambles.

I'd force the food down, no matter what it took.

CHAPTER 14

EMME

When we reached the dining room, the table was already set, and I was relieved to see a glass of wine in my usual place. If there was ever a night for wine, it was this one. Thankfully, I'd burn it off long before I returned to Kellan—I wanted to be as alert and coherent as possible in case anything went wrong through the night.

As I headed for my usual seat, Hunter all but lifted me and whirled me around until I sat in the chair right beside his, at the head of the table. By the time my head stopped whirling too, he'd retrieved my wine. "I need you close tonight," he said with that same quiet intensity he'd been wearing like a cloak all evening.

Before he sat, Hunter poured a generous shot of Glenfiddich forty-year-old single malt into a whiskey glass, sinking into his chair as he sipped his drink. I joined him by sampling the deliciously crisp white wine.

During my second sip of wine, the door swung open, and Florence rushed into the room, her face ashen. "Emme," she burst out, wringing her hands together. "We've been so worried since you were taken. And now Alpha Kellan is hurt."

Her voice broke and I remembered the day she told me how much she enjoyed working with these alphas, moving from the South just to be with them. I'd seen her love for them that day, and I wished that she didn't suffer with us now.

I stood to give her a hug, her devastation bringing my own strongly to the surface once more. "Thank you for caring," I rasped, my throat aching until I almost couldn't get the words out. "We're going to bring him back. I don't care what it takes."

She sniffled roughly before her professionalism kicked in and she pulled away. "I have all the faith. He's a fighter, our Alpha Kellan. I know he won't give up if that means leaving you behind. He loves you, Emme. Don't forget that."

I was sniffling now, but determined not to cry in front of Hunter again. Kellan had never said those words to me, but his actions spoke much louder than three little words ever could. "Thank you." It was a whisper and a sigh in one sentence.

Florence nodded, and then scurried from the room, returning a beat later with a full tray that she set in the middle of the table. Hunter watched me closely as I settled into my chair, swirling the golden liquid around his glass. "It's time to eat, little omega," he said, nudging the silver tray toward me. "You won't be leaving this table until I'm satisfied that you've had enough."

It was such a Hunter line, and since Kellan wasn't here, I had to be the one to say, "Is that an order, Daddy Alpha? Because I don't remember asking for a keeper."

He dropped his glass with a thud, and a choked gasp escaped me when he wrapped his claim around my throat, capturing me in *his way*. He leaned in closer, his voice a purr of dominance. "You have a keeper, Babygirl. You are kept. Owned. Claimed. *Mine*." His voice lowered even more, and as I melted into my chair, he released me just as suddenly, retrieving his drink once more. "And don't you ever forget it."

There was literally no way, outside of a lobotomy, to forget Hunter Reeves and his claim.

The intensity eased up at the clomp of boots, and I wasn't surprised when Slade entered the room, but he also had... Finley... right behind him.

This was the first time I'd had dinner with either of these alphas, and Hunter ignored them completely, his attention burning into the side of my face. He'd issued an order to eat, and despite my thoughts earlier that I would choke it down no matter what, Florence's sorrow fueling mine had me sick to my stomach again.

"Why haven't you eaten anything, Emmeline?" Slade asked, looking between Hunter and me. "You've been sitting here for a few minutes drinking wine, but no food was touched."

My brow furrowed as I glanced up to the ceiling again, searching for cameras. How did these alphas keep stalking me so thoroughly when I never saw a single camera. "It's Reeves technology," Hunter told me, and when I met his gaze this time, the burn deep in those stormy depths almost undid me. "You're never going to find the hardware."

These stalking assholes *would* have been pushing on my last nerve, but Kellan had me fully occupied worrying about him. I'd deal with the rest of my pack another time.

The alphas watched me closely, even Finley, expression closed off but not angry. I was well aware that they'd wait forever to make sure I ate first, and as frustrating as they were, this was the part of being with a pack I loved the most. The care and consideration.

The little gestures meant the most to me; I'd never had anyone care before. Living or dying, hungry or full, as long as I stayed out of the way, no one gave a shit.

These alphas gave a shit, and it was disconcerting.

Leaning closer to the tray, I breathed in the delicious scents, touched that Florence and Gerry had included all the starters that I'd ever shown an interest in: bacon-wrapped chicken, turkey meatballs, beef skewers, prawn cocktails, and an array of cheeses. Not a single fruit or vegetable touched the delicious meat selection, and I tried very hard not to cry again at the thoughtfulness.

No one cried over cheese, and this was about way more than that, but the cheese was nice too.

Grasping one of the serving tools, I took a selection and then shoved the tray toward the boys. None of them touched the food until I lifted a chicken scroll and took a bite. My stomach cramped immediately, and I wasn't sure I'd be able to eat, until the salt and juice of the meat hit my tongue, and my stomach eased up.

I closed my eyes to savor that taste, having learned not to make any sort of appreciative sounds while in the room with these alphas. Food would be enjoyed in silence, lest I caused their beasts to go a touch feral. It was a scented-mate quirk, and nothing to do with me personally.

At least not for two of the four alphas in my pack.

When I finished the scroll, I opened my eyes to hunt out my next selection, pausing at three sets of blazing gazes locked on me. "I didn't moan," I blurted out, looking between them. "I didn't make a single sound."

Finley averted his eyes fast, taking a gulp of his beer, while the other two didn't even attempt to look away. "We can feel your enjoyment," Slade told me, and there was an intensity in his voice that he rarely let himself reveal. I had no idea where my coldly contained dragon was, but this alpha was all fire. "Your emotions are potent. I can't imagine the strength of it when a bond is completed."

My mouth fell open; I was thankful I'd already swallowed my food. "Even unbonded you can *feel me*?"

I couldn't sense their emotions, outside of dominance and scent. Okay, and that slight tugging in my chest as our beasts attempted to drag us together, but again, that wasn't akin to *feeling* their emotions.

Hunter nodded, and as he tilted his glass, I was stuck on the strong lines of his throat as he swallowed the last of his whiskey. *Goddess be damned.* "Yes, alphas can feel their scent-matches' beasts. That's how the four of us knew we were meant to form a quintet. It's a draw that supersedes everything else. The four of us bonded through a magical connection ceremony, because we're brothers and decided that the bite wouldn't join us. Not until we found our fifth. We all sensed the final of our quintet would be a female we'd share. So, you'll be the only one we bite, which will make you the core of our quintet. The... heart, if you will. As an omega, once you bond with all of us, you'll feel us more intimately."

Fighting the urge to fidget on my seat, my body heavy and throbbing, I considered what this truly meant for me. And my future.

It wasn't that I hadn't thought of sharing the four alphas sexually—it was the only real quintet experience I'd grown up with, so while my mom's had been a toxic setup, it didn't feel odd. But I didn't know about them being able to *feel* my emotional upheavals. "My mom was bonded with a full pack of alphas, and they never acted like they could feel her emotions. Or at least they didn't care about them if they did. She was there to serve them and their needs."

Actually... I'd never even seen them *offer* her food, let alone wait for her to eat first.

No wonder my pack continually took me by surprise. They

were smashing every one of my preconceived notions of an omega with four alphas right out of the water.

They observed me in silence, and I realized I'd just spilled a fairly private detail about my mom and her pack dynamics. Information I didn't usually freely offer.

"If what you say is true, then your mom's pack could not be true alphas," Finley said finally, shaking his head and taking another swig of his beer. "They're a pathetic example of our designation, and shouldn't have been blessed with a quintet, let alone an omega."

I blinked at him. "You... you think an omega is a blessing? I mean, you've hidden it *really* well."

He hadn't done anything tonight to deserve my sarcastic response, but parts of me were still bruised and battered from his previous attitude.

He ran a hand over his short beard, and I swore I caught a brief glimpse of a brittle smile before he wiped it away. "You rejected us, Icy the Ice Queen. Or did you forget the part where you refused us like we were nothing. I don't see why you'd think I'd welcome you with open arms. Honestly, I kind of wish you'd never come into our lives and brought all of this... pain... with you. But it would destroy Kellan if you left him now, so I won't drive you away. Even if I can't imagine us ever being more than simply pack mates."

Pack mates was better than enemies, but if I was also *being honest*, it bothered me to hear his dismissiveness of anything more between us in the future. Even though *I didn't want anything more*. Or more accurately, I couldn't want more.

"You need to tell us everything you know about your mother's pack," Slade said, steepling his hands in front of him and peering over the tips. "We need all the information at our disposal to effectively deal with them."

None of the guys were eating yet, so I kept picking at my

food in the hopes they'd take the hint and eat their share. "I was young when my mom met them. I had no idea who my father was, and I don't remember much about my years before the pack, only that we moved a lot. Like... every few months we'd be in a new place. Mom was always cold with me, almost like she hated or resented me, and it only got worse when she met the Rogers pack."

"They were already formed?" Hunter asked, and I nodded, chewing through a turkey meatball I'd generously dipped in red sauce.

"Yep, fully formed, and at least twenty years older than her. She wasn't the first to be part of their quintet. They'd had an omega female lion shifter who'd *died* from lupine flu many years before they met us. Another omega death under their care."

At least that was their story. Lupine flu was a legitimate disease, and one of the few that affected all shifters. While it originated in wolves, it didn't discriminate as it evolved to be able to infect all of our kind. But I had my doubts that was the truth for the Rogers pack.

"How did your mom meet them?" Slade continued. "I could not find much of a history within the shifter cities for you and your mom, but the pack has an old record, then a gap when I assume they were with you, and then back to the cities over the past twelve years. It was as if they knew to keep you and your mom hidden... but why?"

"I have no idea how she met them," I said, having eaten through most of my plate by now. Thankfully, the alphas were eating now too. "She left me home alone all the time, even when I was a toddler. We lived in this dingy little basement room, and one day she left, and when she returned she told me to pack up my shit because we were moving. The next thing I knew we were in a dingy apartment." I met Slade's gaze. "That one I told you about with the mechanic's workshop below. We lived there with the pack for years, without even moving once."

"Your mom lived with them for years, and yet you still blame them for her death?"

The harsh statement slammed me in the gut, and I almost lost the food I'd just eaten. Keeping my gaze firmly locked on the white tablecloth, I took a few fortifying breaths before I faced Finley. "Not that I owe you any explanation, but I'm going to give you one so you can have a rest from being angsty and broken. After Mom bonded with them, the abuse started. It was subtle at first, but as with everything, it escalated. As an omega, she could ignore the commands of dominance, but as a bonded omega, she didn't want to. She gave every part of herself to those assholes, until eventually it killed her."

Finley shot to his feet, his food all but untouched. "We're nothing like them. We've never shown one ounce of violence or abuse toward you."

Debatable, depending on how you looked at it, since I wasn't exactly free to leave. But I understood his sentiment— the Reeves pack was vastly different to the Rogers pack.

The two weren't even comparable.

"They didn't show any violence or abuse toward her at first either," I bit out, knowing that wasn't completely true. They'd never showed the caring my pack had either, even in the early days. "Their alpha sides were corrupted by the omega energy —" I skirted as close as I could to the truth "—and I might do the same to you. I refuse to take her life path. I refuse this fate's design. I refuse to be a victim."

Finley examined me for many long seconds, and I couldn't manage to calm the heaving of my chest. "My mom was truly evil," he told me in a soft, shattered voice. His dark lashes lowered to briefly hide whiskey depths of pain and fury. "She killed my father right in front of me, and then my brother."

With each revelation, I felt as frozen as the Ice Queen he called me. "She kept me trapped for days, torturing me within an inch of my life. Over and over, until I prayed to die." The bitter laughter that escaped him had me thawing, but only to feel the jolts of pain in my chest. "That week ended years of physical and psychological abuse. Of being abandoned by those who were supposed to unconditionally love me. While I survived, I made sure she didn't."

I didn't believe his expression could get any stonier, but he proved me wrong as he stepped away from the table. "I also made myself a promise, just as you did when your mom died. I promised to never let anyone else into my life who was so careless with the emotions of others. Who had everything and destroyed it without thought or care. You're tarring us with the same brush as your mom's alpha pack, and now I'm returning the favor. You mean the same to me as my mom did. Nothing."

When he left the room, I stared at the empty spot as if his energy lingered long after he was gone. I'd been well aware that Finley disliked me, that much was apparent, but the depths of his hatred went far beyond the usual. It went far beyond my reach.

CHAPTER 15

"I'll speak with him." Hunter's rumble brought me back to reality, and I shook my head, unsure if I'd be able to get any words out.

A few sips of wine helped loosen my muscles. "No, it's okay. He's entitled to his feelings, especially when I haven't been the warmest or most inviting pack mate. Not to mention, we have more important shit to worry about."

Finley wasn't wrong; I had tarred them with the same brush as my mom's pack, and it wasn't because I thought they were bad alphas. It was due to the deterioration of the Rogers pack over the years as they siphoned their omega's energy. No pack was immune from the effects of power overload.

"Finley's emotional damage is heavily scarred into his soul," Slade said, and I couldn't get a read from his tone if he was excusing or condemning Finley's behavior. "What he told you was but a fraction of what he experienced growing up."

If there was one childhood scar I understood, it was internal emotional damage. I'd felt that connection to Finley from the first second I stared into his eyes. Unfortunately, my emotional damage had triggered his, and now we were at an impasse.

"Anyway, back to Mom's pack," I said airily, as if everyone couldn't hear the way my heart hammered in my chest. "They were quite powerful when she was alive, and even more so after her death. Don't underestimate them. You're right that they kept us hidden away, and I don't know if it was for the same reason that Mom moved us constantly before that, or because they didn't want anyone to know how they treated their omega. Either way, they're bad news. I can't help with any allies or magical connections though—there was no one when I was with them. At least no one they brought around me."

Hunter leaned forward. "Could they be using magic to increase their alpha energy? It can't be natural, or they'd have registered it with the councils. We're the only powerful, all alpha pack registered. I double checked when we returned home."

Slade's expression was contemplative as he played with his crystal glass. "It didn't feel like magical manipulation. There was a true shifter power in their dominance, which doesn't explain why they're not registered. The two on the council are listed as having a mid-level dominance, which is clearly not the case. Their magical connection is the oddest part. The last time witches aided in destruction like this, it was the Termaine War."

Termaine was the coven of witches who'd helped initiate a war almost two decades ago. Even I'd heard of it after listening in on my mom and her pack discussing it in whispered words. I didn't know much outside of it being a means to overthrow the Alpha Councils. An unknown alpha had gathered a group of witches and rogues to help him destroy the current way and return shifters to a single alpha ruler. Most of those involved in this insurgency were killed in the ensuing battle, but the ringleader was never found.

"Do you think they have more than one witch at their disposal?" I asked, hoping that wasn't the case.

Slade tilted his head, and I got the distinct impression he was surprised. "Absolutely. The one who attacked us in the car was not the same one who spelled the house. You couldn't smell the differences in their magical energy?"

I stared at him, before turning to Hunter, who appeared amused. "Uh, no. I didn't know you could smell the difference in magic. It's all just stinky rotten eggs to me."

Slade huffed, and crinkled his brow like that was news to him. "Interesting."

Hunter's rumble of laughter was a nice distraction, easing up the remaining tension from Finley's dramatic exit.

Deciding it was time for a subject change, I asked, "Did anyone find our phones from where we were attacked? Or... my jacket maybe?"

I'd been trying not to think about—or mourn—the amazing custom jacket Kellan had given me on the day we'd been kidnapped. It hurt too much. I especially hadn't thought about my pretty pink Ducati Penigale V4R motorbike. That, I already knew was toast.

"Yes, I found your phone in one battered piece, but your jacket was shredded by the blast," Hunter said as he pushed to his feet, pausing when Florence hurried in the room, a huge pot in her hands.

"Sorry about the delay," she burst out, sounding harried. "We couldn't find the bay leaves for the beef stew. Gerald almost tore the pantry to pieces."

I reached out to remove the tray from the center of the

table to make room for the gorgeous, burnt-orange ceramic pot, with a notched lid so the ladle could fit. "You're not late at all, Flo," I told her as I forced a smile. "We've been more than well fed on the starters. Thank you."

She patted my arm and whipped the tray off me so quickly it *almost* felt like magic. A second later, my wine was filled, along with both alpha's whiskey glasses, and while she spared a glance at the spot where Finley's half-drunk beer remained, she didn't ask where he was.

No shifter could have missed his outburst.

By the time Florence placed the matching orange bowls next to the stew, Hunter had retrieved my phone, and a spark of joy lit up my insides as he placed the device into my hand. "Sorry, I haven't had time to get you a new one, but it still works if you... want to read the messages."

He knew exactly why I wanted this phone—for a piece of Kellan.

Hunter retrieved his newly filled whiskey glass, the *MINE* flashing at me from his right hand, and I sighed with more contentment than I really had any right to feel. Slade added to that feeling when he reached out to fill a bowl, focusing on the meatier chunks, and then placed it right in front of me. "Thank you," I whispered, finding it hard to believe this was my life.

I wasn't sure I'd ever get used to these alphas or the way they made me *feel* with the simplest of gestures. Slade nodded, sipping his whiskey as well. "You need to eat."

Both alphas were once again content to drink and watch me eat, which should have felt odd, but it just didn't. Life had been a fucking adventure the past few weeks, and I was just along for the ride.

The first bite of stew almost blew my mind. Compared to what I'd made in our prison house, this was a masterpiece of flavor and texture. Every part of it seasoned perfectly, every flavor evenly balanced and fulfilling. "Holy shit," I gasped, scooping up another chunk of meat. "You guys have to try this dish. It's literally lifechanging."

Hunter leaned over, and my entire body stilled except for the frantic flutter of a pulse in my neck. He brushed his thumb across my lips, catching a drop of stew I must have missed, and when he brought that thumb to his mouth and tasted it, my lower half clenched embarrassingly hard.

Feeling any sort of arousal when Kellan was unconscious had me mentally slapping myself. But my hormones did not get the same memo. Or my wolf.

We just continued staring at his sinful mouth.

"You're right," Hunter rumbled with a smirk. "Lifechanging."

Well, fuck a shifter.

Hunter was about to have me moaning, and it would have nothing to do with food.

To keep from embarrassing myself, I dove back into the stew, shoveling in spoonfuls until my stomach started to protest. "Are you two going to eat?" I finally asked, taking a break. "You don't grow and maintain heights and muscles like yours without needing sustenance. What are you both? Six foot eight?"

When Slade smiled, it had almost the same effect as Hunter's little stew trick. "I'm just over six-nine and Hunter is six-six. Poor little guy."

My spoon hovered mid-air, halfway to my mouth. "It's weird when you make jokes. You know that, right? I can never tell if you're serious or not."

Hunter grunted out a dry laugh. "He's serious," he said. "He does consider me a *little guy*."

I tried not to laugh too, but it was impossible in the face of these alphas.

Who knew they'd be so funny? Certainly not me.

Needing to stay busy or I was going to throw myself over the table and into one of their laps, I lifted the lid off the pot and grabbed two bowls for them. I made sure Slade's was mostly filled with liquid and beef, while Hunter was always happy with a mix of meat and rabbit food.

As I served them, Hunter's hands flexed like he wanted to take the ladle from me, but my glare kept him from interfering. I took pride in not spilling a drop as I placed the bowls in front of them, smiling and satisfied with my effort.

All the while the alphas watched me with heavy gazes. It wasn't as if they'd never been served before... Florence served them all the time. But I'd never made any effort to act the part of an omega like this. I wasn't sure what they thought of my gesture, but I didn't regret it either.

"There you go," I said, waving at their steaming bowls. "You're going to love it. Now eat up."

It felt hotter in the room suddenly, and I wasn't sure it had anything to do with the steam rising from the bowls. As I waited for them to recover from my gesture, I wondered if there was another significance here that I had missed. The way they reacted... the deep, focused stares of their beasts in their eyes... it was definitely *more*.

Hunter picked up on my confusion and said, "For our scent match to feed us... it's a gesture of courting. Our beasts are losing their minds."

Slade scoffed, though he didn't disagree. No doubt a dragon felt slightly different about such a simple gesture. "I didn't know it was *that* noteworthy," I said with a casual shrug, though I felt anything but casual inside. "But I'm happy to dish up your stew whenever you need."

My lighthearted words were an attempt to lessen the tension, but it had the opposite effect. Hunter growled and grasped me around my waist, hauling me out of my chair and right into his lap. "I can't eat until you're satisfied, little omega," he said, his voice deep and filled with his wolf.

Between his husky tones and Slade's probing gaze, I was combusting where I sat, needs I hadn't even known existed battering my body.

Hunter spooned some meat and broth from his bowl and he lifted it to my mouth. I opened automatically, too fuzzy to do more than accept his offering. He rumbled in satisfaction, and growled, "Good girl," before spooning another, this time for himself.

I stared hard as he wrapped his lips around the spoon. Oh, *damn*. In my next life, I wanted to come back as that fucking spoon.

Hunter fed me again and I didn't fight, and all too soon he'd shared that bowl between the two of us, leaving me full to bursting. Sated and content, I let my exhaustion press me into his firm muscles, and tried not to wiggle against him.

He'd been hard under me from the second I landed in his lap, but neither of us acknowledged it, and it didn't make me feel even slightly uncomfortable. Nope, I was craving another afternoon of Hunter staking his claim all over my skin.

Only this time, I wanted those marks to last.

Unfortunately, the only lasting mark was a claiming bite, which would bring an end to this happiness and contentment, as the energy slowly corrupted him.

Your mom got years with her pack.

It was a truth I'd been steadfastly ignoring, because it was no better than a Band-Aid over a fatal wound. I wasn't supposed to want this at all, not even for a few years.

But as I sat there cuddled into Hunter Reeves, it grew more

difficult to remember the reasons why I couldn't bond to my pack.

Maybe... a few years would be enough.

After all, a year could feel like a lifetime with the right alphas.

CHAPTER 16

FINLEY

*F*aster. *Harder. Faster. Harder.*

My skates cut through the ice, digging in, destroying what had been a smooth surface, but for once I didn't care. I wanted the ice to represent the chaos inside me, and for that, it must be destroyed.

Faster. Harder.

My breaths wheezed in and out. I'd be worried about my fitness and stamina, except this was my third or fourth hour of sprints.

Why was it so fucking hard to outskate my demons?

I hadn't felt this way since the day my mom snapped and let her bear tear our family to shreds. After *the week* that broke me in more ways than one, I lost control and shifted, living as a bear for almost a month before Kenzo tracked me down. He'd risked his own life and coaxed me back to civilization. Back to sanity.

Even as an alpha wolf he was no match for my feral bear, and if not for advanced healing, he would still bear—*pun intended*—the scars of my rage. Another fucked-up event in my past I wouldn't forgive myself for, even though my brother never held it against me.

"Fin!"

Like I'd conjured him with my dark thoughts, Kenzo's voice rang through the arena. I almost ignored him, but in the end, he was still the only shifter in the world I pushed through my rage for.

As I slowed, the ache in my legs and overall fatigue grew stronger, and by the time I skated to the gate where Kenzo stood serious-faced and arms crossed, I could barely keep myself upright.

Food and water would have aided my healing, but since I'd brought nothing with me when I tore out of the house earlier, it would be a slow, painful process of repairing muscles.

"Brother," Kenzo breathed, shaking his head as he looked me over. "You're about to collapse. Get the hell off the ice."

He unfurled his arms and reached out a hand toward me, which I had no option but to take if I wanted to stay on my feet. He grunted as he took the bulk of my weight, and I snorted. "You shouldn't keep skipping arm day, bro. Or leg day."

His hold on me tightened, and I barely suppressed a groan of pain. "You're an idiot," he said, shaking his head as he dragged me onto the mats. "How long have you been here? Fuck, I should have looked for you earlier."

"Couple of hours," I mumbled. "Got in about nine."

The rumble of his chest surprised me; he wasn't usually a rumbly shifter. "Nine this morning? Are you fucking kidding me. It's six at night, you idiot. You've been skating for nine hours."

Nine hours. Well, that was a new record. "Guess I lost track of time."

Kenzo continued cursing me under his breath as he hauled

my ass to the locker room. I'd have been annoyed to show another alpha any weakness like this, but it was Kenzo. He'd seen me at rock bottom many times, and was one of the two alphas I'd let myself crash in front of.

The other was dying in a bed back at our house.

Hunter and Slade were my brothers too, but they didn't invite us to expose our weaknesses, while Kellan never judged.

I couldn't live without Kellan and Kenzo, and if Kellan died from the witch magic, I would have to fight not to follow him. The only reason I'd stay was for Kenzo, who'd go down with me as well.

We were a fucked-up trio, far too dependent on each other, but such was life.

"Clean yourself up. I'll find food and electrolytes," Kenzo said, still sounding pissed as he left me in front of the showers.

It took a few minutes, but I got naked and under the water, which was hot enough to scorch my balls off. Not that it made a dent in the ice encasing my heart.

From the moment my brother was struck by magic, I'd been in a freefall of pain and misery, with skating doing very little to ease the frenzy inside me.

Perched against the wall, I must have dozed off for a few minutes, only startling awake when Kenzo returned. He held protein bars and an electrolyte drink, which he thrust toward me. "Eat and drink."

Forcing myself to my full height, I downed the blue drink in three large gulps. My body screamed for more liquids, so I drank from the shower, uncaring it was gross. The protein bars were gone just as quickly, and I was relieved to find my strength returning. Within twenty minutes, I'd be ready for more sprints.

Or at least I would have been if Kenzo didn't march my ass out of the shower, watch me like a hawk as I dressed, and then drag me to his rarely used Mitsubishi Lancer Evo VI Tommi Makinen. Kenzo was a lover of Japanese-made cars, but he mostly drove with me, so his collection remained nicely preserved in his garage.

He must have been worried about me if he took his *red baby* out this evening. She was for very special, rare rally days at our track.

"Come on, get your huge ass in the car," he said, and he lifted his foot like he was going to kick my ass in to help. The Evo wasn't modified to fit a shifter of my size, but I managed to squish myself into the passenger seat, after tossing my gear in the back.

When Kenzo was in the driver's side, he locked all the doors, and I shot him a droll stare. "I'm not about to jump from a moving vehicle. For fuck's sake, I had a breakdown, but I'm not ready to end it all." Not that a jump from this car would do much more than scrape me up.

"I know, brother. And I'm here to make sure that you don't reach that point again."

We'd been here twice before, and both times he'd babysat me until I was stable again, and for that I'd forever owe him.

When Kenzo started the car, I fiddled with my phone and found myself once again opening the group chat. I'd had to ask Slade to add me back in because Kellan's annoying ass wasn't here to do it. I fucking hated that. I hated it more than I could express, even though I'd told him a million times to stop adding me. But that was my brother—he got off on ignoring my grumpy requests.

Now I had to figure out how to drag him back to the land of the living, because our pack needed him. I needed him. Even the omega needed him, and I couldn't stand to see her morose expression for another day.

"How's Emme?" Kenzo asked, as if he'd heard that thought.

I responded with a rumble from deep in my chest. "Our resident ice queen is the one responsible for Kellan being in a coma." There was no heat in my words, and the ire was more from habit than any real anger. "Who fucking cares how she is?"

Kenzo shook his head, taking the corner fast enough that I had to brace against his door. "I find it ironic you call her ice queen as an insult, when you personally love the ice like it's part of your soul. Could that name have a different meaning to what you believe, deep, *deep* down in your psyche?"

I shook my head, pretty sure my brother had finally lost his mind. "I call her that because she has a heart of ice, unfeeling and frozen. No other reason. No need to examine my psyche, you weirdo."

Kenzo shrugged. "Look, we're going to have to agree to disagree here. About everything to do with Emme. For real though, when it comes to Kellan's condition, you have got to stop blaming the victim for the actions of others. Emme loves Kellan. I'd bet my life savings that she'd trade positions with him in a heartbeat."

I actually didn't disagree with him. "She should change places with him," I murmured, even as the thought of it burned deep in my chest. My feelings toward her weren't rational... or fair, but hey, life wasn't fucking fair. It was time for Emmeline Anders to start adjusting her expectations about how she'd be treated through life. As an omega, she was a weakness and liability to a pack and should act accordingly.

Kenzo's silence was heavy with his disappointment, which seeped into the well of anger and pain churning inside me. The fact that skating hadn't given me a reprieve was a good indicator that I'd spiraled to the point of concern.

I needed to see Kellan. I needed his soothing presence for a few minutes, and then hopefully I'd be able to sleep. It had been days. Days of an inability to escape my thoughts, which would drive the sanest shifter to the brink of insanity.

It was quiet in the compound when we entered—a lot of our families had been up to check on Kellan already. His brothers had sat with him yesterday. Unlike most of us, Kellan had decent parents, but they hadn't told them yet.

I hoped they would before it was too late for goodbyes.

When Kenzo pulled up in front of my house, he turned toward me. "I'll be back in an hour with teppanyaki for you," he said. "You will eat a proper meal tonight, even if I have to make choo-choo noises and force the fucking train-sticks into your mouth."

A ghost of a smile hovered on my lips. "Like I'd ever turn down your cooking, Kenz. I'll meet you at yours in an hour, though. It'll be easier."

Easier for me to be out of the house as well.

He nodded. "Yep, that works as well, but if you don't show up, I will drag you there. Understand?"

I nodded, understanding all too well. My brother was generally unflappable, a cooling calm to my rage, but when he lost it... well, he didn't do anything by halves.

He waited until I was inside before he drove off. I dropped my gear near the front door and padded up the stairs. I could hear Hunter and Slade in their offices, but wanted to check on Kel first.

Chocolate and honey encased me as I closed in on his room, and I wasn't surprised to see the door ajar, the low light of the moon streaming in through his windows, highlighting the pair on the bed. Kellan hadn't moved, still on his back, eyes closed, chest moving in slow and steady increments. Emmeline was curled up at his side, her left hand clutching his shirt over his heart, and her right gripping her battered phone, even though she appeared to be sound asleep.

The moonlight highlighted the long strands of her hair, which looked paler as it spread out around her face, giving her an angelic look. Feeling uneasy at being near the omega when she was asleep, I crept toward the bed.

Her phone was still lit up, like she'd just fallen asleep using it, and I could see the same group chat I'd been reading. Under her thumb was a message from Kellan, as if she'd brushed across it while she drifted off. My chest grew tighter, all the rage and pain fading under the evidence of our shared sorrow. She suffered with us, and for that I would make more effort to accept her presence here.

Here where Kellan would want her.

As I crossed to the opposite side of the bed to where she slept, I sat in the chair and reached out to touch Kellan's chest, resting my hand beside hers.

It was reassuring to feel his heart beating strongly.

As I stared into her relaxed features and those freckles visible in the moonlight, I noticed silvery streaks tracing her cheeks. Even in her sleep she cried, and fuck, if that wasn't enough to push me right over the edge.

CHAPTER 17

EMME

The next few days were a blur of sleep, worry, and pacing Kellan's room. All of the pack sat with him at times, but I was the only consistent one. Afraid to leave his side.

Almost literally. I slept beside him, monitoring his breathing between my fitful bouts of rest.

A week after we'd returned, I woke to find myself surrounded by the most delicious warmth. It reminded me of waking with Slade's hand on my stomach, and even though my period was finished now, and I didn't need the dragon-pain-relief, it was nice to feel the comfort of an alpha.

Prying my eyes open, I was hit with all four alpha scents. I had no idea who was at my back, snuggling me into Kellan—until I glanced down to find the early morning light highlighting a familiar tattooed hand resting against the base of my throat. Hunter's other arm was draped across my stomach, pulling me back into his big body.

He must have crawled in with me during the night, and I'd been too wiped out to even notice. *Where were you on that one?* I directed at my wolf, who lazily yawned.

She'd made it clear long ago that we belonged with a pack, and if I chose to ignore the goddess' design, then I would have to deal with the consequences of it. With zero help from her.

After sleeping alone my entire life, I'd never have expected to enjoy the sensation of being squished between giant shifters, and yet... here we were. Absolutely enjoying it.

Enjoying it so much it was difficult to even consider sleeping alone ever again.

Not wanting to disturb Hunter, whose breathing was deep and even, I moved nothing except my eyes as I checked on Kellan, relieved to hear a steady heartrate and pulse.

As I lifted my gaze farther, I took in the large male slouched in the chair beside the bed.

Slade.

The dragon was awake, his eyes darker than usual as he observed the three of us asleep, as if he had been keeping vigil. When our gazes met, there was a spark in his, but he never moved or spoke, just let this tense moment extend between us.

The intensity was broken by a raspy snore, and I lifted my head just enough to find the second chair at the foot of the bed. Finley was asleep and looking uncomfortably squished into a chair that wasn't designed to take his full height or weight.

All four alphas in a room with me while I slept would have been my worst nightmare a few months ago, but I felt no unease or concern by their presence. If anything, it was comforting, which was another *very unexpected* outcome of finding my pack.

My bladder started to protest around the time Hunter stroked his hand across my stomach, and then I was filled with a surge of *other* emotions. Mostly need, desire, want, arousal.

As his left hand stroked my bare skin under my shirt, with sparks of energy following in its wake, his right shifted higher to slot perfectly around my throat, like it had been made to claim me.

"How'd you sleep, little omega?" he murmured. The huskiness of his voice had heat seeping into my skin as my core ached.

This couldn't happen next to Kellan. And with two other alphas in the room.

"F-fine," I stuttered, trying to fight how desperately I wanted to capitulate to his dominance.

Just. Like. Mom.

Thinking of her was a bucket of ice water thrown over heated skin, and I shot up in his hold. The entitled alpha let out a low laugh from behind me, and while he could have easily stopped me as I scrambled over him, he didn't.

I raced out of Kellan's room like my ass was on fire, but before I reached my room, Hunter appeared in the hallway, calling out my name. Turning slowly, I took in his dark, tousled hair and the breadth of his bare chest. The tattoos along his arms twitched as he leaned against the frame. "Remember what I said, little omega," he drawled, his dark gaze locked on me in a way that suggested he would very much like to chase as I ran. "No touching yourself in the shower. Your pretty pussy belongs to me. I will be the one to bring you pleasure."

Slade appeared beside him, and my cheeks were so hot, I knew they were a red flashing signal, even in the dimly lit hallway. "Since Kellan isn't here to point it out," the dragon shifter added, "let me be the first to remind you that Snow belongs to all of us. Even her..." His gaze grew heated as it dragged slowly from the top of my head to my toes. "...*pretty pussy.*"

I died. I was now a puddle of death on the floor.

Hunter's dirty mouth had been my undoing from about the first day I met him, but... Slade.

My breaths huffed in and out like I was asthmatic, and with a squeaking sound that resembled a mouse and not a wolf, I darted into my room and slammed the door closed. I heard low, deep rumbles of laughter from outside, and was almost tempted to poke my head back out to see if that was from Slade too.

I'd grown a touch obsessed with hearing all of them laugh. Kellan was the only one to freely chuckle with real humor—I'd barely even seen Finley crack a smile, and would no doubt die of shock if he ever laughed in front of me.

It'd be the apocalypse if that happened anyway, so at least I wouldn't be dying alone.

With my back pressed against my closed door, I tried to regain composure, but my body was just too worked up. *Damn them.* Damn these freaking alphas and their obsessive dominance that I was exhausted from resisting. It was a task I continued to fail miserably at, and I doubted I'd even get points for trying these days. They kept infiltrating my life and thoughts, and I *kept letting them.*

How was any sane, red-blooded shifter supposed to fight the insane draw I felt for them? *Who could fight this long term?* And with Kellan injured and possibly dying, I couldn't leave or escape either.

Locking my door, which would do *absolutely nothing* to keep an alpha out, I hurried into the bathroom to get ready for the day. In the shower, my fingers skimmed over sensitive skin as I washed myself, and I was rewarded with a deep throb in my center. I was tempted to test out Hunter's ability of knowing if I touched myself, but even as I glided a fingertip across my clit, I found no satisfaction in my own touch. Even my body rejected anything other than an alpha. *Traitor.*

With everything going on, I needed to run my wolf this morning or I'd end up losing my mind. I decided to call Cora and see if she was free to shift with me. We'd need alphas too, of course. None of them would let us go on our own.

When I was dressed in a loose pair of black sweatpants and hoodie, I unlocked my door and headed down the hall in search of my phone. It was a relief to find the bedroom empty of everyone except Kellan, even though we weren't supposed to be leaving him alone. Most likely the guys had just ducked out to get dressed, so I quickly searched for my phone, finding it on the desk next to a few loose scraps of paper.

There wasn't clutter in here anywhere except on his desk, where Kellan had clearly been scribbling while he chatted on the phone or read a book. I liked seeing those little personal touches, and his terrible renditions of wolves and stick figure shifters. It reminded me of the joy I felt when Kellan was awake and healthy. I missed him so much.

Forcing myself not to dwell and cry again, I dialed Cora, and it rang twice before she answered.

"Oh, my freaking goddess, Emme. I've been so worried about you."

In my head, I pictured my friend, looking as per usual ethereal and elegant. "Sorry it took me so long to get in touch," I choked out, pain still threading my voice. "It's been a rough few days."

Cora released a low sob, her voice just as broken as mine. "Warrick and I tried to visit yesterday but Alpha Hunter said you were asleep. I just wanted to make sure in person that you were okay. I can't believe what's happening to Alpha Kellan."

Kellan might not be the entitled alpha of our quintet, but he was dominant enough to garner the respect of the title. Especially when he'd acted like a complete hero and saved my life.

"It's killing me," I whispered, shaking my head at how weird it felt to have a friend to share my burdens with. "He intercepted a spell meant for me, and now he's possibly never going to wake up. How is this happening? I can't lose him."

"He's going to be okay," Cora said, her voice less shaky now. "Trust me. He's strong, and we have all the council and our magical connections working on it. Warrick hasn't stopped since he got back. They're figuring out how to go after this pack without creating a war between cities. They will pay for this."

I'd been too focused on Kellan to even ask what had been happening with the council and Mom's old pack. Hunter would have told me if they were either dead or in custody, which meant they were still out there being evil assholes—searching for the next omega to power their alpha energy. The Alpha Council clearly hadn't gone after them yet either, playing the politics game.

I hated that fucking game.

"Do you have any time for a run this morning?" I asked, as I rubbed my sternum to try and counter the mounting pressure in my chest. "I need to get out. I need to escape from these relentless emotions for just a few hours."

"Yes!" She answered so quickly I suspected she'd been hoping I'd ask to catch up. "War and I can be at your place in twenty minutes."

"Thank you," I sighed, a flicker of relief piercing through me. "I'll see you soon."

"See you soon, bestie."

When Cora hung up, I was surprised by the burst of warmth, chasing away the ice in my heart. I'd never had a best friend. Hell, I'd never really had a friend until I met her, and I'd clumsily called us best friends. Despite my awkwardness, there'd been nothing but comfort and ease between us, and I was forever grateful to have a Cora in my life.

Pocketing my phone, I leaned down and pressed a kiss to

Kellan's cheek. "I'll be back soon, Golden Boy. Don't go anywhere, but feel free to wake up."

Breathing in his cinnamon and caramel scent, I couldn't wait for the day it was no longer tainted with that hint of sulfur. Leaving him was hard—I held a genuine fear that he'd deteriorate while I wasn't with him—but if I didn't run, I'd be no use when he needed me.

Downstairs, I followed the voices into the kitchen hoping to find Hunter. He was there, along with Slade, Finley, Florence, and Gerald.

Florence rushed over to me with a breakfast sandwich already plated. "Eat, sweetheart," she said, thrusting it toward me. "You look pale."

With a smile, I thanked her and took a bite of the sandwich, my stomach no longer protesting regular food. The alphas had made sure of that.

Hunter placed a cup of coffee, perfectly doctored to my sweet, creamy preferences, right in front of me. "Here, little omega. You look like you need this."

"Thank you, sweet coffee gods," I moaned, grasping the cup and taking a sip, finding it was the perfect temperature too, as if he knew how often I burned myself with my first, impatient sip.

"Hunter will suffice," he drawled, sipping from his own cup of unsweetened tar.

I paused, shaking my head. "Is that a thing you do now? You make jokes?"

He lifted one of his broad shoulders. "If the situation calls for it."

I supposed that without Kellan, someone had to step up and bring the humor. Might as well be Hunter—he was practically cheery compared to the other two.

"I'm going on a run this morning with Cora and Warrick."

My blunt announcement had all three alphas pausing, even as Florence and Gerald continued cooking and cleaning around them. "I need to get out before I go crazy and start scratching up the furniture."

"Scratch all you want," Slade said, lifting one eyebrow. "Just don't pee on it."

Okay, now he was making lighthearted comments too. What the fuck was this? *The Twilight Zone.*

Hunter shook his head. "We'll all come with you. Kel's brothers just messaged to say they'd be by to sit with him again."

I barely acknowledged that, too busy trying to come up with a snappy response for Slade. Nothing worked quite right to match his wit. *Dammit.* No doubt I'd stumble upon the perfect zinger in two or three business days. He'd just have to be patient.

Wait... Had Hunter said the whole pack?

Despite my every intention not to look his way, I glanced at Finley, surprised to find that he wore a neutral, unaffected expression as he ate through two sandwiches and drank his green glass of death.

Was I really about to go on a run with three of the four members of my pack?

Holy shit.

A real pack run.

If only Kellan could be there with us.

CHAPTER 18

EMME

Cora and Warrick showed up in their very shiny Range Rover, and I spent the few seconds it took for them to stop in front of our house, trying to figure out who cleaned all of these alphas' cars. I couldn't imagine them out there washing and waxing them, and yet they always looked so shiny. Maybe it was magic. A far nicer magic than the one Kellan dealt with.

Hunter approached the driver's side before I even made it down the outside stairs. I heard him inform Warrick that they would be taking me to the forest, and to meet us there. Ignoring him completely, Cora tumbled out of the car and raced up to meet me.

We collided in a mess of limbs and tears; it was hard to tell at this point who was crying harder. It wasn't that I'd been holding it together with my pack—the shower breakdown with Hunter was evidence that I wasn't holding anything, but there was just a weird freedom in blubbering on your girlfriends. The comfort as Cora held me and rocked back and forth was nicely different to the guys.

Eventually Hunter huffed. "Time to give my omega back, Cora."

She snorted out a laugh into my neck, and to my surprise, held on for just a few more seconds. It wasn't in her nature to rebel against the very dominant shifters of this city, but for me she made an exception. *You go, bestie.* "She's not just yours. I know you have the strongest claim, but you can't dismiss bestie rights."

It was the most deferential I'd ever heard Cora be, and to my relief, Hunter took it well. Not that I'd have let him disrespect her either. "While that might be fair, you do need to hand her back before my wolf decides he wants to step in."

With a shake of my head, I rolled my eyes at him. "You slept in the same bed as me last night. You've had plenty of omega time."

Cora opened and closed her mouth a few times as she looked between us, but she didn't comment before Hunter leaned down, his face hovering near mine. Despite everything that had happened between us, we'd never really kissed, and having his lips so close had my heartrate spiking hard enough for everyone to hear. My scent grew stronger too.

"I didn't sleep inside you though," he rumbled, and everything went a little blurry as the blood rushed to my vagina. "Therefore, I did not, and *will never*, have enough omega time."

Cora released a hushed gasp, but I couldn't look away from Hunter long enough to catch her expression. The entitled alpha kept me enthralled, captivated, and completely ensnared.

My tongue darted out to moisten my lips, and Hunter's gaze lowered. *Was he going to kiss me?* Our first real kiss, right here in front of everyone?

Before I could hyperventilate and swoon like the most

pathetic damsel, he smirked and straightened. "Come on, little omega, let's go on our pack run."

Too stunned to respond, I barely squeaked when he gripped my waist with both hands and threw me over his shoulder, striding away from Cora and back into the house. He moved fast toward the garage, and I swear I managed less than two breaths before I was gently deposited in the passenger seat of his Bentley Flying Spur. I'd never been in this dark green car with its cream interior, and as I sank into the soft leather, my distracted brain could only focus on the interior of the vehicle. *Oh, this was nice.* Really nice.

The back doors opened as Slade and Finley slid in, or more accurately, wedged themselves inside. Slade was behind me, and I fumbled until I found the control to pull my chair as far forward as I could. "Happy to switch and let one of you have the front," I said, my knees almost in the dash. "I'm the smallest."

Multiple growls and rumbles filled the space, which appeared to come from Hunter and Slade. "Stay right where you are, Snow," Slade said shortly. "I can manage a small space for ten minutes."

Luckily, claustrophobia wasn't part of his touch aversion, and Finley, who was planted against the far door, didn't come close to touching him.

Hunter started the car; the powerful engine rumbled to life, filling the garage with the delicious rev of all those cylinders. Twelve, if I knew my engines correctly. A W12, and it was a beautiful, *beautiful* piece of machinery.

"I enjoy that look on your face," Hunter said casually as he reversed out of the spot and headed for the exit. "It's this mixture of awe and desire, and honestly, as frustrating as it is that a car of *all fucking things* gets you off, it's worth it for that look alone."

A snort escaped me. "You can't possibly be jealous about me lusting after your cars."

Slade leaned forward, just enough that I got a whiff of his toasted marshmallow goodness. "You'd be amazed at what Hunter can get jealous over. Don't look too closely at the toaster or he'll toss it right out the window."

Hunter shot him a dark look, which *oddly* morphed into a smirk. "Now that I think about it, that fucking toaster has been getting a little handsy with our omega lately."

Another. Joke. "The world's ending," I muttered, shaking my head.

Hunter threw his head back and laughed. It was a deep, husky reverberation that sent sparks of heat down my spine and through my limbs. "Feels weird to laugh when Kel isn't here with us," he said, sobering as he turned out into the main street, leaving the family compound, and heading toward the forest where most of the city ran in their beast forms.

"He'd be pissed if he knew we were all moping around because of him," Finley added in the heavy silence. "When they figure out how to bring him out of this spell, he will ask how we all reacted, and it's best if we don't disappoint him. Who knows what his revenge will be."

"Have we had any updates from Jewels?" I asked, a stupid sliver of hope seeping out when I knew better. "She said we didn't have an infinite amount of time, so she must be working on it, right?"

Hunter nodded, glancing away from the road toward me. "Yep, she updated me this morning. Her coven has managed to find a possible counterspell, and she made it clear that it would be his only chance..."

He didn't need to fill in the blanks. I refused to consider this spell failing. I was all about manifesting Kellan's recovery.

We drove for a few minutes in silence, which Finley of all

shifters broke. "Why haven't you asked about our relationship with the witch?"

As much I wished I could just ignore him, because this bastard always knew exactly where to poke to hit my sore spots, I couldn't bring myself to stay quiet. Turning to meet his hooded gaze, I was briefly distracted by how much darker the bronze and gold irises looked against the white of his hoodie. "What do you mean?"

Finley shrugged, his tone remaining even and conversational. "Hunter wants to smash the kitchen appliances for getting too close to you, but you don't even care about a strange, magical female who clearly is comfortable and familiar around us. You haven't asked once, Ice Queen."

His tone might have been light, but that nickname reiterated the fact that it was still another dig. It didn't matter how much I'd changed since our first meeting; he would always point out which of my actions backed his anger toward me.

It felt like all the alphas waited for my response, a newly unfurled tension holding the interior of the car hostage. Too tired and heartsore to bother playing games today, I went with the truth: "Of course I've wondered about your relationship with the witch. She's alluded more than once to a *very familiar* connection in the past, and as far as I know, that could have been as recently as last month. I'm confident that none of the other alphas—*except for you*—have been with anyone else since I came into your lives. Which is the only part that matters to me now. I'm not a virgin either..." That statement set off a bunch of growls, and I was surprised to hear a rumble from Finley too. "But they were before you, and all humans. They meant absolutely nothing to me. What's important is now, and how we treat each other."

I met his gaze full on, feeling the burning stare of the other two as well.

"Names," Hunter bit out. "What are their names?"

Don't laugh. Don't laugh. "You can't kill humans for touching me," I told him, still unwilling to look away from Finley. "It's not worth it either."

"We can kill whoever we want," Slade growled, and fuck if that wasn't the rumbliest he'd been in a while. "I'll find them."

This was bad, but I had come too far to turn back now. "How about you two focus on building a relationship with me and forget about the past. It's done. We can't go back. The future is the most important part."

My brow started to sweat as I kept up the staring contest with Finley. If he didn't tap out soon, I'd probably combust. Unfortunately, he appeared to be content to just stare into my soul.

Hunter and Slade grumbled for a few more seconds, and when I caught sight of Slade pulling out his phone from my peripherals, I really hoped the poor humans who'd stumbled into my life were hard to trace.

"I don't have a right to care about your past," I finally said, hoping to push Finley into a response. "We all have one, and frankly, mine is a shitshow. What would hurt me, and what would cause me to lose faith, was if you pursued a relationship now. While I was here in your lives."

Like the night you came home smelling all gross and floral. Or the time you implied you were still single.

"That would be disrespectful when I'm doing my very best not to even touch another male shifter." I side-eyed Hunter, unable to keep up the staredown with Finley any longer. "Or the toaster."

The entitled alpha's lips twitched, even as the rest of his expression remained hard and annoyed. My entire body sighed when he slid his hand across the console to wrap around my thigh, giving me a brief squeeze. My statements had gotten through to him, and he wasn't quite so murderous.

Unable to *not look*, I glanced at Finley to find his head hanging low, his hands clenched tightly in front of him. Someone needed to give this bear a hug, because I'd literally never met anyone who needed one more. Along with a punch in the face.

"There's been no one else since you showed up," he said suddenly, shocking the crap out of me. "I implied there was to hurt you, but my bear is loyal to you, even though we both know you plan to leave us. It feels... selfish... to expect respect when you don't intend to return the favor and abandon us."

His words really shouldn't bring the joy they did, and I pretended it wasn't due to his admittance that he'd been faithful to our bond. "I promise not to just up and disappear on you all," I said, which was the best I could offer. "If I need to leave, for my own safety or yours, I will tell you about it. I won't just disappear like a thief in the night. I won't show you that disrespect, because you all deserve more. I've grown to see that my initial actions were ill thought out and cruel, and I won't—" My breath stuttered from me, and it took a few seconds to catch it again. "I'm grateful to have found you. You make me wish for a different future."

Hunter lifted his hand and grasped mine, twining our fingers together. "Fuck the future you think is yours," he growled. "Fate does not control us. We control ourselves and our future."

Slade leaned forward to add, "And you're going nowhere, Snow."

Oh goddess. Was that *a claim* from the dragon himself? Or was he just annoyed that one of his possessions might choose to leave before he was ready to finish playing with it? One could never tell with Slade Riverson.

Finley's energy was calmer as he settled back in his chair and stared out the window for the rest of the drive. Hunter never released my hand, even as he drove at insane speeds, weaving through the town and toward the forest.

When he parked, I didn't get a chance to touch the handle before Slade was there, pulling the door open and letting in the chilly air. The scent of snow drifted in with the breeze, though none had fallen yet. We were well into November, and I expected winter pack runs would start taking place sooner rather than later.

Warrick's car slid in next to the Bentley, and the mated pair jumped out. "Cores, you need to wait for me to open your door," Warrick huffed, and Cora laughed him off.

"Sorry, babe. I'm just so excited to have Emme here to run with us again. I haven't been out since the last time we went. My wolf is quite literally somersaulting inside me."

Mine had also upped her game of swirling and twirling and scratching at my insides to get free. Slade crossed his bare arms, seemingly unaffected by the freezing winds cutting through the air. "Are you planning on shifting?" I asked, trying to figure out the logistics of a dragon on a pack run. Especially fitting through the tightly packed sections of the forest paths. Maybe he just knocked everything down and made it easier for all of us...

The green of his eyes appeared lighter out here, and I was surprised by his slight smile. "I can keep up in this form." I'd just bet he could.

Cora and Warrick undressed where they stood, with Warrick's bulk shielding her from the other alphas. Nudity might not bother shifters, but alphas were possessive of their mates no matter the circumstances. As I started to lift my sweater over my head, the cool air hitting my nicely warmed boobs, I found myself surrounded by my pack. They turned their backs to give me privacy, forming a circle around me. Hunter's shoulder even touched Slade's as they blocked me from view. None of them had said a word, moving in sync, like they bore a single mental thought.

My hands shook from more than the cold as I shucked my clothes, the frosty air biting until I shifted into my beast.

I'd been worried for a second that with the alphas here I'd struggle to shift so quickly, but my wolf was raring to go. She pranced from the middle of their huddle, and they turned to give her all their focus.

My wolf's size wasn't comparable to alphas, but I was still large for a female. Slade reached out and traced his hand over my snout, wrapping his massive palm around the back of my head.

I blinked up at him, wishing I had the ability to talk so I could ask him what the fuck he was doing. The alpha with a touch aversion was threading his fingers into my fur.

"Snow," he murmured, tilting his head in that predatory way of his. "As white as snow."

Finley broke the moment by snorting derisively and walking away, and Slade released me as if he'd never touched me in the first place.

CHAPTER 19

EMME

Finley was a giant in more ways than one: a giant pain in my ass, a giant lumbersnack, and a giant, terrifying bear.

He stood what felt like miles above my wolf form, his fur a deep rich brown, with scatterings of that same golden color that threaded his human hair. He bore no resemblance to any sort of cute fluffy bear. He was exactly how I imagined a crazed murderous monster with a taste for blood would look.

Was it necessary for him to stand seven feet tall and resemble a nightmare creature? One or the other would have been more than enough, but as always with these alphas, they had to be overachievers.

Cora wiggled her small frame, silky strands of fur flying around her gracefully while she got the zoomies out. Warrick remained at her side, his canines on show as he kept an eye on our surroundings.

I'd always thought that Warrick had the most terrifying and vicious wolf form until Hunter's beast strode in. I'd seen Hunter's black wolf from a distance, but nothing could have prepared me for him stalking toward me in the dimly lit forest.

I had to back up many steps to take in his massive length and breadth, and... he was as alarmingly terrifying as Finley.

No. More terrifying.

Holy fuck. He was huge all over, powerful muscles visible under his short, black coat, and as he locked me in those dark as sin eyes, I wanted to run. I wanted to flee in a way I'd never felt.

This aptly named alpha had always given off hunter and prey vibes, and they'd never been as strong as today, when we both stood as wolves. This was nature at its basest form, and there was no doubt who we bowed to.

Then Slade strolled over, and once again, even in his humanoid form, he held dominion over the beasts. How were these alphas *my* pack? It was almost impossible to believe, and yet I felt the connection to them deep in my soul. Especially in my wolf form, as I slid my nose along Slade's boot, huffing in his delicious scent. My beast had always been cautious around the dragon, but less so now that we'd spent time with him.

When Slade crouched down, he met my wolf's eyes. "Ready to run, Snow?"

A little *yip* escaped me, and my tail moved like a fucking windmill, round and round. The wolves around me howled, and Finley opened his massive mouth, displaying long and lethal canines as he roared into the world.

Animals had long ago departed our vicinity, so he didn't scare anything off except a couple of other shifters, who did a double take and sprinted in the opposite direction of our group.

Warrick and Cora took off first, playfully nipping at each other. Or at least one of them was—Warrick tended to be quite serious for the first part of the run. He'd loosen up when his wolf's initial needs were sated.

Hunter nudged me to move, and I bounded into the forest, enjoying the stretching of my legs and muscles. Hunter remained at my side and slightly ahead, keeping an eye on everything. Finley fell in behind us, his form surprisingly quiet and agile despite the bulk he hauled around. Slade looked like he was taking a casual stroll but somehow stayed on my other side.

The alphas were adept at leading while remaining around me in a protective circle.

At first it annoyed me, my beast fighting the restrictiveness of their formation, until I realized that this was what running with a protective pack felt like. My wolf and I had no experience with packs, but eventually we found our rhythm. Abandoning all human thoughts and worries, I sprinted as fast as I could along the well-worn paths, the scent of nature and other shifters everywhere.

The mocha, vanilla, cherry, and toasted marshmallow were comforting as they blended with my chocolate and honey. The only hovering shadow was our missing cinnamon and caramel.

The thought of Kellan had my wolf throwing her head back and howling mournfully into the crisp air. He would have loved this run with *all* our pack. Our first real run, and he wasn't here for it.

With that thought my joy faded, and I found myself slowing.

"Kellan would want you to enjoy yourself," Slade said into the quiet morning air. "Mourning him before he is dead doesn't help anyone. Keep living life for him, Snow. Give him what he needs while he fights to stay alive."

A snarl ripped from me as I spun around, only to find myself pinned by a pair of deep, green eyes. "I know, Emmeline," he shot back with his own snarl. "I understand that feeling of helplessness and despair tearing through you. It won't save our pack mate, so you need to rise above it."

Dammit. I hated when he wouldn't just let me sink into my feelings, whether they were irrational and frustrating or not. If I had the ability to flip him off, I would have taken the risk. I was almost certain he wouldn't kill me over a simple middle finger. *Almost* certain.

Hunter's growl and bark of command got us all back on track, and we ended up in a section of forest by the stream, similar to where I'd first met Kellan. That was a nice memory, and I wrapped it around myself as I tried not to dwell on our missing alpha. Whether *he'd* want me to be happy running without him or not... I just wasn't. It felt as if an essential part of me was missing, like a limb or a quarter of my heart.

Cora and Warrick, who'd diverted from the main path at some point, burst into the clearing, and I wasn't surprised by Warrick playfully nudging his mate. He rolled her over onto her back to nuzzle against her throat.

Hunter did the same to me, his massive head firm against my side until I went down, and he licked along the edge of my jaw. His rough tongue felt good, and I yelped lightheartedly, trying to bowl him over too. With his boulder-like density, I had no hope.

He didn't budge even when I ran full force into his side, bruising only myself and my ego.

I swear he laughed a little, his lips lifting as his chest rumbled.

Warrick and Cora headed for the stream, and I watched them, happy to see how strongly their bond shone. To the point I *almost* caught a glimpse of what appeared to be tangible connections as they lapped up water and splashed in the shallows.

My observations were interrupted by Slade gracefully

sliding to the ground, his long legs sprawled out in front of him as he leaned back against a nearby tree in the shade. As promised, he'd had absolutely no issue keeping up with us, and through a few of the denser paths, the branches appeared to all but shift out of his way as he moved. If I didn't know better, I'd say that Slade commanded nature, and nature obeyed.

When Hunter finally allowed me to regain my footing, I padded toward the stream to find Finley, in his bear form, perched in the middle. His huge paws plunged into the current, and for all his terrifying grizzly form, he looked cute as he swiped through the water, like he was trying to catch a—

He stabbed a dark pink fish with his eight-inch claws and lifted it to his mouth, tearing the head right off it. *Well…* that was one way to fish.

My wolf was thirsty, so we moved downstream and lapped at the frosty water, enjoying the fresh taste of the stream. Hunter remained close by, ever vigilant as he observed the clearing, scented the air, and kept a general eye on our surroundings.

It reminded me of a story Ophelia Locker, a lady I worked with in Vegas two years ago, told me. She said whenever she went out at night with her husband, she switched her brain off. I never truly understood what she meant at the time, but she explained that when she was alone she always kept a close eye on her surroundings, calculated the risk of every path she took, and always held her keys or mace in hand to use as a weapon.

Human women didn't have the luxury of just strolling around at night without fear, but when she was with her big, burly, tatted husband, he was the protector, and she just got to… exist.

At the time, I'd internally laughed at the thought of ever

trusting a male shifter enough to switch off my own protective instincts. But with Hunter and this pack... I mean, I didn't just stop overseeing my own safety, but I shared it, which allowed moments of enjoying my run without fear.

For the first time in my life there was a pack at my back, and considering how hard I'd fought against this fate, and how wrong I'd been about it, I was starting to wonder if I'd been wrong about more than just that.

Could these alphas truly turn on me one day and become a threat?

They were *nothing* like the Rogers pack, and therefore... maybe... they could handle the power.

It was a terrifying, alluring thought.

When I'd drank my fill, and was sated and relaxed, I padded back toward Slade. My wolf understood not to touch him as she lay down, leaving a few inches between his legs and our body. Hunter settled in on my other side, and he had no qualms about space, pressing into my side, the heat of his energy countering the chill of the air.

Even at a distance Slade gave off just as much heat, and I was relaxed and drowsy, resting my head on my paws as I drifted off into a snooze. In my half-asleep state, a solid but gentle weight pressed to the base of my skull, and my wolf internally preened at Slade touching us. The pressure against my head was soothing, regulating my beast.

Finley's scent drifted closer, and while he didn't touch me, his presence helped me drift off to sleep. Sleep away my pain and worry, and fears over Kellan.

Sleep away the concern that my presence in these alphas' lives was going to get one of them killed.

Finley blamed me for Kellan, and deep inside I agreed with him. I kept that pain and anger tucked away with the memories of finding my mom hanging like a husk in the street.

She'd never been a good mother, and I wasn't sure she deserved a different ending to the one she got, but we continued to share the same fate. Even if mine already felt different with this pack of alphas who brought me moments of peace and protection.

Her pack had never done that for her. Not even once, despite her dependency on them. It was always her sacrificing everything, and them taking and taking.

They'd been assholes in the truest sense, and when they'd stood there and laughed as I tried to cut her down from her place of death, I'd known I had to run.

From them, and all the alphas I believed were the same.

I'd been successful for a while too, until fate chose a different path for me.

Did that mean my fate no longer aligned with Mom's?

Would I get a different ending?

CHAPTER 20

After our run, Hunter and Slade said they needed to head into the office to deal with work they'd been neglecting, and Finley had an afternoon game he couldn't miss, which left me on Kellan duty. Along with the dozen or so enforcers prowling the outside of the family compound.

"Are you sure you don't want me to stay?" Warrick asked Hunter. "We can keep her company while your pack is out, even though half our squads are patrolling your street."

Hunter crossed his arms and raised one eyebrow until Warrick let out a sigh. "You know I'm not a threat to Emme in any way. I've already found the love of my life and a scent match. I've got a completed quintet. She's my frien—"

Hunter and Slade snarled together, and Warrick threw his hands in the air. "Call if you need anything, Emme."

With that, he spun on one booted heel and got into his car. Cora was inside already, having hugged me ten times before she left. "Thank you!" I called after him. "Sorry about the Neanderthals."

Neither of the alphas denied their cave-shifter tendencies, and when Warrick's car was out of sight, they both relaxed.

Our drive home was quiet and comfortable, all of us content now that we'd let our beasts run free. Except for Slade, but he must have been channeling us all the same.

When we were parked in the garage, and I'd just gotten out of the car, Hunter said, "Don't leave the house for any reason today."

I narrowed my eyes and took a step into him, our chests almost touching. I had to tilt my head all the way back to keep his face in my line of sight. "It's in your best interest to rephrase that statement." I jabbed a finger into his chest, which hurt me more than him, but I had a point to make.

"Did you not understand my order?" Hunter asked softly, brow furrowing as he faked confusion. *Asshole.* "And here I was thinking that was a perfectly clear and non-negotiable statement."

Hunter and his exceptional grasp on sarcasm. "You don't own me, Hunter Reeves. You don't get to control me. You don't get to order me around. You should know by now that I don't even need these warnings as I'm not the type to run into dangerous situations without thinking it through."

Slade, the annoying dragon he was, decided to pipe up. "You did wander off to the guardhouse on your own without letting any of us know."

Of course, he had to bring that up. "*Your* guard house. Why would I expect that the shifters you employed were in with my mom's evil pack to kidnap me."

Not that we'd had that theory confirmed, but it was pretty much the general consensus. They'd put a call out, offered a shit-ton of money for my capture, and good old Jones-beta-fuckface had jumped at the chance.

"You shouldn't trust anyone *but* your pack," Slade said with a shrug, like it was pure commonsense.

"Which includes Warrick and Cora," Hunter added, and for the love of shifter babies, these two were ridiculous.

I jabbed Hunter's hard chest again, and debated jabbing Slade too, but couldn't quite bring myself to step over the line with his boundaries. "I will trust whoever I want to trust, and let me tell you, I'm still not sure I should even be here with *this* pack. Can I trust you four?"

It was a nonsensical question, because I already trusted them more than I'd ever trusted anyone. They'd proven themselves worthy through their care, consideration, and protectiveness. But allowing them to know that gave them way too much power, and it was already unbalanced.

Hunter's hands wrapped around my waist, and he hauled me up until my face was even with his. My gasp was a muffled sound as his lips crashed against mine and oh my freaking life I was *kissing Hunter Reeves.*

Hunter Reeves, who tasted like sinful dessert, and everything deliciously wicked in the world.

Every thought escaped my mind except the taste of this alpha as he kissed me.

No, not kissed, devoured.

My lips parted and his tongue collided with mine, consuming me with force. Hunter kissed like he did everything else in life, with complete control and skill, and an edge of ferality that destroyed my ability to reason.

The moan that escaped me was obscene, and I didn't care that we had an audience as I wrapped my legs around his waist and ground myself against his hard muscles. I had no idea what part of his body was between my thighs, and I was too fucked up to care.

Was it his cock? Ribs? Abs? Who cared? I just needed relief and friction, and I rocked like my life depended on it.

The intensity eased up as he pressed small kisses and nips against my lips, the edge of pain in his bites bringing a gush of arousal to my already very damp panties. My scent was everywhere, edged even sweeter as my desire heightened to levels I'd only ever experienced with this pack.

Slade and Finley. I remembered they were right there, and unless they'd walked away, they'd just witnessed this drugging, perfect kiss, which left me a shaking, needy mess.

"Eyes on me, little omega," Hunter commanded, and my gaze snapped up to meet his stormy gray irises. "You can absolutely trust us. There are no shifters in this world who you can trust more. Do you know why?"

My brain remained a ball of mush from that spectacular kiss he'd just bestowed on me, so I kind of mumbled, "Not really," and wobbled my head.

Hunter released an amused rumble. "We're part of your soul. We're matched in a way that not even the gods can destroy. To hurt you would be akin to hurting ourselves... actually more than hurting ourselves, because I would sacrifice myself for you. I would sacrifice the entire fucking world, including everyone else in our pack *for you*. Understand?"

It was another version of what Kellan had said, right before he'd thrown himself between me and an unknown magic. The thought of another one of them having to make the same choice made me physically sick.

"I don't want that," I whispered, my voice breaking as I stared into the blazing charcoal and gold of his eyes. "I'm not worth that, and I don't want it for any of you. I'm the least worthy of this pack, and I wish I could take Kellan's place. I deserve to."

When the temperature shot up, I took in Slade's form. The

dragon hadn't left, standing six feet away, but there was no sign of the bear shifter. Not that I could focus on anything other than the burn in Slade's gaze.

"Slade," Hunter warned, his voice low and irritated. "Calm down."

"She needs to learn," the dragon rumbled back in a voice too deep to even comprehend.

It shouldn't be possible for a shifter to reach an octave that low, but it was exactly how I imagined it would sound if his beast form spoke. "She's the heart of our pack, and without her we will crumble. I refuse to be bonded in a weak pack, and for that, she must *learn her worth*."

Hunter's exhalation was filled with both exhaustion and acceptance. "She won't learn through you scaring it into her. We must build her up. She's never had anyone build her confidence until it was unshakable."

"She also doesn't like being spoken about like she's not in the room." I wiggled in an attempt to get down from Hunter, but he didn't release his hold. "I am strong on my own," I continued. "I have always known that I could step up and do what was needed, no matter the circumstances. But I'm also aware that you four are exceptional. I'm the outlier in the shifter world, and this is not a woe-is-me, pick-me-girl moment. It's a fucking fact. In a fight or a battle, you four would be the ones to step in front of danger to protect me, and I fucking hate it. I can't live with that. I don't want to be put first... I want us to be equals."

When I wiggled to get down again, Hunter held me tighter while releasing an annoyed grunt. "We are equals in the pack. Even as the entitled alpha I acknowledge that. The only reason there is any hierarchy at all is for our beasts, but you must know you're the core and heart of the pack. Always protect your heart."

"Because you can't survive without it," Slade finished, and I was absolutely fucking gutted.

These alphas continued to be my most beautiful destruction.

Slade reached out to touch me, stopping just short of my cheek. "You *are* strong on your own in survival mode," he agreed with me. "But this is about pack strength together. You need to learn how to rely on us emotionally... which, understandably, with your upbringing, will take more time." His dragon fire died down, as if he was now satisfied with our discussion.

"Are you sure you'll be okay here on your own?" Hunter asked, drawing my gaze back to him. Back to his lush mouth and the memory of the kiss that would be forever seared into my brain.

I had no doubt he'd stay home with me, and as nice as that sounded, I needed a little space to think and breathe. "Totally okay. I'll be with Kellan, and I'm still tired, so I'll catch up on sleep."

Might fit in a sobbing session or two while I was there.

Hunter's all-seeing stare took me in for many long seconds, but he did eventually return me to my feet, his hand drifting up to cup my throat. "Don't forget who you belong to, little omega," he whispered, leaning in until our lips touched. "*Mine.*"

His thumb scraped over my skin as goosebumps covered me from that simple touch. "I won't forget," I choked out.

"Once again, it's *ours*, you possessive bastard," Slade drawled, back to his usual calm, logical shifter. "But as the entitled alpha, I'll let you have that today."

Neither of us missed the unsaid reminder that he'd let him have the *entitled* part as well.

Hunter didn't take offense as he brushed his thumb across

my throat once more and released me. The alphas stood side by side as they moved together, and I couldn't stop staring at the masculine beauty. I mean, it was like an all-you-can-eat buffet of my favorite foods, and I was suddenly starving.

Despite the lack of blood ties between them, Slade and Hunter could have been true brothers with their dark hair, bronze skin, huge frames, and piercing gazes. Even if Slade did have the *poor little guy* beat on height.

Goddess, it was a lot being around them like this, and it was good to have a reprieve from the intensity.

I also needed a hit of Kellan, because it had been too long without my golden boy.

CHAPTER 21

EMME

Once the alphas left for work, the house felt empty. I should have been used to that feeling, having experienced it for most of my *almost* twenty-six years, but weirdly, it bothered me.

In Kellan's room, it was clear that Florence had been in to freshen up the space. The bay windows were open, letting in the crisp air, and there was the faint scent of lemons from her cleaning products. Only the best, natural products without synthetic scent for these billionaires.

"Hey, Golden," I called as I wandered over to sit beside his bed. "Still not waking up for me, I see. We really need to do something about that."

There was the faintest twitch along the lid of his closed eyes, but no other sign he'd heard me. I took his hand, frowning at the unusual warmth under my touch. Ever since the spell had hit him, he'd actually been on the cooler side, and as I reached out to check his forehead, my phone chimed. I carried it around in case of a Kellan emergency, and expected it would be Hunter or Slade checking in.

I blinked at the name which popped up in the group chat.

Grouchy Bear: *Image attached*

I clicked the image. It took a second to load before the entire hockey team appeared on the screen, all kitted out on the ice, heads back as they appeared to be howling toward the roof of the stadium. There was another ding, and this time Finley sent a video.

This was slower to load, but when it finally popped up, it was the Celtic Wolves skating in a circle and chanting Kellan's name. They all took a moment to throw their heads back, howling for their teammate, and just before the video finished, Finley's face appeared in selfie mode.

With no one here to judge me, I drank in every detail of the bear shifter, from the golden brown of his hair to the richer brown of his beard. His eyes were somber, the whiskey depths filled with the swirls of pain I'd come to associate with him. "Show Kel for us," he said into the camera. "Tell him we're playing the Warriors, and that we're going to kick their asses. This game is for him." He tilted the phone and Christian appeared, dark circles under his eyes and his face haggard.

"We love you, brother," he said hoarsely. "We need you back. Don't give up. You promised me that we'd grow old, wrinkly balls together, and I'm forcing you to keep that promise." His voice broke, and he handed the phone back to Finley, who shot one last look into the camera before the video cut off.

I choked in air, having barely breathed through the footage. I hit play again and held the phone near Kellan's face. "Golden Boy, your team love and miss you," I said through my tears. "That's a mourning wolf cry. They need you back, just like the rest of us. Keep fighting."

I played the video for him a few times, and maybe secretly

for myself, because Finley was so lovely to look at. Especially when he wasn't growling or snarling in my direction.

Part of me was disappointed not to be at the game, even though he wouldn't have appreciated my presence. There was another chime as I exited the video, and I let out a sad chuckle at the name that popped up. The voice to text read it for me, because I was way too emotional to slowly decipher the message.

> Daddy Alpha: Kellan will be perfectly fine. He's strong. He's more than capable of holding on. Jewels said she has news and will be by tonight. Nothing to worry about.

It was in Hunter's usual blunt, confident style, and the most telling part to me was that he hadn't changed his name. Even though Kellan wasn't awake to change it back.

Finley hadn't either.

Another ding and...

> Scary Shifter: Correct. I'm formulating my own plan to give him a boost of energy, but it might require Emmeline's help.

And Slade was using *Scary Shifter*. Kellan had these big, bad alphas acting like they had real feelings and weren't dominant beasts. It was the most heart wrenching, perfect way for them to act.

> Pretty Girl: I will do absolutely anything to help Kellan. You don't even have to ask. Just point me in the direction I need to go.

> Scary Shifter: Yes, I know you will.

Slade's reply was almost instantaneous, as if he had

already been following along as I slowly typed and corrected my words before I sent it.

Staring up at the ceiling, I made another half-hearted attempt to find these super-tech Reeves Industries cameras. *Ding!*

> Daddy Alpha: You'll never find them, little omega. But we are always watching.

> Pretty Girl: That's creepy as fuck. You know that right?

> Daddy Alpha: *shrugging emoji*

That arrogant asshole would be the death of me.

> Scary Shifter: You won't love my plan, Snow. Prepare yourself.

That had me slightly worried, but I couldn't really think of anything I wouldn't do for Kellan.

> Grouchy Bear: The omega might not be the strongest of our pack, but she shows genuine care toward Kellan. In this, I trust she'll do the right thing.

That bear was getting on my last fucking nerve.

> Pretty Girl: *middle finger emoji* Suck a dick, Finley Thornton.

I sent it before I even considered the ramifications.

> Grouchy Bear: *bear raging emoji* From what I've heard, you're the one with the dick sucking skills, Ice Queen.

No. The fuck. He didn't.

> Pretty Girl: Pretend all you want you're not jealous that I wouldn't touch your dick with a ten-foot pole.

My reply was fast and furious, and if I didn't have all the tech help on the phone, not one of those words would have been spelled correctly. I didn't have time for spelling or grammar when I was pissed off.

Finley's reply was super quick as well.

> Grouchy Bear: How'd you know I had a ten-foot pole in my pants? You been spying on me, Icy? Why are you obsessed with someone who is not interested?

I was about to shoot back a long-winded message where I called him for every fucked-up thing he'd ever said and done, before I paused. I took a few deep breaths and thought about what the best response would be. Finley wanted a rise out of me. He wanted to make me look pathetic and childish. I would not give him the satisfaction.

> Pretty Girl: You're entitled to your opinion, Finley. I have nothing further to say.

When the reply came, I almost didn't open it until I saw Hunter's name.

> Daddy Alpha: That's my good girl.

Whoa, now that was an ending to the text wars I hadn't expected to receive.

But... it felt hotter in here suddenly.

Wait... Heat. Kellan. I'd been about to check his

temperature when the first message from Finley showed up. I dropped my hand on his cheek and flinched at the slap of heat against my palm.

Whipping out my phone, I quickly voice-chatted the message because I was too shaken to type and google to figure out spelling.

> Pretty Girl: Guys, Kellan is burning up. I just noticed when I put my hand on his cheek. I don't know if this is a normal part of the spell's process, or if we should be worried, but I'll try and cool him down until you get back to me.

Hunter rang and I answered straight away. "Emme, tell me exactly how he looks."

Running my gaze over Kellan, I said, "He's paler than usual, and there's no sign he's flushed, but I can feel the heat coming off him. His heart's beating a little faster than it has been as well, and—" I paused to listen again. "And there's a slight skip every three or four beats. He's not doing well, Hunter." Panic sent my voice into higher octaves, and I couldn't sit still, jumping up to pace back and forth.

"Jewels is on her way. We'll be there in twenty minutes," Hunter replied, his voice low and reassuring. "The magic is reacting strongly to Kellan's alpha essence, but that doesn't mean he can't fight it. He can and he will. Put me on speaker."

Removing the phone from my ear I hit the speaker button and held the device closer to Kellan. "Listen to your alpha," Hunter commanded, and even I wanted to obey that deep rasp. "You will not get worse. You will keep fighting the magic. You will come back to this pack. We are not complete without you, Kel, and I refuse to let you fade into the magic. Fight, brother. Fight for us all."

The line went dead, and I clutched the phone tighter than

ever, trying to calm myself enough to do what was needed. I had to cool this fire burning beneath his skin.

Pocketing my phone, I rushed into Kellan's bathroom and grabbed a hand towel, running it under the cold water. Back in his room, I placed the cloth on his forehead, before repeating the process with all the hand towels I could find. The next twenty minutes were spent switching out the cloths for newly cooled ones, while I dabbed down his cheek and neck.

He wore a soft cotton shirt that I got quite damp, and as I debated stripping it off, he released a soft groan. I stilled, unsure if I'd heard that or just wished it into existence. "Kel," I whispered. "Can you hear me, love?"

The endearment slipped out, and I prayed that one day soon he'd be awake to hear it. I'd never said *I love you* or any other variation of it to anyone before, and I couldn't only be brave when he was unconscious.

"Come on, Golden," I continued, dabbing him with the cool edges of the cloth. "Make another sound. Wake up for me."

The heat of his skin leached the coolness from the cloths fast, so I kept racing back and forth to the bathroom. Florence would have provided ice water, but I was scared to leave him and ask for help. For some stupid reason, I felt like it was my presence and hard work with the towels that kept Kellan from falling victim to the flames beneath his skin.

On my twentieth trip from the bathroom, hurrying faster than ever, I clipped my toe on the edge of Kellan's rug, landing on the bed and half on top of the alpha himself. A rush of heat washed over my skin as I tried to scramble off, unable to find traction. My hands rested on his bare forearms, and I was surprised to find that after a few seconds there, his skin felt cooler, as if my palms had absorbed the heat and dragged the potency of the spell from him. The irritating scent of magic grew stronger in my nostrils, but I ignored it in the hopes of helping Kellan make it through this new attack.

Hunter burst into the room a beat later, Slade right behind him, neither of them blinking an eye at the sight of me sprawled awkwardly across an unconscious shifter. "What happened?" Hunter bit out quickly, looking around the room.

Maybe he thought there was a threat, and I threw myself on Kellan to save him. If only the story was that heroic.

"Uh, I tripped over the rug as I rushed back and fell on him. But..." I cleared my throat. "My bare skin touching his appears to be dispelling some of the heat. Certainly more than the cool cloths did."

Hunter and Slade exchanged a quick glance, and I swallowed my gasp when Hunter shucked his suit jacket and started to unbutton his shirt. "We need to pack huddle," he said quickly, looking down at Kellan and me. "He needs our energy to fight the witch magic, and the best way is for skin-on-skin touch. As you've just discovered."

Spluttering, I blinked at him. "Are you serious?"

"As serious as Kellan's death," he shot back. "Now get your clothes off or I'll get them off for you."

Well, okay, then. When he put it like that...

As I lifted my shirt too, I almost choked on air because Hunter and I weren't the only ones undressing. Slade was also.

CHAPTER 22

In my time with the Reeves pack, I'd seen Slade dressed in sweats, leather, or his enforcer getup. In all outfits there was only a hint of his tattoos peeking out from the neckline and sleeves of his shirt, with most of his bronze skin hidden away. There'd been the time in the clearing of Silver City too, but I'd been too distracted by the pierced cock hanging over my head to take in any other part of him.

Today, though, I got the full show.

I forgot to take my pants all the way off as I stood in shock, staring at the glorious planes of his chest as they emerged. *Shifter saints have mercy.*

None of the alphas in this room were slouches in the muscles department. Hunter, who was also shirtless at this point, was big, beautiful, and a work of art I still couldn't afford, while Kellan had the smooth, muscled physique of a professional athlete.

Slade, though. Slade freaking Riverson. There was no way he was real.

Firstly. He. Was. Huge.

The actual breadth of his chest and arms were... *a lot.* A

whole lot. Topped off by the fact that he had *both freaking nipples pierced*. I hadn't noticed that the last time, but clearly this alpha enjoyed a dose of pain and piercing.

My gaze caught on the silver bars through both brown nipples and held for longer than was probably healthy. Eventually I continued down the lines of his chest, over intensely carved abs, and along the defined V that led to the waistband of his black pants. There was a trail of dark hair directing me to the center of his V, and I was reminded that his nipples weren't the only part of him pierced. The monster in his pants was as well.

With a shake of my head, I forced myself to stop staring and breathing heavily, which was no doubt getting weird for all of us involved.

"You've got a little drool," Hunter said, and he sounded amused rather than annoyed, which was a lovely change. No one outside of our pack was allowed to so much as breathe in my direction, but within our quintet, there was very little jealousy.

"I mean, can you blame me? How the fuck is he real?"

Slade's sinfully full lips curved into a devastating smile. I'd seen him smile before... No, wait, had I ever seen him properly smile? Either way, it had my legs trembling as I clutched my sweats around my thighs like they were a lifeline keeping me standing. "Dragon genetics," he rumbled with a shrug of perfect shoulders.

Speaking of dragons, his tattoos needed their own moment...

"Your tattoos are not what I expected." They were even more spectacular than Hunter's, and that was saying something.

I fought the urge to step into him so I could trace my fingers along the lines. "Who does your work?" I said, more to myself than anything, because the beasts across his chest were so incredibly lifelike.

Two large dragon heads spanned across either side of his broad pectoral muscles, facing each other. Their bodies trailed up and over both shoulders, their tails curling around his biceps.

On the right side, the dragon was predominantly green with heavy, black-tipped scales, and on the left was its opposite: a mostly black beast with just hints of green to emphasize scales and size. This darker dragon had smoky shadows spanning its form, while the right was lighter, with sparks of what looked like starlight around it.

The greens of both were the exact shade of Slade's eyes and dragon, and I was drawn to the way the pair faced off against each other, jaws wide and snarling, flames curling around their razor-sharp teeth as they met in the center of his chest, foes about to battle.

"A psychologist would have a field day with that tattoo," Hunter said, his gaze also locked on Slade's chest. I nodded, having formed a few theories already.

"What do you see?" Slade asked, tilting his head a touch, which wasn't his predatory move. It was his curious one. "What does it say about me to you?"

Swallowing roughly, I tried to loosen my grip on my pants as my fingers were starting to ache, but none of my limbs remained under my control. "You war against your dragon. Both sides of you are not at peace, the dark and the light, which makes existing between them the most dangerous place of all."

At the center of the two beasts, there was this hollow gap with just a spattering of dark ink—a tear in the fabric of existence that could never be breached.

Slade didn't comment, but his gaze was heavier as he watched me like I was the greatest curiosity in the room.

When Kellan made a slight noise, it broke the moment, and all of us snapped into action to help our pack mate. I yanked my pants down, leaving myself clad in a matching black bra and panties set. Crawling across the bed to Kellan, I draped myself down his left side, gasping as Hunter, who had followed right behind me, lifted me on top of Kellan's chest.

"We all have to fit," he reminded me as I tried to adjust myself so I wasn't quite so intimately sprawled across an unconscious male. "He won't mind, trust me."

Slade sat on the right side of the bed, dipping it with his weight. "Oh, he'll mind alright. But only that he's missing it. I'll have to show him the video footage when he wakes up."

I'd circle back to that video footage comment soon enough, but for now we needed to help our golden boy. The heat of his skin scorched me briefly, and I sighed in relief when it started to cool.

Hunter slid down Kellan's left side, his arm draping over my back, as he held both of us.

I shuddered at the sensation. Being hugged so thoroughly still shocked my system, until I let myself fall into the sensation, allowing a whole bunch of warm gooey feelings to spread from my center. I was supposed to be cooling Kellan down, but this was the healthy sort of heat.

One built of care and... *more*.

When Slade moved closer, my breath caught in my lungs. Everything stopped moving—I was fairly sure the world stopped spinning.

"Do not move," he warned as the hard muscles of his body slid down Kellan's right side. He was so huge that he had to touch me when he touched our fallen alpha, and I choked back a guttural sound when his arm landed on my back, flexing right below Hunter's.

The sensation of his weight pressing me into the unconscious alpha was too much, and in my head I started counting to a million, attempting to get myself under control so I didn't moan or have a spontaneous orgasm. Which would be highly inappropriate considering the circumstances.

At least both alphas kept their pants on, which was for the best when it came to my shaky self-control.

As I continued to mentally count, Hunter chuckled softly, but for once refrained from revealing whatever had amused him. No doubt there was more than one facet to our current situation to find humor in.

I remained tense and off-kilter as I counted like it was my life's work, only starting to relax around the time the heat finally left Kellan's body. Hunter and Slade remained silent on either side, surrounding me in their scents and energy.

I had no idea why I wanted to cry as I lay there, feeling safer and more terrified than I ever had in my life, but there was no denying the burn behind my eyes.

Finley not being part of the pack huddle flickered momentarily through my counting haze, but after everything he'd said and done, it was hard to imagine ever being comfortable enough to cuddle with the bear. My feelings toward him were convoluted and unsure, but deep in my heart I admitted that there might be too much history now for us to ever be more than distant acquaintances.

Finley still needed a few high fives. To the face. With a chair.

I understood that I'd hurt him with my actions, and I regretted my blunt dismissal of the pack when we first met, but Finley's trauma went so much deeper than my rejection.

His healing needed to begin with his past, long before he met me, and I refused to be his punching bag on his way to peace.

It was around a thousand in my counting that I finally fell asleep, snuggled between three alphas. When I woke later, unsure what time it even was, the room was completely dark and Hunter was wrapped around one side of me, with... *what the fuck?* Vanilla and cherries hit me right in the face, and there was enough light in the room to glimpse golden hair and brown skin.

Finley... was here.

Unlike Slade, he didn't wrap his arm over my back, but he was close enough that our bodies touched, his energy and heat different to the fever Kellan had been fighting.

Part of me wanted to escape.

To crawl out from under Hunter's hold and race from this room *and* from this ache in my chest. It was a vise squeezing me until I felt like I'd explode into pieces. The longer I remained where I was, though, the more clarity broke through my panic. There was none of the usual tension that existed whenever Finley and I were close, as if in sleep he couldn't hold on to his anger. It was peaceful as both alphas slumbered soundly on either side of me, their breaths deep and even, their hearts calmly beating in sync.

Prying my gritty eyes open—I had not slept nearly long enough—I lifted my head from Kellan's chest and met Slade's gaze, who was sprawled in the chair, watching the four of us closely.

"He never sleeps," he said, his voice softer than usual. His expression was as well, as if facets of this scene had pierced his coldly contained emotions.

My gaze flickered toward Finley's face, which was mostly hidden by the arm he had thrown up over his head, as if he slept the same way toddlers did. From what I could see, though, he did look peaceful.

Slade shifted closer, resting his elbows on his knees. "His family were particularly good at subtle tortures. Never letting him sleep easily was one of their favorites. Even now, after years of being safe from them, he remains in a constant state of fight or flight."

The more of his past that was revealed, the more concessions I made for Finley and his shitty behavior. Of all the alphas, he was the one who understood what I'd suffered from my mother. On the other hand, that also made his reaction toward me *that much worse.*

It wasn't that I was comparing our upbringings, because it wasn't a competition, and he'd clearly had it worse. But I did understand. I ached at the thought that what should have been shared experiences to bond over had turned into the trauma that kept us apart.

I had no doubts that his pack barely knew a fraction of what he'd gone through, except for Slade, who would have hacker-spied his way through all their pasts.

"How did you know my birthday?" I asked, desiring a glimpse of his secrets too. "It's not recorded anywhere, and I absolutely did not tell any of you, so... how?"

Had the dragon shifter uncovered anything else about me? Did he know the circumstances of my mom's death? Did he know everything, and I'd kept this stupid secret for no reason at all?

CHAPTER 23

EMME

Slade didn't adjust his gaze. "I know almost everything about you, Emmeline Anders. The secrets I haven't uncovered yet remain only because I've been too busy keeping you safe to dig through my sources. But rest assured, I will figure it all out."

This fucking dragon.

"Did it ever occur to you…" I started way too loudly, cutting my annoyance back only when Hunter stirred behind me. Weirdly, Finley didn't move at all. I lowered my voice to a hiss: "…that if you wanted to know about me, you should have just asked. I don't like you prying into my past."

The dragon leaned even farther forward in his chair, and whatever relaxed casualness he'd displayed was gone. "You're my fated mate," he said, and his tone instantly sent goosebumps over my skin. Hunter's hold tightened over me as he pulled me onto his side of the bed and away from Slade.

I had a very brief freak-out that I'd pushed the dragon too far, before remembering that he'd never hurt his brothers. Or me.

I was almost positive.

"And you're keeping secrets from us." His tone remained flat, but with an undercurrent that had my quite full bladder ready to evacuate its contents.

Kellan and Hunter were in real danger of being peed on if Slade continued in the same reverberating tone. Which he absolutely did. Of course.

"It's my role as your mate to ensure that you are safe, and to do that, I need all the information about you. I need to know the threat before it shows up. *Fuck!*" Fire flashed in his eyes. "I need to eliminate the threat before it shows up. I almost failed at that once already, and not even you can stop me from protecting you." He paused briefly, and a fraction of his dominance crushing the room eased. "As I said, I know almost everything about you, Snow. You better get used to it, because if I could crawl into your fucking head and live there... I would. Hacking into your past is a poor, second-best option."

My heart slammed in my chest, but when Hunter's hold relaxed, I figured Slade was no longer in danger mode. I took the opportunity to roll over Hunter and slide to the floor. Not only did I desperately need to pee, but I also desperately needed to escape this room. And my feelings.

"I'm going to shower," I mumbled, feeling pathetic as I fled Kellan's room clad only in my underwear.

As I exited into the hallway, I heard Hunter say, "When is her birthday? You haven't told us that or updated her file."

My file. Yeah, these fuckers were all going down. I needed to figure out a way to get back at all of them—not Kellan—for their various and varied assholeish behaviors. It would take some planning, and maybe a little help from Cora, but there would be a way.

I'd figure it out. Starting with Slade Riverson.

In my room, I decided I needed more than a moment to get my head right, which led me to the bath—my place of relaxation and rejuvenation. With how off balanced I currently felt, I'd never needed this reprieve more. It was hard to believe it had been less than a month since my entire life was upended.

I'd thought my life was over the day I got captured and charged as a rogue, and then again when Hunter had scented me as his mate, along with the unsuccessful *and* successful kidnappings.

I'd fit a lot of drama, stress, and fear into my time in Golden Claw, but I'd also found real joy. Real friendships. And a pack who treated me like I was important and worth their time and care.

Pack, my wolf whispered, her tone content after our run and pack bonding session in Kellan's bed. *Our pack.*

I know, I told her, and for the first time in a long time it felt like we were on the same page when it came to being part of this quintet.

After I got the water running to fill the massive tub, I searched through the jars of oils and salts sitting on the ledge, noticing a few new selections. One was a light brown salt mix, and when I removed the lid I was hit with the scent of chocolate and coffee. The oil next to it smelled like toasted marshmallows, and I wasn't surprised to find the other new addition was caramel and cinnamon. The alphas had snuck in their scents, with Finley's the only one missing.

As the scents of pack filled the room, I debated what one to use. My favorite was Kellan, of course, because I missed him so damn much. I could really use a hit of him on my skin.

Not that I wasn't tempted to add all three, because the other two weren't far behind in the favorites scale these days. Hunter and Slade had wrapped me up in their particular brand of *care* lately, and it was destruction and perfection in one.

When the water was full and steamy, I added the caramel salt, stripped off my underwear, and sank into the heated depths. The stress and unease that had been plaguing me vanished as fast as the salts into the steaming depths. There was very little in the world that could compare to this feeling.

A groan slipped out as all my tense muscles relaxed, and when there was a responding rumble, my eyes shot open to meet a stormy gray gaze. I jerked up splashing water over the side of the bath and onto Hunter's pants.

"Shit. Fuck. What the fuck are—?" My breaths heaved in and out, and I had no idea why I was so shocked—these alphas had no boundaries. "What are you doing in here, Hurricane?"

Gold flickered in his eyes as his wolf came out to play, and I remained motionless under his predatory stare. The CEO, suit-clad, highly controlled man was no longer here... I had the beast.

Hunter's long legs propelled him the extra step to the side as he snatched me up. My wet, naked body was plastered against his bare chest, and when he kissed me I forgot everything.

My name. My past. My worries.

Hunter's kiss was my entire personality until he stopped devouring my mouth like it was the literal air he needed for existence. "Little omega," he murmured, his chest shaking. "I fucking knew it would be like this. *I knew you would wreck me from the depths of my soul.*"

I'd never seen his control snap so thoroughly, and it both terrified and thrilled me. Along with a healthy dose of lust and need. The ache in my core was so intense that as Hunter tightened his hold on my ass, until his strong hands bit into muscle, I rocked against the hard length pressing into my center. Yep, I was about to come with very little other stimulation.

I'd never been able to bring myself to orgasm—even with the help of toys—as quickly as Hunter managed with a single fucking kiss. He thought I was wrecking him, but this alpha was about to obliterate me, and I was ready to sign myself up.

"Sleeping next to you," he thundered, kissing down the corner of my lips, his tongue tracing every inch of my skin that he touched, "was beyond my fucking control. I need you in my bed, Emmeline. I need you naked and under me every damn night, before my beast goes completely feral. The man as well."

My core spasmed, and I arched harder against him, the swirls of pleasure in my gut building and building. When he bit into my neck, almost breaking the skin, I cried out and came so hard that my vision went blurry and dark.

Hunter's growl echoed loudly around the room, and I whimpered through my continued pleasure, trembling and shaking in his hold. He didn't stop marking and kissing along my throat and onto my shoulder, and I leaned back until I got my tits right where I wanted them. In his mouth.

He sucked my nipple, his teeth pressing against the areola until I wanted to scream. Pleasure or pain, they were both perfection.

"I need to see my bite on your skin," he said, moving on to my other nipple. "Are you ready to beg for my claim, baby girl?"

Yes. No. Yes. No. The dueling emotions were a continuous chant in my head.

"Fuck, Hunter," I cried, and he slowed his assault, his teeth grazing over the tip of my nipple.

"What is it, Emme? Use your words, baby girl. Tell me what you need."

I needed him to fuck me. *I needed it now.* I needed it to happen even if it meant he was going to bite me during the throes of pleasure. Dramatic or not, there was a real sense I'd die anyway if this intense, churning need inside me wasn't met.

"Hunter, please. Alpha, I need you to fu—"

There was a loud rapping on my bedroom door, interrupting me as I breathed heavily and tried to figure out what just happened. The lust had my brain clouded and slow.

Hunter's mouth and teeth grazed between my tits as he lifted his head and snapped, "What is it, Finley? You better be dying."

There was a brief pause, and then Finley shouted back. "The witch is here. She's got information about Kellan's condition."

Hunter stilled, and then a long exhalation of air escaped the alpha. "Fuck," he groaned, his head falling against mine as he straightened. "Only for that asshole would I interrupt our time together, little omega. For now, Kellan comes first."

His expression was creased in disappointment and reluctance as he lowered me to the damp tiles. "Finish up your bath and come find us. I won't let them make any decision until you're in the room." His gaze leveled me, eyes filled with dark swirls of gold once more. "And Emme…"

He paused, and I swallowed roughly, surprised to find my voice still worked. "Yes?"

"Use the mocha bath bomb."

When he was gone, I remained in a trembling mess, clutching the vanity and staring into the slightly steamy mirror. I'd had one orgasm, but it hadn't remotely taken the edge off—if anything, it was worse than ever.

I needed hours with these alphas without interruption, where they fucked me into exhaustion. All of which could absolutely wait until Kellan was whole and healthy once more. He was one of the alphas I desperately needed.

As I slipped back into the still-warm water, I reached out and lifted the white and mocha speckled bath bomb and dropped it into the water. Chocolate and coffee rose up around me as it dissolved, and with Kellan's scent still present from earlier, I found a place of peace and serenity once more.

Just with shakier thighs this time.

CHAPTER 24

HUNTER

My wolf howled relentlessly as I marched back down the hall and into Kellan's room. My damp sweats needed to be changed, but I wasn't ready to give up the sweet scent of Emme's release just yet. It was as soaked into my pants as the water from her bath.

I needed it to get through the next few hours, since I'd barely gotten the taste I craved.

Jewels had better have good news, or I was likely to be a worse nightmare to deal with than Slade, and as the entitled alpha of this pack, I couldn't devolve to that. But if there was any situation that smashed my control to shit, it was one of my pack hovering between life and death, along with my dick attempting to punch through my pants, and my balls firmly in the *blue* category.

"Speak to me," I growled as I entered Kellan's bedroom to find Jewels hovering over his still form, Slade and Finley watching her closely.

None of us fully trusted this witch. Not in the past or now, but she was our strongest ally in the magical world, and we'd exchanged multiple successful favors over the years. I had to play nice. Well, as nice as I could manage.

"We've created the counterspell," she said as her head shot up. "But I needed to examine him first to determine his strength, and after the fevers which indicate the original spell has infiltrated deeper, I don't think he's strong enough. The counterspell will most likely kill him."

Not a fucking chance. "He's going to die without the counter," I reminded her, barely keeping my wolf restrained. "It's better to take the risk versus letting him just deteriorate into death. He's strong enough."

I knew my pack brother better than most, and Kellan would fight with everything he had to stay with us. To stay with Emme. He'd literally never had more to live for.

Jewels didn't look convinced, her expression torn as she glanced between Kellan and me. "Judging by your current mood, and your actions in the past, I have no doubt you'll kill me if my spell *kills him*. I'm not sure I'm willing to risk that." Her eyes narrowed a touch. "I mean, unless of course you want to offer up a few very big favors from everyone in your pack to sweeten the task."

My wolf howled again as she finally admitted the real reason she held back from handing over the counterspell: she wanted to make sure she got her full pound of flesh from each of us.

Slade was on her so fast she barely managed a pip before his hand was around her throat. The dragon never allowed others to touch him—except in the few rare instances they got past his guard during training or fights. But if he touched you, it was never for a good reason.

As Jewels was well aware.

Her face paled as she stared up at him, unmoving and completely unable to speak. She could have used magic, but against Slade, she'd need more than just her normal defenses. If you tried to take on his dragon with magic, you better have a veritable atomic bomb worth of power.

"No favors, and if you don't give Kellan the spell asap, you're going to die." His voice and expression were neutral, if you discounted the faint burst of flames in his eyes. "At least if you *do* give him the spell and he survives, you will also survive."

Normally, I'd step in and defuse the situation, but as my wolf raged against the cage of my skin, I found very little inclination to save the witch. She parted her lips, but he held her too tightly for words. Her face was a dangerous blue when he finally loosened his hold, allowing her to splutter. "I-I will do the s-spell."

With a huff of fiery, ash-scented air, Slade relaxed his fingers and Jewels hit the floor hard. "See that you fucking do. Today."

He returned to where he'd stood a moment ago, arms relaxed at his side, no sign he'd almost choked her to death with one hand. Jewels remained sprawled on the floor, her eyes wide and glassy as she sucked in a few ragged breaths and coughed with each one.

It was finally registering with her that we were not the same pack we'd been the last time she saw us. We had found our final mate, the heart of our quintet, and until our bonds were complete, our beasts would be feral. Probably after as well.

"We have no choice but to ensure Kellan survives," I told her, making no move to help her off the floor. As far as I was concerned, there was no reason to ever touch another female who wasn't Emme. "How do we strengthen him using the pack bonds?"

She coughed again and rubbed her throat. "A completed quintet is really the only way."

Emme entered the room at that moment, dressed in blue sweats, her damp hair darker than usual as it hung around her heart-shaped face. Her crystal-blue eyes were wide, and her expression distressed as she stared at Jewels on the floor.

"Are you saying that it's our lack of a bond that's weakening him?" she choked out, moving her gaze to me in a search for truth.

I held my hand out, and like Thor's mighty hammer she crossed toward me without hesitation. Like I was finally fucking worthy.

When I tucked her close to my side, I noticed her scent was mixed with coffee and caramel, the combination enough to finally calm my beast.

Leaning down, I ran my nose along the soft, smooth skin of her throat, groaning deep in my chest. "Good fucking girl," I murmured, pleased she'd obeyed my command. No omega had to obey, so it was that much more satisfying when she did. "I need you covered in my scent now and always." She shivered against me, and I caught the moan she suppressed. "And no, this is not your fault. Not now or ever. We have no idea if a completed quintet would make any difference to his ability to fight this spell. Magic is unpredictable and Jewels is guessing."

She sank into me and my still-hard cock kicked in my pants, but I didn't bother to adjust myself. I was proud to show the world how much I craved her, my perfect mate.

"Jewels found a counterspell," I said, updating her on the new information. "But with the strength of the original spell infiltrating Kellan's energy deeper, and how potent this counterspell is, there are some concerns he might not be strong enough to survive the process." I could tell that Jewels hadn't been lying about that part.

Emme hyperfocused on the bed, her eyes wide and red-rimmed. I could smell the tears she stifled, her sorrow tainting the air with bitterness, which added to my already unhinged emotional state. "He'll die without the spell though," she murmured. "We would be stronger as a complete quintet?"

For some fucked-up reason, she turned to Finley, clearly seeking out the one who'd give her the whole truth. Not that I lied to her, but I tempered my response when the bear wouldn't.

Over Emme's head, I glared Finley into submission, silently reminding him that if he hurt her unnecessarily, I'd beat his ass until he prayed for death. I couldn't use dominance to force him without clueing Emme in on my pull of rank, and I wanted her to believe his response was genuine.

"As Hunter already said, we don't know if he'd be stronger fully bonded," Finley finally muttered. "This is all guesswork and hope. Like most fucking magic, if it's not annoying and dangerous, it's useless. There's no real in between."

Emme frowned, her freckles bunching together as she blinked and then turned to Slade next, before lifting her adorably confused expression my way. I remained calm as she ran her gaze over me like she could uncover my secrets with a simple look.

Having her complete focus while I stared into her striking blue eyes was second only to tasting and touching her. Our omega was so beautiful that I found myself stunned like a fucking pup when she gave me her full focus. It hurt. In the best way.

"How do we help him, Hunter?" she whispered, her expression begging me to have the answers she needed. Usually I'd be full of options, but today I had fucking nothing.

My wolf flipped out again, and my hold on Emme tightened until it had to be painful. Not that she made a noise or tried to step away. With effort, I loosened my grip and sucked in a deep, calming breath. "We have no choice but to attempt this spell and hope he's strong enough. His fever is gone, and he has taken energy from us, which will go a long way toward helping him."

Jewels dragged herself to her feet, moving closer to Kellan again. "We should do it now, then," she said, her voice huskier. "Every minute we wait, the spell grows in strength and is infusing deeper into his shifter essence and energy. If you all are fine with this decision, then I'll start preparing."

Emme's chest heaved, her sobs trapped inside as she clung to me. I had no idea if she knew she held on so tightly, her tiny hands wrapped around my forearm, taking my support. I'd be here to support her for the rest of our existence. "Yes, we should do the spell now," she murmured.

My gaze met Slade's, and he nodded slowly. Finley looked like he was about to either throw up or shift into his bear, but he nodded as well. The decision was made, and I would give the command as the entitled alpha.

"Yes. Do the counterspell. *Now*."

Jewels ran toward the door and picked up her brown leather satchel. Finley and Slade moved closer to us, forming a united pack. Emme, her expression still wreathed in pain and despair, turned to Slade: "You said you had an idea that might help him, but I wouldn't like it. What was it?"

Slade hadn't discussed it with me, but I had a strong inkling of what his idea was.

"It's a moot point anyway, now that the spell is stronger," my brother said with a shrug. "It would have required you to bond with him, which couldn't happen until Kellan was conscious to complete his side of the connection. I was theorizing a way to infuse him with energy and return him to consciousness long enough for the bond. But it's too late for that path. We don't have the time."

Emme's expression was a myriad of shattered pieces, and I couldn't stand to see that look on her face. "It's not a possibility, so don't even think about it," I told her, guiding her closer to the bed. "Let's pack huddle again until Jewels performs the spell."

"I've called in a few more from my coven," the witch said stiffly, pulling ingredients from her bag. "They'll be here shortly."

"We have time, then," Slade said, joining us near the bed. "Hunter is right, we should give Kellan as much strength as possible."

Emme was on the bed, draping herself across Kellan before he even finished his sentence. His shirt had been removed when we'd huddled earlier, and Emme openly sobbed into his skin. Witnessing her pain and not having a solution for it was an unbearable situation.

Speaking of bears, I caught the flinch of agony in Finley's features as he watched her with his brother, before he schooled his expression back to indifference. He strode over and placed his hand on Kellan's arm, careful not to touch Emme. Slade and I did the same, all of us touching his skin. "Your entitled alpha commands you to fight this," I rumbled near Kellan's ear, letting the dominance of my beast slide into those words. "You will be strong enough. You will not let this magic win. You will return to our pack because we need you, Golden Boy. We need you here."

Emme sobbed harder, burying her face in his chest and wrapping her arms around him. "Please be okay, Kellan," she whispered. "Please. I beg the goddess. I can't do this without you."

Kellan had that way about him. Emme might be the heart and soul of our pack, but Kellan was a close second. He'd kept us from drowning in our fucked-up darkness, and for that we'd owe and love him forever.

CHAPTER 25

EMME

I *can't fucking do this!*

I couldn't do this.

I could not sit here and watch Kellan die from magic meant for me.

How did I fix it?

I would have done anything. I would have formed a complete quintet in a heartbeat if it meant saving Kellan's life. But as Slade said, it wasn't an option with him unconscious, and we had no more time to fuck around. The spell was progressing faster, digging its lethal hooks in deeper, and we couldn't wait any longer.

My tears ran along his skin and onto the sheets, and in normal circumstances I'd be annoyed at thoroughly breaking down in front of the other alphas, *especially Finley*, but today I didn't care. My sweet Kellan did not deserve this fate, and it brought with it a pain that could not be contained.

The alphas believed that a completed bond wouldn't have made a difference, but they didn't know the true strength of an omega. If Kellan died here today, it would be my fault for fighting this bond. *My fault. My fault.*

Rough fingertips brushed against my cheeks, and my eyes opened to find it was Slade of all the fucking alphas. The tingles his touch left was enough to shock me out of my panicked sob-fest.

"We don't have many in our lives who would cry for us," he noted clinically, lifting his fingers away from my cheeks and examining the moisture lingering there. I blinked as I watched him closely, embracing the distraction.

Then, to my astonishment, he pressed his fingers to his lips and tasted my sorrow. His chest rumbled slightly, and I felt the dragon pushing against the man.

Goddess be damned, he was unearthly.

The moment was broken by Jewels dropping a bunch of magic paraphernalia on the end of the bed. The alphas backed up, releasing their hold on Kellan, and I pressed my lips to his cheek, lingering for one more second to breathe him in. "I love you," I whispered, aware everyone in this room could hear me. "I will kick your ass if you don't survive this, Golden Boy. Please don't make me do that."

I pushed myself up off his body in time for Hunter to scoop me into his arms. I expected him to drop me to my feet when he moved out of Jewels' way, but instead I was lifted higher until our faces were close. He nuzzled against my cheek, and then in a similar move to Slade, tasted the lingering moisture on my cheeks. "You taste like sweet despair," he murmured against my skin. "When I see you cry, I want to destroy the fabric of our existence." His tongue swiped across my cheek again, and despite the situation, my body responded as if he'd touched me much more intimately. "Stop crying now, Emme. Kellan will not want to miss out on tasting you, little omega. He will fight for you."

Between Slade and Hunter, I was shocked from those relentless tears, and found the strength to pull myself together, ready to fight beside Kellan. "Let me down," I said with a decisive nod. "This is about Kellan." Hunter set me on my feet without argument for once, but he remained at my side.

"All of you need to stay at least three feet back," Jewels warned as she shifted her magical equipment closer to our mate. "I can't have any interference."

She started to sketch a pentacle on Kellan's chest in charcoal, and then arranged white and purple candles around the five-point star. Within the circle she placed a bundle of herbs and a few tiny bones, which would most likely be from a small bird or rodent. The candles were joined by a dark, shimmering string, and while I had no idea what the material was, it was threaded with gold. When this string was secured, and joined all five points of the pentacle, that gold brightened until it hurt to look directly upon.

The candles lit with a snap of her fingers; the scent of sulfur, lavender, and frankincense filled the room, almost overwhelming in its intensity. A cool breeze drifted through the open door, and I expected it to wash away the scent of the candles, but it only grew stronger. *And hotter*. Until we were bathed in a magical sauna.

With the next breeze, three witches drifted into the room. A male and two females. They varied in size and skin tone, but all of them exuded that same bitter, unearthly scent of magic. The scent of those who dabbled in energy that wasn't freely available to all of us.

"Hurry," Jewels snapped, the heat picking up as she swirled her hand over the top of the pentacle. "I need you to join in and reinforce the spell now."

The witches' hands joined with a snap, as if they'd practiced that move until it was perfect and in sync. They started to chant in another language, low and murmured. If my limited knowledge of the magical community was correct, most spells required an ancient dialect of Latin.

The heat picked up as their chanting grew louder, and if Hunter hadn't been a solid weight at my back, I'd have been buffeted around by the winds. There was a heaviness to this magic, pressing against us, reminding us that we were mere mortals *allowed* to exist in this world. Magic was eternal, and we were blips in life.

The chanting reached its pinnacle, and as the final note died off, they wrenched their hands apart, and Jewels palmed a large, ornate dagger. Instinct had me lurching forward, disturbed by her holding a weapon so close to Kellan, but he wasn't the one to come under the sharp blade.

The dagger bit into Jewels' palm, which she held over the top of the pentacle and Kellan's chest. Exactly eight drops fell, and when they sizzled against his skin, I held my breath.

This was it. The moment the spell took.

This was when we'd know if he was strong enough to embrace the counterspell and destroy the magic holding him hostage. The witches remained silent, eyes closed for many tense seconds, and I was forced to suck in the hot, scented air... Passing out wouldn't help Kellan.

Jewels waved her hand over the candles and the flames died out. "The next hour is crucial," she said, meeting Hunter's gaze. There was a fine sheen of sweat on her brow, and she panted slightly. "I'll see the others out and then return to help you keep watch."

The witches turned to leave, as silently as they'd arrived, and I hurriedly added, "Thank you for offering your energy and magic to save our pack mate. We appreciate it."

Hunter's chest moved against my back, and I heard his wolf growl in response. *Whoops.* Had I just unintentionally overstepped and undermined the entitled alpha?

"Yes, you have our gratitude," he finally said, and I relaxed once more. "I will have our accountants send the usual fees for this type of work today."

I'd never heard any mention of money, but Hunter knew how this shit worked. All three nodded their heads respectfully and exited the room.

The oppressive magic and rotten eggs scent left with the witches, and I was glad they were gone. I didn't love strangers or magic, and they were the worst of both.

"Can you feel any changes with Kel?" I asked, unsure if we were allowed to approach him now.

Slade moved to the side of the bed and dropped his hand right on his brother's chest, smudging through the pentacle. "There's a battle within him. The two magics war, and I can't tell which side is stronger."

"Kellan will be stronger," Hunter said without an ounce of doubt in his tone.

I stumbled into Kellan's side and reached out to grasp his hand. It was hot to touch again, but not in the same way as before. This heat was moderate, warming my hand without burning. "Come on, Golden," I breathed, squeezing his fingers. "You've got this."

"I'm going to grab us some food," Hunter said, heading for the door. "Don't go anywhere until I return."

Finley sat on the other side of Kellan, and grabbed the hand I wasn't holding. "I don't think food is that important," he said, glancing up at Hunter. "The witch said this first hour was critical."

"A few minutes to ensure all of us are fed won't hurt," Hunter shot back quickly, and while I couldn't see Hunter's expression—he was behind me—I noticed Finley look at him and then at me.

Should have known that it wasn't *all of us* he was intent on feeding. "I'm absolutely fine," I huffed, tilting my head back to meet his dark gaze. "I can wait an hour or longer. We all need to be here with him."

Hunter pressed his hand against my shoulder, the firm touch grounding. "I can hear your stomach rumbling. With Florence's help, I'll only be a few minutes."

I honestly didn't have the energy to argue with him, so I just shrugged, and when he left the room, I tried to ignore how much I missed both his presence and his touch.

Slade took the chair while Finley and I remained on the bed, clutching Kellan's hands, the three of us silently staring at our pack mate. It was astonishing that despite the internal battle he fought, Kellan looked perfect. His skin was healthy and tanned, hair thick and shiny, muscles and frame still broad and defined. Except for the growth of dark blond hair on his cheeks, and the off scent in his caramel and cinnamon tones, you'd never know anything was wrong with him.

He couldn't be dying. How could anyone this strong and healthy fade from existence?

Silently, I urged him to fight, sending my own energy into him. If we'd bonded, I would have figured out how to literally transfer my essence and strength into him. I'd seen my mom do it more than once, sometimes by choice, often by force. There'd be no need for force today.

"The magic grows stronger," Slade said, jerking forward in his chair. "He's weakening as he fights."

My heart plummeted and the panic was a real, tangible explosion within me. Helplessly, I looked around the room, desperately trying to find a solution, but there was nothing.

"Read one of his books," I said suddenly. "Read *to* him. He needs calm, and to know he's not alone."

Slade was on his feet in a second, Finley right behind him. They hurried to Kellan's shelves and perused them for about ten seconds before the bear shifter yanked a book free. "This is his favorite," he said, hurrying back to the bed. "I will read it to him."

My frustration at not being able to read reared up once more, but the fact that it was Finley with the book felt *perfect* somehow.

He settled in at Kellan's side and opened the first page. "*It was a coldly bitter night when I found the love of my life. Found and lost her. I was part of the Night Realm pack, and we'd been out in the Forest of Hellsward fighting against the dark elves, who were warring us to the edge of extinction...*"

His low rumbly voice was soothing, and I found myself wanting to curl up at Kellan's side to drift off to the sound of Finley's disturbingly sexy voice. This bear confused me more than any other shifter or human I'd ever met. He was built of shadows and sharp edges, but then he had these moments of softness and emotional depth that completely altered my perception of him.

But whatever the case, his perfect voice did exactly as I hoped, and calmed the shifter on the bed. Me too, if I was being honest.

CHAPTER 26

EMME

Kellan's energy had evened out by the time Hunter returned with Florence, both carrying plates piled high with food along with bottles of water. "It's going to be okay," their housekeeper announced after she handed me a plate and a bottle, her face pale and eyes red-rimmed. "I believe in my soul that Alpha Kellan is strong enough to win this battle."

With that said, she ducked out of the room, and I did my best to manifest the same confidence. Ignoring the swirls of dread in my stomach.

"Eat."

I jerked toward Slade, my sandwich almost spilling off my lap. Hunter generally took point on protecting the pack, but today all three of them watched me closely.

"You've lost weight since you got here," Finley said simply, sandwich in his hands though he hadn't taken a bite yet. I found it hard to believe he was waiting for me to eat first, but still, he didn't take a bite.

"Thanks for pointing it out," I replied shortly. I had lost weight, but it wasn't really his business to comment on.

Hunter sank down beside me on the bed. "You're always perfect, Emme, but your energy feels weaker. It's not safe to starve your beast, you know that, and you won't be able to help Kellan if you're not at your strongest."

It was hard to argue with that logic, even if I did want to curse him out for being both wise and attractive. The goddess had really given with both hands in this pack. "You're right, and I'm trying. My stomach is churning hard, and has been since he got struck by that witch."

Slade shifted his plate from one hand to the other in an almost absentminded manner, his expression contemplative. "It's possible that it's more than grief affecting you. You might be experiencing side-effects of the spell wreaking havoc on Kel. Fully bonded or not, there's a connection between all of us. I've personally felt a strain on my beast and power since the attack."

Hunter's expression was sharper as he examined me from the top of my messy hair down to my feet, which dangled off the side of the bed. "You might be right," he murmured, brow furrowed as his scent grew stronger. "I hate not knowing exactly what we're dealing with. Fucking magic."

Jewels strolled into the room then to provide a target for all the magic hate, but none of the alphas even looked her way as she crossed to Kellan. Needing a distraction, I picked up the sandwich, which was thankfully plain roasted chicken without any unnecessary grass filler.

I took a large bite and chewed, tasting nothing, but I kept eating anyway.

After another bite, the alphas started to eat as well, all three of them finishing multiple sandwiches before I got to the last mouthful of mine. Hunter took my empty plate and dropped it with the others outside the door. Finley and I returned to holding Kellan's hands, while Slade and Hunter pressed their palms to his biceps.

"Can you tell how it's going?" I asked Jewels, voice so high it was almost at a pitch only wolves would hear. "He's not moving..."

"The battle continues," was her cryptic reply.

Oh, great. *Thanks for that...* Feels like you painted me a fucking picture and annotated every scene.

We settled in for the wait, and as I stared relentlessly into Kellan's beautiful, still face, he jerked in my hold. A small movement at first, but not even a few seconds later he jerked again, harder, and it was only that I was prepared this time that I kept hold of his hand.

When he started to flail, his huge body almost knocked me to the floor. Hunter caught me and shifted our positions so he could use his bulk as a barrier between Kellan and me.

"What's happening?" he roared, glancing toward the witch.

Jewels' hands shot out and dropped onto Kellan's chest, right above his heart. "The original magic has finally realized it's under attack and is fighting back." She cursed roughly. "I hoped the counterspell would have more time to infiltrate before that happened. The pair are equally strong foes and they're fighting for survival. It all comes down to Kellan's strength now."

My panic, which let's be real, hovered at a consistent eight these days, ramped right up. A red flush spread across Kellan's skin. The heat of the magical battle appeared to be scorching him from the inside.

"It's going to kill him," I cried, trying to crawl toward him, but Hunter held me back. "We have to save him. I have to boost his energy with my own."

Jewels' head jerked up, her expression both distraught and contemplative. "Maybe... I didn't think of it before, but there might actually be a way to boost his energy using the alpha bond you already possess." She was up and off the bed in a flash. "You three need to follow me down to my gear. It'll be faster than hauling it all the way up here again."

Hunter strode around the bed and dropped me into the chair. "Stay with Kellan, but don't get close when he's thrashing about. We'll be right back."

He wouldn't move until I nodded, and when he took off after Jewels, Slade and Finley were right behind him. Deciding there was one action still available to me, I raced into the bathroom for a stack of washcloths, running them under the cold water.

"Come on, Kel," I murmured, dabbing at his forehead, which for the first time was sweaty and pallid. "Come on, Golden. You've got this. When you're better, I'm ready to stop fighting fate, and hope that the outcome is different with you. I need you." Despite Hunter's warning, I couldn't help but lean down and press my forehead against his. "I need you."

"Shortcake."

The room tilted as I lurched up to meet a pair of dark blue eyes. Eyes I hadn't been sure I'd ever see again. As our gazes locked, my wolf howled and smashed against me, desperate to touch her mate. Kellan's irises turned violet, and I felt the presence of his wolf close by as his face scrunched in pain. "Oh fuck. What's happening?"

"You've got magic warring inside you," I told him as fast as I could, wincing as he gripped my hand so tightly I couldn't feel my fingers. Not that I'd have pulled away even if he broke every bone in my body. "You're so strong, Golden. You have to keep fighting and stay here with us."

Discomfort lined his face as he held my gaze, desperate pants spilling from his dry lips. "I'm not sure I'm strong enough, pretty gir—" He coughed, and my heart dropped into my stomach. "Baby… there's an inferno scorching my insides, and it's—" Another cough. "It's too much. No mortal could survive this."

This time, when I stared into his eyes, all I saw was glassy regret, engulfed by pain and unshed tears. "I wanted mo… more time with you."

"You will have it." I choked on my words and sobs and my own anguish. "I don't care what it takes, you have to live. I can't be here without you. I can't do this without you. I will literally lay down and die next to you, Kellan Jackson, so you must live for both of us."

At that statement he attempted to sit, a weak but rage filled rumble escaping his chest. "You will live for me," he rasped. "Please. I need to know you'll live for me, and keep my pack safe and happy, and… you guys better name your first kid after me."

My stomach lurched, and I leaned over the side of the bed and vomited up my sandwich. *Fuck.*

Kellan tugged on my hand, pulling me back around so we were face to face once more. "I need to see you, pretty girl," he whispered, his voice weak as his eyes fluttered. For a horrifying moment, I didn't think he was going to open them again. "I need this to be my last sight."

Tears streamed down my cheeks, and barely holding on to the urge to vomit again, I remained right where he wanted me.

Mate! My wolf surged forward with force and power, taking me by surprise as I partially shifted. She knew exactly what to do, lunging to bite the base of Kellan's neck, on the join near his shoulder. Like I'd shot him with adrenaline, Kellan roared, and blood filled my mouth, metallic with a hint of caramel. My beast remained in control, howling as she held on until his tanned beast rose up to meet her. She released him then and returned control to me.

When I lifted my head, I flinched at how deep the bite was.

Kellan's eyes were open, the blue almost black in intensity. "We can't," he whispered, sounding a touch stronger than before. "If we bond and I die, you might follow."

"Bite me," I ordered, knowing I'd follow anyway. "Please. Give me this one last request."

I had no intentions of it being a last request, but he didn't have to know that. A hint of gold streaked through the dark purple of his eyes, and then his jaw shifted as he sank his teeth into the same spot I'd bitten on him, in the join between shoulder and neck.

My wolf remained close as her mate rose and met her, our essences merging.

This moment intertwined our power, lifeforce, and future.

In that bonding, I finally felt the full force of the battle inside Kellan, and understood why he'd been unable to fight it alone.

Oh goddess.

It felt like I'd fallen into a volcano and had to swim through lava. No one could have survived these fires alone, and luckily for him, he was no longer alone.

I had no idea of the intricacies of sharing power, and it was all instinct as I pushed my wolf into the newly formed connection.

Take from me.

I urged him to draw on my power, and at first he resisted, unsure what was happening. As the magic struggled inside him, his own survival instincts took over and he accepted my gift.

Darkness danced on the edge of my vision, and I wasn't

sure if it was due to the magical exchange, or if I was dying from a catastrophic loss of shifter essence. Either way... I gave Kellan everything I had to ensure he'd survive. And if he didn't, well, we'd be together in our final moments.

Humans always said "till death do us part," but in the shifter world we meant it.

CHAPTER 27

SLADE

Energy crashed through the house right when we were neck deep in a spell to use our alpha essence to bolster Kellan's. Volatile, unpredictable energy. "We need to get upstairs," I bit out, my dragon restless and uneasy at the thought of Emme up there without us to help her.

I'd already been walking a fine line of control in convincing my beast to release our essence, and it was only for Kellan that we'd ever share our precious power. Power that would regenerate within a few days, but when we claimed anything, dragons became unparalleled possessive bastards. Me and my beast.

"What's happening up there?" Hunter asked as we picked up muffled screams. His gaze cut to the witch. "You have two seconds to finish the spell. Emme needs our help."

The omega's heartbeat and breaths were rapid, but she wasn't in mortal danger. Yet. "She's hanging on," I told them. "Hurry and finish the spell because I think Kellan's... awake."

Finley almost jerked his head off his shoulders as he turned toward the stairs, his desperate need to see his brother creasing his face. "If he's awake, this might be our only chance to say…"

His voice broke and he couldn't finish. *Goodbye.*

Jewels' entire focus remained on the spell she was in the middle of weaving, visible light forming in the center of the pentacle board she carried around specifically for spell work. Our energy was held within that magically contained center, unable to be influenced or stolen by another.

"Almost done," she finally muttered, face wreathed in annoyance. After this was all over, the once easy relationship we'd shared with her would be no more. We'd already used up all good-will that had been banked. Not that I gave a single fuck.

I could count on one hand the shifters I cared about not seeing again.

My pack.

Everyone else was so insignificant to me that I didn't even bother to stalk them via security cameras or their banking information. Except for the Rogers pack of course. Those fuckers were absolutely under surveillance so I knew exactly what it would take to rid the world of their existence.

"Done!" Jewels declared a second later, drawing closer the ball of energy, now freed from the spell board. "You three are very powerful. I barely skimmed your energy, and this spell is maxed out on what it can hold."

"Why didn't we try this earlier?" Hunter oozed his annoyance and dominance without even trying.

Jewels shot him a droll stare. "I've been under a lot of pressure from you already to form this counterspell. That's where my thoughts and energy were. Not to mention this is a long shot. You can't share power in a quintet, but this might bolster Kellan long enough to kickstart his own alpha strengths. There's a small hope—"

I was gone before she finished her sentence, taking the stairs four at a time to make it to the second level and Kellan's room. In the hall, the scent of blood grew stronger, and it wasn't that I was panicked, but I did burst into the bedroom like it was an enemy force I had to plow through.

The scent of vomit mingled with blood, and I ignored it all to focus on the pair on the bed. Emme was unconscious, straddling Kellan, her face buried against his neck. With gentle hands, I lifted her off my pack brother, noticing the deep bites both now bore.

Kellan was awake, eyes open wide, jaw still partially shifted. When his beast sank back inside, fading from his features, he said, "Holy fuck."

I was *almost* startled by how strong he felt, his energy sufficient now to power the counterspell and destroy the foreign magics.

"What the fuck happened?" Hunter snarled as he entered the room like a force of nature. "What's wrong with Emme?"

"They bonded," I said shortly, holding the tiny omega against my chest as I focused on Kellan, cataloguing the changes within him. "It strengthened him somehow, and now he's about to destroy the spells."

The blond strands of Kellan's hair lit up as energy exuded from him in a rapid wave, powerful enough that Hunter took a step back. The magic easily flowed around my dragon resistance, unable to touch me, but I still turned to block Emme in my arms.

"What happened to the Ice Queen?" Finley asked, and I almost detected a note of concern in his voice, which was rapidly hidden by his scowl. "Bonding doesn't usually render one unconscious, right?"

Ice Queen. He called her that to remind us all she was cold and unfeeling. My nickname for her *could* technically fall into the same category, but to me it represented the opposite. Snow transformed the world into a wonderland of beauty. Fresh and pure.

Like the white of her wolf, and the purity of her soul.

Far too fucking pure for my darkness.

Still, I couldn't find the strength to release her from my arms, no matter how destructive my dragon and I would be for her.

"I swear that somehow she shared her wolf with me," Kellan bit out gutturally, energy still expelling from him.

It almost looked like his hair was lifting as he powered up; our brother was about to go Super Saiyan Ultra Instinct, and the fact that I even knew what the highest level of powering up a Saiyan in *Dragon Ball Z* was had me needing to kick Hunter's ass.

Jewels entered the room last, gasping when Kellan came into her line of sight. "Oh praise the moon goddess," she cried, and with a snap of her fingers she crushed the magical ball of energy she'd been holding. I felt my share of power return to me, sliding right into the endless pit of fire in my center. "We don't need a power up. He's almost free."

It felt like a mountain had been lifted from my shoulders. It took a mountain to crush a dragon, and though I'd never admit it, a part of me had floundered under the weight.

Kellan's power surge died off in slow increments, and I turned back to face him, adjusting Emme so she sat higher against my chest. Hunter held his arms out for me to hand her over, but again, I couldn't bring myself to release her from my protective hold. The itch beneath my skin from touching her was so minimal that... fuck, it felt good to have her in my arms.

"I've got her," I said shortly, and his eyebrows shot up as he examined me with one of his annoying and all-knowing stares.

I narrowed my gaze. "Don't fucking read into it."

Hunter held both hands up in front of him. "Let me know if it gets to be too much for you."

A rumbled snarl was my reply, but he took the hint and backed off.

Jewels threw her hands in the air, all but dancing across the room. "I can't believe it! It feels like a miracle, but he's going to be just fine. The magic is gone. His energy has never felt stronger. It's like he absorbed a city worth of power."

Emme. I glanced down at her pale face, the freckles standing out starkly, her head flopping forward against my shoulder. Somehow she'd given him her energy, leaving herself weaker and fragile.

"It was Emme," Kellan confirmed, his voice growing stronger with each word. "She bit me, and that was enough to jolt my system as our wolves collided. But when I bit her back..." His desperate and earnest gaze locked on the omega in my arms. "The connection formed between us, and she shared her shifter essence and strength with me. I tried to stop it at first, but she wouldn't give up, and I finally let her in." He'd never been able to deny her anything, even if it got her killed.

"How is that possible?" Finley whispered. "It's not possible, right? We can't share energy in a pack."

Jewels stopped dancing and squinted at Finley. "It must have been the magic," she finally said, her forehead crinkling. "It opened up pathways that would normally be blocked. Let's not question the miracle."

Kellan held a hand out toward me, his face crumpling. "Is she going to be okay? Can I hold her?"

He was alive and filled with energy, and it was the best sight in the world. "Only because you almost died, and... I would have missed you," I told him shortly, depositing her into his hold, while attempting to ignore how empty my arms felt without her in them.

Kellan wrapped his arms around her back, dragging her into his body as he buried his face into his throat. "Please, Shortcake. Please don't have hurt yourself to save me. I couldn't live with it."

He pressed his lips to her skin, and I was reminded of Emme doing the same when Kellan had been fading. These two had found a symbiosis from almost the first moment they'd met. I'd never seen such a pure relationship. The golden boy and our snowy omega.

"She needs to sleep," Jewels advised, tilting her head and observing the pair on the bed. "I would need to touch her to confirm—" Growls rumbled through the room, and she held her hands up. "—and I already know better than to do that, but it appears she's going to be just fine. Let her sleep so her energy can regenerate. Kellan, you should rest as well, even though you feel like you're rocking enough power to light up Golden Claw."

"Can I share the energy back with her?" he wondered, looking between Emme and the witch. When he stared at the omega, there was such desperate longing in his gaze that it even stirred my cold heart. "Give her my essence..."

"I doubt it now the magic is gone," Jewels said with a shrug, "but who the hell knows with you five. I wouldn't suggest trying it though, just in case anything goes wrong. She'll recover on her own."

Finley moved over to place his hand on Kellan's shoulder, gently squeezing it. "I'm glad you're okay, brother. I'm going to head to the rink and let them all know the brilliant news. I'm assuming you'll be back at training tomorrow. We have a game the next day."

Kellan was silent for a few seconds, his gaze on the omega in his arms, a hint of a smile on his lips. "If Emme is okay, then yes, I'll be back. She's my priority."

Finley, for once, didn't show any annoyance that Emme was Kellan's first priority. "I understand. Keep me updated."

When he left the room, Jewels said with a wild flourish of her hand: "I should go as well and complete coven duties I've been neglecting. Call me when you're ready to deal with the other pack. We owe their magical connection a visit."

"Thank you," Hunter said, nodding as respectfully as he ever showed another. "We won't forget your help."

"I won't let you forget," she said with a smirk, before pushing back her wavy hair and heading out of the room.

Kellan, still cradling Emme as close as he could without actually crawling under her skin, said, "You need to tell me exactly what happened from when I was hit with the magic. That's the last thing I remember before I woke up *on fucking fire* with my soulmate crying on my chest. I *do not* want to ever experience that again."

"The fire?" I asked him, and he shook his head.

"Fuck no. I'd take the fire if it meant I never saw Shortcake as distressed as she was. The fact that I almost wasn't strong enough to stay here with her will haunt me for the rest of my days. I said my fucking goodbyes, brother. *My goodbyes*. She told me she would follow me into our next life. We cannot let that happen again."

His arms shook, but he remained gentle in his hold. Not that she was going to stir, her exhaustion had secured her deep in an unconscious state.

"She's been a wreck without you," Hunter informed him, keeping his own emotions locked down under an impassive expression. "We all were. You've lingered on the edge of death ever since you were hit, and it was only our presence and skin on skin pack bonding that kept you here this long."

The relief on Kellan's face lit up the room. "I can't believe I missed the naked pack bonding. *Fuck*. We better repeat that again, minus the almost dying part." His smile grew and grew as he looked between us. "Tell me the truth, though…"

We waited as he dramatically paused, and I found myself delighted by his stupidly mischievous smile. "You missed the group chat the most, didn't you?"

Hunter snorted and shook his head, and I felt like light pierced through the darkness of my soul once more, allowing me to pretend for a short while that I wasn't a literal living nightmare.

Kellan shot us all an indulgent expression. "Don't worry yourselves, Daddy Alpha and Scary Shifter. Golden Boy is back, and all will be right in the world as soon as I have my phone in hand."

Hunter reached out and grabbed the device off the dresser, handing it to him. "You might want to check the current message thread. Our little omega was pouring her emotions out in messages. I don't think she realized she posted them in the group chat rather than privately. They're well worth a read."

I'd read them more than once, needing the hit of purity that was Emmeline Anders. Between Emme and Kellan, my dragon scales would be greener the next time I shifted. That was what happened when there was light in your soul.

Even if it was borrowed light that I'd never truly keep.

CHAPTER 28

KELLAN

Pretty Girl: Hey, Golden Boy. I'm lying next to you, and I wish you were awake so we could chat. I could really use a dose of your positivity and humor. This fucking sucks. I can't believe you jumped in front of that magic for me. If you ever do that again…

My left arm tightened as if to bring her closer, but she was already sprawled across my chest. As close as I could physically get to her without this shit turning awkward and weird… *though*… Tempting.

My sweet, perfect mate. I'd fucking stand between her and anything. She could never stop me from doing it again and again.

Pretty Girl: Okay, so maybe threatening you when you're possibly dying isn't exactly appropriate, but just know, I'm very mad at you. We're in a fight, okay. And right now I'm winning and you're losing, so I need you to wake right up. Immediately. Like now. Please…

My heart thudded roughly in my chest, the ache so acute that I would have rubbed my sternum, except both hands were occupied with the two most important things in the world. Emme and her thoughts.

> Pretty Girl: Okay, so, let's talk about something else because I need my mind off what's happening. I'm sorry about the bike… my poor, pretty baby. I'm assuming she got totaled when they blasted us, and I never even got a chance to tell you how much that gift meant to me. Along with the helmet and jacket. Goddess, it was more than anyone has ever done for me, you sweet, beautiful shifter, and I need you to know that it broke me. In the best ways.

I'd already sent out a few messages to get her bike replaced, and this time I'd be the one to give it to her. I needed to absorb her emotions in person rather than via security footage that Slade *reluctantly* shared with me after. Greedy fucking dragon.

Focusing on the phone again, I savored these messages, saving them into another private chat. These tiny snippets were glimpses of *my* Emme, and she was never this open normally. I was experiencing the tiny cracks in her chest as she bled out her emotions.

The fact that I'd almost died and missed this was unacceptable.

Turning my face toward her, I breathed in her scent, letting my wolf calm. He was prepared to escape from my skin and storm Silver City until we tracked down the fuckers who almost stole me from my mate. I understood why my pack hadn't done anything while I was unconscious and on death's door, but now there was nothing to stop us.

I pressed my lips to her brow, and again between her eyes, and down her perfect, cute little nose, tracing each of her freckles. I had them memorized by now, and as I pulled away, it hurt to see her normally rosy tanned skin so pale. Even during rest, exhaustion lined her features, and I wished I could erase everything I'd put her through.

Or go even further back and start with her mom.

Unfortunately, reversing time wasn't one of my talents, but I could ensure that the rest of her days were filled with so much love and happiness that it drowned out her past until she couldn't hear it at all. No matter what it took or who I had to destroy along the way.

Tucking her against my chest once more, I returned to the phone.

> Pretty Girl: The witch didn't have good news, baby. But I know you're strong enough to fight. To stay here with me. It's not just me either. Finley is a mess, and our two stoic alphas are keeping up their usual gruntiness, but they're struggling as well. We all need you and your sunshiny ways. YOU HEAR ME, GOLDEN BOY. Do. Not. Fucking. Leave. Us.

At the start of her next message, my heart skipped a few beats, and I was fairly sure it was about to pound out of my chest as I read on.

> Pretty Girl: I've told you this many times in your unconscious state, but I love you, Kellan Jackson. I think I fell in love with you the first day you stalked me in the forest, shifted into one of the hottest golden men I'd ever seen, and all but flopped your penis out in front of me like it was just a regular Tuesday. It is a really nice penis, btw. Anywho. You're not going to die, and I will delete all these messages in that case, but I have to put it in writing. I love you. You're one of the best things that ever happened to me. The end.

The tightness in my chest overwhelmed me as the heat in my eyes rivaled the fire of my previously fought magical battle. "I love you too, pretty girl," I whispered, dropping the phone by my side and wrapping her up with both arms. "I love you so much it hurts. You're the other half of my soul, and now I need you to wake up so I can tell you that."

My emotions were a swirling pit of warmth, love, and despair, and I wasn't sure how to let them escape without howling to the heavens. It almost slipped free when I felt the slightest movement in my hold...

"Kellan." Her rasp was barely audible, but I heard her. Choking back a *very manly* sob, I was just so goddess-be-damned thankful she was awake.

"Baby," I breathed, joy piercing through my chest until it felt like my heart was as tattered and bleeding as hers had been in her messages. I rocked her back and forth, before pulling away to see her eyes slowly open. "Are you okay?" I demanded, assessing her vital signs, which were all stable. "Do I need to call in healers?"

Another slow blink, then she shook her head, tongue darting out to moisten her lips. My gaze locked on that tiny pink tip, and I almost leaned down and tasted her. Now was not the time, but as the bite on my neck pulsed, reminding me of our new connection which I felt all the way to my wolf soul, I wasn't sure how long I'd be able to hold back.

From my mate.

"I feel weird but okay," she mumbled as she tried to moisten her lips again and groaned. "Need water."

There were a few bottles on my desk, which I could only reach by bringing her along with me. I sure as fuck wasn't about to let her go. Cracking the lid, I sipped it so it wasn't so full, and then lifted her upper half closer. She closed her eyes as she drank, and when she'd had enough, I recapped it and threw it to the floor, letting Emme slump into my hold once more.

"What happened?" she whispered, sounding marginally clearer. "Did we bond, or did I dream that?"

Pure bliss was a shot of adrenaline to my body. "Baby, we absolutely bonded, and you saved my life. Again."

There was a pause as her eyes widened and her cute little brows wrinkled. "When did I save your life the first time?"

Fucking hell she was adorable. There had to be a way for me to bottle her up and keep her with me always. I was hooked. I refused to spend even a single day without a dose of Emmeline. "You saved me when you arrived in Golden Claw. My existence was empty, and I didn't even know how pathetic it was until you filled it with... well, you. With warmth and love and perfection. With the other half of my soul."

Her wide eyes bored into me, a murkier blue than usual. When her lips trembled, I shook my head and cupped her face with one hand. "Oh, Shortcake. Please don't cry. Your tears elicit two reactions in me: I need to beat someone to death, or cry with you. Neither of which are appealing when I have you here, alive, in my arms."

"You almost died," she croaked, that tremble more pronounced, heavy moisture rimming her lash line. "You almost left me, right after you made me love y—"

She cut herself off, breathing deeply, and I laughed as I leaned down and kissed her lips. Tasting her soft sweetness. "I've read your messages, my perfect mate. You didn't get a chance to delete them, and for that I'm eternally grateful. You don't need to hold back how you feel. I fucking love you too. More than anything in existence, more than this world, more than I thought was possible. You will never get rid of me, baby. You have to know that. We are one now, and I can feel you deep in my wolf essence... in my soul."

The heat of her tears slipped between our lips, and we tasted her salty sorrow as we kissed. "I love you, Golden Boy," she breathed, her words strangled. "I've never said it out loud to someone who was awake before, but I can't wait another second to tell you. Please don't ever leave me again."

Fuck my heart. It shattered in my chest, and each piece glowed with the knowledge that she loved me. "They will have to tear me away," I whispered back. "Cleave and tear me from you."

Her ragged breaths eased as she leaned back, and while the remnants of tears remained, she was calmer. "I can't believe this is happening." She lifted her hand and pressed it against the now healed mark on her shoulder. My wolf howled at the sight of her wearing our claim, and whatever possessiveness I'd felt before was a million-fold now. A billion even.

Fuck. There wasn't a number high enough.

"Mine," I rumbled, my voice low and threaded with my beast. "My pretty mate."

Emme's breaths quickened again, but in a completely different way as her pupils dilated. "Yes," she whispered. "As you are mine."

I was. Completely and irrevocably.

This time when our lips met there was desperation between us, and I sucked her tongue against mine, needing more. When she moaned against my mouth, my cock kicked hard in my boxers, and I groaned in return. Knowing I'd been in this bed for days and was no doubt gross as fuck, I hauled her tiny frame into my arms and lifted us from the mattress.

We didn't stop kissing even as I strode into the bathroom, pleased to see my strength had returned to normal, with no apparent lingering weakness from the spell. When the water was warm, I stripped off our clothes and stepped under the spray.

Emme arched against me, and I barely held on to my control as my dick jerked in an attempt to get closer to the warmth between her thighs. Emme's perfect, pretty pussy had a manicured strip of dark blond hair leading to paradise... *Fuck.* I could feel her arousal, and smell it, against my stomach, but I refused to claim her for the first time in the shower.

She deserved more than a quickie. She deserved hours of me worshipping her as the goddess she was.

"Please, Golden," she cried, arching again as she tore her mouth from mine and threw her head back under the spray. Sliding one hand higher up her back, I supported her as she ground her core against me. "I need you inside me. Now."

Gah. She was going to kill me again if she wasn't careful. What a fucking way to go though.

With a strangled laugh, I dropped my head and sucked one of her tight pink nipples into my mouth, consumed by how delicious she tasted. She was sweet chocolate, and I was enthralled. This siren had me completely under her control, and I'd never been happier. "I will be inside you, baby. For hours. Don't worry about that. I just need to get cleaned up first, then we're heading right back to bed."

The snarl that erupted from her had my dick kicking harder against her soft skin, and when she turned needy and demanding, I was even more of a goner. "Please, Golden. Please, please, please."

The begging, that was it, the best moment of my life. "Patience, my little wolf. You know I've got you."

Her pupils were blown as she slowed her thrusts against me, the smallest of sigh escaping. "I did actually throw up earlier, so maybe some teeth brushing wouldn't go astray."

I hadn't noticed any vomit; my sole focus always on Emme. Florence had probably cleaned it up at some point. "Why were you sick?" I took in her drawn features, happy to see a little color already returning.

"Distress over you," she whispered, no longer moving against me at all. She just studied my face as though she'd never see it again. "You were dying."

Her lip tremble had returned, so I quickly reassured her, "I'm alive and well, and I'm not going anywhere." With her still firmly in my arms, I stepped from the shower and grabbed my electric toothbrush and a new head if she wanted to switch it out.

"Thank the goddess," she whispered, accepting the brush, and I wasn't sure why I was pleased as fuck when she didn't switch the head, but I was. Every part of her was mine, and the least of the germs we would share was via a toothbrush.

Finishing my own shower took a few minutes longer than usual because I refused to let her out of my arms. When we were both clean, I got us out, dried, and back in my room. Somehow, I knew that the sheets would have been changed by Florence, our absolute miracle worker. Sure enough, we found fresh sheets, blinds drawn, the door closed, and no vomit.

The perfect setting for me to love my mate.

"Baby," I said as I lifted her onto the middle of the bed and crouched over the top of her on my hands and knees. I got distracted by the sight of her long, naked limbs spread out below me, the wet strands of her strawberry hair bright against the white sheets.

A cheeky smile lit up her expression, and I was relieved to see that the icy blue of her irises had returned. "Yes, Golden? Though I do like when you look at me like a starving shifter."

Holy fuck. Starving didn't even come close to the desperate hunger I had for her. "Shortcake…" I pressed my lips to her shoulder, and then down to her throat. "I'm ravenous. I'm going to eat you like you're a buffet and I have an all-day pass."

Her pupils dilated as she reached for me, her fingers grazing over the bite mark she'd left on my throat, and her lips parted as she panted. "Good boy."

My cock jerked so hard that I had to reach down and palm the fucker to stop it from jumping out of its skin. Desire, need, and joy merged into a desperate vortex inside me of. "You keep that up, pretty girl, and I'm not going to even get inside you before I'm coating you in my cum."

Emme nodded, her pupils dilating as she parted her full lips and gasped. "Yes. I want you to mark and claim me in every single way, Kellan. You will do that for me, won't you? My perfect, good boy."

Goddess. *Fuck!* My cock leaked pre-cum everywhere. I'd never been this hard in my life. It was a pain that both tortured and pleased me.

Dragging my tongue along her soft skin, I sucked her right nipple deep into my mouth, gently biting around the tip, while my tongue laved as much of her skin as I could reach. Emme let out a guttural sort of scream, lacing her fingers into my hair and tightening her hold until it was almost painful. *I wanted more.*

I kissed between her luscious boobs, tasting every freckle I found on my way, and gave the left nipple just as much attention. Emme writhed against me, desperation clear in her little moans, and when I moved down her stomach, finding more sweet freckles, I finally settled between her thighs. The most perfect pussy, spread out for my feast.

I breathed in the scent of her arousal, a groan building from the deepest part of my chest. Guttural was this need. Desperate and frantic.

Sliding my nose across her lower lips, my tongue darted out to taste her, and my beast roared in my chest. I growled louder than I think I'd ever done, burying my face in her cunt and devouring my sweet omega.

"Kellan, oh fuck!" She bowed her back as I sucked hard on her clit. I was coated in her cum when she squirted, taking both of us by surprise. *The best fucking surprise.* Was it my birthday? Christmas? Did I just get a wish granted, because this was my lucky day.

Refusing to waste any of that deliciousness, I moved faster, my tongue swiping through her sex and across her clit, and when my hands tightened on her thighs, I relished the deep tremble in her muscles.

Determined to make her come again, I shifted my right hand to slide two fingers inside her, curling them up to her g-spot, shuddering as her walls clenched around me. "So tight, baby. I can't wait to feel you on my cock. I need to claim every part of you."

"Y-yes," she mumbled, her mouth open as she palmed her tits and held on for life.

Pre-cum leaked so hard from my dick that I was all but lying in a wet patch as large as the one under Emme. Despite my best efforts to devour all her release, my girl was a squirter, and I was *fucking here for it.*

New goal in life, make sure we both ended up in a puddle every morning.

And night.

And lunchtime.

All fucking day.

CHAPTER 29

Kellan Jackson was a delicious menace with his mouth. Hunter liked to devour as well, but the difference with Kellan was that he had no restraint. Hunter remained controlled and deliberate in his actions, and I loved that because when he actually lost control, it had so much impact.

My golden boy ate my pussy with the same ferocity that he approached all of life: with abandon and zero fucks given about what anyone else thought. *Except me.* He was all in to please me, and the focus he showed was unlike anything I'd ever experienced.

Kellan was the literal definition of a good boy, and he deserved all the praise.

I'd already come twice, and he was winding me up for a third, the pressure building from the base of my spine, until it burst through me in a wave. Kellan growled and buried his face harder against me, lapping up my orgasm like it was a melting ice-cream he refused to let drip on the ground. He was going to kill me. But what a way to go.

"Alpha," I begged, base instinct rearing up as I lost control of myself.

In the back of my mind, a small part of me was freaking out that we'd bonded, tingles of his emotions mingling in the deepest recesses of my own energy. A true joining of shifter essences.

So, yep. Fully bonded. I'd initiated an action I swore would never happen, but even freaking out, there were no regrets. If the alternative to bonding was Kellan dying, well... I'd bond all day every day. We'd just have to figure out the rest later.

Kellan lifted his face, lips shiny and full as he smiled. "I'm not actually sure I didn't die, Shortcake. Can you confirm this isn't eternal paradise?"

My throat grew almost too tight to reply. "It's too soon to joke about that, Golden. Way too soon." I wasn't sure I'd ever purge the memory of his life fading out of him as fire and magic wreaked havoc on his body.

His lopsided grin reminded me of everything right in the world as he crawled up my body and pressed his lips to mine. I tasted myself on his lips and beard. He didn't usually have facial hair, but he hadn't bothered to shave in the shower, and I was into this rapscallion look he had going on.

When he settled his big body between my thighs, the sensation of his weight pressing me into the bed had my head spinning. He was large and muscled everywhere.

"Let me apologize in advance for this first time," he whispered against my mouth. "I'm just too desperate to wait." Before I could respond, he lifted himself, and as soon as the head of his cock stretched my entrance, he thrust hard and I cried out. It took a few more thrusts to seat his length fully, and I was fairly sure that he was almost as big as Hunter, who was a monster.

As our eyes met, his were vibrant purple, and the bite on

my throat pulsed, sending another shot of pure pleasure to my core. *Was I feeling his arousal as well as my own?* "Fuck," I choked out, unable to remain still as I moved my hips higher. "You feel so good."

Kellan rumbled. "I'm going to explode like a teen, baby. Don't judge me for this, because I can back it up."

"No judgement from m—" I cried out as he thrust again, the force almost sending me up the bed. Kellan's strong arms caught me as he wrapped them under my head, bringing us closer. He kissed down my throat, slamming relentlessly into me.

Despite my trio of orgasms already, another was building fast, this one deeper and more intense. "Oh my goddess," I mumbled, half delirious. "I can't—too much—so fucking good."

Kellan rumbled, and lifted his head to lock me in a stare of such intensity that my heart joined in with the sensation of detonation. "Look at me when you come, baby," he commanded, and I obeyed, meeting his blazing eyes. "I love you," he whispered, his movements slower but just as forceful. "I adore you. I cherish, treasure, and prize you. I claim you forever."

I screamed into my orgasm, the force tearing me from the fabric of this reality. My head spun, and my lungs choked over a lack of air.

Kellan shouted my name, and my pleasure increased as his cock swelled and he came, the scent of caramel and cinnamon stronger than ever as it blended with chocolate and honey, until we were one bundle of sweetness.

Just when I thought he was finished, he pulled out of me and jerked his cock hard to release final spurts of cum across my pussy and stomach, marking me in another claim.

"Shit, you are a good boy," I said between ragged breaths. "Always keeping your promise."

His hand stilled, massive chest heaving as he stared down at me. He remained like that, hard cock in hand, observing me like I was a fairy-tale that had burst to life right before his eyes. His nostrils flared as he shifted forward in his kneeling position, leaned down, and swiped his cock over my stomach and through the mess he'd made. "You'd be running if you knew what I wanted to do to you, pretty girl," he murmured, and I realized he was drawing his name on me in his release.

Fuck, I loved this alpha.

"Mine," he growled, and it reminded me of Hunter's tattoos. These alphas and their claiming were perks of this pack I hadn't expected. It was pure perfection.

"Yours," I confirmed breathlessly.

He shifted his weight back again, and as I reached out, not ready to be apart, he palmed his hands under my ass and lifted me up off the bed. He was so strong that I didn't have to do a thing other than let myself be handled, and fuck me dead, he knew how to handle his mate.

Bringing me with him, he settled on his ass, and I ended up straddling him, his cum a sticky, delicious mess between. He thrust up against me, and I responded by shifting my hips slightly until I was able to slide down his length. The pulse of pleasure across my already sensitive walls was instantaneous, and when I was seated, with him buried so deeply it felt a tiny bit like my insides were being rearranged, I gulped in air to catch my breath. I ended up breathless more than was probably normal around these alphas, but who could blame me.

"I'm not sure it's safe having a cock this large *this deep* inside me," I said with a choked laugh. "But whoa, it's too much fun not to take the risk."

The heavy-lidded arousal in his expression lightened as he tipped his head back and laughed, shaking me like a puppet attached to... well, an unlikely appendage.

"Ready for more fun, then?" he finally said, a twinkle in his eye and mischievous grin.

"Yes," I said, sure I'd never been as ready for anything in my life as I was for this.

He settled his hands on my hips, moving us together in a slow rhythm. He didn't thrust all the way in and out like before. He kept us completely connected, buried all the way to the hilt as we rocked together. With each rotation of my body, my clit was stimulated, helped along by Kellan as he slid his hand between us and stroked me as well.

Losing any grace in my movements, my hips rotated faster as I chased my release.

"That's it, baby." Kellan's deliciously husky growl trailed down my spine, leaving goosebumps in its wake. "Use me. Make yourself come. Fuck me as hard as you can. I'm not breakable."

He had his own version of praise and command, and it tightened everything in my lower half as I cried out. He thrust up roughly and we came together this time, our breaths mingling in kisses and sobs and praise until we were both spent and exhausted.

Only a few hours ago Kellan and I had both been on the edge of death, mine from sharing my energy and his from magic. Which just made this moment so much more poignant. We collapsed on the bed, sated, mated, and covered in sweat. Along with joy. A purity of joy that I had been unaware was possible to achieve.

And I had no regrets.

As promised, Kellan was near insatiable, taking me every which way. We went from hard doggystyle fucking, where I held on to his headboard and he slammed into me from behind with enough force that his *equally as impressive* balls slapped my ass and I felt like I was getting spanked and fucked at the same time, to devouring me and edging me for an hour until I exploded with an orgasm so intense that we had to change the sheets after.

By the time he finally dozed off, wrapped around me, I wasn't sure I'd ever be able to walk again. Could you dehydrate from losing fluids via the vagina? Or did the overload of his release inside of me balance it out somehow. Thank the goddess I wasn't in my fertile period any longer, because there was no way I wouldn't be pregnant by now. Probably have a damn litter at the rate he liked to fuck.

Not that I was complaining. *Nope.* My good boy knew exactly what he was doing.

After a few hours nap, restless energy had me slipping out from under Kellan's hold to head for the bathroom. My skin was a gunky, dried-out mess from our hours of sealing the mate bond, and while that should have felt gross, it didn't bother me. I enjoyed smelling Kellan all over me, and if it wasn't literally in my eyebrows, I wouldn't have even showered.

When I was finished, I dried myself and threw on one of his hoodies, before kissing both his cheeks and thanking the goddess once more that she brought him back to us.

Kellan slept deeply, no magic tainting his scent now, and I

almost crawled back into bed, until my stomach growled harshly, reminding me I needed to eat after hours of sharing energy and being fucked into oblivion.

I wasn't sure yet if the energy I'd shared would return fully to my essence, but I felt fine and so did my wolf, so I figured it was regenerating. Judging from Mom and the years with her pack, it took more than one moment of sharing to make a permanent mark.

The test now was how Kellan dealt with that power, and if it corrupted him into wanting more. During sex would have been a prime opportunity to ask, or attempt to exchange, but he hadn't even mentioned it. I expected the others would have some questions though.

Mate, my wolf howled, strong and satisfied. She wasn't exactly present during the sex, remaining deeper in my subconscious, but she was happy with the deepening of the bond.

Of the connection that we felt in the bite we'd wear permanently now.

When I reached the first floor, I'd just turned toward the kitchen when I heard a curse and shout from the opposite side of the house. Worried it was a call for help, I changed directions and hurried toward the disturbance. When another crash rang out, I realized it was coming from the garage.

Even though I was only dressed in a hoodie, with no underwear or shoes, I didn't hesitate to race down the stairs. At the base of the staircase the heavy door was closed, and when I pushed on it, it took a bit of extra effort to open. Not only had I shared my essence, but I'd been horribly neglecting my food intake lately, which was never good for shifters. Now that Kellan was safe, I could focus on building my muscles up again.

The door eventually opened, and I stepped into my favorite area of the house. Another clank rang out as I moved into the dark room, and with a quick—sad—glance at the bikes, I headed toward the back of the garage, where the older cars and trucks were parked.

The smooth, stone flooring was cool under my feet as I padded along. It was climate-controlled here to protect the babies, but there was no underfloor heating. When I passed Finley's TRX, I wondered if he was home. Like the others, he had more than one car, but I hadn't bothered to learn which were his. Okay, not totally true, but I didn't know *all* of them.

The next clank and curse were louder, and I froze at the familiar deep rasp.

Shit. I backed up a step, already huffing in the faint whiff of vanilla and cherries. It was too late though, as Finley rounded the back of an old Chevy, his glare prepped and ready. "Is Kellan okay?" he asked, his gaze dragging briefly down the length of my exposed legs, before he returned his focus to my face.

I nodded, feeling stupidly tongue-tied around the bear. His reaction to my presence was unpredictable, and I wasn't really in the mood to destroy my post-fucking-glow with sharp, mean jabs. I might have softened slightly toward him over the past few days as I watched his love for Kellan, but it wasn't enough to erase everything that happened *before*.

"He's fine," I replied, relieved to sound somewhat normal. "I just heard banging and cursing and came to check that no one was in trouble."

Shadows flashed in his eyes, which looked darker than usual. "And what if it had been another pack breaking in, or a threat? You'd think you'd have learned by now not to wander around alone, unless you're trying to get another one of us *almost* killed to protect you." His glare deepened, and weirdly he kind of looked concerned.

"It briefly crossed my mind," I admitted, "but what are the

odds anyone could get in here without Slade or one of you knowing? I calculated the risk and decided that it was worth it to make sure none of you were hurt."

That momentarily stopped him, before he shook his head. "Maybe you wanted one of us to be hurt. Do you need to be forced into the claiming, Ice Queen? Can't admit you actually want us?"

My hand shot up to rest against Kellan's bite, and instead of following that movement, Finley's gaze dropped to where the hoodie had lifted enough to flash my vagina to the world.

Whoops.

Releasing my shoulder, I cleared my throat. "No, I don't want any of you to ever step between me and danger again. Almost losing Kellan is the hardest thing I've ever gone through, including my mom's death. And not that I owe you any explanation, but the fact that I would bond with Kellan when every part of me fears the consequences should reassure you that I'm not here to hurt any of you. I never wanted to hurt you. It was pure self-preservation."

Finley watched me in a way I wasn't sure he ever had before, a consuming, drowning sort of stare that tightened my center. It was odd being down here without all the big industrial lighting to light up the place. Almost eerie. "What changed?" he finally asked, in a low, confused tone. "Why did you give up on putting yourself first?"

That was the easiest question to answer. "I didn't want to live if Kellan didn't. I guess... there was nothing more important than making sure he survived."

The conversation was getting too heavy between me and a bear shifter I did not trust with my darkest secrets, so I searched for a distraction. Finley wore grease-smeared jeans and a red and white checkered flannel; there were a few spots of black on his cheeks too. Add in a backwards baseball cap holding his glorious hair off his face, and it was easy to forget he hated me. Or at least to wish that he didn't. "What are you working on?" I asked, genuinely interested in this new topic. "I didn't know you tinkered with cars."

His expression didn't soften. "An old Ford. I'm sure you're not interested."

Well, well, Grouchy Bear, you prickly bastard, you could not be more wrong.

"What year?"

The twist of his smile twisted my insides as well, for no good reason. "Why don't you tell me? I mean, if you have a genuine interest in cars, you should have an idea."

Oh great. It was a test. "Sure, lead the way."

I waved my hand like I was a queen and he was my minion, but for once he didn't call me out on my bratty, *Ice Queen* behavior. His boots clanked on the floor as we passed a few rows of modern trucks and American muscle cars, leading me toward a section that was clearly designed for mechanic work. I noted the hoists and walls of tools, along with a bunch of computer equipment I wasn't familiar with. A lot of the gear in here was more modern and expensive than the old garage I'd spent years in, but the feel and scent remained timeless.

Oil, fuel, leather, metal, and cleaning fluids.

Finley led me toward a huge, faded red truck with the hood up. "Oh, shittt," I said, rushing forward to run my hands just above the bumper. "Ford F-100, right? And the year has got to be..." There were a few years with this shape, so I took a guess. "1956?"

There was no response, and when I turned to meet Finley's gaze, he stared at me like he'd never seen me before. "Fifty-four," he murmured. "How in the fuck...?"

It felt nice to surprise him, and not in the way I usually did. "Does it have the 317 in it?"

He nodded slowly, eyes wider than usual as he fiddled with his hat. "Yep, the 317, and she's giving me some grief. I've been trying to keep her original, but the parts aren't the easiest to come by."

Unable to help myself, I stepped closer, peering into the engine bay. "I'm here to help if you ever need anything. I'm no expert, but I know my way around basic tools, and can assist."

The moment the offer left my mouth, I regretted it. Had I lost my mind along with my omega energy when I bonded to Kellan? This was Finley, and he hated me.

I'd hazard a guess that he enjoyed fixing cars in a similar way to how he enjoyed hockey. A cathartic release from his darker thoughts and memories. I recognized the signs because I'd had them myself, though mine came from baking, riding my bike, and sneaking audio books when I could afford them.

No doubt my presence in his space would have the opposite effect of the escape he'd been searching for.

Before he could reply with his usual mean rejection, I spluttered, "Sorry. That was stupid of me. Good luck with the engine."

I spun on my bare foot and raced back through the cars and up the stairs.

CHAPTER 30

EMME

My head remained a fuzzy mess of confusion and self-recrimination as I made my way through the house. What the hell had I been thinking? Why had I even stuck around when I figured out who was in the garage?

I should have run the moment I scented him.

Fuck, it was probably half his scent's fault, the connection between us pushing our beasts to be together, while blurring the memories of him being a raging prick with anger issues.

Despite *zero regrets* with Kellan, I wasn't prepared to bond with the rest of them unless necessary. At least not until I better understood the consequences of Kellan's claim, and whether he showed any signs of being corrupted by the energy.

I could feel tendrils of his calm, sleeping mind as I reached the foyer, and I found myself once again pressing my hand to the bite on my neck. The urge to return to him was strong, but I fought against it, needing food first.

I did end up taking a side quest to my room to put sweatpants on, and when I entered the calm of my space, I exhaled out my tension from Finley. There was a nice distraction in the form of a small pile of glossy magazines on the end of my bed, right where the basket of period supplies had been. *Another gift?*

The cover on top was a familiar publication even though I hadn't seen a copy of *Muscle Cars Monthly* in years. There was also *Bike Talk, Supercars of the future, Rebuilt,* and a few other Ducati-specific ones.

There was no scent attached, leaving me with no idea who'd been thoughtful enough to leave them here. Clutching them tightly to my chest, I tried not to let more tears spill free —I was a walking water factory at this point. But could anyone blame me when I had a pack of alphas out here *doing the things?*

Leaving the magazines on the end of the bed to read later, I threw on panties, black sweats, and socks to finish off the outfit. On my way out, I opened the windows to check out the day, relieved to see the sun shining over a perfect fall morning. It was peaceful at first, staring into the leaves that were almost all gold and orange, but after a few minutes there was this odd sensation of being watched. I'd felt a similar tingle down my spine when Hunter had been stalking me at Warrick's home, but this was different.

This was no one in my pack.

With a yank on the shutters, I blocked it out, which dulled the sensation. I was probably still jumpy from everything that had happened over the past week, and as I'd told Finley, it wasn't easy for anyone to get inside this property without alerting one of the alphas. Especially Slade, who was our guard dragon and security expert.

Leaving the window, I ducked into the bathroom to check my appearance, relieved to see I looked normal, my hair was finally dry after my shower, loose and hanging down my back.

There was a slight flush to my skin, and I felt rather energized despite having recently shared my power.

I blew Kellan a kiss as I passed his door, because I was a lovesick fool, but I didn't let myself get distracted from food again.

In the kitchen I expected to run into Florence or Gerry, but found myself staring at a strange woman, sitting at the bench and reading Hunter's usual paper while she ate *four* of the breakfast sandwiches. She had strong alpha energy and was definitely a wolf, her scent giving off a faint hint of strawberries.

Okay, who in the fuck was this shifter? She was clearly comfortable enough with the pack to sit in their kitchen and eat their food, and I wasn't sure which part pissed me off more —the fact that she was eating *my* favorite food in the house, or that she was so comfortable here when I'd never met her.

Comfortable and pretty, with long, tanned limbs, black curls, and a heart-shaped face.

When I stepped into the room, her head shot up and I almost took a step back, because pretty did not cover it. She was absolutely stunning, with huge blue eyes and full red lips.

Her face lit up when she saw me. "Emme!" she cried, like we were old friends.

She unfolded herself from the bench and hurried toward me, standing only an inch or two shorter than me. Along with her beautiful face, apparently she also had curves to absolutely die for.

Eating *my* sandwiches and *also* having perfect tits and ass...

Excuse the fuck out of me.

Her smile grew and grew, and the longer I stared into her features, the more I was reminded of someone. She had a more feminine look of—

"I'm Kassidy. Hunter's sister."

Four little words and all my anger toward her vanished. "Shit, I'm sorry," I said quickly, returning her smile for the first time. "I'm not sure if you could tell from my glaring, but I kind of lost my mind there and went weirdly territorial about another female shifter being in the house. I mean, it was mostly over the breakfast sandwiches, but a little over the alphas too."

It was a huge overshare, but to my relief she snorted and let out a loud laugh. "Oh, damn. I see why my brother is so obsessed with you. You're perfection."

I froze at her freely offered compliment; my brain moved slowly as I attempted to process how I should take those words. Was I supposed to respond in kind with my own praise for this confident alpha? Friendship rules were hard, and I often felt like a fish floundering on land.

Kassidy saved me from overthinking when she placed her hand on my arm. "I'm a huge believer that women should always build up other women." I was surrounded by her sweet, husky laughter. "And we also need to be honest with each other. Which is why I'll tell you how amazing you are... *and* if the dress makes you look like a bag of potatoes. It's balance. It's trust. And it's honesty. I value all three."

"Me too," I said, feeling comfortable with her already. Kassidy had a strong personality, like her brother, the hurricane. I'd already known that to some degree, after Kellan explained her decision to shun quintet life and live on her own without any pack. And not for a reason like mine, but because she valued her independence and privacy.

"In the face of honesty," I continued, "I have to say that you're quite possibly the most beautiful, intimidating female I've ever met. I really need to meet your parents and assess the genetic combination that created the perfection of you and Hunter."

Kassidy's face shuttered, but before she replied, a mocha scent wrapped around me, and a wall of muscles pressed against my spine. "You will meet my parents over my dead body, little omega," Hunter said shortly, wrapping his arms around me. "Their particular brand of evil will never taint your particular brand of sweet innocence."

I spluttered and tried to turn in his arms, but he was far too strong. He kept me locked against his front, his hands sliding under the hoodie and across the bare skin of my stomach. "I'm far from innocent," I protested, squeezing my thighs together in an attempt to counter how good his touch felt. Kellan had flipped the switch, and whatever hold I'd had on my sexual needs was gone. "I found my mom's body when she died, and went on the run, and lived like a rogue for years. I've seen some shit."

Even if most of my adult life had been more about loneliness and boredom, the earlier years with Mom and her pack had left scars. Most internal, but I'd always have one large reminder on my back. My innocence had slowly bled from me in those years. Now I was a broken mess who couldn't even bond with her pack except under duress.

Kassidy, who watched me closely, shook her head. "It's not about discounting what you've experienced in your life, Emme. Hunter understands that you've been through hell too, right, brother?"

Hunter grunted, and we nodded along with the universal sign for agreement from an alpha. Or disagreement. Or anything, really. In this case, though, it sounded like the affirmative.

"It's the purity of who you are in your essence," Kassidy continued with a very brief smile. "Our parents are not good shifters. I'd go as far as to say that there's true evil within them and their quintet. Hunter has the right idea in keeping them far away from you."

Hunter brushed a thumb over my cheek, and I glanced up to find him smirking. "Your cheeks are pink, baby girl. You can't take compliments, that's for sure, but I do enjoy this flushed look on your face." His thumb scraped lower and lower, until it brushed over the mark on my shoulder, shifting the hoodie to reveal the bite. "How are you feeling after this?"

"I think that's my cue to leave," Kassidy said as I remained caught in Hunter's predatory gaze. "I just popped in to check on our Kellan. Tell him I'll see him tomorrow at the family barbeque."

Shit, it had been almost a week since we got Kellan back here, and tomorrow was the Sunday family event.

"Tomorrow is hockey," Hunter said softly, gaze remaining on me. "They had to shift the game back a day."

"I'll see you there, then."

"See you tomorrow," I called to Kassidy, tearing away from her brother. "It was really nice to meet you."

She darted over and pressed a kiss to my cheek, which had Hunter growling and lifting me away from her. "Mine," he added, in case his actions weren't clear enough.

His sister's smirk was so similar to Hunter's that I almost did a double take. "I know, brother," she said, patting him on the cheek. "I've seen the tattoo. But you also need to learn to share. Emme is my new sister, and I will love on her as much as I want. Don't even think about fighting me on that, or I'll destroy you. Entitled alpha or not."

My responding smile was broad and amused, and it only grew as Hunter groaned. "I'm ordering you two not to gang up against me. You're not allowed. That's a fucking command from an entitled alpha."

Leaning away from his hold to meet Kassidy's gaze, I said,

"Well, new sister, I feel it's my duty to inform Hunter that you're technically an entitled alpha as well."

Hunter looked aghast. "But... she's in a pack of one."

"Still counts," we said together, and Hunter dropped his head back and pressed his right hand to the bridge of his nose, muttering *goddess be damned*, which set Kassidy off into laughter once more.

"Oh, she's not going to be any help here, *Alpha* Hunter. You're well and truly fucked."

With that, she laughed all the way out of the kitchen, a real pep in her step.

Hunter remained in the position of half despair until I patted his chest, and his gaze snapped down to mine. "I've really been looking forward to meeting her, and that did not disappoint in any way."

With a shake of his head, he lifted me higher, burying his face in my throat as he breathed me in. The fire of his dominance died down with each inhalation, until eventually he placed me on the stool Kassidy had left pushed away from the counter. "Just know, little omega," he said, leaning down to my height, "that whatever you two cook up, you'll be the only one who gets punished."

His eyes darkened, and the flash of gold had me squirming in my seat.

It was hard to tell if he was kidding or not, but in reality, I really didn't care. Hunter's punishments took on a whole new meaning these days, and I was *here for it*.

Time to start my plan to stir up these alphas' lives. Slade might be the first on my list, but Hunter, the domineering asshole, was second.

I couldn't wait.

CHAPTER 31

EMME

I spent most of Saturday with Hunter and Kellan. We swam, ate all the delicious food, watched movies, and existed in a bubble where we dealt with nothing and had no serious conversations. Neither of them asked me what had happened during the bonding, and I got the sense they feared spooking me by demanding answers.

I had no idea how long it would last before they pushed, but I enjoyed the peaceful day.

I stayed in Kellan's room that night, and he loved every inch of me until I fell into an exhausted sleep in the early hours of Sunday morning. It felt like I'd been asleep for seconds before a roughened hand slid down my spine and I jerked awake. I hadn't had to use my *sleep lightly and come awake at a dime* instincts for a while, leaving me at a disadvantage.

"Snow," Slade rumbled when I managed to focus on his giant form beside the bed. "I need you to look at some security footage for me."

Blinking to clear my gaze, I whispered, "Is—Is everything okay? Hunter and Finley?"

"Yes, both okay. I found a new piece of history on your

mom's pack, and I need to know if you have any additional information to assist my investigation."

The mention of Mom's pack was a shot of adrenaline to my system. I gently dislodged Kellan's arm and jumped out of bed, forgetting I was butt-ass naked. It was dark, but not dark enough to hide from shifter sight.

Slade's gaze slowly slid down my body, and by the time he returned to my face, his jaw was tight and I was combusting. I tried not to full-body blush, which would really highlight all the naked parts, but was fairly sure I failed. *Shifters.* We were shifters. Naked was normal. Naked wasn't inherently sexual.

Still, the way the dragon *stared* didn't feel even remotely platonic.

Blindly, I reached out to grab Kellan's shirt from the floor, pausing when Slade rumbled. Glancing up, I had no idea what was happening until he palmed the back of his plain black shirt and yanked it over his head. With the soft material in hand, he reached out and draped it over my head, surrounding me in his sweet scent. "Arms up," he ordered in a low voice, and I obeyed like he had the master controls to my body.

The length fell well past my thighs, and I was so frazzled by my proximity to his unbelievable chest and intriguing tattoo that I blurted out the first words that came to mind. "Next thing you know, you'll have me tattooed on your body like Hunter."

I was an idiot. There was literally no other explanation for that comment.

Slade had only just started to tolerate me, and I was well aware that his bursts of possessiveness were a product of him being an alpha and my scent match. We were nowhere near the stage of tattoos or claiming bites. We probably never would be.

In the darkness, I caught a slight twitch of his lips. "How do you know you're not already marked on my skin?"

Wait. Wait a hot freakin' minute...

My sight was laser focused on the dueling dragons, but if there was anything new there, I couldn't see it in the dim light. "Are you serious?"

Slade shrugged. "One day you'll find out, Snow. But not today."

I... *Oh, yeah*, I was definitely in trouble. Now all I could think about was exploring every mark and tattoo on his body.

When he turned to leave, I wasn't sure if it was relief or disappointment that hit the hardest. With one last glance at Kellan, who remained peacefully sleeping—he'd told me his beast only woke him when danger was present, and clearly he trusted his pack brother with his life—I followed the dragon shifter.

His broad back was as much a piece of art as his chest, and I hurried closer to make out the swirls of his dragons' bodies that continued over his shoulder blades and down either side of his spine.

"Who does your tattoos?" I asked. "How can you handle being touched for so long?"

Slade glanced over his shoulder, and the shadows playing across his features added to his dark-god vibe. "Finley, and when I'm prepared for it, I can handle touch from our pack."

I ground to a halt, wondering if I'd misheard him. "Finley?" It was a harsh word of disbelief.

He didn't stop for me, and eventually I had to move again to catch up. "Finley's an artist? Does he even have any tattoos?"

Kellan didn't have any; I'd quite thoroughly checked over the past twenty-four hours. While I'd caught glimpses of Finley's chest once or twice, I'd never seen any obvious tattoos.

"He has a couple," Slade said. "Which he doesn't share with many. They're not for everyone to experience."

Considering my relationship with Finley, there was no doubt I fell into the *everyone* category, which didn't sate my curiosity one bit. And that was a worry. Finley was heartbreak in six-and-a-half feet of growly goodness, and I couldn't let myself go there. I had to stop desperately clawing at brief snippets of a connection amongst the carnage of our interactions.

He wasn't for me.

Slade took the stairs to the third floor, and when he opened the door to his room and entered, leaving me standing on the threshold, I tried not to freak out. Hesitating, I explicitly waited for his invitation, my focus locked on him as he strode toward a bank of computers.

At least six large screens filled a wall in the corner near his windows, which were covered in a heavy curtain of dark-gray material. The desk was clearly custom built to handle all the technology, and fit the expanse of Slade's room, which was at least four times the size of mine. Despite the vast square meterage, the room itself was sparsely furnished, with a massive bed dressed in gray and white bedding—again, twice the size of my king bed—some shelves with books, a few small plants, and a dresser.

A quick glance didn't reveal any photos or personal effects, and once again, I had no idea who Slade was from this room.

"Come in, Emmeline," Slade called impatiently, already seated in front of a screen.

I lifted an eyebrow as he shot a hard stare over his shoulder. "Listen here, Scary Shifter," I said, stepping onto the same soft carpet of my room, "you're the one who has everyone pissing themselves when it comes to you. I was warned no less than seventy billion times to never step into your dominion without your express permission."

His eyes burned into me as I hurried toward him, like his room was boobytrapped and a randomly swinging blade was about to cut me in half. "Good," he said, a smirk tipping up the corner of his lips.

Good...? Yeah, he more than enjoyed the fear slash respect he commanded in the city, and having met his dragon, I completely understood its origins.

When he returned his focus to the monitor, I was able to breathe more freely. The intensity of his unwavering stare was too much.

"Closer, Emme," he commanded, and I jerked out of my trance and stepped forward until I felt the heat he exuded. "I've been tracing back through the years, and I found an odd image."

I snapped to attention as I was reminded of the reason he'd gotten me out of bed at the crack of three a.m.

His fingers moved over the keyboard so quickly that whatever he typed into the screen blurred. Not that I could have remotely kept up, even if he didn't type as fast as a bolt of lightning.

From what I saw, it was computer gibberish—what did they call it... code? Along with other boxes within boxes that had security footage and webpages. Everything moved around his screen until it all stopped on one grainy image of a man. "Do you ever remember seeing this shifter before?"

Leaning forward, I was careful not to touch Slade as I stared at an unfamiliar face. Along with the graininess, it was also in black and white and clearly old footage. Slade pointed toward the date printed in a neon orange on the bottom right side. The image had been taken almost twenty-six years ago on... "That's the day I was born," I said softly.

The quality was so bad that I really couldn't make out the finer details, but I felt no jolt of familiarity as I examined the nondescript face. I'd have guessed he was a shifter, just from the way he stood and his general broad, muscled build. His hair appeared to be blond or light in the image, and there was no way to determine eye color.

He appeared to be a normal male shifter; nothing stood out at all.

"Yes," Slade confirmed. "He was there the day you were born. This is where your mom gave birth." He clicked a few more buttons; the image expanded to reveal a small shack in the background. "Just outside of Georgia. This shifter was there, and then two days later…"

He clicked another couple of buttons, and everything changed on his screen again to reveal the same background, but this time four *very familiar* faces were in the frame.

Confusion had me shaking my head. "But Mom didn't meet them until I was older. I remember…"

I shifted through every one of my earlier memories, but there was nothing of the Rogers pack until we moved in with them. "Are you sure that's where I was born?"

Slade responded by speed typing his way to another photo, this one showing my mom in front of the shack, her face drawn, and in her arms a small bundle that clearly looked like a child. "There's no other footage," Slade said softly. "I found these by scrolling through security footage from a convenience store across the street, and I had to dig deeper than I ever have before to find the deleted footage from that time."

He didn't elaborate on how he knew when and where to search for the footage, but I got the feeling it hadn't been easy.

"What do you think it means? The guy is my dad, and the pack was in my mom's life long before I was born? Or… could one of those assholes be my actual father after all?"

Slade let out a frustrated huff, running his hand through his short hair, the thick strands disheveled for him. "I don't believe any of the Rogers pack is your father, but there's no evidence to suggest the other male is either. I was hoping you had some insight, or it might have triggered a memory of meeting the other shifter before. I can't find an identity for him, except for a possible connection to this image from the past…"

He slid his chair a few spots along and typed into one of the other computers. It booted up immediately, displaying dozens of photos scattered across it. He pulled up an image of the first shifter again, clearer this time, dressed in an older fashion style. Including a large top hat and coattails.

"That looks like the same guy," I noted, feeling stupid as soon as I said it out loud; Slade's mega brain would easily be able to tell that.

Slade nodded as he leaned back in his chair to meet my gaze. "Yes, but this is Valdor Breinstine, born 1802."

Which explained the outfit. "Eighteen hundreds… So, an ancestor? Or I guess that first photo is grainy, so maybe they're not even that similar looking."

Slade didn't appear convinced as his brow furrowed. "By my calculations, based on height and facial features, these two are genetically identical. I just don't know how or why. It is at least giving me a place to start searching as I trace through this family line. I'm not sure why they're shrouded in secrecy, but I *will* find out."

There was a spark of excitement in his tone that I rarely heard, but I wasn't surprised that Slade enjoyed this sort of deep diving investigation when unravelling a mystery. "I wish I was more help," I told him. "I don't remember ever seeing him before, but then again, I don't remember the Rogers pack being around in my younger years. Why were they there when I was born?"

I shook my head, frustration rearing its head. I'd ignored a lot of shit in my life in the hopes of living past my twenty-sixth birthday, but to know they'd been in the background, manipulating Mom long before we lived with them, really scared me. "Has there been any follow-up by the Alpha Council yet? Shouldn't they have done something about their attack on us by now? Why aren't those assholes in jail or dead?" I wasn't familiar with the punishments doled out by the councils and cities, but considering rogues were generally killed, why shouldn't evil, kidnapping murderers get the same fate?

The mouse cracked under Slade's hand, loud enough to indicate it was more than superficial damage. "The Silver City council is insisting we provide evidence before they allow us to take any further actions. Our word isn't enough, and even though I've pulled up all the security footage from when they entered Golden Claw, there's nothing that shows the Roger pack's faces. The shifters we do have footage of are mostly dead now, thanks to me and Hunter, so the council is calling it a settled matter."

My heart sank, and I reached out to clutch the back of a chair, knuckles tightening until my fingers ached. Slade noticed. Of course he noticed. "It's not over, Snow," he said, in a quietly dangerous tone. "We're making our own plans, which do not involve the council's approval or knowledge. Hunter will give final instructions, as he has a more level head to maneuver through the politics involved."

"You have a very level head, Slade," I told him, voice strained. "I don't know where you got the idea that you're a raging beast without reason or control. If anything, you're so contained at times that I want to shake you a little and wiggle parts of you loose."

A strange, broken sound echoed from his chest, and I jumped back as he stood. "It's control or destroy. There's no in-between for me."

With that blunt statement, he left his desk and headed for the door. At first, I thought our meeting was done until he called back, "Wait here while I grab a new mouse from the storage cupboard. I'll be a few minutes."

When his overwhelming presence was gone from the room, I sank into the chair he'd just vacated, my heart slamming in my chest. *Fuck.* That was intense, and I wasn't even sure *why* it was. Slumping forward, I lay my head on the desk and sucked in more calming breaths.

Which did fuck-all to help.

Jumping to my feet, I paced back and forth, my wolf rising to check in and see if I needed her. She'd shift and run if that was what it took to calm me down.

I don't even know if it's Slade, or the photos, or the weird guy who looks like the weirder older guy. But all of it is fucked up. She howled in response, agreeing with my assessment. What Slade had uncovered here had a deep-seated unease rising, and if I'd been in my beast form, all my fur would be standing on end.

I almost wished Mom was here to ask, but even if she had been, she'd be no help. She'd die again before revealing any secrets to me. She *had* died due to those secrets, I was certain.

I'd thought I understood exactly what contributed to her death, but maybe I'd been the one fooled. She knew the Rogers pack before I was born. Otherwise, why would they have been there? Had they truly been scent matched but let her have a child to another shifter? It made no sense.

As I paced, a sliver of light caught my attention between the joins of two of the gray curtains. Wondering if the sun was finally starting to rise, I decided that a glimpse of nature would help calm the panic racing through me.

When I slid the heavy gray curtain, with its intricate gold stitching aside, I expected to find a bank of windows like mine, only... it was another wall of screens. He had windows as well, but the first sheath of curtain concealed eight wall-mounted screens.

It took a few seconds for me to understand what I'd uncovered, but eventually I recognized the scenes playing across the screens—it was our pack house and yard. One of the screens near the middle repeated footage from earlier today when I'd been in the kitchen with Kassidy and Hunter; another was me in the pool this morning; a third was Hunter kissing me before bed tonight.

Oh fuck. I knew exactly what this was: security footage. But not just any old footage.

This was Slade's stalker wall, and I was on every single screen.

I was his prey.

CHAPTER 32

In my daze, I yanked the curtain back, intent on returning it to its original setting before Slade dragon-fried my ass for snooping. This wall might have shown me his stalkery ways, but it didn't tell me *why* he stalked me. For my protection, or was this evidence that he still didn't trust their newest pack member?

As the curtain settled back in place, I heard a very slight rustle that I should have ignored, but *fuck*, curiosity got me. A curiosity that would no doubt kill a shifter if I kept it up.

Ducking my head behind the curtain, I took in the new facet of his stalker game, and when it fully registered, my gasp was loud enough to alert half the city.

Pinned to the back of the curtain were photos of me.

Dozens of them.

In chronological order from when I was quite young, to more current ones taken in Golden Claw. Almost all of which came from what looked like security footage in the city where I'd lived with Mom and her pack. Though, there were quite a few from my time here with the Reeves pack.

When did Slade take photos of me?

I was asleep in some of them, and others were candids from moments I couldn't even remember.

With a shake of my head to clear the confused thoughts, I stepped out from behind the curtain, checked it was all in place, and raced back to his computers. When I collapsed in the chair, my chest heaved and my head spun.

Slade had always seemed indifferent toward me, his actions born from pack obligation.

But the *wall of Emme* revealed another side. I just didn't know how to feel about it.

A part of me hated this level of invasion into my life—he'd unraveled every broken piece and secret I'd ever kept. While another part was thrilled that he felt strongly enough to keep an eye on me. For whatever reason.

A therapist could step up at any point and sort out my mental state.

"Emmeline…" I jumped about a foot off his chair.

I hadn't heard the stealthy dragon return, and as he strode toward me, my gaze darted briefly toward the curtains to double check everything was in place. Slade paused, and the green of his eyes deepened as he too glanced at his stalker wall.

I braced myself for his next comment, but he just held up the new black mouse, as calm and cool as ever. "Got the replacement."

"Oh, yes," I said breathlessly, internally screaming at my lack of poker face. *Get it the fuck together.* "Sorry, I got tired while waiting and used your chair."

Slade brushed past me, our bodies almost touching. "Understandable."

"So," I squeaked, still not getting it *the fuck together*, "is that all you needed from me?"

He nodded, and I tried to breathe evenly, all the while knowing my scent and elevated heartrate would clue him in on my uneasiness. "I'll keep tracking the history of that shifter and let you know what I discover. The council has also requested a meeting on Monday for a formal statement of events. Hunter was vetoing, the last I heard, still pissed off that they aren't pushing harder against Silver City. I'm not sure where it will end up falling."

"Right. Thanks."

Unable to handle the tension for a second longer, I spun to leave, Slade's shirt swirling around me. I didn't even make it two steps before a steel band wrapped around my wrist and I was yanked back to stare into the eyes of a predator.

I hated that instinct had me frozen in place rather than fighting for my life. "Did you snoop while I was gone, Snow?"

His voice, low and lethal, dripped down my spine and into my soul. His pupils flared as the green of his irises burned me, and I could see dragon flames in their depths.

"I... I don't know what you're talking about." Nails on a board would have been less high pitched than my voice as I choked that out.

Slade tugged once and I was unable to resist falling into him. When the hard planes of his bare chest collided with my softer curves, I was scorched. "I'm a dragon, Snow. I ferociously guard what is mine, and right now, *you are my possession*. I *own* you. I watch over you. There's no part of you that will remain separate from me. Do you understand?"

Was the air thinner in his room? Why couldn't I breathe?

I managed another squeak, and for the first time in existence, I think I saw a true, genuine smile from Slade Riverson. Bastard looked positively pleased with himself. "I'm glad you understand," he murmured, and just like that I was released as he returned to his computer. "I'll see you in a few hours."

My head was a screaming wall of static as I stumbled from

the room, moving on autopilot until I ended up in my own bed, bypassing Kellan's room completely. I expected to lie awake for hours, consumed by what had happened with Slade, but instead I drifted off so fast it was almost as if his stalker wall really didn't bother me.

Not like I wasn't already aware that these alphas kept a close eye on me. If anything, it was reassuring to know Slade was in the background playing dragon-Batman. *Dragonman?*

I'd circle around on that one when I'd slept and had a stronger mental capacity.

When I woke hours later, I was surrounded by alphas. Hunter and Kellan had both found their way into my bed, and while my first instinct should have been panic—waking with an alpha on either side of me was not my normal—all I felt was contentment.

Sprawled between them, my body was more than comfortable. My right leg thrown over Hunter's, his hand possessively gripping my thigh. His hold slipped very close to the low throb in my core, and with Kellan wrapped around my left side, his hand on my ass, I couldn't help but shift against them.

"Mhmmm," Hunter mumbled as he rolled closer and all but crushed me under his bulk. "You need something from us, baby?" He pressed his lips to my throat, and a needy groan spilled from my parted lips.

The delicious rasp of his voice did not ease that incessant throbbing drumbeat between my thighs. Surrounded as I was, the bite on my throat pulsed to remind me our quintet wasn't complete. I needed three more marks to appease fate and our goddess, and I had no idea how I would resist them.

"Nope," I choked out in response, unsurprised when he laughed.

Ugh, his laugh was one of my favorite sounds, second only

to that deep groan he released whenever he was eating me like I was his favorite meal.

No, Emme. Why oh fucking why did I add that to my horny thoughts.

"What do you think, annoying pup?" Hunter asked, lifting his head from where he'd been scenting my skin. "Is our little omega lying to us, or herself?"

Kellan yawned and chuckled, tucking his head into the side of my neck, his lips grazing over the bite, which had my core clenching violently. "She smells needy," he murmured, voice deep. "That sweetness invaded my dreams last night, and I'm so damn happy to wake up to this." He pressed kisses to my burning skin between each word.

Hunter slid his lips over my cheek and down my neck. The scrape of his beard against my sensitive skin created a delicious friction that had me clawing at the sheets, needing to ground myself. "Wait, no," I gasped, choking on my own damn arousal. "We can't. I can't bond with Hunter too... fuck."

Hunter's response was to grip Slade's shirt and pull it tighter until my hard nipples were visible. His eyes were stormier as he leaned down and lapped at one's peak, sucking it into his mouth through the material. It felt so good that I clutched my right hand into his hair to hold him there. "Baby girl," he rasped, "You're giving off mixed signals. Do you want me to make you come or not?"

"Yes!" I burst out. "But... no sex." I would beg for his claim during sex. I would beg and cave.

Hunter's rumble emerged from deep within his beast, and when he lifted his head, his swirling gaze was all wolf as he observed Kellan kissing down my throat. "You know the deal, Emme. You will beg me for the final claiming, and until then, this is as far as it goes."

That statement had Kellan lifting his head and blinking at

Hunter. "Are you angry that I claimed her first? I didn't even fucking think about the fact that it was your right as the entitled alpha." Kellan paused and shook his head. "I'm not going to apologize for it, though. I will never apologize for anything shared between Shortcake and me."

Hunter snorted, running a hand through his glorious hair, letting it fall over his forehead. "You're still alive, aren't you, pup. You're part of my pack and it's my job to keep you all safe. Bonding saved your life, so I'll never be mad about how it happened. Emmeline and I will have our time."

"Still right here," I mumbled, feeling overheated, horny, and a hundred percent done with this conversation.

"Yes, you are," Kellan joked as he leaned down and kissed my lips. "Why did you leave my bed last night, though? That's the real question."

Hunter distracted me when he lifted my shirt to press his lips to my stomach. "Because Slade hijacked her from your room in the night," he said between kisses.

I jerked, and almost headbutted Kellan. "How the hell do you know that? Do you have a stalker wall too?"

Hunter's laughter trailed over my skin, and it felt so damn good that I forgot everything else in the world but the feeling of his breath and tongue as it darted out to taste me.

"Of course he does," Kellan said, amused. "He's a control freak with a god complex. How could he be everywhere at once without a stalker wall?"

These alphas were too much, but *damn* I liked them.

I liked them more than Twas safe for me or my sanity.

Further conversation was cut off as Hunter slid between my thighs and lowered his head to run his nose along my sex, breathing me in. His chest rumbled my favorite sound, and he buried his face to place a wet, open-mouth kiss on my clit, before he swiped his tongue down to my ass and then back up.

Kellan caught my cry on his lips, and I opened both my mouth and thighs, needing more. The fact that I was in the midst of my first threesome, with alphas I swore I'd never bond with, should have been a concern. But it felt too damn good to do anything except hold on and enjoy the ride.

Hunter swirled his tongue around my clit, and I unashamedly rode his face, the pleasure instant and strong. When he pulled away, I cried out, only to calm when he slid one, and then a second finger inside me, curling them to thrust hard and fast. It sent me reeling into an orgasm so quickly that I briefly lost my grasp on reality as I cried out and clutched Kellan.

"Fuck, I'll never get tired of watching you come, pretty mate," Kellan whispered, staring down at me with the softest eyes. "I need to be inside you now. Please."

Pretty mate. My heart swelled, and I couldn't help the tears that sprang to my eyes.

He'd upgraded *pretty girl*, and it was another completion of our bonding that felt so fucking perfect.

"Pretty please, baby," he begged again, and I had to upgrade his begging to one of my favorite things too.

I nodded. "Yes, I'd like that very much."

Kellan's entire face lit up. "Give her to me Alpha Hunter," he said as he all but bounced his ass off the bed. "I need my mate."

"Our mate," Hunter growled, and I groaned as he slid his tongue through my release once more, before he lifted his head, lips glossy and eyes feral.

"Right," Kellan chirped. "Our mate. Our forever."

My emotions overflowed like a dam that had burst its banks, but I was able to keep the tears at bay by focusing on the pleasure. I'd deal with the other complexities of this bonding later.

Lifting myself, I got onto my hands and knees and pressed my aching core into Kellan's face. His groan was deep and guttural. "Still think I actually died."

His hands slid over my ass as he moved forward and glided his tongue through my folds, lapping up the last of my orgasm. I arched back into him, and when I lifted my head to find Hunter watching us, his gaze predatorial, I gestured for him to come closer.

The entitled alpha moved forward on his knees until he knelt right before me. The broad head of his cock poked up from the band of his boxer-briefs, the pre-cum seeping from the swollen tip tempting me in every way. I couldn't wait to taste him again.

"Oh fuck. I need more," I breathed.

The gray in Hunter's gaze darkened, and he shifted positions until I was face to cock, letting me breathe in his mocha scent. Kellan buried his face in my core, lapping and sucking, and I almost died of sadness when he pulled away.

Thankfully, the thick head of his dick replaced his mouth fast, and when he pressed against my entrance, I cried out as he slowly, inch by inch, pushed inside me. Hunter drew my focus, his fingers threading through my hair as he pulled me to his cock, which was now free of his boxers.

When Kellan was fully seated, his size was enough to have my muscles protesting the invasion, even as the pleasure struck me down. When I rocked against him, I licked across the tip of Hunter, before attempting to fit as much of him into my mouth as I could.

There was no easy way to take alphas of their size, but as Hunter palmed his huge hand on the back of my head, thrusting down my throat until my eyes watered and jaw ached, and Kellan pulled all the way out to drive into me again, the pure pleasure had my body opening for them both.

Kellan's heavy balls slammed against my clit as he buried himself fully inside me again, and I gasped around Hunter's length as he thrust again. The sensation was too much as they moved in tandem, fucking me into a second, devastating orgasm.

This was one of those deeper, more intense releases, and I felt the gush of my cum seeping out around Kellan's cock. He reached down and swiped through my release, holding out a glistening finger toward Hunter.

"You want to taste her, Hunt?" His voice was strangled, and I wasn't sure the entitled alpha would be into that, but then he leaned over and licked across Kellan's hand, groaning in response.

"You two want a moment?" I choked out, my core tightening at the sight of that interaction.

Hunter growled. "We don't swing that way, but we will happily share every single part of you, little omega. You're the center of our quintet. Our core."

"Our heart," Kellan breathed. "And soul."

I shattered again, and this time Hunter fell with me, rasping my name as he poured his salty sweet release down my throat. I devoured every drop, and when Kellan's thrusts turned jerkier to follow us, I wondered how I'd ever top this moment.

CHAPTER 33

EMME

My phone chimed multiple times as I got ready for the game.

Back From the Dead: It's fucking game day, pack. You know what that means. Everyone wears a jersey with 22 on it, and you all must worship me as the hockey god I am for at least twenty-four hours.

Care Bear: Kel. I swear to the hockey gods. Do not fuck with the routine. Don't do it. I will cut you.

Care Bear: What. The. Fuck. Is. My. Chat. Name? You will change it back or your new name will be Texting from Hell.

Back From the Dead: You know I'm going straight to Eternal Paradise. I'm a good boy after all.

Kellan's praise kink was turning into a bit of an obsession for me, and I laughed out loud as I read through the message thread. I didn't have to use voice-to-text as often since Slade had shown me a *dyslexia* font on my phone that changed the size and shading of the messages. He'd promised more lessons soon, and for once the prospect was exciting.

BACK FROM THE DEAD HAS CHANGED CARE BEAR'S NAME

Fluffy Care Bear: Refer to yourself as a good boy one more time, Golden. One. More. Fucking. Time.

Fluffy Care Bear: KELLAN. That's it, I'm smashing you into the boards today. Screw the other team. I'm gunning for you.

Back From the Dead: Aw, you wouldn't do that. You love me, you big old softie. I bet you cried when I was dying.

BACK FROM THE DEAD HAS CHANGED FLUFFY CARE BEAR'S NAME

The swirl of anticipation of what Finley's name would be this time indicated that I was far too into this conversation. I did love these text threads, and today the feeling was stronger than ever because Finley hadn't left the chat yet.

Big Daddy Alpha: Little Omega, we'll be ready to leave in about twenty minutes. These two morons are already on their way to the game. The bus is taking the full team since it's not at our home rink this time. It's at Golden Dashers' rink on the other side of Golden Claw.

BIG DADDY ALPHA HAS CHANGED HIS NAME

> Pretty Mate: I'm just getting ready. Will be
> down in ten minutes.

My heart jolted at my new name in the chat, and I wondered if I'd ever get used to being called mate in the way Kellan used it. A claiming. A forever.

> Build a Bear: They have home ice advantage,
> but you know what we have…

> Back From the Dead: Emme's face on your
> cock to bring you luck?

My face flushed, and I was very happy there was no one in the room with me to see my flustered features. Though, my various stalkers were probably watching anyway.

BUILD A BEAR HAS LEFT THE CHAT

Well, it was nice while it lasted, and honestly, that still felt like huge growth for us as a pack.

> Slade: Most of the family will be with us today
> for Kellan's first game back. Prepare yourself,
> Snow.

Aw, Slade was in the chat too, even though he no longer used *Scary Shifter*.

Fuck, was I sitting here with heart eyes? Were they all watching said heart eyes via invisible security cameras?

> Pretty Mate: I'm prepared. Looking forward to
> meeting them all.

Needing a minute, I threw my phone on the bathroom cabinet and ignored the next chime as I blow-dried my hair and applied minimal makeup. I wore Kellan's jersey again, but had decided to also add a tiny teal thirty-four to the corner of my cheek. Not that I was particularly fond of Finley, but I felt the need to show pack support and unity today. Especially in the face of everything that had happened lately.

I hadn't been out of the house or family compound to experience it firsthand, but Cora had told me that the rumor mill was in full force around Golden Claw. Everyone was speculating about what had happened in Silver City, who I really was, and why my mom's old pack was trying to steal me. Questions I would also like answers to.

When I was ready, I picked up the phone again and let it read me the next few messages.

> Slade: Famous last words. The family can be a lot, but I will keep them in line.

> Call Me Daddy: Do not kill anyone today, Slade. I don't have the time or energy to clean up the mess.

> Call Me Daddy: Fucking hell, Kellan. How did you change my name again? Listen, you have one more day of leeway because you almost died. But come tomorrow, you better sort your shit out, or I'll make that witch magic feel like a bubble bath.

I snorted at his newest name for Hunter, and the fact that only Slade was scary enough for Kellan not to mess with during these chats.

> Pretty Mate: Why is Slade the only one without a cute nickname?

Where my need to shit-stir dangerous alphas came from, I'd never know. But here we were.

Unrepentant.

Back From the Dead: He has one!! I've
changed his name so many times… It just
never takes.

In my head I pictured Slade's responding smirk, which reminded me of his stalker wall and the way he manipulated technology.

Slade: *Smirking face* *Skull emoji*

He was scary, but that didn't mean he was untouchable.

After coming face to face with his *wall*, whether his intentions were good or not, I'd been finessing the final steps to my plan, which would add a little *upheaval* to *his* life. Someone needed to shake up his routine, and that someone was me.

The issue I kept running into was these *Reeves Industries cameras* that filled the house. After failing to figure out a solution myself, I'd asked Cora if she knew of a way to hide from them, and she messaged back that she had an idea and would chat to Warrick.

She'd also ordered the other supplies I needed, so there was no online Emme trail for Slade to track.

Back From the Dead: We're at the rink now.
Time to head in. I'll be looking for your faces
in the stands. Especially you, pretty mate. I
love you. *Red heart emoji* *pink heart emoji*
*red heart emoji**pink heart emoji*

My breath caught in my chest as I stared at those three words. In this new font, they were solid and unmoving. A permanent statement, visible to the world.

Sure, Kellan had said them out loud multiple times since

we'd bonded, and I'd said them back, but to see his love in writing. It felt... permanent. More than whispers lost in the breeze.

Tears streaked down my cheeks as my fingers flew across the phone, and if spellcheck hadn't been on its game, I doubted anyone would have understood a word of my blubbering mess.

> Pretty Mate: I love you too, Kellan Jackson. I'm so proud to be your mate, and I'm so proud of you. Kick their asses today.

After almost losing him, I'd decided not to hold back my feelings any longer. You never knew when the last moment you had together would be, and I needed to say everything in whatever time we had.

And while I had fairly strong feelings for two other alphas as well, the three of us just weren't quite *there yet*. Slade especially, even if he did stalk me like his life depended on it. And with Hunter... I still wasn't convinced that his actions weren't products of obligation and a desire to keep his pack mates safe, rather than actually wanting me for me.

After shoving my phone and cash into the pocket of my jeans, I wiped away the remaining moisture on my cheeks, fixed up Finley's number, and stepped out of my room.

Hunter and Slade stood waiting for me in the hallway, and I ground to a halt, not expecting them. Their giant shoulders filled the hall space, and I tried to look beyond them. "Wh- what's happening? Is everything okay?"

"Everything is fine," Hunter said, brushing back strands of my ponytail that had fallen loose. "You're just not leaving our sides today. Our enemies are still out there, and you can think of us as your new shadows."

"We will kill anyone who gets too close," Slade said, his eyes shining against his neutral expression.

With a shake of my head, I sighed. "How about we make *killing anyone who gets too close* plan B, and slot *scaring them away* into plan A."

Slade tilted his head as he considered my proposal. "Yes, I guess that's acceptable. It would only take a fraction of a second to kill them anyway if they ignore plan A and decide they are suicidal."

Don't smile. Don't encourage his psycho side. Why was it so adorable though? This had to be some sort of trauma bond after we'd been trapped together. A one-sided bond anyway, since I doubted Slade held any trauma from it.

Hunter ruined my composure when he laughed, one of those rare, genuine laughs that I doubted many had ever heard. "Well, with our plans settled, let's head for the game."

Small sparks of excitement danced in my stomach, and I found myself randomly asking, "Can I drive?"

The alphas tended to act like I was a permanent passenger princess, and while I didn't hate it, I missed being behind the wheel. Or bike. Even if the last time had been a bit of a disaster.

Today felt like a great day to have a little extra fun.

Kellan was alive.

And we were about to watch our top seeded pack destroy the Golden Dashers, who were currently fourth in the league. Not to mention that no one had attempted to kidnap me in well over a week.

Hunter tucked me under his heavy arm as we walked down the stairs. "You know what, Emme..." He sounded cheery, which was fucking weird. "...you can drive today. The only rule is that you have to choose one of our new, reinforced vehicles. We're taking no chance on anyone blasting you with a fucking rocket again."

As I would also like to avoid that, I wasn't about to argue. "What are my options?"

Slade glanced back toward us. "We had four delivered yesterday. There's a black Gelandewagen, a Range Rover, a Cullinan Rolls, and a Hummer."

The fizz of excitement from before turned into fireworks. "I don't want to choose," I said eagerly. "That's like choosing between children. How can we drive them all?"

"You didn't even ask me what a Gelandewagen was," Slade huffed, like he'd hoped to catch me out on that one.

Crossing my arms, I peered around Hunter's bulk to shake my head at him. "Always underestimating me. But I know my Mercedes, dragon. The G-Wagen is one of my favorites. Have you seen that baby offroad while still looking like a badass piece of beauty."

Slade's answering smile held a hint of pride, and when he nodded, I tried to ignore the surge of warmth in my chest.

"Sounds like you've already made your choice, then," Hunter said. "The Merc is our winner."

"But the Rolls..." I fake cried.

Hunter laughed again, and at this stage, I wasn't sure if this was the apocalypse or hell freezing over. Either way, it was cataclysmic.

"You'll have plenty of occasions to drive them all. For now, let's get you into *your* Mercedes."

I stilled, and if he hadn't outweighed me by two hundred pounds, I might have dragged Hunter to a halt. As it was, he kept us moving forward, my feet barely on the ground. "My Mercedes?" It took a concerted effort to get out those two strangled words.

Hunter's grin was slow and languid, and I felt like a rabbit stalked by a wolf once more.

"Yours, baby girl. And you'd better get used to it, because we're about to buy you the damned world."

But... but... "I can work and buy stuff," I spluttered. "I need to earn my own money." I mean, I didn't have G-Wagen money, but that didn't mean I couldn't try. I'd never expect them to just fund a lavish lifestyle for me; I'd survived on almost nothing my entire life, and it had been fine.

I kept up my protests until we were in the garage standing beside the shiniest, prettiest, most exquisite black G-Wagen I'd ever seen, rendering me completely silent. As I stared and drooled, Slade leaned over and pressed just the tip of his finger to my chin, closing my mouth.

"No more working unless you want to, Snow," he said. "You're part of our pack, which means you're a billionaire now. Hunter has all your bank cards ready to go."

My throat was dry, and as much as I wanted to stare at the exquisite German masterpiece in front of me, all I could see was my reflection in the shiny black surface, between two even more exquisite alphas.

"What if I can never truly bond with you all?" I murmured, needing to remind everyone about the complexities in our relationship. The fact that I'd bonded with one of them, and we were all still alive and okay, might be leading all of us—*mostly me*—into a false sense of future happiness.

"We'll figure it out," Hunter said, and he didn't sound angry or upset as he pressed a brief kiss to my forehead. "Us sharing our pack money with you is not contingent on you bonding with us, or obeying us, or making any choices you wouldn't normally."

"There are no strings attached to what we're offering," Slade added. "It's freely given, and it makes us happy to provide for you."

I wanted to do the same for them. The thought of providing for the alphas, even if it was only support and understanding, filled me with happiness and contentment.

Now I just had to figure out how to keep it all from crashing down around us.

CHAPTER 34

FINLEY

Kenzo dropped down next to me, leaning back against the locker as he laced his skates tighter. "It's so good to have Cap back," he said, sounding relieved.

Good was a poor descriptor for how it felt to have my brother joining me on the ice today. His cheeriness already filled the locker room as he moved amongst our team, slapping shoulders and chatting to the guys.

We'd won one and lost one of our games without him, and I'd played like a bucket of shit for both. All over the place, missing easy marks as the puck and team glided right by me like I wasn't even there.

Part of it was the lack of my normal pre-game routine. Without Kellan, I'd lost all sense of time and place, and had even strolled in late without my jersey to our last game. I'd had to wear a spare with a quickly ironed on number, but it wasn't the same. My jersey had been through all the games with me, and while it was frayed and patched, I wouldn't let them upgrade it.

You didn't get rid of shit just because of tarnish.

You loved it for all its flaws.

So, yeah, it was partly my lack of routine but mostly... my heart hadn't been in it without Kellan. Turned out hockey didn't come before my pack, which was a hard *and important* lesson to learn.

"You ready for today?" Kenzo asked when I remained silent, his worry for me not completely abated. I might have been in a better place, but it still wasn't a good place.

"Ready," I confirmed, forcing a smile. "I'm excited to be able to play without the stress and worry over Kellan. Even leaving the house felt wrong when Kel could take a turn and be gone from us at any moment. Now he's here, annoying the crap out of everyone, and it just feels right."

Kellan appeared like I'd summoned him by rubbing a magic lamp and making a wish. "He totally cried when I was dying," he said to Kenzo, dropping heavily on the other side of me.

Carlson, our goalie, let out a loud laugh. Fucking lion shifter sounded like a hyena when he cackled like that. "Baby bear was even more grouchy than usual. Just ask Lewis."

Lewis was another defenseman, and despite having played together for years now, we were casual enemies. Occasional allies. "He got in my face when I was trying to move the puck," I reminded them. Lewis called out his own bullshit version of events, before the locker room erupted into laughter and argument, everyone chiming in with their two cents of what happened.

"What did you do?" Kellan asked, turning so a hint of Emme's bite was visible as he scratched his hand over it, obsessive as ever.

"Knocked him on his ass during the game," I said shortly, shaking my head. "I shouldn't have to battle the other team and *my fucking own* when trying to clear the net. He knows that."

Kenzo snorted. "But for real, I need to know if he did cry when you were dying. I've never even seen him cry. You should ask Slade for the video footage." My *former* best friend held his stomach as he laughed harder. "We could have blackmail material forever."

No one had seen me cry since I was eight years old and my mom stabbed my dad, almost killing him. That was the first time, and it was my weakness that had cost him. I swore never again to allow my emotions to put others at risk.

Christian was a great distraction as he pushed through the room, most of the team having moved on from the Lewis argument. It felt right for the four of us to lace up before a game again, as we waited for Coach to appear.

Kellan leaned back with his hands behind his head, stretching out. "As if Slade has any footage that's not Emme-related. I swear he's just up in his lair jerking off to our pretty omega sleeping every night."

Right. Sleeping.

Even from down the hall I'd heard her with Kellan and Hunter, and I was fairly sure sleep didn't factor into their nightly activities. Thank the goddess for noise-cancelling headphones and sleeping draughts. Not that they worked much these days. The healers had warned me I'd eventually develop a resistance, and apparently, the time was now.

Kellan pressed his hand to the bite once more. "You should feel how happy she is right now." He released the most contented sigh I'd ever heard from another shifter. "The alphas let her drive, and she's zooming through the streets, turning both of those lucky assholes on with her skills behind the wheel."

I slid forward, my body jerking toward him. "You can tell

that much about her through the bond? Even without the quintet fully formed?"

The corner of his lips twitched until he laughed out loud. "Hunter might have sent a few messages and an image to fill in the blanks, but I can absolutely feel her joy. It's weird, but also *everything*. I know it's not my emotion when it blazes through me, but we're also linked, so it feels like my joy somehow. My wolf is a contented ball of fluff. When Emme's feelings seep through, it's like I stumbled into the warmth of summer after being lost in a snowstorm."

The Ice Queen shouldn't feel like summer. It just didn't mesh with her personality.

"Speaking of, we're actually scheduled for a snowstorm tonight," Christian piped up. "I think they're working to organize one of our winter runs as soon as the first flakes fall."

Further conversation died off as Coach appeared. "Listen up, Wolves," he roared, his lion flashing in his eyes. "Firstly, let's give a moment of thanks to have our captain back and ready to go."

Kellan waved his arms in the air as everyone shouted and called out. "Thanks, Coach," he said, pretending to wipe a tear away. "I'm thrilled to be playing again, and it'll be even better to have my girl, pack, and family in the crowd. We're going to destroy them tonight."

More cheers and shouts, and I slapped him on the shoulder as my adrenaline started to build. The excitement that hockey and skating usually brought me had been duller without Kellan, but it blazed as bright as ever today.

"Yes, we are," Coach continued, shutting down the cheers. He never had to raise his voice, having long ago earned our respect—helped along with suicides until we puked if we talked over him. "This team is one of our greatest rivals, especially now they've got *Henderson*, who is an absolute machine at center. He's fast, built like a tank, and without mercy. Do not underestimate him."

I'd been studying game tapes of Henderson, and he was a worry. Matching me in size, he played like it was his last day on Earth, and to make it to eternal paradise he had to take out as many of his opponents as he could.

It wasn't that I was worried about stopping him, but it wouldn't be as easy as usual. My eliminator socks felt a little extra snug as I flexed my toes, hoping they'd come through as always. I didn't even want to think about my boxer briefs and what they represented, but for the rest of this season at least, they were important. I carried the omega with me, whether either of us wanted it or not.

Knowing she would be in the stands again gave me mixed feelings. She'd saved Kellan's life, and I'd owe her forever. For that, I'd decided that shit had to change between us, and while we might never be a fully mated portion of this quintet, we could learn to be civil.

I'd mentioned as much to Kellan and the fucker had thrown his head back and laughed. "Emme is always civil with you, bro. You're the jerk here. It's your attitude that needs adjusting."

My bear had reared up, but it was a fair call. She'd triggered my trauma, and I'd been clinging to my anger to ensure that I never softened and got hurt again. Letting her close and then losing her wasn't a survivable option for me.

And I was still sure we'd lose her. It was the inevitable future that she'd been preparing us for since she'd first arrived.

When Coach was finished, we headed out for warmups. I grabbed my stick and jumped to my feet, bouncing on the rubber floor, ready for the game. We might not be on home ice, but we'd have plenty of support out there in the stands.

The moment we hit the ice, and the chill washed over my

face, I breathed more freely. There was no feeling comparable to this—I didn't care what anyone said. I'd had plenty of sex in my life, and I fucking loved sex, but the first glide across smooth ice was better.

Moving with Kellan and Kenzo on either side of me, we skated in zigzags, loosening our muscles. The other team were at their end, and noise erupted around the stadium as the crowds cheered and shouted for both of us.

I felt her out there, in the stands, and despite my best efforts I searched the seating reserved for players and family. Half of our compound was already seated, and Emme was right in the center between Hunter and Slade. Kassidy had the seat on the other side of Hunter, and no one sat on the other side of Slade, which was business as usual.

As I stared, Kellan popped up beside me, and I prepared myself for his commentary. "She's so fucking gorgeous," he gushed, eyes dreamy. "I feel like my heart is about to explode. I kinda wish I was in the stands with her."

Ignoring his need to leave hockey for the omega—I could not deal with that—I kept my tone light. "Sure, it's your heart that's about to explode."

Kellan shot me a satisfied smirk in return. "Okay, it's my heart and my dic—"

"Jackson! Thornton!" Christian shouted. "Get your asse— uh, butts over here for a second."

He was near the gate with a couple of kids holding out jerseys. Kellan and I shot over in his direction and spent a few minutes chatting to fans and signing some gear. Layla, our promo and public relations manager, stood off to the side taking photos, and even though we didn't normally meet and greet fans during warmup, I figured this had been set up in advance for a specific promo opportunity.

When we were done, I bopped a girl, who looked about

five, gently on her head. "You stay safe out there, sweetheart," I said as she shot me a gappy smile, at least two of her teeth missing.

"I hopes you wins, Mr. Eliminator."

Fuck. She was cute.

"You got it, sweetheart. Now head back to your family."

Kellan and Christian had already returned to their warmups, but I watched to make sure she was safe before I resumed mine. A gaze burned into the side of my head, and I knew it was Emme before I turned in her direction. Her face, which was undeniably beautiful, creased into a look of confusion as she looked between me and the little girl.

Clearly, she'd expected me to be an asshole toward kids too, but I saved that shit for flighty omegas who'd rather run than trust us. We all had our trauma, and I wasn't one who should point fingers, but I also wasn't the one who'd used my trauma to reject her before she'd even met me.

I might be embracing my new plan to keep the peace, but I still believed Emme was too weak for our pack. She couldn't handle the hard shit, and the rest of us would have to keep pulling her through life.

She handled Kellan just fine.

My bear wasn't always vocal, but when he spoke up, it held weight—a weight that settled deep in my subconscious. I couldn't argue with him about it either.

As she'd pointed out to me, Emme had never tried to run. Not even when shit got hard and dark with Kellan. I'd watched her closely, waiting for her to break and leave us, but she barely left his side, let alone the house. She's also gone against everything she believed in and bonded his ass to save his life. All actions that indicated I hadn't judged her accurately or fairly.

Still, that particular pack brother brought out the best in

everyone, so it wasn't a huge surprise Kellan brought it out in the omega too. For him, I hoped that Emmeline stayed in our lives as part of our pack. She was bonded to Kellan, and it would hurt them both to be separated for any decent amount of time. Which meant she was here to stay. For better or worse.

I'd learn to live with her for the pack's sake, and maybe one day we'd even be friends.

Weirder shit had happened.

Unconsciously, I'd been skating closer to the side of the stadium where our family sat, and I forced myself to smile at all the familiar faces before I reached Emme's. Her lips tilted up just a touch, before she smothered the smile, as if it had appeared without her consent.

For some reason, that made me happier than it should, and I shot her a wink. No doubt it looked as stiff and stupid as it felt, but I couldn't help myself.

Her eyes widened minutely, and I didn't want to stick around to see more reaction. As I went to turn away, I caught a glimpse of the tiniest thirty-four drawn in teal on her cheek. The sight of my number on her face brought a weird lurching sensation to my chest, and I had to shake the confusion off as I skated away.

Now was not the time to analyze the what and why of her actions, but eventually I'd have to dive deeper into my tumultuous feelings for the omega.

Thankfully not today though. Today we had a game to win.

CHAPTER 35

EMME

He... *winked at me.*

Wait. Had I just imagined Finley skating closer, smiling at the family members in the stands, before he winked *while looking at me?* "Did I have a stroke?" I murmured, patting my chest to ensure my heart still beat.

Hunter shifted his huge shoulders, which jostled me into Slade, who stiffened but otherwise didn't react. "Shifters don't have strokes. Our bodies heal before a stroke would occur."

"I don't think she was posing that as a serious question," Slade replied with a shake of his head.

Hunter examined me, and I hoped I managed the neutral expression I aimed for. "I might have been serious."

Both alphas tilted their heads, and even if I wasn't held in my seat by their bulk on either side, I couldn't have moved a muscle under those domineering stares. "No," Slade finally said. "I think she was trying to slot Finley into his usual place in her brain, but he's not quite fitting as well."

Damn him. "I hope you know it's very irritating the way you correctly dissect and categorize my thoughts and actions."

Slade looked pleased with himself as he hummed in agreement. Better than a grunt, I supposed.

"As I keep saying," Hunter added as he sprawled back deeper in his chair, long legs smashing into the row in front of us, "our pack dynamics will all work out the way they're supposed to, in the time they're supposed to. This isn't a sprint... it's a journey. And we all started at a different place."

Yep, both were too wise *and* annoying for their own good.

Barely resisting the urge to jam my elbows into their sides, which, let's be real, would hurt me more than the alphas, I shut my mouth and watched the rest of warmups. Enjoying the playful way the hockey boys raced around the ice.

The game itself was serious most of the time, but this just looked like fun as they stretched and let off steam. It took a concerted effort not to react to Slade sitting right by my side this time, his jacket pressed against my jersey. Our skin didn't touch, but the solid heat and weight of him was enough to have my wolf losing her shit.

Me too, if I was being honest.

There was a spare seat on his other side, and then we had Kenzo's mates—Vanessa and Luce—who I'd briefly met. Ness was a gorgeous brunette with brown skin and eyes, and Luce was a vivacious blonde, with pale skin and hazel eyes. At the moment, they were focused on the ice and the warmups, watching Kenzo as he shoved Finley into the boards, before taking off with a laughing bear after him.

This carefree side to Finley was disconcerting, and I was absolutely struggling to slot him back into his regular place in my mind—firmly separated from the other three alphas in our quintet.

Focusing on the rows of chairs around us, I enjoyed seeing Kassidy beside Hunter. I couldn't wait to catch up with her again. Beside her were Kellan's brothers, who'd arrived with their pack mates and their gorgeous baby boy, Declan. I'd had no idea that Kellan was an uncle, and as I'd stared at the golden-haired little boy, there was a brief moment where I imagined another golden-haired little boy.

Who knew if babies were in my future, and I certainly didn't want them now, but... maybe one day...

It was nice that the whole family had made the effort to be here today, driving the hour across the city to this rink. I'd personally thought it was far too short of a drive as I tore through the streets in the G-Wagen.

I'd met most of the family as they arrived, not that I could remember names, but they'd all been curiously polite in greeting. As expected, Hunter and Slade didn't let any of them get close enough to touch me, which suited me just fine as it kept my skittish wolf from freaking out at being in a crowd again. So many strangers around us bothered me, and I had to consider that on top of the trauma from my upbringing, I likely had new trauma from my kidnapping.

My soul was littered with broken pieces, but I was confident that with time, I'd find my new normal.

I could feel the curious gazes on us, all of them wondering how our pack was making this semi-bonded quintet work. Most of them knew the circumstances of my arrival in Golden Claw, which explained a few cool stares from Kellan's Aunt Georgia. She was single too, her mate having died in the last war. According to Hunter, she hadn't been the same since, and I didn't care how suspicious she was of me; my heart ached for the older shifter.

Kellan's brothers though, had gushed all over me, and I would have been engulfed in a double-sided hug if Hunter and Slade weren't doing their staring and growling thing—my possessive and obsessive stalkers.

Slade and I still hadn't mentioned his stalker wall yet,

though we were clearly both aware that the other knew. It was as if we played a game of uncle, to see who would remain quiet the longest. I was determined not to break first.

I straightened when the teams left the ice, the teal, white, and gold jerseys of the Celtic Wolves, along with the white and brown of the Golden Dashers. The crowd held a fairly even spread of team jerseys, and the energy contained more of a buzz than the last game I'd watched.

Hunter had told me on the way here that these teams were true rivals, both from the same city, and close in the league ranking. They'd actually met in the Shifter Cup last year, which was the pinnacle of the league. The Celtic Wolves had come out as victors, which explained the tension today... their first game since the cup.

"Their new center plays like a machine," Hunter said, leaning forward in his seat as he closely observed the Golden Dashers leaving the ice.

"Finley can take him," Slade noted without a shred of doubt in his pack mates. "He's got more experience and heart, and both of those will make a difference in how it all plays out."

Hunter grunted, and I assumed that was an agreement. Studying the side of his face, his five o'clock shadow was heavier than usual, but the tension that had lined his eyes while Kellan was under a magical attack had faded. His pack was currently safe, and he could finally relax.

A relaxed Hunter was an extra sexy Hunter, which didn't bode well for me. He was dressed casually in a teal Henley and jeans, and I wanted to climb all over him like he was an adults-only jungle gym.

I couldn't pinpoint when my feelings toward Hunter had changed so drastically. At first he'd been a scary, dominant alpha, who pushed me *well* past my comfort zone. But the more I got to know him...

It started with the way he'd pursued me without remorse or hesitation, letting me know in no uncertain terms that I was *his*. Continuing with the care and effort he put into looking after me, without ever showing an ounce of irritation that it was his responsibility. He appeared to enjoy it actually.

I was aware that a lot of his actions could be attributed to his entitled alpha obligations. He would always do what was right for his pack, and as the fifth of the quintet, he needed me to complete their bond...

A realization hit, and I stiffened in my chair as I finally figured out what had been holding me back from Hunter, when I'd gone all in with Kellan. I feared that my feelings outmatched his, and that to him I was an obligation. Whereas to me... he was my heart. Just like Kellan.

I had genuine feelings for the grouchy, bossy entitled alpha.

The start of the game was a thankful distraction from my thoughts, as the teams were announced, skating onto the ice in a flurry of green and blue strobe lights, doing a quick lap around the rink before it all got underway. Kellan won the first face-off, taking the puck through the other team quickly, before passing it off to another wolf.

The Dashers easily blocked their first attempt at goal, and then they had possession, racing back along the ice. It was a fast-paced game, and I was trying to keep up with my limited knowledge of hockey, only taking my eyes off the players when snacks arrived.

Delivered to us by Gerry, of all shifters.

"You're supposed to be watching the game, not working," I said with a frown as he handed Hunter hotdogs, fries, nachos, and drinks. "We can get our own food."

He scoffed, shaking his head with a scowl. "I needed to ensure you got the best quality of what they had to offer. This is all made by my hand, and is as good as we can get here. The Annandale pack keeps our rink's catering up to scratch, but here I don't trust these Dashers."

Three of Warrick's pack ran the hospitality sector at the Celtic Wolves' stadium, and I had to remember to compliment them the next time we caught up. Their food had been excellent.

"Well, thank you, Gerry," I said as he tucked his empty tray under his arm. "Where are you sitting?"

He pointed to the row in front of us and down a couple of seats. Florence was seated in that section, a teal scarf wrapped around her neck, and a giant foam finger on her hand. She was laser-focused on the ice, while simultaneously stuffing a hotdog into her mouth with her free hand.

Goddess, I loved that shifter.

"Flo is a hardcore Celtic's fan," Gerry said, following the direction of my gaze. "And I'm a hardcore Florence fan. It all works out."

My eyes widened, because that was news to me, while also making perfect sense. "Don't leave your lady waiting, Gerry," I ordered, shooing him away. "And thanks for the food."

He tipped his head and then hurried back toward his seats, sliding in next to Florence. "Did you know about Flo and Gerry?" I murmured, looking between Hunter and Slade. They'd been quiet during the exchange, but I'd felt their stares as they kept me in their focus.

Always in their focus.

"We knew," Hunter said as he held out another hotdog for me to take. "And you need to eat, little omega. I can feel your hunger."

"That's disturbing. You know that, right?" I glanced down at all the food precariously perched in my lap. "It's actually not that easy to eat while balancing this much food. If I promise to eat, will you guys please take some of it."

"We will *hold* it for you," Slade told me as he lifted a few of the cardboard boxes off my lap. Hunter also took a few, and I could finally relax and enjoy my fully loaded hotdog, nachos, and icy cold beer. This was the freaking life.

Neither of the alphas took a single bite until I'd made it through a hotdog and nachos. Hunter tried to hand me another hotdog, but I shook my head. "One bite," he purred close to my cheek, and I wondered if he was aware of just how many eyes were on us.

If he was, he absolutely did not care as he coaxed me to eat from his hand.

"I have nachos still," I protested, gesturing to the third left in my disposable carton.

"One bite," Slade murmured, his tone even deeper, the rumble more commanding. Like an absolute sap, who couldn't refuse these alphas when they cared for my well-being, I bit into the bun.

"Good girl," Slade said, and at the same time Hunter rasped, "There's our good girl."

I almost slipped off my chair as my panties took part in a slip-and-slide contest we were clearly winning.

Hunter's nostrils flared; the gold in his eyes more pronounced. "Your scent, Emme, is going to start a war."

"Destroy stadiums," Slade confirmed, and I was surprised by the strain in his voice.

"Your fault," I mumbled, and needing a distraction started shoveling the last of the nachos into my mouth like there was in an eating competition to go along with the slip-and-slide. It took a few seconds of laser-focusing on the ice again before Hunter and Slade returned to eating their own food.

The Dashers were an aggressive team, and within the first ten minutes there were multiple fights, with Christian ending up in the penalty box along with number seventy-four on the other team.

Both teams had great attempts at goal, but by the time the buzzer sounded on the first period, the score remained at zero.

"Is Finley hurt?" I asked, my food all gone now, which gave me plenty of time to nervously chew my nails and bounce my right knee. "He took a really hard hit from that Viking-looking asshole of a shifter."

"Henderson's a fucking pussy," Tyson, Kellan's brother, called from his seat. "Our boys will take him out at some point. I'm sure of it."

"He's hot," Kassidy piped up, leaning forward so I could see her, "but I'd still like to beat him with a hockey stick."

Henderson was number forty-six on the Dashers, and he reminded me of an ancient Viking warrior. As big as Finley, or even a little bigger, the alpha had blond hair tied back from his face, with multiple strands braided in his team colors. From here I wasn't sure of his beast, but I'd guess wolf as he rumbled his way across the ice.

"Finley is fine," Hunter said, but he sounded annoyed that anyone would dare beat up on his pack mates.

Without a word, Slade rose from his chair, and Hunter's arm shot out around me to grab his brother's shirt. "Do not fucking move," he barked. "You need to let them fight their own battles here. This is sports, not combat."

Slade stared into the empty rink, his expression hard, until he shrugged off Hunter's hold and retook his seat. "No one fucks with my pack."

I cleared my throat. "Are-are you planning on just straight-up murdering Henderson?"

Slade shrugged, and Hunter sighed like this wasn't the first time the dragon had been halted from going on a little killing spree. He was a worry, for sure, though secretly I'd have paid good money to watch him beat a little humility into the arrogant center. Just a little.

CHAPTER 36

EMME

Half my beer went flying as I leapt to my feet and screamed with the other twenty thousand Celtic fans in the stadium. Kellan scored in the dying seconds of the game, giving us the 1-0 victory as the sole puck to pass a goalie.

Hunter removed the plastic cup from my hand while I continued to jump up and down, relief coursing through me. The game had been tense, with neither side giving an inch, and so many fights and penalties. Half of both teams spent significant time in the penalty box.

The stands vibrated as those of us in teal, gold, and white shouted the stadium down, and the guys did victory laps on the ice. The Dashers skated off with their heads low, faces creased in exhaustion. The Wolves were exhausted and beat up too, but the win sent a new surge of adrenaline through them.

Kellan slammed into the glass, his helmet tipped back and the biggest grin on his face. One of his hands pressed against the glass while the other crooked a finger in the come-hither gesture. My feet moved before my brain caught up, and Hunter and Slade were on my ass all the way down the stairs.

I stopped in front of Kellan, my hand resting against his, the glass between us. "Did you see me score, pretty mate?" he asked, gaze intense as I was caught in the deepening blue. "That one was for you."

I shot him a cheeky grin. "Of course I saw you score, Golden. And let me tell you, after that victory, that's not the only time you're going to score today." Fuck, I was cheesy, but it felt nice to have these cute little moments.

Kellan threw his head back and whooped loudly, and when he met my gaze again, the heat in his stare had me ready to leap over the barrier and into his arms.

His coach shouted for him to get off the ice, but Kellan didn't turn away from me. "You've got press," Coach added with a growl.

Kellan's bottom lip jutted out as he pouted. "I've got to go, Shortcake, but later we're celebrating. Get ready, because I'm taking you out. We have a lot to be thankful for."

Hunter tapped the glass, momentarily stealing Kellan's focus. "Where are you taking her?"

"Luxuria of course," he said without hesitation. "It's ours, secure, and has the best whiskey collection in Golden Claw. No brainer."

A small lick of excitement lit up in my belly. I'd never had a night of casual fun with friends or lovers. The closest I'd come was the nights I worked Luxuria when Kellan and Christian kept me company. Tonight, though, I didn't have to leave or serve.

Maybe I'd even dance with my mate. Another first.

"We'll be there too," Hunter said, "so plan accordingly." I shook my head at how seriously my new bodyguards took their jobs. With pretty good reason, I supposed.

Slade released a huff, surrounding us in his sweet, smokey

scent. "I have patrol duties this afternoon and evening, but I can make it around midnight."

Hunter nodded. "You leaving now?"

"Yes. I'll shift and fly over to save time." He leveled me with his generally unreadable stare. "I'll remain overhead until you and Hunter are in the car. Stay out of trouble, Snow. I'll be keeping an eye on you."

Nice to know he wasn't about to lose his stalking touch. "I'm well aware."

Another unspoken understanding passed between us, but still, he never mentioned his stalker wall, and I was yet to figure out how to break him. It felt like it might be an impossible task.

Slade left us as the coach shouted once more, "Jackson, I won't fucking tell you again. Get your ass off the ice."

The stadium was all but empty by now, and with a final kiss blown in my direction, Kellan reluctantly left. "See you in a couple of hours. Dress sexy," he called as he skated off, shooting me sad puppy eyes over his shoulder.

Hunter scowled, and that had Kellan laughing the rest of the way off the ice and into their locker rooms. "You two will be the death of me."

I gently punched him in his massive biceps. "Come on, we can't be worse than Grouchy Bear and the scary, murderous shifter who will be *watching us*." I lowered my voice in a very poor imitation of the growly dragon.

Hunter shrugged like that was debatable, which amused me all the way out to the parking lot, where my beautiful car sat untouched in our reserved spot. There was no logical reason for why she already felt like *mine*, but here we were. I glanced up to see if I could spot Slade, but there were too many low clouds scattering the sky, and no sign of a massive, scaled beast.

"You want to drive again?" Hunter asked, bringing my focus back to land.

I appreciated him giving me the option when he'd normally just take control, but found I was happy for him to drive home. His unease at being out here in the open was clear; a little return of control would help his equilibrium. "I'm good to play passenger princess."

Hunter opened the door for me, and as I climbed in he placed a hand on my ass to boost me inside. A gush of air escaped my lungs, mostly from surprise. The alphas understood I was capable of performing these actions on my own, but they wanted to help me anyway.

Which was odd. I didn't fully understand what they got from making my life easier, but I'd be a liar if I denied my enjoyment of the way they shifter-handled me.

Being cared for was completely underrated as an aphrodisiac.

Don't get me wrong, I *really* enjoyed traditional foreplay, but true seduction began long before the bedroom. And these alphas were experts.

Despite the rush of shifters attempting to leave the stadium parking lot, Hunter made it out in under fifteen minutes, capable and calm behind the wheel—despite the slew of drivers around us who clearly had a death wish. "You're more patient than I expected," I said, finding myself staring at his side profile. "Which might have been an unfair expectation, but as entitled alpha I was prepared for a lot of demanding and rage when you didn't get your own way." Instead, I'd gotten a patient hunter, calculated and intelligent in his approach.

He met my gaze, and by now I'd stopped worrying that he would crash us into a pole. "You didn't have the best examples of alphas growing up," he said, the darkness in his eyes cutting into me. "It's no surprise that you expected us to be monsters."

There was no lie in that statement, but I remained disappointed in myself for judging them so harshly before we'd even met. "I understand that for the most part I've been an obligation for you." The truth slipped out as I sank into the heated seats, my exhaustion dragging me down. "That you're ensuring I don't want or need anything so I'll stay and be part of your quintet. I understand that, but I'm still thankful for your support. It was obvious from our first meeting that you don't generally compromise, but for me you have. You're nothing like my mom's pack, or the alphas I expected, and I should have told you sooner how appreciative I am."

Hunter's eyes were on the road again, and I noticed his sudden death grip on the steering wheel. "You're not an obligation, Emme." His words were clipped, and I hurried to explain.

"I just meant that I might not have been your first choice. I mean, you could have had a strong alpha like Sissily instead of a traumatized omega who fought you from the first interaction. You didn't have to be so kind and generous with your time, money, and attention, and... I'm sorry about how I acted when we first met. It was pure survival instinct, and it bothers me that I might have hurt you all with my actions."

Hunter hit the brakes hard, and the car slammed to a stop in the middle of the street. Horns blared behind us but he didn't give a fuck as he breathed deeply, his hands crushing the steering wheel as he strangled it. *Don't hurt my new baby.*

"I'm going to say this one time, Emmeline Anders," he murmured softly, with that undercurrent of ferality that told me he was closer than he appeared to losing himself to his wolf. "And one time only. You are not an obligation to me. Not anymore."

My heart started performing an Olympic acrobatic routine in my chest as I waited for him to continue.

"At first you were a duty to our pack, before I truly knew you, but now... now *you* are as essential to me as the fucking air that I breathe. Now... I can't imagine my life without *you* specifically in it. You burst into my life like a fucking solar flare, and everything that was dull before turned brighter. There's not another shifter in the world, including Sissily, who I'd want or prefer over you. In truth, they don't even exist to me. You are all I see."

Releasing the wheel finally, he turned and I was hit with blazing gold eyes, the essence of his alpha wolf capturing my own beast. "I'm sorry," I whispered, overwhelmed and wondering if I could finally let myself fall into this alpha. Let my feelings for him flow free from where I held them tightly contained.

Hunter shook his head. "Don't apologize. I understand why you came to the conclusion you did. Our path to this point hasn't been smooth, and you've lived most of your life feeling like a burden in your own home. But I need you to understand, Emme, that I would choose you in every situation. *In every life.* The goddess knew exactly what she was doing bringing you into my life. You're my perfect match and the other half to my soul."

As Hunter Reeves poured his heart out to me, I shattered like a fragile glass dropped off a mountain. "I would choose you too," I told him with force, through tears I hadn't even realized were falling. "If I'd ever had the freedom to wish for a pack, I would have chosen this one in every lifetime."

Hunter pressed his lips to mine in an urgent but gentle kiss. This alpha did not ever do submission, but I enjoyed the liberty of embracing my more feminine energy around him, allowing him to take control and knowing I could trust him with it.

When I groaned, and another horn honked behind us, Hunter pulled away. "We're going to seal the mate bond," he promised me, pressing one last kiss to my lips. "But the rules have not changed. You will beg me for it, and it will be before your birthday."

"That's in like eight days," I choked out, and his smile was positively devilish.

"I know, little omega. I know."

There was another honk, and without any urgency, Hunter got the car moving again. It took me a long second to get myself under control, only to have the entitled alpha undo it all by wrapping his right hand around my jeans-clad thigh, flashing his claiming tattoo at me.

This was too much for a mere mortal shifter. Too much, and yet not enough at the same time.

"You know, you can tell us the reason you've been running," Hunter said suddenly, the silence of the car wrapping around us and echoing those words louder. "There's nothing in your past that would turn us away from you. *Nothing.* As a pack, we will fight whatever battles we need to, and it will be much easier if all of us work together. I mean, we're aware that it's regarding your mom's death and that fucking pack. A pack I don't need to remind you is still out there, waiting to make another move. No matter what we're doing behind the scenes to prevent that from happening, without all the information, we're working at a disadvantage."

"You think they're going to try and take me again?"

There was no hesitation in his response: "Absolutely. You're important to them for some reason, and they will not stop now they've tracked your location. You've been off the pack's radars for years, but now you're registered with Golden Claw and our pack, you won't be able to run from them again."

It was terrifying to think that I would never have freedom

from Blaine and his minions again. Always looking over my shoulder and keeping out of evil alphas' clutches. My best hope was Hunter and our pack, and for that I needed to trust them with every part of my past—in the hopes we might have a future.

"I will tell you," I promised, "the next time we're all together. I was going to the day we got smashed into by the witch, and then our lives briefly went to shit, but I agree that it's safer for you to know everything. I just—I just hope it doesn't change our dynamics."

Hunter flexed his fingers on my thigh, drifting his palm higher, his finger pressed against the heat of my core. "There's no chance it will change us, Emme. But I acknowledge and understand your fear. Let's just take it one day at a time."

I wasn't sure I shared his confidence, even though Kellan was *so far* unchanged in characteristics, but I desperately wanted to believe him. So, for now, this would have to do.

CHAPTER 37

EMME

For the rest of the drive I was more relaxed than I'd ever been in Hunter's presence. The wall between us had crumbled piece by piece, and it was like a breath of air when I'd been struggling under water.

We filled the time chatting about our lives, and I enjoyed learning different facets of what made up Hunter Reeves. "Your favorite color is black?" I said with a snort. "Could you be more of a brooding alpha cliché."

He growled playfully. "Slade is the broodiest of the lot, and his is green."

With a shrug I said, "Based on his wardrobe, I'd have said black too. But his eyes and dragon coloring are stunning, so it makes sense."

Hunter's smile was gentle, and I barely managed not to crawl across the console and into his lap. "What are your guesses for Fin and Kellan?" he asked, slowing for a light.

I thought about it for a second. "Maybe red for Finley, and teal or gold for Kellan."

Hunter nodded like he was somewhat impressed. "Kellan's is yellow, sunshiny bastard that he is."

Where was the lie? "And the bear?"

This got me a side-eye and smirk. "Light, icy blue. A color *very* close to your eyes, actually."

There was a jolt in my stomach, and for my sanity, I pretended it was food poisoning from the stadium food. "How long has it been that color?"

His smirk grew. "A long time, Emme. What a delicious coincidence... or not."

"He does love ice," I reasoned, "so I would guess that was where it originated."

That got me another raised brow and a slightly impressed expression. "You appear to have a pretty good read on him already."

The satisfaction in his tone annoyed me. "Don't make more from it than is warranted."

Hunter was choosing his battles wisely today too, and just nodded. "As you wish, little omega."

Our conversation shifted to the places we'd lived over the years, and I was surprised to find that outside of the first ten years of his life in Golden Claw, Hunter had spent the rest of his youth in Europe, following his dad on scavenger hunts.

"If he wasn't making money, he was excavating for ancient and unearthed shifter cities," he said, tone flat. "That was how he found Slade. He'd heard the stories of a treasure buried beneath this ancient volcano, and when it erupted, he knew it was his chance. I wasn't even born when he found Slade's egg about to hatch."

"Was he surprised when out popped a beast instead of a baby?"

Hunter laughed, a dark, raspy sound. "He loved it, the evil bastard. Allowed him to treat Slade like a dumb animal rather than the genius shifter he is. He deserves to die for how he treated my brother, but for some reason, Slade won't take him out. And he won't let me either."

Knowing Slade, it was either a misplaced loyalty to the man who found him… or it was because of his loyalty to Hunter.

"How did you handle rolling around with a baby dragon as a wolf pup who couldn't shift yet?" I asked, hoping the subject change evoked happier memories. "What was Slade like when he first shifted into his human form?"

A wistful expression crossed Hunter's face, and I got a sense of those happier moments intermingled with the darker. "He was wild. It took years to domesticate him. My father used specific techniques that I won't ever speak of without Slade's permission, to break the dragon in him. It didn't work of course, but he did teach my brother how to control it in the worst possible way."

"He destroyed the connection between Slade and his beast?" I guessed, my words a whisper of horror. And now *I* hated Hunter's father with the same fervor as I hated my mom and her pack.

Hunter's jaw tightened, and he didn't deny it.

"What did he do to you and Kassidy growing up? Why did your mom never stop him?"

I was captivated by the way his bronze throat expanded as he swallowed roughly. "He ignored Kass, as females are only good for one thing. With me, he ensured that any shred of weakness was stripped from my soul. Apparently, I was quite a sensitive little asshole, which was unacceptable to my family. My mom is just as bad as he is, or maybe worse, because we barely even existed to her. She gave birth to us and then never looked at us again. We were born to carry on the family name."

"Reeves," I whispered, trying not to hate the name I'd already fallen in love with.

For the first time since this conversation began, Hunter smiled. "Actually, it's not. I changed my name as soon as I grew strong enough to claim the status of entitled alpha. *Reevesen Latia*, or "Reeves" were the name of these tall, willow-style trees that surrounded our land. Trees that Slade and I escaped into when we were younger. They represented our freedom, and my father hated them, so it felt fitting to create a new life under Reeves. His pack name is Davenport."

The name *Davenport* tickled the back of my mind, and I wondered if I'd heard it somewhere before. Where, though, I had no idea. "I'm glad you changed your name. Why does Slade use Riverson though, if he grew up with you?"

Hunter shifted lanes, smoothly merging us onto the road near his offices. "When Slade was about sixteen, he felt a calling to shift and return to the place of his origin—the volcano where our father found him. The area was called Riverson Canyon, and etched into the walls in the dialect of the dragons, which to this day he's still the only one to speak and understand, was the same family name. Slade felt like there were more of his brethren out there, and it was they who called to him, but he never found evidence of more eggs. Or dragons."

My chest ached at the thought of him making the journey alone. "It must be lonely to be the last of your kind."

Hunter inhaled deeply, before he released it as a sigh. "There's a part of him that mourns his dragon side, but he has us, and we're his family."

Knowing that Hunter and Slade had each other growing up brought me a sense of comfort. My existence had been eternally isolated. I would have loved even one sibling to call family. "We all have our hidden traumas, don't we?"

"Except for Kellan," Hunter said with a broken laugh, pulling into the family compound. He turned to me while he waited for security to open the gates. "He grew up in a functional, loving family."

"Thank fuck he did," I said, my own laugh shallow and forced. "Imagine if he wasn't around to lighten our day. We'd live in a house of morose fucks."

Hunter didn't deny that either, and soon we were back in the garage, parking in the Mercedes' new spot. Once the car was silent, Hunter turned to me, his hands capturing my face. I gasped as he dragged me into a kiss. "What was that for?" I breathed against his mouth, lightheaded and aching for more.

He brushed his thumbs down my cheeks, over and over, in a soothing and somewhat *stimulating* rasp. "You offer just as much lightness as Kellan," he said. "We're a lucky group of morose fucks to have you in our quintet, Emme. You're strong, resilient, kind, and one hell of a driver. You know cars as well as us, ride motorbikes like a fucking dream, and I have no doubt would kick our asses around the racetrack." He kissed me again, like he couldn't help himself. "I'd really love it if you begged me now," he whispered against my skin.

Oh goddess. I wanted to so badly, and honestly, couldn't remember any of my very good reasons for not rushing into this with him.

"Hunter..." I whispered, meeting gold eyes.

He was so fucking gorgeous that I was opening my mouth to beg when my phone rang. It broke the moment, and I turned away, sucking in rapid breaths. Blindly, I reached into the center console to grab the device, seeing Cora's name pop up.

My arousal was doused with worry that she was in trouble, and I quickly swiped to answer. "Bestie," she trilled, her voice high and excited. "Your glam team is here to get you ready for tonight."

"Glam team," I repeated in confusion.

Her laughter rang down the line. "Well, yeah. Kellan told

War that we're heading for Luxuria tonight, and I figured it was my best friend duty to help you get ready. Plus, we have that *other thing* to discuss."

The other...? *Ohhhh.* The *thing* she referred to was part of my silent battle with Slade, and hopefully if Cora had what I needed, I could enact my semi-evil plan today. Just in time for him to discover upon returning from patrol.

"See you in a few seconds," I said as I hung up.

Hunter opened my door and held his hand for me. "Come on, little omega," he said. "Let's get you delivered safely to your friend."

"I have a friend," I chirped, feeling pretty proud of myself. "A best friend. I've never had one of those before."

There'd been acquaintances and friendly coworkers in my life, but no one who would ever show up to help me get ready for a night out. Probably because there'd been no nights out.

But still, I'd never been close to anyone like this before, and it felt nice.

Hunter grunted into a rumbling growl. "I'm your best friend. She can be your second-best friend. Or fifth, once our pack gets their shit together. Make sure Cora is aware of her status."

With a peal of laughter, I threw my elbow into his ribs, and Hunter's smirk was his only reaction. Bastard could at least pretend he felt it.

"I will not make her *aware of her status*. Even I know that's not the way to enrich a friendship."

"She's part of a quintet," he said with a shrug, like he didn't give a fuck. "She knows how it works."

That much was no doubt true.

She'd been pushing me into my pack from the start, knowing that it was the right place for me and my wolf. It was clear she romantically loved Warrick with every part of herself, and the others in her quintet she loved as family. They would be her first best friends too, and after finding my own quintet, it made perfect sense to me.

Hunter must have alerted security that it was okay to let Cora in, as she already waited in the foyer. Dressed in a multi-layered violet skirt and a simple white tank with a cream cardigan over the top, she looked as gorgeous as ever.

When she saw me, she squealed and threw her arms around my shoulders, the bags she carried flopping heavily against my spine. "I'm so excited that we're heading out tonight," she said, dancing on the spot. "Come on, girl. We don't have much time. We need to get ready."

It was barely five p.m., and from what I knew the club wouldn't be busy until ten, but she was the expert here.

As we wandered past the living room, the television was on *Shifter Sports Broadcast*, as per usual in this sports-loving house, and I paused at Kellan and Finley on the screen.

"Hang on," I said as I hurried to find the remote and turn up the volume. "I want to watch this."

Cora dropped her bags on the couch and joined me in front of the screen. "You've got it bad," she teased, and I could feel her watching me while I stared at the screen like a creeper. Speaking of creepers, was Slade currently staring at me through a screen, while I stared at the rest of our pack through a screen?

We'd reach a point soon where it would be hard to tell who the bigger stalker was.

"Not that I blame you," Cora continued conversationally. "And don't think I didn't notice that bite on your neck, *friend*. You need to spill."

I tore my gaze from the reporter who was asking about the fights during the game, and said, "This is one of those sex sharing conversations, isn't it?"

She chuckled. "Of course. These are the details we share with our girlfriends."

I had a lot to learn about friendship, but I felt no embarrassment as I quickly detailed what had happened with Kellan's magic battle which resulted in my decision to bond with him.

"How did it strengthen him?" she asked, forehead furrowed.

She was the first to ask that question, and I still couldn't believe the alphas just let it go. Did they already know the truth? Or were they content with not knowing, since it had saved Kellan's life, and that was all that mattered? Once I came clean about my past and my mom's, that was a question I'd be able to ask them.

"I'm not really sure," I lied, wishing I didn't have to, but I refused to tell Cora before the alphas. "I'm just happy it happened."

Her face crumpled; her eyes were watery as she nodded. "Oh, goddess, me too. I was so scared for you and Kel. It was heartbreaking to not be able to help."

I turned back to the screen, needing to see Kellan's healthy and happy face. Anything to clear the memory of him almost dying from my mind. "He wasn't really aware enough for true consent in bonding," I said softly, "But I don't think I forced him into anything he didn't want."

Her tears dried up in the face of her laughter. She even went as far as to slap a hand on her knee when she hunched over. "Forced him...? Girl. Please. You are literally his reason for being alive, and I'm not even talking about the way you saved him from the magic. He must be overjoyed."

Even with my doubts, I agreed with her. "Yeah, I think he is."

Cora regarded me for a second, and then waved her hand toward the television. "Call him."

Wait... what? "*Call him*... isn't this live?"

She nodded before I even finished. "Yep, this is live. Call him and then you'll never again have to wonder if you're his one and only reason for existence."

Unsure whose face this was about to blow up in, I pulled my phone from my back pocket and hit Kellan's number. It rang and I watched the screen closely. The reporters had just asked about his recovery from the magical attack, when Kellan jumped and glanced down at the table. He held a hand up to halt the rest of the question, lifted his phone, and answered it with the broadest of smiles gracing his lips. "Pretty mate," he crooned down the line, on live fucking television, in the middle of a press conference. "Is everything okay?"

There was a long, extended silence before I remembered I was supposed to talk and not just stare at his handsome face. "Oh, uh. Yes, totally okay. I just wanted to check in and make sure you were safe."

Cora took the remote from me and turned down the TV volume so it didn't echo back as he answered. On the screen, his expression softened, and he leaned on one hand, staring into the main camera. "I'm more than safe, Shortcake. I'm just in a press conference about to tell everyone about how you saved my life, and that I'm one lucky son of a shifter to have the most perfect mate."

Oh goddess. These alphas were determined to elicit the deepest of emotions from me today. "I see you," I whispered, drinking him in like I was parched, and he was the only water available. "Sorry to call while you're doing press, I should have checked first."

Kellan released a gentle laugh. "You can call me any time of any day or night, and I will answer. No exceptions."

Truth rang in his voice, and I'd never been surer that there were no exceptions to his feelings for me. My voice caught. "I miss you, Golden Boy."

On the screen, he jumped to his feet in a graceful rush, and everyone around him went crazy, except for Finley, who just shook his head and leaned back in his chair. Reporters' shouts rang out as Kellan spoke directly to the camera. "I'm on my way home to you right now," he said as his long legs maneuvered him around the table. "Don't move a muscle."

"Wait," I called with a laugh, and he slowed as he waited for me to continue. "Finish your press conference, mate. I'll be here waiting for you when you're done."

Kellan blinked, his mouth dropping open in a sexy dip. "Say it again," he whispered, his voice wavering.

I knew exactly what he wanted to hear from me. "Mate. You're my mate, Golden."

He lit up the room, and some of his external warmth crept a little deeper into my heart. "I love you so much, pretty mate. So. Damn. Much. Wait for me. I'll be home soon."

With that, he blew a kiss at the camera and hung up the phone, retaking his seat as if he hadn't just created a frenzy with his dramatic exit.

"Em," Cora choked out as she pressed a hand to her chest. "That was the most romantic thing I've ever seen in my life. I need your alphas to give War a few lessons."

Still feeling overwhelmed and dazed, not to mention filled with the sort of joy I thought only existed in fantasy stories, I tried not to bounce on the spot like a puppy. "Warrick does just fine," I said with a grin, giving her my full attention. I needed a distraction until Kellan returned home. "Now, show me what you're wearing tonight. I'm sure it's going to knock his fur off."

Cora shimmied, her layered skirt swirling around her. "You know it. And I have the perfect dress for you as well."

She dragged me out of the room and away from the television, where two of my mates continued to answer questions in front of the press. *Goddess*. I had it bad when I was reluctant to walk away while they were visible on the screen.

But it was only an issue if I made it one.

Right?

CHAPTER 38

EMME

With bags in hand we headed upstairs. I heard Hunter in his office chatting to someone on the phone, which should give us time to discuss the *thing*.

I'd noted in my brief glance at Slade's stalker wall that there was a corner of my bathroom which appeared to be outside the security footage. The rest, of course, was all there for him to observe, the creepy dragon. Not that I wouldn't have watched him shower if the opportunity presented itself, but that wasn't the point.

The point was, I had a little dead zone to put everything into play.

"How are Richard, Sierra and Marcus?" I asked Cora as we hurried up the stairs. "It feels like forever since I had dinner at your place. What with all the kidnapping and unexpected bonding."

Cora threw her head back and laughed. "You know, what initially drew me to you is your touch of self-deprecation and humor. It's similar to how I deal with trauma."

My snort was filled with disbelief. "All I've done is run from my trauma. Don't be fooled, it absolutely controls me."

She shook her head and pursed her lips, giving the impression she was thinking it over. "You might run from a situation that's outside of your control, like another pack claiming you. But trauma exists internally, and as far as I can tell, you're grounded, realistic, honest, and kind. You haven't let that trauma turn you into an untrusting, bitter shifter. Which it quite easily could have."

Hunter had given me a similar compliment, and honestly, I didn't know how to handle their assessments. It was one thing to be called beautiful, and I enjoyed that as much as any female, but to have them see deeper... no one had ever done that before I met these shifters.

"Thank you," I whispered, feeling choked up and overwhelmed.

Cora didn't appear to need more than that, understanding in her gaze.

When we reached my room, she glanced around at the decor. "This house is incredible," she said brightly. "The trims and detailing on the sconces are perfect with the style of home."

As an interior designer, she no doubt noticed a lot more than I ever had, but I agreed with her. This house was stunning, and I loved it as much as the pack in it. Most of them anyway.

"I'll give you a full tour one day soon," I promised her. "It literally has everything you could want in a dream house."

"And more, I'd bet," Cora said, leaning closer to one of the edges, running her fingers over the engraved details. "These edgings..." She groaned.

With a laugh, I gently shoved her through my door and

into the bathroom. "Come on, show me what you've bought for us to wear."

She patted the bags hanging over her shoulder. "I've got everything we need."

She hung the dresses on one of the towel hooks, before handing me a duffle bag. I backed myself into *the corner* near the shower and gestured for her to do the same. "We're being watched and listened to," I whispered, barely making a sound.

Cora didn't even blink an eye, her response loud. "I brought my full range of *Essence* makeup, and of course, that body spray you love so much."

She gestured for me to open the duffle, and I choked on laughter at the contents. The giant plastic bag was filled with exactly what I'd requested. I was about to become a very minor annoyance to one dragon shifter.

In the bag was a note that I had to slowly read, hoping Cora wouldn't think anything of the time it took. Thankfully she'd written it in large, block letters, which made it easier. *Use the spray to block your scent. It should last about an hour. This is Reeves tech, and the device will briefly knock out the cameras. You'll have ten minutes.*

Slade would notice the security system go down, but I was banking on it taking him longer than ten minutes to get home. More than enough time for my first prank.

Lifting the spray, I quickly doused myself, and when Cora sniffed me, she nodded. "Safe."

I grabbed the device from the duffle next. "It's already connected to this system," she murmured as we both pretended to peer into the bag. "Warrick got Kellan to help, and he said this device would get us where we needed to go. It's patented Reeves tech, and not even out in the world yet."

She spoke so softly that there was no way anyone could overhear, but I remained paranoid as I looked around.

"I knew Kel would be in," I whispered back, "He's been dying to mess with Slade, and believes I'm the only one who'd get away with it."

What I had planned was an inconvenience at best, and nothing that should piss the dragon off into a murder spree. I was at least seventy percent sure of that assessment.

Taking one last fortifying breath, I tucked the plastic bag under my arm and hit the button on the device to scramble the security. Cora met my gaze briefly, and she nodded before shoving me toward the exit.

Out of my room and through the hall, I raced like my ass was on fire. I took the stairs to Slade's room three at a time, attempting to keep my footsteps light so as not to alert Hunter. Like all brilliant, barely thought-out plans, this one had a lot of holes, but it appeared that luck was on my side today. I didn't run into anyone on my way to his room, and the door was unlocked.

Cora had included a kit to pick the lock, but it would have eaten up valuable time. My stealth skills were a little rusty—it'd been years since I'd needed to escape my mom and her pack.

Slade's confidence that no one would overstep his boundaries worked to my advantage, leaving his room open and ready for me to explore. When I stepped into the dark, cool space, I half-expected to hear a blaring alarm, alerting the dragon to my presence, but there was only blessed silence.

The bank of computers caught my attention, and as much as I wanted to have a little peek at what he worked on, my time was limited. Opening the zip lock on the bag, I got to work, placing each of the items into the perfect spot, which would ensure he saw them only when he was lying down ready to sleep.

Once everything was in place, I glanced at the stalker wall, curious if he'd added anything new. There was no time for that either, so I sprinted from his room, ensuring the door was closed behind me. By the time I made it to my bedroom, the device was beeping, which I could only assume meant security was up and running again.

My phone rang right as Hunter slammed open my door and raced inside. "Emme!" he shouted, and I poked my head out of the bathroom, forcing myself to breathe evenly.

"Hunter, what's wrong?" I called back, a faked hint of worry in my tone.

He ran his gaze from the top of my head to my toes, as if searching out an injury. "Slade called and said the security system went down for a few minutes. He rebooted it from his device but wanted me to check on you."

A quick glance at my phone showed Slade had called me too. Six times actually, starting about a minute after I hit that button. "I'm perfectly fine," I told Hunter. "We've just been gossiping and figuring out what to wear tonight. Maybe it was a glitch in the system?"

Hunter stepped closer and peered into the bathroom, relaxing when he found only Cora inside. "Yeah, you're probably right. We'll have to fire the company who installed them."

Okay, Mr. Jokester. "Wasn't that Reeves Industries?"

With his worry fading, Hunter's smile was dark and sexy. "I've heard they've been occupied with their new omega. Might be slipping."

There was absolutely no slipping when it came to anything Hunter touched. "Somehow, I doubt that. They appear to be pretty on top of it all."

He reached out to snatch me up, but I darted out of his grasp. "No," I said, pointing my finger. "I've got to get ready,

Hurricane. You can't distract me, or we won't make it out tonight."

Hunter didn't appear to care in the slightest. "Fine with me. I'd rather keep you to myself anyway."

"Yes, but this is for Kellan too." I shooed him away and he left with a grumbling growl.

Cora's eyes were wide when she met mine in the mirror. "Close," she mouthed.

I nodded, pressing my hand to my chest, pleased that my pulse was relatively normal. Hopefully, Hunter thought the slight elevation in heartrate was just my usual reaction to being around the alphas. Charismatic bastards that they were.

Getting ready ended up being an excellent distraction, and I immediately fell in love with the black and gold dress Cora had for me. "It'll go perfectly with all that gorgeous strawberry-blond hair and tanned skin," she said.

"I think you're as good at designing outfits as you are at designing houses," I said, twirling in front of the mirror, the short skirt flaring around my thighs.

The dress fit perfectly, the top half a bodice with corseted back and thick black straps that tied into bows on my shoulders. Cora curled my hair into loose waves and added heavier makeup than I'd normally wear.

She'd just stepped back to declare me perfect when I heard Kellan and Finley arriving home.

Noise picked up on the lower level, and I recognized a few voices: Warrick, Kenzo, and Christian for starters—along with other unfamiliar males. Possibly more of the team.

Slade had texted me after I'd missed his calls advising that he would see me tonight at Luxuria, and that next time I'd better answer my damn phone. *Bossy fucker.*

"Okay, you ready to drop those alphas' jaws to the floor,"

Cora said, doing her own little twirl, her lavender silk dress floating nicely around her body. We both wore heels, though mine were in the form of little black boots and hers were purple stilettos.

"You did an amazing job glamming me. This dress is so perfect that I want to be buried in it, okay?" I looked around for what I needed to bring and asked, "Should we grab coats?"

Cora shook her head as she left the bathroom. "Nah, I don't want to cover these gorgeous dresses. We'll go from the car to the club in seconds." Our metabolisms kept us warm most of the year, though mine was never quite as efficient as other shifters.

In the black wrist purse Cora provided with the dress, I added my phone, a lipstick for touchups, and cash. Hunter had left a bunch of cards on my side table earlier, and I eyed the shiny Amex sitting amongst many other shiny credit cards, all with my name on them. I wasn't quite ready for that part of pack life yet, but it was nice to know they were there in case of an emergency.

At the top of the stairs, laughter and rumbling voices grew louder, and I tried to ignore the flutter of butterflies in my stomach. This was a night to celebrate and count our goddess-given blessings that we were alive and together.

The Rogers pack might be out there, hiding behind their council, but we'd eventually figure out how to take them down. I should have made them pay years ago for what they did to Mom. Not because she deserved revenge, but to stop them from ever hurting another shifter. By staying quiet, I'd allowed them to continue in the world, wreaking destruction and havoc.

I shuddered to imagine what they'd been up to in the last ten years.

"Are you okay?" Cora asked, and I realized I was clutching the railing at the top of the stairs, lost in my darker thoughts.

"Oh. Yeah." I shook my head and loosened my grip. "Sorry, got lost in the past for a second there. I think I need a drink."

She linked her arm through mine. "You and me both, girl. Come on, let's get our guys."

With the first click of our heels on the step, the noise cut off below, and a crowd of giant males made their way to the base of the stairs to wait for us.

Warrick stood front and center, his eyes wide and his smile wider as he dragged his gaze over Cora, eating her up with eyes that were liquid pools of darkness. "That's exactly how a mate should look at you," I murmured.

She released a few heavy pants before nodding. "My alpha certainly has a way with non-verbal communication."

"He does—"

Hunter and Kellan pushed in through the crowd, and I was seized by a pair of hungry gazes. Kellan had his hand pressed to his chest, jaw slightly unhinged as he stared up at me. I took in his blue button-down shirt and black slacks, and felt my heartbeat quicken. Whenever I saw him dressed up, it all but took my breath away. Goddess above... he was stunning.

The lights from the foyer highlighted the gold in his blond hair, casting a glow over my golden boy. He watched me as if I were beyond his belief, a sight he never expected to encounter and had no idea how to process. It was enough to have me stumble over my own feet.

Then there was Hunter, whose predatory stare had my breaths coming out even faster than Cora's.

The darkly handsome shifter wore an inscrutable expression. His eyes blazed with gold, and he looked... ravenous. Hunter was also dressed nicely in a black button-down and slacks, his hair tousled and ready for me to run my hands through it.

With a sudden lurch forward, he stalked up the stairs, and I was frozen to the spot, locked in the stare of a predator.

CHAPTER 39

EMME

Hunter hauled me up into his arms, hands tight on my ass as he charged up the stairs, and I swore I heard Cora's laughter following us. I found myself pressed against the wall just out of sight, with a background symphony of Kellan's rumbling growls as he warned the others to *shut the fuck up*. There were shuffles and mumbles as the crowd dispersed.

The pack didn't really let outsiders into their house much, and I doubted this group would make it past the front foyer.

Hunter buried his face against my throat, biting down into the skin, and I let out a low shriek, but he didn't break through. It was another one of those temporary claims, situated on the opposite side of Kellan's permanent one. "Mine," he snapped, his chest heaving. "You can't go out looking like that tonight without my claim on you."

My core clenched on nothing as my hips surged forward, desperately searching for any sort of friction to ease the need, but Hunter had me pinned thoroughly, his massive frame holding me in place. "Hunter," I moaned, my voice growing harder as I demanded, "Make me come."

His face remained buried against my skin, and I swore he let out a low laugh. "I like when you use your words, little omega. Makes me want to give you exactly what you demand. While also leaving me with a need to punish you for your smart mouth. It's a quandary."

"Is it though?" I gasped, half out of my mind. "You can easily do both."

He rocked back, and I was left panting and staring up into black eyes. There was no chance to catch my breath as he reached out in a slow, deliberate movement and grasped the edge of my thong. When he jerked his hand, my panties tore right off me, and I gawped as he tucked the destroyed lace into his pocket.

His hand slid between us again, his roughened fingers stroking gently over my clit, and I gripped his shoulders to keep myself steady.

"You want to be punished, baby girl?" he whispered in a dangerous tone that was a warning I was about to ignore. I was too far gone to care about the *consequences of my actions.*

I needed whatever he was offering.

He lifted his hand and lightly slapped my pussy, and I jerked with a moan, surprised at how fucking good that felt. This time I was sure of his laughter as he kissed me, lips moving against mine, his tongue dominating as it drove into my mouth.

I cried out as he slapped me again, closer to my clit this time, and I felt a burst of release that wasn't even an orgasm yet. Pure arousal slid down the top of my thighs. I was a desperate, shaky, needy mess.

"You are going to smell like sex and pack, little omega," Hunter rumbled, sounding pleased with himself. He slid two fingers inside me and curled them. When he added a third, his thick fingers stretched me to the point of pleasure-pain, and I... came so hard my head slammed against the wall.

Hunter didn't stop there, his hand continued to pump into my body, slower as I moved through my orgasm, and then faster, until I was gasping and gripping his shoulders. The last orgasm was never ending, and more than that, it built to an intensity that could quite possibly kill me. At least, that was how it felt. I wanted it to build though—I never wanted this touch and pleasure to stop.

Oh, goddess. I needed Hunter's destruction.

"Eyes on me," Hunter commanded, and my gaze jerked up to meet the tumultuous storm of his. "Watching you fall apart is the best sight of my existence," he whispered, the deep rasp of his voice adding more stimulation.

My gasping moans grew louder and louder, and not that we'd been quiet before, but no one in this house would be unaware of what was happening up here.

"Come for me," Hunter directed again, and my screaming orgasm burst from me until my head spun and I lost control. I almost faltered on our eye contact, but somehow, I found myself clinging to his gaze and those flares of addictive gold.

"That's my good girl," Hunter growled, pressing kisses to the corners of my lips. "Such a good girl, coming so prettily for me."

His fingers continued to stroke perfectly inside me, and then over my clit when he eventually slid them free. "You... your pants," I huffed, breathless and boneless.

It was hard to tell on the black material, but I had soaked him.

Hunter smirked as he brought his hand to his mouth and slid his tongue over my release. I found myself mesmerized by the pink length lapping at my cum. "I get to wear your scent all over me tonight," he said throatily. "Almost as good as a claiming bite."

After he'd finished tasting me, he steadied me on my booted feet, my legs weak and wobbly. "Do you need me…?" I gestured to the massive erection tenting his black slacks, hoping he'd say yes.

Hunter wrapped an arm around me, and before I knew it, we were heading for the stairs. "I'm more than satisfied, and we'll be late if we don't leave soon. I know you're looking forward to this night, and I want you to have the full experience."

Hunter Reeves, my secret knight in shining suits.

"What about underwear?" I asked, my bare thighs brushing, my release still sticky.

Hunter paused, as if debating, before he finally nodded. "If anyone caught a glimpse of you without them, Emme, I'd have to murder that shifter where he stood. Let's save the bloodshed for another time."

He stayed with me as I dashed on wobbly legs to my room, and when I went to slide on another thong, Hunter grasped them out of my hand and to my utter fucking shock, knelt before me. He held the lace out, his hooded gaze dark and locked on my face. My heart slammed in my chest as I automatically lifted one boot and then the other, unable to believe what was happening.

Hunter maneuvered the underwear to fit over my boots, and then slowly slid the lace up my bare legs. His eyes never left my face, and even on his knees he was massive.

With a final graze of his fingers over my core, he gracefully rose, and I tried to calm myself, though we could both hear the racing of my heart.

"They're waiting for us," Hunter said, in a deep rasp. "Come on."

My head spun at the implications of what Hunter had done, and we were silent as we exited my room and made our way to the foyer. Entitled alphas knelt for no one; it was pretty much part of the package. They submitted themselves to no one, standing as the head of the pack.

But he'd knelt for me. There was no mistaking his actions.

I just didn't know what to make of it.

Downstairs, we found all the guys and Cora climbing into a row of black Escalades, there to take us to the club. Each car had a driver, dressed in black suits, holding open the doors. Most of the hockey bros minus our friends and core group filled the first few vehicles.

"Don't you smell, delicious," Kellan said as he hurried over and spun me around, planting a heavy kiss on my lips. "And you look like a fucking goddess. More than that. You would put the goddess to shame."

"Shush, don't insult the gods," I said with a choked laugh, giving the sky a quick glance like *Forsana* or *Hecatana*, the goddesses of shifters and the lunar cycle, were about to smite him where he stood. I didn't exactly worship in the old ways, but I appreciated the sentiment, and tried never to bring disfavor from the deities. "But thank you. Cora did an amazing job."

Hunter's chest rumbled, and his mirth held a hint of derision. "It has nothing to do with Cora or makeup."

When he lifted his hand and brushed his thumb over my cheeks, I could smell myself on his skin, and fuck, it was a turn on. Kellan's nostrils flared as he chuckled too. "A very nice scent."

Hunter ignored him as he continued to rub away the powder over my nose and cheeks, even though I'd told Cora to use a light touch. "Much better."

"My freckles." Kellan's laughter faded into a sigh. "I swear, when I'm not kissing my way along all the delicious connect-the-dots on your body, I dream about them."

It hadn't escaped my notice that Kellan enjoyed kissing his way between my freckles. By now, he had my whole body mapped out. Not that I was complaining.

"Come on, lovebirds," Cora shouted, half hanging out of the last car. "You can obsess over her gorgeous butt when you get home."

"Oh, that's a certainty," Kellan replied, sliding his hand down my body and over my ass. "I'll be obsessing every day for the rest of eternity."

I remained flushed and breathless even once we were seated in the middle row, the two massive alphas on either side of me. Cora, Warrick, and Finley were in this car as well, the mated pair squished in the back, and the bear shifter taking the passenger side.

My gaze met Finley's as he turned, and for once he didn't scowl at me. He wasn't smiling either, but his expression remained neutral, and I held on to a small hope that for tonight we could pretend everything was okay in the pack.

The wink. I still had no idea what to make of it, so I shoved it deep inside and locked the lid on that memory. For now.

It was a twenty-minute drive to Luxuria, and in that time the conversation centered around hockey and how fucked up some of the plays had been. When they moved on to the first scheduled winter pack run on Tuesday, Cora leaned forward and said, "You have to be there, Emme. There'll be hundreds of us out for the first snowfall exploration. It's my favorite run of the year."

"I'll be there," I assured her, already excited by the prospect. My wolf had been desperate for a run with more of the city's packs, and this sounded like the perfect opportunity. Add in the snow for us to frolic, and I was bouncing like a pup.

"Wait, do we still need to meet with the council tomorrow?" I asked, angling myself toward Hunter to read his expression.

He had an annoying habit of dropping shit on me at the last minute and giving me little time to mentally prepare. I presumed it was his way of taking the bulk of the worry and preparation, but I couldn't always play the helpless female omega letting her alphas deal with life. Occasionally, I needed to be the one who handled my own problems, especially when it pertained to the fucking Rogers pack.

Warrick released a low, warm laugh, as if he already knew the answer, but I didn't remove my focus from Hunter. "The meeting is scheduled, but I'm not sure it's worth showing up," he said with a shrug that sent me into Kellan. "I was going to wait and discuss it with you in the morning."

"What he actually said," Warrick began, his voice still filled with humor, and I had a feeling we were about to learn why he'd laughed, "was to shove their orders up their asses and not to bother his fucking pack again until they worked out a satisfactory consequence for the Rogers pack."

"Which is death," Kellan grumbled, his arm wrapped around my shoulders from where he'd steadied me a second ago. "I'll accept nothing less."

Hunter nodded, as if that settled it. "Anyway, let's not discuss that shit tonight. Tonight is about freeing your beast and having fun. No one will ruin this for Emme."

Hunter's way of showing he cared was different to Kellan's, but both made me feel... *everything*. It was frankly terrifying. How did shifters just wander around with all of these emotions spilling out them like a leaking faucet? It couldn't be natural.

The vehicle came to a halt, and I glanced out the darkened window to the familiar entrance of Luxuria, with its red carpet and gold-tinted, cathedral architecture. There were dozens of shifters standing in line, waiting for entry, and I wasn't surprised by its popularity. The interior was just as stunning, with gold chandeliers, red velvet, runners on the floor, and drinks that were more than a generous pour.

Of course, no one made us wait as we strolled along the red carpet, and it didn't escape my notice how the shifters in line stared at the alphas, taking photos on their phones like they'd run into celebrities.

When Kellan and Hunter closed in on either side of me, linking my hands in theirs, there were shouts of my name. I didn't turn to the crowd; Hunter had told me not to engage with them, and I chose to follow his orders. I'd like to say *for once*, but so far he hadn't demanded anything I wasn't happy to comply with. I'd never felt the need to rebel for the sake of it —the very thought was exhausting.

"Wait," Cora called, stopping us in the candelabra-lit entrance, the heavy beat of the music pulsing behind us. "Let's get a photo."

She pulled out her phone, and Hunter and Kellan pressed in even closer to either side of me, until I felt heated and breathless at their scent and energy surrounding me so thoroughly. Cora sighed and started to snap away.

"You too, Finley," she ordered after a few more photos, and I barely managed not to glare at her. It helped no one to keep forcing our proximity, especially if poking the bear brought out the grouch. Chilled-out Finley was my favorite Finley.

To my surprise, he just offered a brief smile and stepped in on the other side of Kellan.

"Perfect," Cora gushed as she snapped a dozen or more pictures. "You four are far too attractive to be in one pack. It's criminal, really."

Warrick smirked as he wrapped his arm around her

shoulder. "Love, you're one to talk. Your beauty has no comparison."

She scoffed at him, but I could tell she was pleased, as her pretty face lit up. "Thank you, mate. You'll be rewarded for that later."

His eyes darkened as he leaned in to kiss her lips, and she returned that kiss before jumping away. "Oh, I need a photo with Emme. Besties must take at least one photo together a year. It's the rule."

She handed her phone to Warrick and hurried over to me. The alphas were slow to move from my side—except for Finley, who'd already headed into the club. I noticed him make his way to Christian, who was perched against the stunning mahogany bar that ran the full length of the wall.

"Smile," Cora cheered, and I returned my attention to my friend, laughing as Warrick jumped around pretending to be a professional photographer as he took the photos.

"Cora will message them to you," he said as he handed her device across. "I have no idea how to share from that model."

His mate nudged him playfully. "You and your old school tech. It's almost as if you didn't live in the cities your whole life. I swear you have the heart of alphas who existed in the wild in tiny packs hidden from humanity."

"I'll show you a wild alpha," he growled playfully. He scooped her into his arms and strode across the club, disappearing in the darkness.

It was dimly lit inside, the array of chandeliers adding a soft golden light. As a new song started, my hips shook to the beat, and Kellan placed his hand in the small of my back. "Come on, baby. Let's get you a drink. I need to dance with my mate."

"Ours," Hunter told him. "Say it with me, annoying pup. She's ours."

Kellan shot him his brightest grin. "Aw, come on, Daddy Alpha. You know I'm a good sharer. There's plenty of Emmeline to go around."

I tapped him *hard* on the shoulder. "Please, never reference our shared sexual relations in that way again. Otherwise, you'll be sleeping in the doghouse."

He sobered a touch. "Is it weird for you? Being in a multiple mates situation? We've never really discussed it, but I mean… outside of your mom, you wouldn't have much reference for this sort of dynamic in the human world, right?"

It hadn't felt weird to me, not even for a second. "I think there's been such a natural progression of our emotional connection that the sexual part has fit in just as seamlessly." My voice was quiet, and the music was loud, but both alphas heard me. "I can't imagine being in a pack any other way."

"We're meant to be," Hunter agreed, his nod decisive. "Always have been. Always will be. Nothing more right than that."

As much as I wanted to argue the point, I couldn't. This pack was nothing like my mother's, and that was reason enough for me to start trusting in the bonding process.

My omega energy might even be safe with them.

For the first time, I was willing to risk it all to find out.

CHAPTER 40

EMME

I'd never been inside Luxuria when it wasn't packed to capacity, and tonight was no different.

Half the town was out to either celebrate the Celtics' win or commiserate the Dashers' loss. Either way, the drinks flowed, and the music moved from one dance beat to the next, mixing between fast and slower sensual numbers.

In the VIP section, the couches generally cost a few grand a night, but on the main floor there were tables where you could hang out for free. Nothing these alphas did was ever exclusive to the rich and connected, ensuring a portion remained accessible to all.

For billionaires, the Reeves pack were surprisingly grounded.

From what I knew, Kellan and Finley hadn't grown up rich, and Hunter and Slade had grown up with an asshole of a "father", all of which had shaped them into the alphas they were today.

Alphas I happened to like very much.

"What do you want to drink, Shortcake?" Kellan asked as we claimed one of the VIP couches. A red velvet sectional wrapped around us, and there were a few plush chairs opposite the small table in the middle. "The world is yours to command," he added, waving his hand to encompass the room, "and we have all the shifter serums and additives to ensure whatever buzz you're after."

"Uh…" Outside of wine, I wasn't much of a drinker, and it felt reckless to lose control tonight, especially when I teetered on the edge of begging Hunter to seal our bond. "Maybe wine to start. Something sweet."

Kellan dropped a kiss on my cheek. "You got it. I'll be back in a minute."

Others called out their orders as well, and Kellan nodded as he strolled toward the second, slightly smaller mahogany bar, which curved into a large horseshoe shape around the VIP area.

There was table service here, of course, and we'd already had Hadley, a tiger shifter I'd worked with before, come by to welcome us. But when I'd been his server, I'd noticed that Kellan often ordered his drinks at the bar while chatting to his friend Jimmy. The head bartender was a blond, burly beta wolf who took no shit and could mix cocktails faster than I'd ever seen before.

The music shifted to a new song with a slower beat, the bass settling in my chest as I leaned into Hunter, whose arm was slung over my shoulder. As I relaxed fully, he pulled me straight up onto his lap, expelling a small huff from me at that unexpected move.

Across from us, perched in her own mate's lap, Cora grinned and waggled her eyebrows at me. She loved when these alphas went all possessive. According to her, no one had ever seen them act this way, and it was definitely stoking the city's curiosity.

Warrick's fingers traced across her bare shoulders, and of

all the new experiences and knowledge I'd gained during my time here, my favorite was seeing how true quintets and scent matches acted together. Whatever my mom and her pack had going on was wrong and toxic. It pissed me off to no end that I'd spent years believing that was the norm. It almost cost me everything. It almost cost me the chance to know my mates.

The thought of never meeting the Reeves pack sent sharp pains into my chest, and for a brief second I couldn't breathe through the panic.

Hunter felt the new tension in my body and wrapped his arms tighter, pulling me firmly against him until I had no choice but to sink into his hold. His hand traced along the outside of my thigh, bringing my focus to his touch and *how damn good it felt.*

"No more thinking, baby girl," he murmured, breath caressing my cheek. "Enjoy the moment. This is your night, and I will fuck up anyone who upsets you."

Ironic when I was the one upsetting myself, but his soothing touch and soft words did help calm me. Hunter had an uncanny knack of knowing what to say and do to bring me back to myself. I was completely fucking gone on this alpha.

There was no point in denying it, and as badly as I wanted to spin on his lap and straddle him, I couldn't here, which meant I needed a new focus.

Across the table, Finley sat next to Kenzo, Vanessa, Luce, and Christian. The rest of the team were at nearby tables—this entire area was pretty much dominated by the hockey team tonight. Some had their mates with them, but for the most part, the boys were celebrating their win.

Hunter slid his hand higher on my thigh, lifting the edge of my dress, right as Finley's gaze snapped in my direction. The bear shifter's expression remained neutral... but his eyes drowned me in their whiskey depths. Between his gaze and Hunter's touch, I was about to detonate.

"You're wiggly," Hunter mused, his tone light. "What's wrong, little omega? Do you have a need to share with me?"

This asshole knew exactly what he was doing, and there was no way he'd missed Finley's focused stare on us. "No idea what you're talking about," I rasped. "Maybe it's just that your overabundance of muscles isn't that comfortable."

Hunter's laughter was low and satisfied. "Oh, I think you enjoy my *overabundance* of muscles, Emmeline. You certainly weren't complaining when I used said muscles to hold you high enough in the shower to eat your pussy."

Heat flared in my cheeks, and I coughed to cover up my shock. Just the mention of Hunter and a shower had me squeezing my thighs together. I noticed Finley's nostrils flare, the honey depths of his eyes darkening. My scent match had not missed my burst of arousal as he continued to watch me, that tinge of darkness and curiosity playing in his gaze.

Kellan interrupted whatever fucked-up foreplay was happening here, grinning as he caught sight of me perched in Hunter's lap. The tray laden with drinks was deposited on the table as he headed straight for me.

Leaning down, he nuzzled into my throat. "You smell like fucking nirvana, pretty mate. I need to eat you right up or I'm going to die."

Hunter snorted, and removed his hand from my waist to shove Kellan away. "Hold the dramatics, pup," he ordered. "This is just the prequel. Let our omega have a chance to relax before we devour her."

Kellan pouted, but complied as he dropped down beside Hunter, reaching out to thread his fingers through mine. To my surprise, Finley was the one who leaned forward and handed us our drinks so we didn't have to leave our cozy cuddle.

For a second, as he passed me my wine, he eyed up the empty spot on the other side of Hunter, as if he contemplated sitting there too. He didn't, of course, and I shook my head at that ridiculous notion. "Thanks," I mumbled, confusion slipping out. To cover it up, I took a large gulp of the fruity, sweet wine. Finley nodded as he held up his beer like a toast, and that was the last time he looked at me all night.

After an hour, Kellan dragged me off Hunter's lap to dance on the main floor, and when Slade showed up a few hours later, we were still drinking and dancing. The dragon, in his black enforcer outfit, downed two whiskeys in minutes.

He was terrifyingly beautiful, and my currently tipsy brain had me *almost* crawling into his lap where he sat, his long legs and thick thighs relaxed in front of him. Fuck a wolf.

This was why I couldn't let myself get drunk.

Slade watched me closely, but didn't invite my touch. He never reached for me, but fuck, that heavy stare felt like it covered my skin and burrowed into my essence. Still, there was no doubt that invading his space to crawl into his lap would either get me thrown to the floor or there'd be a scaly beast destroying the club.

"Emmmmmeeeeeeee," Cora shouted, swaying into me on the dance floor. She'd danced as much as me, and was as disheveled as I'd ever seen her, curls everywhere and her dress hanging off one shoulder. "We have time for one last dance."

I took her proffered hand without hesitation, even as my feet ached and my head swirled from the copious drinks. As exhausted as I was, nothing in the world would stop me from having this last dance with my friend.

She pushed me back out onto the main floor, but no one touched us, already understanding that to do so would incur the wrath of our alphas. It had really made our time here tonight run smoothly.

As we danced, I marveled at how much I'd enjoyed hanging out with Cora tonight. It was intoxicating, really, to have a real friend. One I could share my life with and never feel judged. She might not fully understand my reasons for holding out on my pack, but that was my fault, and hopefully one day soon I could share it all with her.

"You might be my soulmate too," I said, draping my arms around her shoulders. "Platonic soulmates are highly underrated."

"They totally are," Cora agreed, flinging her head back as she twirled around me. "Besties for life. We'll be two hundred years old and I'm going to be glamming your ass and telling you how pretty you are."

Tilting my head back I laughed, drunk enough to forget my worries and feel all the joy and happiness. "You're the one who is stunning. I don't know how Warrick lets you leave the house most days."

This set Cora off; she bent and laughed until she cried, tiny streaks of makeup lining her cheeks. "You know what, some days he doesn't." I wasn't remotely surprised by this truth.

"It's nice seeing you like this," I noted, amused by her rare lack of refinement. "You just feel so... free."

Cora spun, arms held out on either side of her. "I think that's the true beauty of my mate bond."

She slowed and lifted her head to seek out Warrick, who stood at the railing of the VIP level beside Hunter, Kellan and Slade. The four of them watched over us on the main floor, just as they'd done every time we'd danced without them.

We both knew they'd be here in seconds if needed, which was half the point Cora made.

Her whole face softened as she stared at her mate. "It's a privilege to have a mate at your back and know that it's an unconditional support. When I'm with War, I don't even look over my shoulder. I could walk along the path with my head buried in my phone, headphones on, my mind in the middle of a daydream, and know I'm safe. War allows me to find strength in other ways that have nothing to do with survival. I do the same for him as well, giving him a soft place to come home to."

"Isn't it terrifying though?" I asked, words grating against my dry throat.

My gaze roved over the alphas, and when I pressed my hand to the bite on my shoulder, Kellan mimicked the movement, his expression soft. "It scares me to know that I could tie my happiness to another." *Or four others.* "They could betray my trust at any point and completely tear me to pieces."

Cora grasped my hand and squeezed it tightly. "That's the part that makes it so special. They *can* tear you to pieces. They could easily do it, actually, but they choose not to. Every single day they choose to put you first, and after a few years, you learn that it's not an act. It's the real alpha, and he would burn the world for you."

I want that. It was a sudden and ferocious thought.

My heart bled at the very thought of losing this pack. "I'm not sure I'll ever let go enough to truly trust in a pack," I admitted, undecided if this was still my truth or not.

"I know, and with your past, that's understandable. My only advice is to let yourself believe in fate and your mates. The rest will work itself out."

Put like that, it sounded simple, but she didn't know everything. When I spilled the full truth of my past to the alphas and Cora, their advice might be different.

When the song ended, lights slowly lit up the edges of the room, reminding everyone that it was time to start heading their drunk, happy asses home.

Warrick, Kellan, Hunter, and Slade appeared, blocking us from the shifters exiting the club. "You have fun, pretty mate?"

Kellan asked, brushing back a strand of hair plastered down my sweaty cheek. The curls had fallen out long ago, and I had no doubt I looked a mess, but you'd never know from his expression.

"So much fun," I trilled, sadly sobering up already. "Though I will be glad to get out of these heels. My feet are killing me—"

I choked as Hunter, for the second time tonight, lowered himself into a half-kneel crouch before me. He gestured for me to lift my foot. "Come on, baby girl," he murmured. "Let me help."

An entitled alpha does not kneel.

But he had.

There was no denying it this time. I almost fell to my own knees in front of him and begged him to take me. Fuck waiting for my birthday; I couldn't wait another damn second. My wolf howled in my chest, scraping against the hold I had on her.

Hunter's nostrils flared as he stared at me, the drowning darkness of his eyes hypnotic.

Slowly, feeling dazed, I lifted my right foot, and Hunter slid the small zip down on my boot before removing it. He ran his thumb over the arch of my socked foot, and I closed my eyes at how good that felt.

When he released me, I dropped my foot on the floor, which was no doubt gross as fuck, but who really cared. When he removed my left boot, my feet screamed in happy relief. Hunter tossed the boots over his shoulder, letting them clatter across his empty club floor. *Shit.* I'd have to figure out how to get them back for Cora—not that she appeared remotely worried, too busy gawking at Hunter.

My entitled alpha's expression exuded a sliver of darkness as he stood and swept me into his arms, cradling me against his chest as he headed for the exit. "I can walk," I said with a nervous chuckle. Did I really want to get down? Nope. But I had to at least make an attempt at independence.

"There might be broken glass," he said, tone brooking no argument. "I won't let you get hurt, little omega. Not now. Not ever."

Damn him.

This alpha was getting lucky tonight, and I would beg for his claim before the sun rose.

My days of denying Hunter were done.

CHAPTER 41

HUNTER

Her wolf was vibrating, fighting harder than I'd felt in a while. My beast howled back, ready to claim its mate. I might have accepted Kellan being the first to bond due to sheer necessity—saving my brother's life trumped everything else. But the fact that I still hadn't claimed my mate was a restless energy inside me. An energy that grew worse every day.

We were on the way home, but there was no fucking way I'd rest tonight without a run. My wolf was determined to tear the compound to pieces, so I directed Marco, our driver, toward the forest. "I need to run," I told him, my beast heavy in those words.

Emme's head shot up from where she'd been resting against Kellan's shoulder, almost asleep.

"On your own?" she asked, concern lacing her sweet tone.

I'd never had anyone other than my brothers give a shit about me before, but Emme had stormed into our lives, sassed the hell out of us, and then started caring. *Seeing us* with her ethereal blue eyes. It messed with my control, and tonight I was too on edge to risk returning to the pack house.

"Yeah, my beast is restless. I need to free him before he makes a mess that I'm forced to clean up."

As entitled alpha, I'd learned control and how to harness my power but this was an exceptional circumstance. An exceptionally adorable, freckled, frustratingly sexy circumstance.

"I'll come with you," she declared suddenly, any fatigue she'd shown vanishing as she sat straighter.

My beast howled, and it was all satisfaction unfurling through my chest. "You want to run with me?"

She nodded, a determined glint in her eyes. "Yes, I've always loved a night run, but it's never been safe enough."

At this stage, it was an early morning run, but we'd have darkness for a few more hours.

"I would love to—" Kellan piped up, but when my gaze slammed into him, hard and unyielding, he cleared his throat. "*Never mind.*"

The deep menacing sound that had filled the car faded as I calmed. Our annoying pup had figured out that this was my time with Emme. Running with our omega would be my only way to find peace.

"Okay, little omega," I said, my chest heating as I drawled her nickname. Emme's lips parted and her heartrate picked up, which was a usual occurrence when I called her *little omega.* "We will run together. You and me."

Forever, baby girl.

"I'll send the squads around the perimeter," Slade said as he turned in the passenger seat. "No one will enter the forest while you let your beasts free."

I'd tear anyone apart who even glanced in her direction, but I couldn't be too confident after those fuckers stole her out from under Slade. They'd clearly studied our pack and knew who they were up against. For that sole reason alone, I'd allow the extra patrols and males in the vicinity of my mate.

When Emmeline Anders had first appeared in Golden Claw, my focus was on bringing her into the pack and securing our quintet. I wanted to control her, claim her, provide for her… because she was pack.

I was a fucking idiot.

Knowing her now, having her in our lives, I couldn't remember how we'd existed without her for all these years. Emme brought warmth, light, and a sense of home to my world.

My parents were the worst of our kind, and living under their command was the darkest of my days. Slade kept me from spiraling at first. Then I found my pack and threw myself into that responsibility. Still, the darkness of my youth remained.

Until Emme. My perfect mate.

A mate as essential to my existence as food, water, air, and sunlight.

I would never let her go now. *Never.*

She'd have been more hesitant to run alone with me if she knew the lengths I'd go to keep her with me forever—the ferality of my thoughts when I considered a life without her.

The restless demons would only ever be sated by one shifter now. Poor Emme.

When we reached the forest, Kellan planted a long kiss on her lips, leaving her dazed as she stumbled from the car. "Have fun, kids," he called after us with a smirk. "Don't do anything I wouldn't do."

Emme turned her wide, gorgeous eyes on me as she stared like I was her fucking god. The satisfaction and awe I felt at being able to claim and be claimed by this stunning female was overwhelming.

"I can't tell if you're going to run or let me devour you," I murmured, and when her lips parted, breaths harshly grating from her mouth, my cock jerked in my pants as the predator inside rose for the hunt.

Oh, little omega. You will beg me, and then I'm going to claim every inch of you.

My wolf howled, sending my chest rumbling, and when I held my hand out for her, she didn't hesitate to take it. Her instinctive response to this pack had changed dramatically from the first time we met, when she'd been standoffish and skittish. Tonight, there was trust in her gaze as her wolf and emotions opened to our pack.

Very soon, she'd wear all our bites. Even Finley's. The bear shifter spent more time than he'd ever admit watching the omega, analyzing her every action. She upset the status quo for him, disturbed his hard-fought peace. He'd fucked up more than once in the early stages of their relationship, and while it would take him time to earn her forgiveness, I had no doubt it would happen eventually. I didn't fail at anything in life, and securing our quintet wouldn't be the place I started.

Emme shivered as flurries of sleety snow fell onto her bare arms. "Give us your phones and gear," Kellan said, leaning through the door. "We'll be back at dawn to pick you up."

I handed him my phone, and Emme held out her little bag. Kellan shot her a warm smile and wink as he took them, and then he closed the door.

The vehicle pulled away, leaving me alone with my mate, the dimly lit forest our backdrop. "I'm surprised you wanted to run with me," I said, unbuttoning my shirt. "Out here, all alone, with no one to hear you scream."

Teasing her was my new favorite hobby, and I wondered how she'd take that statement. The screams I spoke of had nothing to do with pain, and I was sure she understood my meaning.

She stepped toward me, her socked feet already wet, and I was hit with the urge to get her into her wolf form before she got any colder. "Maybe I don't want them to hear me scream," she murmured, pressing her tiny hand against my bare chest. A spark of energy and warmth passed between us and my cock kicked even harder.

"Maybe," she continued, leaning down to press her lips to the very spot her hand had just warmed. "I'm curious to see what big bad Hunter Reeves does when he has me all to himself."

Oh, she had no idea the inferno she'd just ignited. My poor, precious little omega.

Leaning down, I cupped her face with my right hand, scraping over her soft cheeks until I collared her throat. The tattoo sent a shot of satisfaction through me and my beast. *Mine.* "I'm going to give you a five-minute head start, baby," I murmured, tasting her sweet lips, barely stopping myself from tearing her dress off her luscious curves.

"Head start for what?" she replied breathlessly, pupils dilated.

My wolf pushed at me leaving my words rougher. "To escape me. I'm going to chase with the intent to claim you, Emmeline Anders. I'm going to hunt you through this forest." Her breath caught as she licked her lips and watched me like I was the only thing she could see. *Fucking intoxicating.* "If I catch you before the sun shows up, then you will beg for my claim, and I will take you in the forest against the most ancient tree in the area. One of the western redcedars that were here long before Golden Claw, where the blood of our ancestors run."

Her pupils blew out as she panted. "And… if you don't catch me?"

There wasn't a chance in hell that would happen, but letting her think she had a real shot only added to the thrill. "If you manage to hide from me, without leaving this forest, I will give you whatever you want. With no limitations."

"What if I still want to escape?" she whispered, and for the first time I was sure she didn't mean it.

"Sorry, little omega. That's non-negotiable, and will never happen. You can't leave Kellan, even if you wanted to. Which I know you don't."

She didn't try to lie or argue that truth. "Okay, Hurricane Hunter. You have a deal. You give me a head start, and if I stay out of your grasp, you'll owe me a huge favor. Without limitations, except for not leaving permanently."

It wouldn't matter. She'd barely last the five minutes head start, so I could agree to anything. "It's a deal."

Emme looked pleased with herself as she jumped away, as if she was going to undress herself. *Oh no, sweetheart. Not a chance.*

When I stalked toward her, she backed away until her ass hit the railing that separated the parking lot from the forest. Her expression remained calm and open as I reached for her, and there was no rejection in her gaze. With slow, deliberate movements, I pulled the ties on her shoulders and loosened each strap. She turned without prompting, presenting the laces that secured the back of her dress.

Slowly, taking my time, I unraveled and loosened the bodice until the entire top fell from her body. Emme made no move to catch it, comfortable enough to bare her breasts to me and the icy darkness. I'd devoured her body enough times now to know perfection didn't remotely come close to describing Emmeline.

I reached out to cup her full, heavy breasts, pink nipples puckered in the cold and under my gliding touch. It was the same pink as her pretty pussy, and fuck, this omega was just pretty all over.

Through sheer force of will I released her and finished the process of stripping her dress away.

When she was naked, the long lengths of her limbs gleaming in the low light, she shifted into her white wolf. Her beast quickly shook off the change, and I noted how well she blended into the wintery forest.

There'd been no white wolves where I grew up. No omegas in our area, no matter how hard my father searched for them. He'd been obsessed with omegas and dragons, and I still had no fucking clue why. Why did he care more about two outliers of the shifter world when he had sons and a daughter who needed him? When I'd first changed our name and moved to Golden Claw, I'd expected him to fight. Not just to keep me but also Slade, his greatest discovery.

But he never did.

Keeping Emme away was a new priority for more reason than one, and if I had to kill that old bastard to ensure he never touched my omega, then I'd do so without regret.

"Run, Emme," I ordered as she pranced on the snow. "Your five minutes start now."

With a yip and then a quick howl, she took off into the forest, and I lurched forward, instinct guiding me to follow. With squads patrolling the forest perimeter, we were as safe as we'd ever be. Still, it was a risk to have her on her own. Already, I'd stripped off the last of my clothes, prepared to bolt as soon as the five minutes were up.

After I placed our items into one of the wooden boxes set here for personal items, my beast rose to the surface. We shifted fast, a base, animalistic nature to our thoughts.

I threw my head back and howled long and loud into the night as a warning to anyone out there who might be hovering in the darkness, debating if they should touch what was mine.

Touch her and die was my new motto.

The howl was also a tiny warning to my omega. The predator inside me was about to hunt her, and then she would be claimed.

CHAPTER 42

EMME

Hunter's warning howl rang out in the distance, and it spurred me on faster. My body was nimble as a wolf, and smaller than Hunter's beast, which was why I chose the most overgrown, least accessible part of the forest to escape into.

He'd made it clear that there was no chance I'd outlast him in this primal chase, but I wouldn't give up without a fight.

As I barreled deeper into the forest, my surroundings grew darker, the natural light eliminated by a heavier canopy. My wolf's sight was strong enough to keep us from getting into too much trouble, and it was both soothing and a touch unnerving to hear only my panting and the soft pattering of paws over the icy ground.

The few rabbits and foxes I'd disturbed were long gone, leaving me alone... for now. Hunter was already behind me, tracing my scent and path, and while he didn't feel close yet, an eerie feeling of being watched persisted.

Snow fell in soft drifts around me, most of it blocked by the foliage. Covered by fur, I barely felt the cold at all. When I reached an open section of forest, the ground was muddy from melting ice and flakes of snow, and I rolled in the muck until my white fur was brown, hiding my unique coloring and scent in one action—another part of my plan to remain out of his clutches until sunrise.

A crash echoed behind me, and whether it was Hunter or another creature, it jolted me to keep moving. My fur stiffened as the mud dried, and with each step the fear in my chest grew and grew. I couldn't figure out why my beast was afraid, the fur on the back of my neck standing up as I sprinted, my tongue lolling from my mouth to keep cool.

My heart raced until it was all I could hear, this frantic *thump thump thump* in my ears. Shadows rose up around me as the foliage thinned out, leaving me feeling exposed and vulnerable.

By instinct, I changed directions, and another shadow washed over me. My wolf struck first, and I ended up with a mouthful of big cat. Big *non-shifter* cat.

The cougar was close to my size, already snarling and swiping at my face. This must have been what stalked me as I ran, but I was a wolf shifter, and wouldn't bow to no fucking feline.

We tumbled together and my jaws clamped on to its throat, tearing through the fur. I didn't go for a killing bite yet, giving it a chance to respect my dominance. Thankfully, it did just that, scampering away when I released it.

It was odd that these larger animals remained within shifter territory at all, which made that one a confident, top tier predator. Just not top tier enough.

Mild fatigue hit me as the adrenaline eased, and when I moved again I chose strategic rather than in a flat-out sprint. Another tingle ran down my spine as I lowered myself to my belly and crawled through dense bushes. I got the sense that this tingle was from Hunter.

Dammit. I hadn't even been running for twenty minutes.

If I ever had to flee the cities, I needed a plan for how to keep myself hidden. These alphas were locked on to me now, locked on and unwilling to let go.

A rumble filled the forest; he was even closer than I'd thought. Just out there, playing with his prey. *Asshole.*

Unwilling to roll over and surrender, I changed trajectory, heading for a row of huge trees I'd passed earlier. One of them had a hollow log spanning across its base from a long-ago fallen trunk. I should be small enough to hide in it, and hopefully Hunter's beast would be too large to follow. Even if he found me before sunrise, he wouldn't be able to *catch me*, which should satisfy the rules.

When I felt him breathing down my neck, I picked up the pace. The log came into view, and a burst of adrenaline had my legs moving so fast that I was in real danger of tumbling over my own feet. Just as my head reached the opening of the trunk, Hunter leapt from the bushes and barreled me over. We rolled across the snow and undergrowth, and the whole time that fucker smirked a wolfie smirk. Yeah, he'd been playing with me. I'd never stood a chance.

When we came to a halt, I was sprawled on my side with Hunter's weight holding me down. It would be futile to struggle, so I lurched up and locked my jaws around his throat, which he'd left woefully unguarded. These dominant, arrogant wolves always underestimated other shifters, too used to letting their dominance do half the work in a battle.

Hunter stilled as I tasted the first drop of his blood, warm and rich, with just the hint of his mocha scent. My chest rumbled, and I wasn't sure if it was due to a desire for more blood or more Hunter, but either way, my wolf was content to lie under the bulk of her mate.

The way he'd hunted us had her all but ready to lift tail and give him exactly what he wanted.

I yipped when Hunter shifted back, leaving me pinned under a very naked male. "Oh, my stealthy little omega," he drawled, big hands running through my mud-caked fur. "You did much better than I anticipated. I'm impressed."

My wolf preened under her alpha's praise, and I felt the same, even as I held on to a sliver of annoyance at being bested so easily. When I forced out a growl, Hunter's touch slowed, gentling, and his expression was a mix of desire and need. My wolf arched, and I decided it was time to switch back.

My beast didn't fight, content with what had happened this evening, leaving me to deal with the human side of our claiming. She'd claimed this pack long ago, and now it was time for me to do my part.

Hunter's eyes darkened as he examined my face, like he committed every single detail to memory. "You've never looked more beautiful," he rasped, his nostrils flaring as he leaned down and dragged his nose along my throat. "Even covered in mud, you can't hide your scent from me. I could follow it through multiverses."

A chuckle bubbled up from me, even as my cheeks pinkened and core throbbed. "Nerd," I teased. "Always thinking in terms of multiverses."

He nudged more firmly against my cheek, scraping through the dried mud, which was rough against my sensitive skin. I gasped when he licked me, no doubt tasting half the forest at the same time, but Hunter didn't appear to care. I wiggled against him, my center throbbing, but he had me pinned as he kissed and licked a path down my throat and over my chest, until his tongue encircled my left nipple.

"Hunter," I cried, wound up, swirls of desire growing in arcs through my core.

There was a real possibility I might explode if he didn't claim me this second.

"What do you want me to do, Emme?" he murmured against my breast. "You know the deal, baby girl. Use your words to tell me *what you want.*"

His voice lowered over those last words, and as he rocked his hard, naked length against me, I was nearly delirious with desire. "I want you to claim me, Hunter. Please. *Claim* me. *Bite* me. *Fuck* me. I want it all."

His chest rumbled in a deep, satisfied purr, and I felt his pleasure even though there was no tangible connection between us yet. "Ah, my sweet omega. I've waited a long time to hear you say that. Before I could even put a face to my mate, I knew your soul. And it's mine."

He kissed me hard and I cried out, wondering if my drenched lower half was about to explode like a freaking bomb and kill us both. As dramatic as that sounded, the pressure felt like destruction at its purest form. I wanted to scream and thrust against his hard thigh just for some relief. "Hunter, please," I cried, dragging myself against him, "I can't wait. We have to seal the bond."

Fighting fate had been the hardest path I'd ever taken in my life, and after what happened with Kellan, I hoped I could change paths. Kellan hadn't lost his mind and started taking my power. In fact, none of the alphas had even tried to dig deeper into what I did that day, accepting that whatever it was, it had saved Kellan. It was as if the power didn't matter to them, and I had to trust my gut here, which told me to claim a second alpha. *Now.*

When he leapt gracefully to his feet, Hunter dragged me up with him, and I groaned as we crashed back into the huge tree that sheltered the fallen trunk. His hands cushioned my landing, and I craved every part of this moment. Even the pain.

"How did you know this was the exact ancient band of redwoods where I wanted to seal my claim?" he rasped, kissing my lips between each word.

I'd had no idea of course, but fate was in control today, so it made perfect sense to me.

"I know you, Hunter Reeves," I told him, believing with every part of me that was the truth. "I know your soul and heart, and I fucking want them both."

With a rumble, our lips clashed, the kiss rough and desperate. Growls ripped from our throats, and I knew this would not be a gentle, sweet claiming like Kellan's. This was animalistically fueled by the primality between predator and prey.

My body was on fire, the wet heat of my need dripping down my thighs as Hunter and I battled... for *something*. Control, pleasure, relief, need. When his strong hands gripped my thighs, tearing them apart, he thrust up in a mindless movement.

Despite my delirium, arousal, and need consuming me, there would always be pain with an alpha of Hunter's size. The first stretch of him against my inner walls was a delicious burn, and I threw my head back to scream my way into an orgasm. He never even made it a third of the way inside, but the decadent feel of his body entering mine was enough to send me reeling.

His irises were gold at this point, threaded through with stormy darkness, and as he thrust again, he dropped his head to my throat. My body opened to him, piece by piece, the pleasure and pain intermingling into a hurricane—a fitting sensation for this alpha.

The bark of the tree bit into my back, the mud on my skin cracked and shattered around us. I had never felt wilder or freer as Hunter seated himself fully inside me. When our bodies were joined as intimately as was shifterly possible, my mate threw his head back and howled to the sky, bringing the ghostly visage of my wolf to the surface, where she frolicked with Hunter's beast. They'd formed a bond long ago, but after this claiming, their souls would have the tangible connection to go along with it.

I tilted my head to the side and presented him the unmarked shoulder. "Please, Alpha," I begged, recalling our deal and how I would capitulate. "Please claim me. *Claim us.*"

Hunter's voice seeped out in a deep, overpowering growl of dominance. "Tell me why now, Omega? Why did you change your mind?"

There were a million reasons, but in my sex and desire addled brain, I revealed what tipped me over the edge. "You knelt for me," I sobbed, arching into his hold. "An entitled alpha never kneels for another, and yet you did... You—" His hips moved against mine and I cried out. "Oh goddess. You showed me that—" He thrust again and I was just senselessly babbling, but he didn't seem to care.

When I finally stopped word-vomiting all the reasons he'd destroyed me, his unwavering gaze held me. "Keep your eyes on me, baby girl," he said, voice a deep, hypnotic rumble. "Even a king should kneel before his queen. You will never accept anything less, from anyone, including those in our pack. Promise me."

I couldn't speak, my voice lost in the sensation of his cock buried deep enough to hurt. Pleasurable pain.

Hunter pulled half out of me, and then thrust in again, and again, over and over, claiming my body with his. "Promise me, Emmeline Anders. Promise me you will make them all kneel."

"I... I... *AHHHHH*," I screamed as another orgasm ripped through me, Hunter's length pulsing inside to prolong the pleasure.

His lips tilted in a satisfied smirk. "You will make them all kneel, because you're the fucking queen."

"I promise," I gasped. "Please, Alpha. Bite me. Claim me. I need you…"

He thrust hard, a frantic energy taking him over until I panted and shouted his name, the building pressure indicating my next orgasm would be of the gushing, squirting variety. These alphas played my body like they held expert knowledge of every nerve ending.

Hunter's right hand slid up my side and across my chest, wrapping around my throat. As he tightened his hold on either side, the air restriction heightened the sensation of building pleasure, and I embraced the darkness dancing in my peripherals.

"Mine," he growled, his gold gaze branding my soul.

My wolf howled in my chest, and I heard Hunter respond as he tilted his hand collar to graze his teeth across my throat: "Mine," he repeated, and there was a tingle of power as he shifted his jaw.

When he pierced the side of my throat, our wolves danced together in a soul-binding moment. My orgasm exploded until I was calling Hunter's name and writhing against his firm hold. Pleasure consumed me for what felt like an eternity, and yet it was far too short.

Hunter remained locked on my throat for just as long, sealing the bite as he thrusted inside me. If he kept that up, he'd have me coming again. Even as wrecked as I was, I never wanted this to end. He was everywhere all at once, filling me in more than just the physical sense.

My jaw ached as I longed to shift and bite him too, but I was at his mercy until he decided to release me. My previous orgasms made a wet, dirtily delicious squelch between us as he fucked me like both of our lives depended on it. When his jaw finally unlocked, and he licked across the wound, sealing his bite, I felt the shimmer of his power and need, deep inside where my shifter essence resided.

Fuck me. Hunter's desire was like a depthless pool of lava, burning and destroying everything in its path. I'd had no idea how he'd felt, not really, but now we were bonded, Hunter's feelings filtered through our connection.

So strong that my eyes burned, and my jaw shifted to claim him just as thoroughly.

He tilted his head, and I clamped down on the space between his shoulder and neck, letting his deliciously sweet lifeforce flow into my mouth. Without the *dying* part to impact the moment, this sealing of the bond was cataclysmic in a different way to mine and Kellan's.

With Hunter, I was washed away in a tsunami, or more accurately, a hurricane.

CHAPTER 43

EMME

Sheer overload and the sealing of the bond, stole my consciousness for a time, and when the world righted itself, I was in Hunter's arms as he walked silently through the forest toward the parking lot. Snow fell heavier now, but against the heat of the alpha, all I felt was a warm contentment.

"Hunter, I can walk," I murmured, feeling his own contentment deep in my chest.

I pressed my hand to his bite and his chest rumbled lightly in response. "It's my duty," he said, the words carrying an odd weight. "More than that, I want to take care of you. Let our bond settle, little mate. You have given me the greatest gift, and I will never be able to repay you."

A tear slipped down my cheek, and I forced myself not to sniffle and give away my overwhelming emotions. Stupid, really, since Hunter was connected to my feelings now. He leaned down and kissed away the tear, still powering through the forest. He didn't need to watch the road when he drove, or the path when he walked apparently.

I sighed through our kiss, which was a truly gentle,

loving caress. When I parted my mouth and fell all the way into the kiss, my tears soaked our faces. "Your tears destroy me," Hunter murmured as we parted, a pull of sorrow highlighted on his face in the early morning light. "But this time I feel the happiness behind them. You don't regret our bond."

"Not even for a second."

His arms tightened and his tone turned serious. "What you've gifted me is an honor I can never repay. I need you to know, Emme, that trusting me with your soul and your wolf... it's more than I deserve, but I will work every day to be the alpha *you* deserve."

Oh, Hunter Reeves, you secret romantic.

Lifting my hand, I pressed it to his cheek. "You already are, Hurricane Hunter. From that first day in the council chambers, you blew through the room and tore me to pieces. Then you put me back together. Not many would have looked at all of me and my *messy* life and thought, Yep, I want this mess. That's *my* mess. Despite my fears over bonding, I will never ever regret you."

His grip pulled me higher to his chest. "Why do you still fear this? Now that you've felt how perfect it is."

"You will understand when I explain everything that happened to my mom. Which I will do, as soon as all the pack is together."

Hunter grumbled. "Maybe you should tell me now before another interruption prevents it. If I don't know your truth, how can I protect you? It's my duty, little mate. My duty to keep you safe."

I felt a surge of hot, dominance rise inside his beast.

"I don't think I can tell this story more than once," I admitted, staring out into the snowy forest as we crossed through it. "It's hard to force the words out when I've spent years guarding this secret. A secret that will also explain how I saved Kellan, not that any of you have actually asked me yet."

That amused Hunter, and I liked it when his energy grew lighter. "None of us wanted to push you for an explanation. We don't care what you did, all we care is *that you did*. We can't lose you, Emme. We just can't."

It bothered me that I'd forced them to be so careful of what they said to me. I hoped that some of that damage would be repaired when the truth was revealed. "I'm scared this is all going to come crashing down on me," I admitted, my emotions raw and vulnerable after our bonding. "That the truth will destroy the good in my life. I've never—" My throat tightened, and I took a second to work through it. "I've never had good like this before. Losing this pack would—"

End me.

A deeper, darker sound than he'd ever made rumbled from Hunter's chest, strong enough to lift my body with its force. There were crashes as every creature in our vicinity took off, until we were most definitely alone. "You will never lose us," he said, barely understandable. "We will ensure that this good in your life remains, no matter what it takes."

Hunter had demonstrated possessive and obsessive tendencies from the first moment he'd scented me, but this was next-level. A promise sealed in fate, and with that, the bite on my shoulder tingled.

"The Rogers pack is still out there," I reminded him. "And the witch who spelled that prison house. She's powerful, they're powerful, and we have no fucking idea what they have planned next."

Hunter's reply was instant: "The council has fucked around with this long enough. I'm going to demand they act. If they don't, I will destroy every single one of them. I control this city and they all fucking know it."

A part of me considered acting as the voice of reason here, reminding him it wasn't the council's fault, but I found… I didn't really care to. We needed the Rogers pack destroyed. They were a threat to not only me, but my entire pack.

"We could just kill them ourselves," I suggested, regretting the words the moment they left my mouth. I didn't want to risk my pack by going up against them alone; they'd almost killed Kellan last time.

"That's plan B," Hunter assured me, and I choked down my concern. "It would be cleaner all around if the council dealt with the issue, but if they delay any longer, not only will I rain hell down on all of them, but I'll also take matters into our pack's hands. Now that Kellan's safe, we can give our enemies the focus they deserve."

Experience and instinct told me that being the sole focus of a pissed-off Hunter Reeves was not good for your health.

He reached the edge of the forest, the cityscape coming into view on the horizon. There was a tugging sensation in my chest, followed by a tingle along Kellan's bite, a moment before his Bugatti roared into view.

"Well, well," he said as he opened his door and popped his head out. "Aren't you two a sight. What happened? Did you get dragged backwards through the forest?"

Hunter set me on my feet in a patch cleared of snow, and Kellan leapt from the car to sweep me into his arms. "I'm genuinely worried," I said around a burst of semi-hysterical laughter, "that I might forget how to walk. You two barely let my feet touch the ground."

"What sort of mates would we be if we let your feet get cold?" Kellan appeared aghast at the very thought. "I've already got the heater blasting for you, pretty mate. Let's get you warm."

He walked to the passenger side, and when I expected him

to place me in the chair, he slid in and took a few seconds to adjust me onto his lap. When the door closed, the warmth surrounded us, and I sank bonelessly against Kellan.

A few minutes later, Hunter slid into the driver's side, and I realized why I was in Kellan's lap: this was the only way the three of us would fit in here.

Hunter dropped our clothes into the back and closed the door, sealing us in the warm interior.

He reversed out fast, and Kellan wrapped his arms tighter around me. The fact that two out of the three of us were completely naked, not to mention covered in mud and *other bodily fluids*, should have felt weird, but it was all serenity as the powerful car ate up the road.

The Bugatti's power was *almost* as good as sex. Now that I'd been with these alphas, I knew there was nothing that could compare to sex, not any longer. Not even the sweet sound of a powerful engine.

When Hunter pulled into the garage, I was able to walk on my own two feet all the way up to my room, where Kellan and Hunter ensured I was thoroughly clean before the three of us crawled into bed for some much-needed reprieve from our exhaustion. Getting hunted, and then fucked and claimed against a tree, really took it out of a shifter.

Goddess be damned, what a fucking great night.

Sleep took me under fast, nestled between two naked alphas. It was hard to believe how comfortable I now felt with them. I could barely remember my life before they came into it, and the parts I could remember... I didn't want to.

It felt like I'd been asleep for two seconds when a heavy hand landed on my shoulder. With a gasp, I jerked up in the bed, knocking Hunter's arm off my stomach. Blinking to clear my vision, the heavy fatigue passed as I panicked, but my racing pulse eased when I noticed Slade at the end of the bed.

He took me in fully, and until his eyes darkened, I'd forgotten I was naked.

"Get dressed," he told me shortly. "We have training."

"We have training?" I repeated mindlessly. "Wait, we have—?"

"Training, yes," he shot back. "You have five minutes to get ready, or you'll be tested wearing what you have on."

His expression remained neutral as he strode from the room, and I let out a long sigh.

Hunter ran his hand down my spine and murmured. "You want me to interfere?"

"No, it's okay," I replied, shaking my head as I leaned down to kiss his cheek. "You go back to sleep; I'll see what this training is all about."

Kellan rolled closer and ran his hand over my side. "I'll be there in a couple of hours, Shortcake," he mumbled, voice filled with a delicious rasp. "But Slade's got you first."

Great. What could possibly go wrong with that scenario?

Kissing them both, and feeling a little annoyed at leaving two rumpled, gorgeous alphas in my bed, I rolled over the top of Hunter and dragged myself into my wardrobe. Grabbing the first workout gear I could find, I was relieved to see it was all black. Saved me trying to co-ordinate colors when half asleep.

In the bathroom I peed, brushed my teeth, and washed my face, before tying my long hair back in a braid. Whatever this *training* entailed, keeping my hair off my face felt like the right move.

No doubt Slade was going to kick my ass and make no apologies for it.

He had seemed extra short with me as he growled over the end of my bed— *Wait...*

A few more cylinders of my brain came online, and I was reminded of what else had happened yesterday. Before the club and the mating. *The prank*. I'd left Slade's *gifts* to be discovered last night, and now he was here demanding I train with him. *Oh. Shit*.

Could training be code for *taking me back out to the woods for another hunt?*

One that would end in an entirely different, far less pleasurable way...

CHAPTER 44

EMME

It took all my focus to pull on sneakers and grab my phone before leaving my room. Slade waited at the end of the hall, a giant, intimidating shadow, expressionless and with his arms crossed, allowing no way for me judge his mood.

"So," I chirped, forcing a smile, "training, hey? I don't think we discussed that. Or did I zone out in the middle of a conversation again?"

The babbling filled the silence nicely while also making me look guilty. Might as well admit what I'd done in his room and get it out of the way.

Before sheer panic had me confessing, Slade turned toward the stairs, calling over his shoulder, "I always planned to teach you to protect yourself and manage your reading, but only one of those is essential while our enemies linger in shadows. Defense skills are non-negotiable."

Hurrying to keep up with his long-ass legs, I huffed, "But I'm really not that athletically inclined. I mean, you've seen me swim."

Slade *almost* cracked a smile. "And run. I'm fully aware of what I'm up against."

"Rude," I groused, though he had a point. "Wait, when did you see me run?"

He wore no smile this time. "I gathered footage through our street's security to follow your trajectory the day you were attacked at the guard hut. Additional cameras have been installed now, to ensure that nothing is out of my view."

Had I scrambled all the streets cameras yesterday during my prank? How was Slade not ripping me a new one, especially with the Rogers pack still out there and apparently gunning for me?

I wasn't even sure if he was angry, his emotions concealed behind the stoic expression. If Slade's plan was to freak me out by *not* leveling accusations at me in the hopes that I'd inadvertently reveal my own crimes... well, it was absolutely working.

Not quite ready to give in yet, I forced a smile onto my face, and chatted my ass off *all* the way into the garage. Slade chose the reinforced Range Rover today, and held my door open for me and everything. I continued my random babbling about the weather, Luxuria, how many drinks I'd had last night, and the trouble I went to organizing my wardrobe into colors and material. "By season, really," I continued, plastering the fakest smile on my face. "Because it's important to be seasonal, you know? What if someone met me for the first time and couldn't for the life of them figure out my season. Disaster, am I right?"

For a second, I caught a glimpse of him clenching his teeth, but he smoothed that movement just as quickly. "A true disaster," he replied, going as far as nodding along like he was in complete agreement.

On the way to the training facility, he listened to and *even replied* to my inane chatter, driving so sedately it was almost as if he wanted to hear the ridiculous shit coming out of my mouth. This little game we played would eventually run its course, but for right now neither of us wanted to break. Mentally sparring with Slade had my blood buzzing with adrenaline, and despite my lack of sleep, I felt alive and awake in ways I hadn't for a long time.

When Slade pulled up at the large training facility, he was out of the car and opening my door before I could suck in a few fortifying breaths. "Out, Snow," he commanded. "We've already wasted too much time."

"Keep your panties on," I griped, swinging my legs out the door.

"I don't wear underwear," he shot back, and my mouth was bone dry at the mental image of a naked, pierced Slade. It was permanently branded in my brain. "Now move your scrawny ass."

Oh, okay, then. He'd gone too far now; my ass was perfectly... I glanced behind me to find my rather scrawny butt clad in black gym pants. It wasn't my fault that food had come second to shelter and survival for most of my years. "For a taller female, I have plenty of curves," I called out in false confidence, Slade already heading for the front doors. "Asshole."

"I heard that," he growled back, and I gulped down my next insult. "And if you want to keep those curves, you'll eat full meals rather than picking at your food like a fucking bird shifter."

I stumbled a little, feeling hurt that he'd criticized my looks. "I've been trying," I whispered, and once again he heard what he shouldn't have.

Slade slowed, giving me a second to catch up to his long-legged stride. "You need to be healthy," he said to me, looking less like a sociopathic asshole. There was even a sliver of compassion on his face. "You need to be strong."

I nodded, feeling tired again for no reason at all. My energy shouldn't be so tied to these alphas and their moods, but here we were, the scent match once again driving me past the brink of sanity.

The rest of our journey was silent as we moved past empty reception desks and through the halls. When we reached the training field, Slade said, "Today, I'm going to assess your skill and ability level in relation to strength, endurance, reflexes, and natural fighting."

The field looked massive without all the squads filling it, and I wondered how long we'd have the place to ourselves. "I'm not sure an assessment is necessary," I mused, ignoring the frustrated stare and stiff shoulders from the dragon shifter. "I can easily rate myself in all of those categories."

Slade didn't disagree with me. "Be that as it may, I will be conducting my own set of drills. Now, let's start with a warmup." He dropped his arms and jogged away, gesturing for me to follow. *Fuck.* Was it too late to have Hunter deal with this?

Not wanting to disappoint our resident scary shifter, I put all my effort into keeping up with his long legs as we jogged around the stadium. Twenty minutes later, he was done with the initial warmup, and I was done with living.

My stomach heaved as I fought to stay on my feet, and I was fairly sure that I'd broken all the bones in my legs. There was no other reason for them to hurt this much.

"Stretching now," Slade barked, and I coughed and wheezed, leaning forward in the hopes it would ease the sharp cramp in my side.

"You're cranky," I coughed, too wrecked to care about

sassing him. "Didn't get a lot of sleep last night? What kept you up?"

At this point, I was past waiting for this bastard to confront me about my prank. I needed him to yell, for me to yell back, and then we'd move on. The prank had not had my intended effect, and I wondered why I'd ever thought I could get one over on him.

This shifter was the master of concealing his emotions and torturing me through prolonged silences.

"I slept perfectly fine," he said simply. "My room is my sanctuary, and no one would dare mess with my place of refuge. Now, let's stretch."

Internally I screamed, but externally I dragged my broken ass closer to him and followed his movement as we stretched our limbs.

"How are you so bendy with all those muscles?" I grumbled. "It's not normal. You know that, right?"

Slade shook his head. "You have the flexibility of an octogenarian. That's not normal for a shifter."

I narrowed my eyes on him. "What in the world is an octogenarian?"

Whatever it was, it didn't sound good.

Slade smiled, and I swear my heart stopped. It wasn't anything ground-shattering, just a slight tilt of his lips, but for this shifter it was practically a beam. "A human between the ages of eighty and eighty-nine."

Oh, excellent. I wasn't even as flexible as an elderly shifter. Nope. I was an elderly human, close to death.

"Possibly true, but rude to point it out," I muttered, before raising my voice. "I will admit, my wolf and I have a bit of catching up to do."

Slade didn't disagree, and *was it too late* to change my opinion about enjoying his honesty? "With my help," he said, "you will catch up. Now that you've warmed up, we can head into the first obstacle course."

"Okay... *wait*, did you say *obstacle course*?"

Slade ignored me, already halfway across the field, and once again I followed like a little lost duckling. On the way I debated my odds of murdering him in his sleep, and came to the unfortunate conclusion that there were exactly zero chance that I'd even get close enough to touch him, let alone kill him. Bet he slept with one eye open and a weapon in hand. Wait, he was the weapon in hand. *Fucker.*

As I grumbled under my breath, Slade led me to a large set of roller doors, which opened via a red button on the wall. This part of the training area was almost as large as their outdoor facility, and from where I stood I saw a range of obstacles with ropes, tires, ladders, and so much freaking *pain.*

It was a kid's paradise, and my worst nightmare. "Let me tell you, trainer," I said, trying to keep the hysteria from my voice, "no octogenarian would be able to make it through this. You might have to take your assessment back."

This time I got a laugh out of him, and I almost flew over the first obstacle via butterflies in my tummy and sparks in my veins. "You haven't made it yet either," he said with one final amused stare, "so I wouldn't start subtracting years yet."

Oh yeah. Good point.

He led me farther into the building, stopping before a row of white and black tires spread out across the ground. "It starts here. You'll need to move between these obstacles without touching the ground. Jump from tire to tire and flip the ones that aren't close enough."

"Just flip the tire," I said, sarcasm rearing up to aid me in my disbelief. "Easy. What if I just carry one on my back through the whole obstacle to use when needed?"

Slade didn't even bat an eye. "You can take anything you can carry with you."

I threw my hands in the air and conceded another point to him. "I was obviously kidding. Those things must weigh a ton."

"One point two actually. How heavy can you lift?"

Oh goddess. He was going to make me lift weights too? *Nope. No.*

Without another word crossing my lips, I raced toward the tires, relieved not to fall or trip over the first few. The second section, where the tires were farther apart, I had to flip them to move along. Only I couldn't budge the heavy rubber circle. Not even one inch off the ground. "Put your back into it," Slade bellowed—the smug prick.

"I'm putting my entire fucking body into it," I shouted back, and I heard a whispered curse on the breeze, which I maturely chose to ignore.

Deciding this was stupid, I gave up fast, hopping on the fake grass between the tires, while secretly flipping Slade the middle finger every time I jumped. There was no way for him to see the gesture, but it made me feel marginally better.

The next obstacle after the tires was a vertical wall with a rope dangling to assist in scaling it. It looked easy enough as I grabbed the rope, hoping that for once, my lighter stature would come in handy. Only it turned out pulling one's body weight up a wall was not as easy as it looked. Who'd have guessed it...

Through sheer force of will, I made it halfway before my arms started to shake. *Shit.* Shit, shit.

Risking a glance below, I started to debate the safest way to fall and land with minimal injuries.

Eventually, Slade called out, "Push through the pain and fatigue, Emmeline."

His voice was closer, as if he'd crossed to stand near me. The thought of falling in front of him had a surge of energy propelling me forward, and after forcing myself to take one step at a time, closing my eyes and chanting through the pain, I *actually reached the freakin' top.*

Hanging over the narrow ledge, I huffed in air, internally fist-pumping at my ability to do the hard things today. All ruined by Slade fucking Riverson.

"Any time today, Snow," he called.

My arms refused to obey me when I attempted to release the wall, and with great reluctance I called, "I might be stuck."

The rope burns on my hands were already healing, so surely if I hung around here for a few more minutes, the strength would also return to my arms. There was a low rasping laugh from below, and I almost fell off the wall when a huge body landed beside me.

Landed beside me... "What in the Olympic high jumper was that?" I glanced down for sign of another rope, but there was nothing. "Did... did you leap up here?"

He shook his head like I was ridiculous. *You're* ridiculous, buddy.

"You're a shifter," he told me, nostrils flaring. "You should be able to out-Olympic any human in the world. Are you not concerned by your weaknesses? Even the smallest vulnerability can be used against you."

Adjusting my body on the wall to ease the ache in my ribs, I said, "I probably should be concerned, but honestly, I've managed to keep myself alive without any special muscles or skills for years. I wasn't raised with shifters. I've never let my wolf out much, and I'm weaker for it. I won't apologize for what it took to survive."

He tilted his head, and I ignored the jolt in my gut that happened whenever his probing stare dissected me. "That's fair," he finally said, sounding softer. "But it doesn't mean we rest there. I will make you stronger, and I will teach you how to harness your reading difficulties. These two areas of your life will improve through me. This is a promise."

He pressed his hand to his chest, and I had no doubt that on the rare occasions this dragon made a vow, he followed through with it. No matter the personal cost.

"Just—" I huffed, "—try not to kill me along the way."

His response to that was strolling across the top of the wall like it was flat ground, plucking me up from my precarious position, and dropping both of us off the side of the thirty-foot drop.

"*Ahhhh!*" I screamed all the way down, bracing myself for impact.

Not that I needed to bother.

Slade absorbed the impact and landed like he'd stepped off a two-foot wall.

When he placed me on my feet, I caught the tightening around his eyes, the touch aversion striking him hard enough to leave a visible strain. "Time to assess your fighting skills," he said abruptly, already striding away.

"I have no fight skills," I shouted after him, my legs protesting as I hobbled along.

Stubborn dragon. He was going to learn the hard way.

Or... I was.

CHAPTER 45

EMME

Muscled thighs clad in blue sports shorts came into my blurry view as Kellan lowered himself next to my broken body. There was a large, black case in his hand, which he placed next to him, his expression filled with concerned amusement. "Shortcake, you know you're lying in a pile of snow, right?"

"Umph," I gurgled, unable to coherently form words after Slade's fight drills. We'd only worked on stance and technique, for fuck's sake, and I was still mostly dead. I hadn't managed to lay one hand on the shifter the entire time, and he'd managed to drop me to my ass *multiple times* via nothing more than a few brief touches over my clothes. Which was a relief... and a bother.

A part of me was desperate to experience the first time I touched him without a reason behind it. To feel his skin under my hands because he wanted me to touch him and not because I needed help or fixing. It'd never happen at this rate, and my stupid hero worship of the dragon shifter hadn't decreased with my ass-kicking. It was quite possibly worse.

"Snow helps," I managed to say, enjoying the cool, melting slush easing the pain in my muscles.

"Would you like some food before we move on to the next round?" Kellan asked, and I didn't miss the waver in his tone as he attempted not to laugh at me. Without waiting for my response, he slid his hands under my arms and hauled my floppy body off the ground. "I'm going to hazard a guess that a little energy boost *might* be required before my lesson."

"Slade is getting food," I huffed, shaking my head to keep my eyes open. My lack of sleep really wasn't helping the whole situation either. "Even my eyelids hurt, Golden. Don't let him train me again. I beg you."

Kellan tried so hard not to laugh; he pressed his lips together and closed his eyes, but it could not be contained. I must have looked like a right old bag of dicks, and when he finally let loose, he howled and crouched forward, taking me with him like I was no heavier than said bag of appendages.

"Oh, Shortcake. You're fucking adorable. If you're still walking, Slade didn't go too hard on you. He knows better."

Waving down at my useless legs, I snarled. "What part of collapsed in the snow screams *I can walk* to you?"

Kellan released me suddenly and my legs caught, the ache in them not quite as pronounced as before. "You're stronger than you believe, pretty mate," he told me, eyes sparkling as his laughter faded.

"I've never had anyone believe in me," I replied, with a shake of my head. "You'd think I'd have learned to believe in myself to make up for it."

Kellan brushed back the loose strands of my braid. "You do believe in yourself. If you didn't, you'd never have had the strength to fight our bond and stay out of the cities. You're not weak, you just show your strength in different ways. Ways that I, personally, love."

Gah, Kellan was my destruction and salvation wrapped up in one shifter. "You know I bonded to you not even a month after we met, right? I'd hardly call that *fighting a mate bond*."

When his expression shuttered, I hurried to add, "Not that I have any regrets or would change a thing, I promise. I just wanted to point out... fuck, ignore me. I don't know why I'm babbling like an idiot."

Slade's deep rumble saved me from further word vomit when he appeared seemingly out of nowhere, food in hand. "You saved Kellan's life despite your fears and misgivings. I'd say that qualifies as another form of bravery and strength. It's all about perspective, Snow, and at times, yours is skewed."

I barely managed to contain my eyeroll. "Why, thank you, oh wise one. Any of my other flaws you'd like to point out for me?"

It wasn't like I wanted these alphas to spend all day every day showering me in love and compliments—wait, I didn't *not* want that, but reality dictated that it wasn't possible. Today, though, after his ass-kicking, I didn't need one more negative word from Slade Riverson.

"Well..." he started.

Kellan's eyes widened as he made a very subtle gesture to *shut the fuck up*, and Slade immediately complied.

A huffed snort escaped me. "It's okay, Scary Shifter, I'm quite self-aware when it comes to my flaws. I'm working on acknowledging my strengths too, because I do agree with parts of what Kellan said. I have been through a lot, and I kind of feel like I deserve a bit of this happiness."

"You absolutely deserve it," Slade said with force, and for a brief moment his hard exterior softened.

He handed me the plate of food he'd been holding and my mouth watered at the meat-based selection, which included beef, turkey, chicken breast, and sliced sausage.

"Oh, I forgive you," I cried, making weird, happy sounds. "All is forgiven. We're back to being besties who prank each other."

Kellan coughed up a furball behind us, but I was locked in on Slade's expression, determined to notice even the smallest reaction. All morning he'd ignored my attempts to get him to break first and yell at me over my prank, and even now he remained impassive.

"Besties," he murmured, like it was a foreign word he had no understanding of. With a shake of his head, he handed over the water too. "Give your full attention to Kellan. He's unsurpassed in weapons."

When he walked away, Kellan pressed in closer to my spine, his alpha heat easing the chill from my rest in the snow. "He hasn't mentioned your prank yet?" he asked, keeping his voice extra low in case Slade heard, even though the dragon shifter was already gone from sight.

"Not a single freaking comment or reaction," I whispered back. "I mean, unless you count kicking my ass all morning, but I get the sense he would have done that either way."

"Oh yeah, he's the best with ass-kicking," Kellan confirmed. "Just be careful, Shortcake. Slade doesn't usually let infractions against his boundaries slide. I'm not worried he'll hurt you. I wouldn't have assisted you if I thought there was any chance of that, but that doesn't mean he won't find another, creative way to return the favor."

A shiver traced down my spine, and this one had absolutely nothing to do with the cold. I also couldn't tell if it was fear—it didn't quite feel like fear...

Stuffing my face seemed like a great distraction. I chose a piece of beef first, biting into the tender, pink meat. "Oh, so good," I groaned, closing my eyes.

When I opened them again, Kellan was watching me with

a hunger that had nothing to do with food. I did enjoy food as much as the next shifter, but my groans might have been exaggerated for another reason. I needed a tiny hit of that addictive, starving look that stirred my omega essence. "You want to share?" I asked, feigning innocence as I lifted the plate higher.

The blue in Kellan's eyes almost reached that violet hue. "You eat first, always."

Right.

Making short work of the food, I was full after a third of the plate, and when I handed the rest to Kellan, he *wolfed* it down in seconds. I sipped on a bottle of water as he discarded the plate and grabbed his black case. "Come on, we need to head inside," he told me, staying at my side as we made our way into the hall. "They've got a shooting range and sparring mat back here," he added. "How are your legs doing?"

"Back to normal," I said, bouncing a little to prove it. "I swear, my shifter healing is getting faster. The pack runs are strengthening my beast."

His smile was tinged in sadness. "I hate that you spent so many years hiding a huge part of yourself. Years spent containing the wild heart of your beast. That part alone makes me want to tear your mom and that fucking pack apart, although there are plenty of other reasons to destroy them."

Namely that they'd hurt my mate. "I was content to pretend they didn't exist for the rest of my life, even after what they did to Mom. Let's be real, she wasn't really innocent. But when they hurt you... that was where my tolerance ended. They will pay for what they did, no matter what it takes to make it happen."

Kellan dropped a brief kiss on my head. "Fiercely protective Emme is one of my favorites."

It wasn't anything new to want to keep him safe, but after

almost losing him, the feeling had turned into a calling of sorts. I'd never survive going through that again.

When he opened the doors and hit the lights on the shooting range, it looked exactly like ones I'd seen on television: booths with rows and targets at the end. It smelled like metal and sulfur, but not the magic variety, one slightly sweeter.

Kellan gently placed his case on the large table spanning the back wall and used his thumbprint to unlock it.

When he lifted the lid, I leaned forward to peer in. "Whoa," I said, taking in the array of weapons fitted perfectly into individual slots. I counted two handguns along with one larger, more deadly looking gun. There were also three short, ornate blades, and one longer blade that reminded me of a samurai sword. "Just so you know, when I grow up, I want a cool weapons briefcase."

Kellan traced his finger along the top of one gun, a brief chuckle escaping. "Tell you what, Shortcake. When you can hit the middle of the target ten shots in a row, I'll get you one."

Oh, I loved a challenge.

Kellan spent the next thirty minutes running me through all aspects of the guns, one at a time, showing me how he broke them down, cleaned and serviced, and then put them back together. The blades were next, as he went over the ways he kept the edges in prime condition.

Eventually, we ended up in one of the shooting booths, and from where I stood, the targets appeared to be miles away. "As I said, this is a Beretta M9," Kellan said, handing me the black piece. It was heavier than I'd expected, but completely manageable. "Now, I need you to do the checks we went through before, then we can work on stance."

I ran over everything without missing one item off his checklist, and after he corrected my stance and hold, it was time for me to take my shots. We both slipped on protective gear for our ears and eyes, even though as shifters we'd heal any injuries immediately, and I gripped the M9 once more.

I tried to relax and ignore how foreign the gun felt in my hands—Kellan had told me that the best way to instinctively use a weapon was to practice until it felt like a natural extension of your own hand.

Maybe one day I'd reach that point.

Switching off the safety, I breathed out in one deep breath and pulled the trigger, missing the target by a mile. I hadn't been prepared for the recoil and would have dropped the gun if Kellan didn't snatch it from the air.

With a rueful smile he lifted my earmuff. "Sorry, Shortcake. That was on me. I find this one has a moderate kick. Next time I'd suggest easing back on the trigger rather than jerking it hard."

I nodded, my heart beating fast. "Makes sense. Sorry."

Kellan shook his head like I was silly, and then gestured for me to put my ear protection back on. He proceeded to fire off one shot after another, and every single one hit the target directly through the middle of the smallest circle. It almost looked like each shot went through the *same* hole, which had to be nearly impossible. "My dad was a marksman for the Shifter Guard," Kellan explained when we lifted our ear covers again as he reloaded and handed the gun back to me. "He taught my brothers and me how to use every weapon, right around the time we learned to walk."

"I'd love to meet your parents," I blurted, feeling this strange urge to know every part of Kellan's life. Including where he'd been born and raised. Hopefully, the mention of a pack member's parents would go over better today than it had last time with Hunter.

I was relieved to see Kellan's expression turn soft and

hopeful. "They're going to love you, Shortcake. They remained with their pack back in Thorny Gardens, but will absolutely be out for Christmas."

Christmas. One of the few holidays that shifters and humans shared, even though we didn't share deities or other traditions. Mostly, it was a shifters love of gifts that propelled the cities into that holiday. I'd never really celebrated, and I wondered if there were any special events in Golden Claw during that time.

"Okay, sweet mate, I think that's enough chatting." Kellan gestured toward the gun. "It's time for you to take another shot. I need to know you can protect yourself if we're not around."

As terrible as it was to imagine these alphas not being around, I was aware of the crazy shit happening in the world. Learning how to protect myself would never be a waste of time.

Kellan, to no one's surprise, was a patient and easygoing teacher, and at the close of our lesson, I'd hit the target—close to the bullseye—with all my shots. Even managed to disarm Kellan when he "attacked" with a knife.

It was a quiet drive home, and once inside I dragged my sorry ass off to shower, completely wrecked. Wrecked but happy.

Today felt like a small achievement, and hopefully if I kept these lessons up, I'd just continue to grow stronger and more capable.

When I finally snuggled into my soft bed, I let my mind wander, excited by the prospect of Kellan and Hunter joining me soon. I was quite quickly turning into one of those females who could not sleep without her pack. Which should terrify me. But I was taking it one day at a time. Enjoying the little moments.

When I reached over to hit the master light switch beside my bed, I waited for the normal darkness to descend, only to find a wash of green filling the room.

With a shriek, I scrambled up in bed, staring around in horror.

Holy fuck. What…?

"Shortcake!" Kellan's shout echoed, but I was too shocked to form a reply.

My entire room glowed.

From the walls to the bedding to the fucking rug on the floor.

Along with the glow, there was a set of giant, red dragon eyes peering down at me, also invisible until darkness hit. Below he'd written the words *Game on, bestie.*

The red was a stark contrast to the rest of the room, which was greeny-yellow. "Slade," I finally breathed as Kellan burst in through my door, staring around in wide-eyed shock.

Okay, so yep, the dragon had most definitely noticed my prank, and he'd absolutely out-pranked me in return. *Holy goddess.*

CHAPTER 46

SLADE

The meeting with the executives from our Australian offices wrapped up quicker than expected, and as Hunter shut down the projector, I leaned back in my chair and waited for the room to clear.

It was late, well past our usual quitting time, but no one had complained about waiting for our Australian conglomerate. We weren't assholes to work for, or at least Hunter wasn't, and for the most part, if they did their jobs properly we didn't micromanage. At least Hunter didn't.

I enjoyed existing in the shadows, while keeping tabs on our staff via the internet to ensure that none of them ever took advantage of Hunter's trust. No one would dare steal, slack off, or lie and manipulate at Reeves Industries.

They knew the consequences if they stepped over the line. *I* was the consequences.

Lately, my focus had been on internal pack life, but with my surveillance programs doing most of the work in the background, nothing was slacking here either.

While Hunter finalized our last shipments with help from Casey, I whipped out my phone and hit the app to connect with our home security. Scrolling between the various rooms, I found Emme immediately. I'd installed a tracker on her phone, and for once she had it on her.

After ensuring she was safe, I took a second to check for any external threats, not that I didn't trust our security system to alert me, but it never hurt to doublecheck.

Then I could get back to my favorite new hobby: keeping an eye on Emmeline Anders.

The omega was nothing like I'd expected.

I'd thought she'd be weak and meek, ready to cave at any alpha command. Instead, she was strong and feisty, with a vulnerable core that confused as much as it intrigued me. It should drive me—and my beast—out of our minds to have this messy, complicated creature upsetting the status quo. But she had the opposite effect. I was starting to crave the chaos she scattered about my day.

Amusement danced through me just thinking about this little *prank war* she'd instigated. I'd known the second she'd entered my room the other night, and instead of rage I'd found myself curious about what she was up to. The device she'd used to scramble the security feeds, which ironically was Reeves Industries tech, wasn't strong enough to circumvent my setup. I'd watched as she raced through the halls, and then darted around my sacred space, placing small, clear objects into unobvious spots.

Objects I hadn't recognized until that night. I couldn't remember the last time I felt as amused as when I switched off the lights and dozens of tiny green dragons glowed at me from their perches around the room. I'd even left them there to see again tonight.

Emme was, as Hunter said, an anomaly we hadn't expected. She completely disturbed the natural order, and whether it ended up being for better or worse, I was all in to find out now.

On my screen, Emme entered her room, and my dragon stirred in my chest. This was the first time she'd been back since I'd dragged her out this morning for training, and I'd had a little time when she was with Kellan for my side of the next prank.

The simple challenge of a prank war felt odd, but it also stirred a deeper obsession I couldn't explain. All I knew was I could not tear my gaze from the screen as I waited for her reaction.

Besties who prank each other.

My poor little Snow. She had no idea what being my "bestie" entailed, and it was too late for her to take it back now. She had my attention, for better or worse.

"Emme okay?" Hunter asked, leaning against the boardroom table. "As per usual, she's not answering my messages. I swear, she forgets she has a phone at least half the time."

My response was clipped, most of my focus on her hand as she reached for the light switch. "Like you're not watching her as well. You know she's perfectly fine."

Hunter shrugged and didn't deny it: "You watch closer."

Very true.

When she switched off the light, the monitoring system reverted to the greenish glow of night vision, and Emme took a second to look around. As her newly glowed-up room registered, she scrambled up her bed, which got Hunter's attention.

"What's wrong?" he snapped. "Is there someone in the room with her?" Only self-preservation and years of learning the hard way stopped him from snatching the phone from me.

His own device was out in the next second, and I would guess he was dialing Kellan.

"She's safe," I told him, a dance of genuine amusement in my tone. Emme was openly shocked, her eyes wide and her mouth ajar as she took in her room.

Hunter slowly hung up his phone. "What did you do?"

This little war was between Emme and me, but if I didn't explain, Hunter would be quite vicious in tearing the world apart for the truth. When it came to Emme, especially now they'd bonded, he had no composure.

"You know how the security system went down for a couple of minutes last night," I said, finally lifting my head to take him in. "That was Emme. She snuck into my room and planted *glow in the dark* dragons everywhere. I've just returned the favor."

The tension eased from Hunter as he let out a low chuckle, running his hand through his hair, tearing free his waves. "Glad to see you've found a non-violent way to respond to her cute streak of rebellion." His eyes darkened as he stared out the window, taking in the lights of the city below. "I'm constantly waiting to see what she does next. The challenge is... nice."

He pressed his hand to the bite on his shoulder, and I was intrigued, wondering how it felt to bond in the way they had. My bond to my brothers was forged in pack magic, but it wasn't as physical as how they'd connected to Emme.

I felt an odd interest and protectiveness for the omega, but Hunter and Kellan were next-level. They'd been fundamentally changed through this bond, and while I wasn't sure I'd ever be able to make the same choice, there was curiosity.

Hunter reached out and gripped my shoulder, and I fought back the urge to knock his touch away. My dragon and I were used to him, so there were no stronger urges than that. Thankfully.

My brother had been pushing his little touches for years, hoping it would eventually desensitize me. If anything, the sensations grew worse with age. The clawing under my skin, and icy coldness spreading through my chest as my reason slowly bled away. One day I'd lose myself to the beast completely, and then everyone would be fucked.

"Let's go home to our pack," Hunter said, rubbing his hand over his face. "It's late. I'm fucking exhausted."

Easy for him to say; he got to crawl into bed with Emme. "I might hang around here for a few more hours."

Hunter's expression turned sharper. "Not a chance, brother. You're coming home with me. I made a promise long ago to never let you fade into the beast, and to keep that promise I will drag your ass into the pack—into family days, into *real* life, whether you like it or not."

His promise had been sealed in blood by two tweens who'd decided they were done with the abuse of their "father." My dragon had protected me the best he could, and in doing so a part of what had made us equals was broken. The disconnect between me and my beast meant I could never fully trust him.

"Yep, okay."

Hunter was the one constant in my life, the only fucking one who got through to me when I was floundering. Without his influence, I'd teeter right over the edge of my sanity and rain fire and brimstone all over the shifter community. It was a fuck of a burden for any entitled alpha to carry, but my brother rarely strained under the weight on his shoulders.

There was none like him in the world, and knowing he had Emme in his corner made the scattered pieces of my soul feel a little less destroyed.

We packed up quickly, and while Hunter drove us home I watched Emme on my phone. It was intriguing that even as Kellan took in the room with her, they didn't leave. Emme just stared around from her perch in the bed, the smallest of smiles on her lips.

The anticipation of what she might do in response lit a spark inside my chest, and for once it had nothing to do with dragon fire.

After our arrival back home, I spent half the night watching her sleep between two alphas, all the while wondering what it felt like to be able to so freely touch another.

Eventually, my body forced me to sleep for a few hours, before I got up early and headed in for training with my squad, wishing I could drag Emme with me again.

I'd give her one day to recover, but tomorrow her ass was mine again. Her *not so scrawny ass*, as she'd pointed out. By the time I finished teaching her to protect and defend herself, she'd have more muscle and stamina, and I'd be a touch less paranoid.

Maybe.

It was my role to be the immoveable mountain that stood between my pack and danger. The last sight our enemies would face. The one who kept them all safe, no matter what it took.

The morning passed in the office. We had a ton of work to catch up on after being absent during Kellan's recovery. The afternoon consisted of flight training, and when I released my dragon, my squad didn't even flinch. We'd come a long way from the first day I'd stepped up as their squad leader, and even though my pack were the only shifters I trusted implicitly, I'd built a decent bond with my squad. All were strong and capable alphas, and we had each others' backs.

"You're one scary bastard," Horton called as he dodged my massive right claw. The eagle shifter was the bravest on the squad, holding his ground even when I huffed out my irritation.

We took to the sky, practicing our deadly attack combinations, and I released my more civilized side and became the beast. My dragon never attacked our squad, as they knew better than to touch us. Emme hadn't known, and I still couldn't believe she'd just placed her hand on my snout. Without thought or reason.

My dragon snorted and released a blast of molten fire. My beast thought I was a fucking moron, assuring me he'd never hurt her, and for once... I almost believed him.

By the time our training was over, other squads had arrived, and I was forced to converse with Warrick. "How's everything at home?" he asked, bouncing on the spot as he stretched his arms out. "Kellan and Emme okay?"

"They're safe and healthy," I assured him, unwilling to give this alpha any further information. He had an unnatural interest in my omega, and while it appeared to be purely due to their friendship, it still irritated me. Alpha Warrick Annandale needed to learn to stay in his own fucking lane and leave our omega to the Reeves pack.

"Cora said she invited her to book club later this week," he added. "I wanted to assure you that I'll have the squads patrolling around the venue, though I'm sure you'll all be there as well. We can't be too safe."

I'd seen the message from Cora, along with Emme's expression, which was somber as she slowly read it. I hadn't had a chance yet to do more than offer basic help with her reading, but it was next on my list. Tomorrow morning, I'd drag her from bed again, all naked and perfectly adorable as she glared at me. Almost from the first moment she'd met me, she'd lacked a true fear in my presence, and fuck if that didn't add another facet to my interest in unraveling who she was.

"Emme wants to go," I told him shortly. "We'll make sure it's safe."

Warrick nodded, slapping a huge smile on his face, and I narrowed my eyes on the smiley asshole. Outside of Kellan, I trusted no one who was this happy.

Shifters should be fierce, not fucking jolly. Christmas season or not.

"I'll see you later, Alpha Warrick," I told him, effectively cutting off further conversation.

He didn't show any offense as he nodded. "Nice chat, Alpha Slade."

When he left, I checked on my pack via our security cameras. Hunter was in the office, Kellan in his Bugatti, heading out to Stockyard Motors to grab Emme's new custom bike, and Finley was at home with the omega. The bear had been on his best behavior lately, but it wasn't ideal when he was the only one around.

Another scan through more security footage had me satisfied that she was safe.

Nothing was amiss.

In her room, Emme grabbed a familiar black device from her desk drawer and then hurried into the bathroom. Switching views, I smiled as she ducked into the corner with no camera view.

Clever omega. It made me proud that in the relatively short time she'd had to study my security wall, she'd managed to note where cameras were and weren't. I anticipated the scrambling of footage, and sure enough, a second later my screen went fuzzy.

It was the same interference she'd tried before, and when my system overrode it, a bark of laughter escaped me. Every shifter in the training facility jerked to a halt, staring at me like I had two fucking heads.

"Back to training," I snarled, and all of them swung away just as fast, finding anything else to occupy themselves with.

Switching my phone screen off, I decided not to watch her prank this time. I wanted to experience it firsthand. My little omega kept life interesting, and for the first time, I had hope.

Hope that I'd found a reason to keep fighting for my soul—a five-foot-eleven, strawberry-blond-with-freckles, kind of reason.

Bring it on, Snow. Show me your best.

CHAPTER 47

EMME

Slade's prank was probably the best prank in history. I'd been impressed, amused, and highly intimidated by his dedication and skill level, even as I slept with the soft glow around me. With the early morning light filtering through my open shutters, there was once again no sign that anything was amiss in my room. The fact that my glow-in-the-dark sheets, furniture, and accessories all matched my old ones perfectly had me completely bamboozled.

How had he pulled that off in the time he'd had to do it? Was it all painted? Dyed? What were his secrets?

There was no way I could match it, but I did have a couple of ideas of what to try next to keep the game alive. The first step was to recruit Cora once more, and when she dropped off my new supplies she said, "You need to tell me everything at book club tomorrow. I can't stay now or I'll be late to my meeting with Downings, but you owe me an explanation, Ems."

Framed in the doorway, her gaze glanced over the second bite I was sporting, and the deeper meaning was clear. I had to update her completely the next time we were together.

But the thought of attending a book club gave me hives.

When I remained silent, she shot me the saddest face she'd ever shown. "Please be there. It's Sissily's night to choose a book, so of course it's a horror without a single romantic element in sight. I need you to keep me from losing my mind."

She shuddered like *no romance* was a fate worse than death, and from my brief foray into audio, I had to agree. "I haven't read the book, and I won't be able to before the meet up." For the first time, I didn't feel ashamed to add, "I have trouble reading. Slade thinks I might be dyslexic, which makes book club difficult."

Her face softened. "Oh, sweetheart. I didn't know that, but it's honestly not anything you need to worry about. Most of us don't read the books in advance. We just go for socializing and drinking."

That brightened my day; socializing and drinking I could handle. "Well, okay, then. I'll check with the alphas about security measures, and if it's all good, count me in."

Cora cheered and leaned forward to kiss my cheek, taking me by surprise. "I'm so excited. I'll text the details and let you know what time I'll pick you up."

"I can drive," I shouted as she ran down the front walk to her car. "Want me to pick you up?"

I had a shiny new Merc to play with... even if it was only a temporary loaner.

Cora smiled back at me. "Oh, even better! Grab me at seven tomorrow."

"It's a date."

With one final wave, she jumped into her car and took off, and I clutched the bag closer to my chest, ready for phase two of Prank Wars. Still unsure of how far I could push Slade, I was happy with the lowkey, unobtrusive prank I had planned.

It would require me to scramble the cameras and enter his

room again, and I was excited that only Finley was home. A statement I thought I'd never make.

But the bear rarely kept an eye on me, which was exactly what I needed to make this happen.

In my room, I tucked the items from Cora into my pocket and retrieved the scramble device from the side table. In my bathroom, I spritzed myself with the scent-blocking spray, not that it was necessary since Slade knew exactly who was behind it all, but I followed the same steps anyway.

After hitting the button, I sprinted from my room, heading down the hall and up the stairs to reach Slade's room even faster than last time. When I placed my hand on his handle, I knew this was the ultimate test. If he wanted to continue our war, the door would be unlocked. If not, I'd respect his wishes.

Or at least keep the pranks from his room.

As I pressed down, it clicked open easily, and *fuck*, I felt like I'd achieved greatness with the simple act of intriguing Slade into this war. That had to be as great an achievement as Hunter's invention of Shifter Serum, right? One got you drunk and the other one tamed a fucking dragon. Same-same.

Inside the room, I was surrounded by Slade's scent, and I breathed it in, wishing it coated my skin the way Hunter's and Kellan's did. Since our bonding, and sleeping in the same bed, our scents mingled like old friends. Or bonded mates.

It made me wonder if there'd be any major changes when the quintet was complete.

There was very little chance I'd ever find out, and with no time to dwell on what I was missing—I had minutes to get my prank rolling—I shut it out of my mind and raced across the room.

Yanking back the curtain to reveal his stalker wall, I paused to take it in. *Were there more photos and monitors?* Yep. Slade had added to his collection.

With a shake of my head, I pulled out the bag of googly eyes from my pocket and spent precious minutes peeling off the backs and sticking them to every photo of me, so when he checked his wall, all he'd see was eyes bobbing at him. And bob they would thanks to stalker Slade pinning his photos to a curtain.

When I was satisfied with the hilarious wall of wobbly eyes, I returned the curtains to their regular position and raced out of his room, closing the door behind me. My heart slammed in my chest all the way back to my bedroom, and I drew to a halt at the sight of Finley leaning against the wall by my door.

Silence extended between us, as he appeared content to examine me without words until he finally said, "You're playing with fire, you know." His thick lashes fluttered, hiding his beautiful eyes as he straightened. "Just don't push him too far. Slade is not like the other two."

I noted that he didn't include himself in that statement. It was a subtle warning not to *push Finley too far* as well. With a shake of his head, he left the hall, his steps echoing until the garage door slammed closed. He was off to tinker with one of his cars, and I almost followed, before remembering myself. His warning hadn't been put out there for me to disregard, and despite my need to push at the dragon, I didn't feel the same way about Finley.

I actually had no idea what to do with the bear shifter. He certainly wasn't my friend, but maybe he wasn't my enemy anymore either.

In my room, I paced for a while, working off adrenaline from the prank and my meeting with Finley. The rest of the pack would be home soon, and knowing I'd probably missed messages, I was about to grab my phone when my gaze fell on the pile of books stacked haphazardly in the corner. Books that had been there since Chelsea dropped them off at the guard house.

Deciding I had a few minutes to give these books, I sorted through the pile, while taking my time to slowly read the titles. There were a few words I couldn't figure out, but I managed to sound out most of them. *The History of omegas*; *Pack Hierarchy and Omegas*; *Embracing Your Strength as an Omega*; *Strengths and Weaknesses*; *Pack Bonds Through the Centuries*; and *The Magic of Omegas*.

The last book on the magic of omegas had a small sticky note attached, and I squinted to keep the words straight as I deciphered what was written. *Emme, start with this one. It's the most detailed. I think there's even a section on bonded alphas and omegas near the back. Let me know if you have any questions. Chat soon, Chelsea.*

I'd barely spoken to the other omega since the day of the guard-attack, outside of a quick message to thank her. It wasn't like we'd hit it off immediately the way Cora and I had, but she'd been nice and was one of the few omegas in the pack cities. Her entitled alpha was also Hunter's best friend— Sorenson, a charming tiger shifter. For that alone, I should invite that pack over for a meal one evening. It was time for me to start taking a more vested interest in my pack, and the shifters who were part of their lives.

I picked up the book Chelsea suggested I start with, wondering how magic was related to omegas. We held no active magic, outside of the same essence that had *cursed* shifters to begin with. But maybe this was a reference to the sharing of energy, which could be viewed as a magic of sorts.

Excited, I pulled the book closer, rubbing my fingers over the gritty surface of the cover. It must have debris on it from the attack—I'd dropped these books as I fought back, and they'd lain on the ground until Hunter retrieved them from the guard hut and placed them in my room.

My hand tingled as I flipped open the cover, pausing as a puff of white dust erupted from the first page, drifting into my lungs. Dropping the book and scrambling back, I clawed at my throat, which felt like it was already closing over. Every muscle in my body seized up, leaving me unable to move, and only the faintest of breaths entered my lungs.

Then my legs moved... only, I wasn't the one moving them.

With no control over my actions, I marched toward my desk and quickly jotted down a note that I'd never have been able to pen without assistance. *Dear Alphas, I can't do this anymore. I don't trust you all not to force the bonds, and I need to forge a life away from the risk of being part of a completed quintet. If you care for me, you won't come after me. This was never meant to be. Emmeline.*

The pen fell from my unresponsive fingers, and my legs took me to the windows where I tore the shutters open and pushed out the glass.

I tried to scream.

I tried to grasp the window and hold on until someone came for me, but no part of me was under my control. Not even my voice.

Whoever controlled my movement directed me out of the window, dropping me a full story to the ground. I landed heavily, pain shooting up my legs and into my hips. My magical kidnapper wasn't worried about injury though, sending me on a sprint through the immense back yard toward the towering fences that blocked the Reeves' estate from the land behind.

When I reached the fence, I wondered if they could defy my athletic ability and get me to hop over the ten-foot structure. If

Slade had proven anything, it was that scaling walls was not within my regular skillset.

A crack nearby jolted me internally, but outwardly my body made no reaction. The sensation of being trapped in my own skin had a sickening sense of claustrophobia falling over me.

Another crack followed the first, and off to the right of me, a panel of the fence imploded, clattering into nearby shrubs. My feet moved again, and I emerged into the land behind our pack house to find a shifter standing there. One who did not take me at all by surprise, considering the circumstances.

Chelsea had betrayed me. Her involvement in all of it, including the initial attack at the guardhouse, were the only factors that made sense.

She shot me a harried look, and I noticed a crumpled piece of paper in her hands, which she dropped suddenly. I could have sworn, though, that it was the same note I'd just written in my room. "About fucking time," she muttered, distracting me.

There was no sign of the sweet omega in her voice today. I couldn't answer, of course, and when she hurried into the darkness, I followed as if we were tethered.

How in the fuck was this possible? I'd never heard of a magic that controlled a shifter like this. I could only assume it was connected to our designation. Maybe if I'd had a chance to read the damn books, I'd have found out.

"Hurry up," Chelsea snapped, grimacing at me like I was the one running too slowly. "I've already waited weeks longer than I should have because you're a moron who can't crack a book open despite the danger you're in."

A dozen questions pummeled into my thoughts, but I couldn't voice even one of them, forced to listen to her complain as she picked her way through the landscape.

She sighed in relief when an old, beat-up Honda came into

view. The doors were already unlocked, and when she jumped into the driver's side, the magic shoved me into the passenger seat.

Before my door was even closed, Chelsea took off, and I would have jumped at the crash from my door swinging shut, but I couldn't fucking move. This old beater wasn't the usual kind of car that filled Golden Claw, the well-paid shifters driving much newer models, but I got that sense that was the entire point. This Honda was made before electronics and tracking devices.

Everyone knew that Slade controlled anything with a computer, so she'd taken that option away. Along with any hopes I had of escaping.

CHAPTER 48

EMME

Chelsea's angry mumbles quietened as she focused on driving, moving through the dark streets, taking what appeared to be every back road in Golden Claw. When the security fence and city perimeters came into view, I wondered if she'd be stopped at the gate.

Even if she chose to ignore the guards, blasting past them would at least raise suspicions.

As the main exit came into sight, she slowed, and I tried as hard as I could to scream for help, but not even a gush of air escaped me.

Chelsea smiled brightly, and without a word, handed over a thick envelope to a dark-haired shifter, who didn't even investigate the vehicle. This bitch was organized, I'd give her that.

We were out of the city within a few minutes, and I could do nothing but sit rod-straight in my chair, watching the world go by through the front windshield. Hours passed in silence, and just when I hoped she would have to fill up with gas, she turned off the main road and down an overgrown and rough dirt path. The car's old suspension didn't handle the terrain well, and I couldn't reach out to keep myself from smashing into the door as we bounced along.

None of which mattered when a rundown old house came into view, surrounded by forest, with not a single neighbor in sight. Chilling tingles ran down my spine, and if I'd had the ability to scream, I might have started and not stopped. This had *house of horrors* written all over it, and Chelsea bringing me here could mean nothing good.

The other omega breathed a deep sigh when she stopped the car, her hands trembling on the wheel. "I want you to know how sorry I am," she breathed, voice shaking as much as her hands. "I had no choice. It was you or me, and I won't choose me. They needed an omega, and you are more powerful and already able to scent match multiple alphas. They'd have gotten to you eventually, so when they offered me a deal to help, I took it. But I am sorry."

This weak-willed bitch. I would never have turned her in to save my own ass. *Never.*

But now... I'd cut her into pieces and not miss a wink of sleep over it.

I couldn't glare, but I hoped my eyes were spitting fire, because that was how much rage bubbled over inside me.

Chelsea's expression hardened, resolve settling over it. "Okay, let's get this over with. I need to return before my pack notices me missing."

How in the fuck hadn't they already noticed? Were they that distant from each other that she could drive for hours at night and not have anyone calling to find her?

When Chelsea exited the car, I followed. We both stomped up to the crumbling front porch. Inside, the house looked deserted, with only a few pieces of moldy old furniture visible in the light from dirty sconces high on the walls. When Chelsea had flicked them on, they were so coated in grime that they barely made a difference.

Down the creepy hall, everything remained quiet. We entered a room that looked like a living area with one threadbare couch against the wall. Chelsea collapsed onto it, her normally gentle features haggard and worn. She looked like she'd been through hell for weeks, and I wondered how long she'd camped outside the Reeves' estate, waiting for me to open that book and initiate her spell.

Maybe she'd expected Jones' plan to work initially, but when that didn't, she'd gone for her backup. I had no idea if my pack would believe the note I'd written, but at least Hunter and Kellan had no choice but to come after me. *We were bonded.* A fact I wasn't sure Chelsea was aware of, but already there was a burn in my chest from our connection stretching too far.

A connection I prayed they could use to track me down.

I had no doubt they would come for me, which allowed me to remain calm as I sank onto the mildewy couch beside my newest kidnapper. This shit was getting really fucking old, but how was I supposed to fight against magic that shouldn't exist?

My fingers twitched for the first time, and I was jolted with the knowledge that the spell might be wearing off. Forcing myself not to react or give away this little development, I was excited when Chelsea's head dropped back, mouth open as she breathed deeply.

This was my first real chance to escape, but no matter how hard I tried to force my limbs to move, I couldn't do much more than wiggle my fingers. Inch by inch, I started to flex them against my palm, and after twenty minutes of sweating, panicking, and internally cursing, my right hand could move. Then my left. My wrists proved to be harder, so I focused on sock-clad toes, excited when most of them wiggled.

The spell was definitely wearing off, starting with my outer limbs, which led me to believe that eventually it would dissipate completely.

I'd just gotten my wrists and ankles rotating when I heard a bike, and what sounded like two cars pull up out the front.

No! No, no... I needed more time. I was so damn close.

Frantically, I pushed harder against the spell, and managed to straighten my legs as the front door opened. My first attempt to stand was premature and failed miserably, sending me tumbling to the floor, where I barely caught myself before I face-planted.

"Omega." The drawled word sent ice through my veins. I'd know Blaine's slimy voice anywhere. "Nice of you to make this easy for us. Just sprawled there, ready for the taking."

Unlike the last time he'd ambushed me, I refused to let my panic take me over. There was no Slade here to save me, which meant it was up to me to keep my wits and get out of this situation. If I didn't escape, I'd be claimed and drained by the Rogers pack, until I wished for death like my mother.

Blaine clutched my ponytail, yanking my head up until my scalp shrieked in pain. He *tsk*ed as he hauled me to my feet and back on the couch. "You look a right old mess, princess. Is that any way to meet your mate?"

If this entire ploy was for Blaine to claim me as a mate, then I'd rather die—it was an undeniable truth that I'd acknowledged and accepted years ago. I'd choose death every day before bonding to this evil pack.

As anger sent a burst of energy through me, my shoulders twitched, and Blaine noticed, dark eyes locking on the movement. "Alpha," he shouted, "you might want to get in here. The spell is wearing off."

Alpha? He was the entitled alpha in his pack, so there was no one who ranked above him...

Loud footsteps echoed down the hall, and a beat later an older shifter entered the living room. He was tall and imposing, with olive skin, pure white hair to his shoulders, and dark eyes which were vaguely familiar. There was no way I'd ever met him before. I'd remember a shifter essence as strong as his, which rivaled the alphas in my pack.

His shrewd gaze caressed my features, and I felt vaguely dirty when he was done. "Well, well. Emmeline Anders. You've been difficult to track down."

Those words were an almost exact repeat of what Blaine had said when they captured me last time. Did the Rogers pack kidnap me for this alpha? Was he my bad guy in the shadows all along?

My throat and voice remained frozen behind the spell, but I was able to inch my way back on the couch, trying to avoid the white-haired alpha as he stepped closer. "I've been experimenting for many years with shifters and our dominance hierarchy." He gazed, unblinking, at me. "Omegas always eluded me though. There weren't enough of you to experiment with or break open to learn how you work. They were all so fragile." He tilted his head. "Well, at least not until your mother."

Blaine grinned lasciviously, licking his lips as if he could still taste the omega he murdered. "That was one fun experiment."

My stomach swirled, and bile coated my throat, sticking due to the spell.

"It's all going to change now," the white-haired shifter said, crouching down until we were eye to eye. "I might have failed fifteen years ago, but this time I'll have enough power to control *all* the packs and *all* the witches. As it should have always been."

Fifteen years ago...? Was he referring to the last great war?

Was this the alpha who'd been the nameless, faceless evil working with the Termaine witches?

Blaine's eyes widened, and the way he looked at the white-haired male was nothing short of worship. "Yes, Father," he breathed. "You should be the entitled alpha of all shifters, and not these small, insignificant quintets. The power is spread far too thin."

The alpha nodded, but I was stuck on two points: one, Blaine called him *father*, and I wondered if that was where his familiarity came from. And two, they were attempting to gather enough power to turn back the clock to when the packs were governed by one alpha rather than in quintets—before the councils, when a single alpha had the power to make thousands of shifters suffer.

It was a flawed system we could never return to.

White Hair leaned in closer and sniffed my throat, and I flinched into the couch. "You smell like my son. Bonded to him, I see."

In my confused state, I turned my gaze to Blaine, but he shook his head. "Oh, not me, princess. My half-brother... his other son. Hunter Reeves—"

A backhand knocked Blaine halfway across the room, and anger creased the older shifter's face as he hissed, "Davenport. He is and *always will be* Hunter Davenport. No matter what he calls himself now."

Holy fuck. Holy fucking fuck.

The pieces I'd been missing for all of this to make sense crashed into me with the force of a wrecking ball. White Hair was Hunter's father... And Blaine's.

"Wh-what do you want?" I managed to squeak out, fragments of the spell still holding me.

The darkness on the alpha's face vanished, replaced with a geniality that was honestly more terrifying. "You, my dear, will be the power needed to arm my greatest weapon. Omegas can share their powers with their bonded alphas, did you know?"

"Whether they like it or not," Blaine added gruffly, pulling himself to his feet. "Your weak-ass mother tried to fight for a while, but she was no match."

I knew that all too well.

"It was interesting to see how long it took to wear her down," the other alpha said, "while we waited for you to come of age and be claimed. It's all quite exciting, you know. Your bloodline has another element your mom doesn't, an element you inherited from your father. The bastard thought he could hide you from me, but in the end he had no hope."

Mild curiosity reared up at the mention of my father, but I had more pressing questions to ask first: "Do you really plan on bonding me? Even when I'm bonded to your son?"

I'd heard the saying *keep it all in the family,* but this was going way too far for me. I was already racking my brain to figure out how I could fight him. Again, I'd rather die than bond this crazy fuck.

A bond was for life.

The alpha shook his head, and then let out an ear-piercing whistle. The scent of my fear exploded with that sound, and if I wasn't mistaken, both alphas reacted as if it excited them. Pupils dilated, breaths coming faster, invasive stares caressing my features...

Footsteps sounded in the hall again, heavy once more, and when the shifter moved into view, my heart shattered in my chest. As I took in his massive build, face shadowed in the half-light, I thought for a brief moment that Slade Riverson stalked toward me.

But as I examined him closer, I noticed a few subtle differences that indicated I might be mistaken. Slade's doppelganger had his hair shaved so short that only a light layer of dark strands were visible, which did nothing to detract from the handsome and eerily similar features of his face. Except for the long, jagged scar that cut from his ear down to the corner of his lips, adding a menacing quality to his godlike beauty.

Other than that, there was very little to tell this shifter apart from Slade. Just as tall and maybe even more built, he wore all black but showed no glimpse of tattoos along his biceps.

"This is your new mate," Hunter's dad said, waving the shifter closer. "Dragon, claim your mate."

Dragon. What the fuck? Was this actually Slade's twin?

As the huge, scary-ass male stalked toward me, Blaine grabbed Chelsea, waking her with a start. It took her a second to figure out we weren't alone, a small scream escaping her as she panted. "Shift and bite," Blaine rumbled, "before the magic wears off completely."

There was a moment when Chelsea's gaze met mine and her eyes filled with regret, but even as I shook my head she was already shifting her face. My jaw followed suit, the remaining tendrils of magic enough for one final controlling action.

As my canines lengthened, I gave all my focus to Slade's evil twin, scrambling back on the couch once more. The shifter's jaw was all dragon as it elongated his face, and I was halted by an unbreakable grip around my wrists, tight enough to cut into my muscle and bone.

He kept me locked in his dark and animalistic gaze, expressing none of the humanity that Slade bore when he stared into my soul. With a rumble, he bit my shoulder, right beside Hunter's mark.

The pain was instant, tearing deeper than either of my other marks.

Chelsea moved, but I couldn't see what she did until my

head jerked forward, and I returned the dragon's bite, right at the base of his throat.

He tasted like copper and a hint of maple syrup, scents that grew stronger as my wolf rose for the first time. Rose and sealed our mate bond forever.

Catch up on what happens next in the Shifter City Fated Mates series in book 3, A Claim of Fortune, coming in June 2025 Link. You can keep up to date with releases by following me on Instagram, joining my Facebook group The Nerd Herd, or subscribing to my newsletter.

WHAT TO READ NEXT...

I've had a lot of readers contacting me asking for what to read next. Try my complete (MF) romantasy series, the Shadow Beast Shifters. Rejected- Book 1

My father made a terrible mistake. One I'm left paying for.

As a wolf shifter growing up in a strong pack, I should be living my best life. But after my father tried to kill our leader, I'm labelled an outcast, traitor, less than dirt.

When I can't take pack life any longer, I run, but apparently they don't like losing their punching bag. Torin, the leader's son, drags me back before my first shift... a shift that will reveal my true mate. I never could have predicted who mine would be, but the moment my wolf looks upon him, I'm filled with hope for a brighter future.

Afterall, no one ever rejects their true mate, right?

Wrong. Very wrong.

When the wolves attack, my soul screams for vengeance, and somehow I touch the shadow world.

Somehow I bring him to our lands.

The Shadow Beast. Our shifter god. The devil himself.

Turns out being rejected by my mate was only the beginning.

*If you like sexy, dark paranormal romances, with humor, steam, action, a tough heroine and an antihero, this is for you. Rejected is full length (100k) words, is book one of three in Shadow Beast Shifters series, and ends on a cliffhanger. It's recommended for 18+ due to language and sexual situations.

ALSO BY JAYMIN EVE

Fallen Fae Gods (Dark Romantasy dragon shifter/fae 18+) (complete)

Book One: Gilded Wings

Book Two: Crimson Skies

Shadow Beast Shifters (Dark and Sexy wolf shifter/ god Romantasy 18+) (complete)

Book One: Rejected

Book Two: Reclaimed

Book Three: Reborn

Book Four: Deserted

Book Five: Compelled

Book Six: Glamoured

Bluebell House Duet

Book One: Forced Proximity

Book Two: Trauma Bonded (TBD)

Boys of Bellerose (Dark, RH rock star romance 18+)(complete)

Book One: Poison Roses

Book Two: Dirty Truths

Book Three: Shattered Dreams

Book Four: Beautiful Thorns

Demon Pack (PNR/Urban Fantasy 18+) (Complete)

Book One: Demon Pack

Book Two: Demon Pack Elimination

Book Three: Demon Pack Eternal

Supernatural Prison Trilogy (Complete UF series 17+)

Book One: Dragon Marked

Book Two: Dragon Mystics

Book Three: Dragon Mated

Book Four: Broken Compass

Book Five: Magical Compass

Book Six: Louis

Book Seven: Elemental Compass

Supernatural Academy (Complete Urban Fantasy/PNR 18+)

Year One

Year Two

Year Three

Royals of Arbon Academy (Dark, complete Contemporary Romance 18+)

Book One: Princess Ballot

Book Two: Playboy Princes

Book Three: Poison Throne

Titan's Saga (PNR/UF. Sexy and humorous 18+)

Book One: Releasing the Gods

Book Two: Wrath of the Gods

Book Three: Revenge of the Gods

Dark Legacy (Complete Dark Contemporary high school romance 18+)

Book One: Broken Wings

Book Two: Broken Trust

Book Three: Broken Legacy

Secret Keepers Series (Complete PNR/Urban Fantasy)

Book One: House of Darken

Book Two: House of Imperial

Book Three: House of Leights

Book Four: House of Royale

Storm Princess Saga (Complete High Fantasy 18+)

Book One: The Princess Must Die

Book Two: The Princess Must Strike

Book Three: The Princess Must Reign

Curse of the Gods Series (Complete Reverse Harem Fantasy 18+)

Book One: Trickery

Book Two: Persuasion

Book Three: Seduction

Book Four: Strength

Novella: Neutral

Book Five: Pain

NYC Mecca Series (Complete - UF series)

Book One: Queen Heir

Book Two: Queen Alpha

Book Three: Queen Fae

Book Four: Queen Mecca

A Walker Saga (Complete - YA Fantasy)

Book One: First World

Book Two: Spurn

Book Three: Crais

Book Four: Regali

Book Five: Nephilius

Book Six: Dronish

Book Seven: Earth

Hive Trilogy (Complete UF/PNR series)

Book One: Ash

Book Two: Anarchy

Book Three: Annihilate

Sinclair Stories (Standalone Contemporary Romance 18+)

Songbird